Look what people are saying about

LESLIE KELLY

Dear Reader,

I have to confess: I'm a reality-show junkie. I've watched the greats and the stinkers, been enthralled by *The Mole* and disappointed by *Joe Millionaire* II. So when Harlequin gave me a shot at writing my very first single-title-length romance novel, you can bet the reality-show idea popped into my mind.

There was someone else who'd been occupying my mind a lot, too.

Mick Winchester is a guy I've wanted since I wrote about him in my October 2003 Temptation novel *Trick Me, Treat Me* (Jared & Gwen's story). He was so unrepentantly wicked, so sexy and playful and...just *bad*...that I found him irresistible. When he popped up again in my novella "Thrill Me" (Sophie & Daniel's story), which appeared in a Harlequin collection called *Reading Between the Lines* in January 2004, I knew he had to have his own story.

It just remained to find the perfect woman, that blend of sexy, sassy, smart and strong, who could not only capture a man like Mick, but also hold on to him. TV producer Caroline Lamb is just such a woman.

I hope this story makes you laugh. I hope you can't put it down. More than anything I hope I give you a few hours of real reading pleasure. That's all any writer can ask for.

Happy reading, and thanks for all your support!

Leslie Kelly

LESLIE KELLY

Killing Time

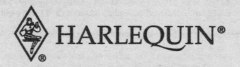

TORONTO • NEW YORK • LONDON
AMSTERDAM • PARIS • SYDNEY • HAMBURG
STOCKHOLM • ATHENS • TOKYO • MILAN • MADRID
PRAGUE • WARSAW • BUDAPEST • AUCKLAND

ISBN 0-373-83615-5

KILLING TIME

www.eHarlequin.com

Printed in U.S.A.

This one's dedicated to all the wonderful,
supportive people at Harlequin,
who have given me so many opportunities.
Brenda Chin, Birgit Davis-Todd, Marsha Zinberg
and Tracy Farrell, thank you for your faith in me.
I won't let you down.

And to all those reality-show contestants
and crews. Thanks for the laughs
and the entertainment.

CHAPTER ONE

"DROP YOUR PANTS."

Today certainly wasn't the first time a woman had told Mick Winchester to take off his pants. From playfully suggestive, to wickedly sultry, the sentence conjured up a variety of pleasant memories. Of women. Lots of women.

He just loved them. And he was a lucky enough son of a bitch that they usually loved him back. Usually.

A lot of people had told Mick that women would be the death of him. He'd heard it from ex-girlfriends, from his mother, from buddies who envied his romantic success. Hell, just yesterday his own grandfather had given him a lecture on settling down before some female went *Fatal Attraction* on him.

He'd laughed off the warnings. How could something he loved as much as women bring about his downfall?

Unfortunately, as he stared down the five-inch barrel of an old Colt .45 handgun, he was beginning to see the possibilities.

"Louise, you don't want to do this," he told the woman holding the gun. "Whatever's wrong, we can work things out."

"Drop 'em, loverboy."

She didn't say another word, merely waiting patiently, watching him the way a hawk might study a tempting bit of prey—with stoic determination and a bit of outright hunger.

He wished he'd opened the blinds as soon as he'd gotten into the office this Monday morning. Perhaps then someone outside might have noticed something odd. Unfortunately, since he had an appointment with an out-of-towner looking for a room to rent, he'd come in early and hadn't opened the office. He'd left the blinds down and the lights dim in the reception area. No one outside would notice a thing. And his secretary wouldn't be in for a little while yet.

The out-of-towner wasn't due for an hour. So whoever the Hollywood woman was, she'd probably walk in after Louise Flanagan finished whatever the hell it was she was trying to do here.

"What are you waiting for?" she finally said, sounding so perfectly reasonable, as if they'd just bumped into one another at the diner or the bank. "I know you're not hard of hearing."

"I'm trying to understand why you want to kill me."

Hell, of all the women in Derryville, this one had the very *least* reason to hate his guts. And that was saying a lot, since he could easily name several females who would probably like to see him strung up by the nuts.

But Louise? He'd always been polite to the woman, giving her a smile when other people had laughed at her. He'd been nice to her in the old days, when the high school hierarchy had liked to crucify the farmers' daughters who wore their coveralls to school and smelled of their daddy's dairy farm.

She gave him a small smile. "Oh, Mick, you old silly, I'm not gonna kill you. Now get naked. Pretty please?"

This was beyond ridiculous, even for *him*. Oh, sure, he'd been caught naked with women before, once even in the coat-check room of an upscale Chicago restaurant. But never so close to home. Never in his own realty office. Never with a local girl whose family would riot at the thought of their darling hooking up with the wickedest playboy in Derryville, Illinois.

And never, *never* with Louise Flanagan, his lab partner from tenth grade biology. Louise not only outweighed him by forty pounds, she was the four-time champion hog wrestler at the state fair. Plus, Mick's and Louise's grandfathers were long-standing enemies.

"Louise, I'm not going to take my clothes off."

She cocked the hammer.

"Shit." He tugged his shirt from the waist of his pants.

"That's good. Shirt first, that's proper. But no more cursing," she said with a tsk. "That's one of your bad habits. That, your drinking and your cigar smoking are going to be the first things you give up when we get married."

That one nearly made him choke. *"Married?"*

She nodded. "Yessir. And soon. Got to get you tied down and rescue you from your overactive manly urges."

Manly urges. If he'd ever had any in his life, the image of marrying Louise wiped them out of his memory banks.

She continued. "I mean, I knew when I heard about those TV people coming here to do their show that I had to step in before it was too late. I can't have you losing your head and giving this whole town more reason to think you're just a good-for-nothing playboy. Not when I know better."

She gave him a worshipful smile that told him he'd been residing on a pedestal and had never known it. That *almost* distracted him from the fact that she'd called him a good-for-nothing playboy. But nothing was distracting him from the loaded gun, which she wagged suggestively toward his body.

"Louise…"

"Come on, your shirt's easy. Just pretend it's Saturday."

The twisting turns in the conversation were giving him a headache on top of his hangover. "What?"

"Half the women in this town make a point of driving down your street on Saturday afternoons because they know you're gonna be mowing your lawn," she explained.

Half the women in town? No wonder his street was like Daytona during Pepsi 400 weekend when he cut the grass. "So?"

She sighed heavily, explaining as if he were a six-year-old and she a weary parent. "So…you always do *it* sooner or later. It's usually after four, when you've finished the cutting and you're just doing the edging and cleanup. And by the way, Mick, you do such a nice job on your lawn, much better than when the Edgertons owned your house."

"*What* do I *do*, Louise?" he asked, still wondering whether she liked him or hated him, wanted to marry him or wanted to kill him. Hmm…when he thought of it that way, she suddenly reminded him of just about every other woman in his life.

"You know what you do," she said. "You know when you're almost done, and you're ready to cool off with a long, wet soak from your garden hose…? That's when traffic's the heaviest."

She gave him a look that said he was supposed to understand what the hell she was talking about. He didn't. Rolling her eyes, Louise said, "You weren't this thick in high school."

"Somehow my brain doesn't work well when it's envisioning taking a bullet."

"Sorry, it can't be helped. I know even as nice as you are you won't get naked and be forced to marry me by my daddy unless I force you to get forced first."

He began to see, as crazy as it was. Louise, the girl he'd been nice to back in high school, wanted to force him to get forced into marrying her so she could help save his unsalvageable reputation. "My head hurts."

"Stop drinking so many beers on Sunday nights with the fellas after your football games."

"So, you know my entire weekend schedule, not just my Saturdays in the yard?"

"Oh, yes, Saturdays. Back to the shirt. You always take it off when you hose yourself down after you're done. Then you get a beer from the fridge on your porch and you pop open the bottle and guzzle the thing down while you're all wet and shiny." A pink flush rose in her plump cheeks. "Tons of women plan their Saturday shopping around your yard work. Except, of course, on rainy days. Then they meet in the basement of the dress shop and play cards."

Welcome to small-town life. Christ, why the hell did he live here again? "That's crazy."

Louise obviously saw his disbelief. "Men. You're *all* thick. Didn't you realize why Mrs. Richardson crashed her brand-new Buick into the back of your neighbor's old AMC Pacer? She was watching you, watching all that sweat mix with the dirt and grass on your shoulders and your arms. Trying to see what we all want to see."

His hands instinctively dropped to the front of his pants.

Louise giggled again. "Not *that.*" Then she stammered and looked away. "Well, yes, that. But also, your, um, you know…"

"My…" Hair? Back? Earlobes? What was the woman talking about? And who the hell knew women were as lewd as men when it came to ogling the opposite sex, even if it was a complete stranger? Of course, no one was really a stranger in Derryville.

"Your *thingie,*" she whispered.

His thingie. A number of thingies on his body tightened up as he waited to hear what all the women in town wanted to peek at.

"My what?" he asked, hoping she meant his checkbook, which should be enough to scare off most women. But he doubted it.

"Your…tattoo!"

He stiffened, his jaw clenching, the response as instinctive as it was predictable. Few people knew the origins of his tattoo, the one spread across his lower back, just below his hips, riding his ass like a low-slung pair of jeans. The tattoo was one subject that was off-limits in his life. As was the woman who'd originally inspired him to get it.

"Forget about seeing my tattoo or anything else. I'm not taking off my clothes."

Her smile broadened. "Oh, yes, you are."

"Put down the gun. You already said you wouldn't kill me."

She lowered the gun and took careful aim at every man's Achilles' heel. The one between his legs.

Muttering another curse—which earned him another tsk—he yanked off his shirt, dropping it to the floor. His

Northern brain had no part in that decision. The Southern one had simply taken over in pure self-preservation.

"That's better. Keep going."

He hesitated, wondering how this could be happening in his nice little real estate office on the nice main road of this nice small town. If any of his poker buddies ever found out a woman had held him at gunpoint and made him strip, they'd die laughing. Of course, if the story had involved one of his more *typical* female friends, they'd probably be jealous as hell.

When he didn't move fast enough, Louise let out an impatient sigh. "You know I wouldn't kill you. But I can shoot well enough to make sure you behave from now on." Her stare followed the direction of her pistol, and she let out a quivery sigh as she looked at his pants. "I guess I'd like to see what all the women fuss and carry on about." Then she squared her shoulders in self-sacrifice. "But if it comes right down to it, I don't mind having a marriage without those carryings-on between the sheets. Whatever it takes, I've got to save you from yourself."

Marriage and no sex. Funny, at the thought of being married to Louise, he could suddenly understand the appeal. "That's very kind of you…but I promise, I really don't mind my reputation."

She frowned and shook her head. "I do," she said fiercely. "You're the nicest man in this stinky town. I'm sick of everyone thinking you're nothing but a walking cock-a-doodle-doo."

The cock-a-doodle-doo bit almost made him laugh, particularly because a brilliant flush had darkened Louise's cheeks when she'd said it, as if she'd uttered an unforgivable swearword. "I'm sure you're exaggerating."

Her expression told him she wasn't. "It's because they're jealous you don't take up with local women. You go casting your rod into the ponds of other towns, 'steada right here at home."

She was right. That was one of his unspoken rules, which he'd adhered to for the past several years. *Never fish in a tiny lake where it's not so easy to throw one back.*

"But I know with those Hollywood floozies coming to town, the urge might be too much for you. So I'm going to save you."

Hollywood floozies. It took a second, but he finally figured out what she meant. Derryville was about to be invaded by a TV crew. A new reality TV show called *Killing Time in a Small Town* was set to film right here. That was the reason for this morning's meeting. One of the producers was looking for a short-term rental, since Derryville's only inn was going to be filled up with the cast and camera crew of the show.

"I know you're not ready to settle down, Mick, but that'll change once we're married. Daddy should be here in fifteen minutes or so, after he takes my brothers to football practice. That gives us enough time to get you naked and me—" she flushed again, more brilliantly than before "—mussed."

Fifteen minutes. Knowing Louise's no-good old man, who was late on everything from his mortgage payments to his own weddings, that equaled more like an hour. Meaning he had that long to convince her to give up her crazy idea.

A number of possibilities quickly ran through his mind. He could sweet-talk her, reason with her, cajole her...

Or, given her brilliant blushes and the fact that she had never had so much as a date, he could do one thing that was sure to send her scurrying out of here like the scared virgin he knew her to be.

Exactly what she asked him to.

Without another word, Mick Winchester dropped his pants.

THE DERRYVILLE REALTY office was easy to spot on the main street of this small town. Caro Lamb smothered a sigh when she saw the sign, complete with engraved drawing of mom, dad, kid and dog playing happily on the lawn in front of their little house.

A sign like that in L.A. would have to show a hillside mansion and a kid being shuffled between Mom and her pool boy, and Dad and his trophy girlfriend. The dog would be replaced by low-maintenance, no-pooperscooper fish. The lawn would become a skate park.

Home. A word of infinite definitions. None of which had really rung her bell as yet.

She parked the rental car, which she'd picked up in Chicago after landing there late the night before. Then Caro grabbed her briefcase and stepped out into the bright Illinois morning. "No smog. I don't think my lungs can take it," she mumbled.

"Eh?"

She hadn't even realized an older man pushing a broom was standing on the sidewalk near her car.

"Nothing," she mumbled, embarrassed to be caught talking to herself. Talking to oneself was something that could *really* start a rumor in Hollywood. Do that on Rodeo Drive and by the time you got back to your studio office, the execs were calling Betty Ford while your office mates planned your intervention.

Nothing was as "in" in L.A. as the occasional breakdown. Of course, as fun as they were, they also spelled death to a production career in TV. Stars, talk show hosts, radio deejays—they "got well" or "got clean" or "got acquitted" and the studio loved them. But lowly assistant producers hoping for a shot at a lead gig on a prime-time network show and an escape from the lowliest cable fodder featuring an '80s one-hit-wonder sitcom refugee?

Huh-uh. Death. Absolute death.

There was, of course, one thing worse than the lowliest cable fodder featuring an 80s one-hit-wonder sitcom refugee.

"You're here for that reality TV show, aren't cha?"

That'd be it.

"I can tell by the rental plates. And your clothes. And the bored look on your face."

Caro's eyes widened. "I'm not bored. I'm just—" *procrastinating* "—thinking."

"'Bout?"

About being stuck here for three weeks with her entire future on the line. About trying to salvage her third-rated network by riding on the reality TV wave that had crested last season.

"About what a nice, normal town this is."

That was true. Derryville certainly seemed to satisfy all the requirements the network had laid down when planning for this next volley into the reality TV arena. *Killing Time in a Small Town* was supposed to take place in an average, all-American place where neighbors were friendly, doors weren't locked and movie stars' wives didn't end up dead in their cars or on their doorsteps.

No crime. Peaceful. Serene. That was what was

called for. And then the show would spice it up with a fake murder mystery, with the contestants competing to solve it before getting "bumped off" themselves.

"You been up to the Little Bohemie Inn yet? I hear there was some camerapeople up't there to do some picture taking."

"The advance team was here a few weeks ago," she told the man as she slammed her car door. "They did some exterior filming of the inn and the town. We've already started working on commercial spots."

He didn't look impressed. That could be a problem, since the town's residents were supplying the backup to the cast. *Killing Time in a Small Town* would utilize the residents of Derryville as often as possible. Maybe even the old man leaning indolently against his broom. But that might not work if the rest of the residents looked as uninterested as this fellow.

"I'm sure the town will benefit from the exposure," she continued. "And America will love this down-home, normal atmosphere." *That's the plan, anyway.*

"Ayuh, she's a normal small town all right. With everything that goes with it," the old man said. He gave her a lazy grin, gave himself a comfortable scratch on the belly, and began to laugh. The sparkle in his eyes showed genuine amusement.

Caro had the feeling he was laughing at her. He'd probably pegged her as a big-city L.A. know-it-all who thought small towns were as sweet and simple as they'd appeared in 1950s sitcoms. If only he knew.

She swung her soft-sided briefcase over her shoulder, locked her car and joined him on the sidewalk. "It's a town like a lot of other ones," she said evenly, letting him know she understood his laughter.

He studied her. "Maybe. Maybe not."

But it was. Transplant this place to Kentucky and it would have been the same burg where Caro had grown up. And from which she'd fled as soon as she'd graduated high school.

Small. Quiet. Boring. Judgmental. Unable to forgive or forget, particularly when it came to town bullies and bad boys.

And their daughters.

Small towns hadn't changed. They all smiled on the outside, but seethed within. She'd never move back to one. Caro Lamb hadn't ever been tempted. At least, she amended, not tempted for several years. In that instance, she had to admit, it hadn't been a *town* tempting her. It had been a man who lived in such a town. The kind of man who could tempt a nun into stripping off her habit to do a bump and grind worthy of the Vegas stage.

Enough, Caro. That subject's off-limits.

"You really think Derryville's gonna make it big on the TV?" the man asked, looking as if he didn't care one way or the other.

"Oh, absolutely," she replied with vehemence. "This place is just perfect for a reality TV show. *Killing Time in a Small Town* will be a huge success."

She prayed it would. It *had* to be if she ever wanted to make it past assistant producer. By nailing this assignment, keeping costs in line and producing a decent show that lasted more than the kiss-of-death four-week replacement slot, she'd have a shot at a prime-time gig.

She could hardly wait. No more road trips looking for funny home videos, or scouting out wacky ideas for the next grand experiment in the reality game. She'd be in a studio, in charge, in a position of power for the first time since she'd hit Hollywood. Eight years ago, right after she'd gotten her heart broken and dropped out of college to head west.

"You going into the realty office?" the old man asked.

"How did you know that?"

He shrugged. "Saw the owner show up early. Only reason to do that is if he had an appointment."

"I guess he got my message," she said. She was only in town for the day to find suitable accommodations. She'd called the realty office yesterday, asking the secretary if she could come in an hour before her scheduled appointment time, since her return flight was earlier than she'd expected.

The woman had promised to try to notify the Realtor. Obviously, since he'd come in early, his secretary had succeeded.

"Enjoy your visit," the old man said. Then he casually stepped away, continuing to push his broom, stirring up nothing but some stale summer air, puffs of dust and a few random cigarette butts.

"Thank you," Caro said to his retreating back. Then she turned toward the office of Derryville Realty. The place looked closed from the outside. The blinds were drawn, with no hint of interior light peeking through to indicate anyone was around. The old man had said there was, however, and he seemed like the kind of person who knew all, saw all. And commented on all.

Unsure whether to knock, Caro first tried the door handle. When it twisted easily in her hand, she stepped inside. The outer reception area was, indeed, dark and deserted. Before she could decide whether to just sit down and wait, or step back outside, she heard voices coming from an inner office.

Glancing at her watch, she made out the numbers in the semidarkness. "It *is* 8:00 a.m.," she whispered. And since she had to first find accommodations, do the paperwork, and then get back to Chicago for her flight home to L.A., she wasn't in the mood to sit patiently.

Following the sound of the voices, she rounded a sofa and coffee table loaded with sale flyers, finance company brochures and photo albums. An archway revealed a back hall, lined with closed doors, one saying Meeting Room, another Restroom. The rest were unmarked offices. One of those doors was partly open, the inside brightly lit. That's where the voices were coming from.

Standing in the darkened hallway, Caro had an easy view of the people in the room. But it still took a moment for her to mentally assess what was happening.

A woman stood inside, with her back to the hall. She hadn't even noticed Caro's entrance. Stepping closer, Caro realized why the woman was so distracted.

She was staring toward a man. A bare-ass naked man.

A bare-ass naked man with a *very* nice ass.

"Son of a…." she whispered.

They didn't hear. Obviously whatever was happening in the room had engaged their complete attention.

"Oh, for God's sake, Louise, haven't you gotten a good enough look yet?" the man asked over his shoulder, his back to his captor.

Though the question obviously hadn't been directed at her, Caro immediately answered for the woman. No. Huh-uh. Not enough. Not nearly.

"Nope," the woman replied.

Good answer, Louise.

"Can I at least turn back around?"

Oh, please please please please please.

"Not just yet."

Argh.

Finally realizing exactly what she was doing, Caro sucked her bottom lip into her mouth and stepped back, pressing herself against the corridor wall. Her heart pounded in her chest, and she struggled to control her ragged breathing, wondering why the duo couldn't hear her shocked inhalations.

Obviously, the Realtor hadn't been showing up early for *her* benefit. He'd had another kind of appointment altogether. The sexual kind. The kind that urged her to move her feet and get the heck out of the building before the panting and moaning commenced. At this moment, Caro really couldn't be sure she, herself, wasn't already doing one or the other.

"Good Lord, no wonder the women in this town are all fools whenever you're around," Louise, the woman in the office said.

One fool standing in the hallway completely concurred.

A discreet person would have left immediately. A calm business executive would have cleared her throat to alert them that someone was present. A sane woman would have resisted thinking about how the rest of the naked male body might look.

Caro did none of the above.

She stayed right where she was. Waiting, trying to work up the strength of will to leave quietly and not steal another peek. Finally, good sense won out. No matter what, she was *not* a Peeping Tom. She hadn't been reduced to the level of a woman who hadn't had sex in so long she had to live vicariously through other people's sexual adventures.

Preparing to walk away and come back later when

the Realtor was less, um, *occupied,* she pulled away from the wall. But before she could take one step, the woman in the office said something that made her freeze in place.

"I hope I don't have to shoot you, because there isn't a place on ya that isn't just about perfect."

At first she wasn't sure she'd heard correctly. She replayed the words in her mind as the truth dawned.

She hadn't interrupted anything as mundane as an office romance. Either these two were playing some kind of fun and kinky sex game—burly prison guard attacks sexy, helpless, naked, studly criminal came to mind—or else a crime was being committed.

One scenario said she had to leave. The other demanded she stay. Because, it was entirely possible Mr. Naked Guy was about to get shot.

CHAPTER TWO

"YOU WERE SUPPOSED to turn tail and run," a male voice said, sounding both weary and amused.

The voice sent a shiver of awareness down Caro's spine. It sounded silky smooth, much too calm for a person being held at gunpoint, which made her think these two were, indeed, playing some kind of game. For some strange reason, the man's voice sounded familiar to her ear. She'd just been too much in shock to pay attention the first time he'd spoken.

The woman laughed. "It takes a lot to make me run away."

Caro inched closer to the door frame. There was just something about that man's voice—not to mention his naked body—that made her itch to take another quick peek.

"That's why you stripped, even though you knew I wouldn't shoot you?" Louise asked. "You thought I'd run away at my first sight of a naked man, even though I have four little brothers?"

Caro took a deep breath and worked up her nerve to steal one more glance just as the man muttered, "Something like that."

Louise had moved slightly out of the way. From this angle, Caro could only see the man from the waist up.

Wow, what a waist. Wow, what an up.

The man had crossed his arms in front of him, so his shoulders and triceps flexed and bulged. His hair was light brown, cut a little long, but not long enough to hide the thick strength of his neck.

Caro gulped. If she'd been the one with the gun, she figured it would've slipped from her hand due to the sweat breaking out all over her body. Good Lord, how could anyone be that close to a man so *hot* and not get weak in the knees?

"Oh, sweetie, you're so funny. I helped raise the boys. Plus I grew up on a farm. I've seen male equipment. And while you're, well, of *generous* proportions, you can't compare to Buddy."

Caro had to wonder who Buddy was. If the mysterious Louise really did know some man named Buddy, and he was better built than the guy in the office, Caro thought perhaps her stay in Derryville might be more interesting than she'd expected. Though she wasn't sure her heart could take it. Not to mention her diaphragm, which had been sitting unused in her medicine cabinet for so long she could probably use it to strain pasta.

Truly, though, she didn't see how anyone else could compare to Mr. Naked Real Estate Guy. At least not from her angle. She doubted *anyone* could look as good from behind as this man did, and she included a number of Hollywood heartthrobs in that assessment.

"Buddy's a bull, Louise," the man said, his voice shaking with what some might have interpreted as fear, but which Caro recognized as unbridled laughter.

Bull-like. There was something a man would aspire to, right? The thought inspired several wicked images. She had to back away again, if only to force herself to stop trying to peer around the armed woman for another tantalizing glimpse of the hips and down.

Wow, what hips. Wow, what *down*.

"I know. But for some reason, you made me think of him," the woman replied.

"I don't know many men who would compare favorably to a bull. But thank you very much, all the same."

Still hidden in the near darkness, and still wondering whether the two were playing some sort of lovers' game, or if she'd really stumbled into a hostage situation, she took a few calming breaths to decide what to do.

Look some more.

That worked.

This time, she gave into her impulse, dropped to her knees, and peered around the door from a lower angle. Definitely a *better* angle. For assessment purposes only, she told herself, knowing she was a big fat liar whose pants, if she had been wearing pants, would be incendiary right about now.

She stayed hunkered down, assessing the couple. The woman was a puzzle. Broad in girth, huge in stature, she wore an unflattering pair of jean overalls, which, Caro was sad to say, seemed to have come back into fashion for some bizarre reason. Not in Hollywood, of course. But they were showing up in the rest of the country—which pretty much meant another planet, as far as most people in L.A. were concerned.

Louise appeared taller than the better-than-average-height man, and heavier by a large amount. So maybe the hunk had a thing for big girls. In which case, he'd never spare a glance at Caro, who only stood five-seven when she wore two-inch heels.

She certainly wasn't an imposing figure now, down

on all fours in a closed real estate office, spying on a pair of lovebirds, or a female rapist. She still hadn't decided which was the most likely explanation. Either the man was a philandering Realtor having a kinky good time—complete with props like fake guns—on a Monday morning. Or he was a poor innocent victim being held up by a naked-Realtor-robbing Amazon.

Not sure which, she curled her back and neck a bit, hunching lower until she was able to see that, yes, the woman was definitely holding a real—if rather old-looking—pistol.

The hostage wasn't turning around. He remained still, his body aligned with the sight of the gun. His back was perfect. Smooth. Sculpted with layer upon layer of thick muscle. Tanned, taut skin glistened with a sheen of sweat that probably had more to do with the situation than with the temperature.

His thick arms flexed with the tension. That, more than anything, convinced Caro that while his tone might be flip, and his voice might hold laughter, he wasn't relaxed. He was, in fact, completely tense, obviously waiting for his chance to extricate himself from this unusual situation.

The overall-wearing bandit was still too busy staring at that naked tush to move. Caro couldn't blame her—she couldn't do anything else, herself.

She'd never really considered herself a butt woman. A man's eyes were so much more important. Or at the very least his smile. A pair of lips that could instill a sense of shimmering heat while widened in laughter used to make her completely crazed. One smile, in particular, had nearly been her undoing.

But as for the rest? Good looks, as she'd found in Hollywood, didn't always equal good men.

That didn't mean they weren't fun to ogle. Particularly in this case, with a man whose backside looked hard enough to crack a walnut, and hot enough to make her legs go weak.

Then the man shifted, as if he planned to turn around. She hissed. *Weak,* nothing. At the thought of seeing the full-frontal onslaught, Caro's legs turned to jelly. If not for her arms holding up the front part of her body, she probably would have fallen face-first on the carpet.

"Don't turn around," the woman said matter-of-factly, apparently noticing her victim making a move. "Please stand there and look away while I get myself mussed before Daddy gets here."

Daddy. Mussed. Caro began to understand. This was strictly TV Writing 101 stuff. Tons of shows, from soaps to sitcoms, had explored this scenario in every conceivable way. This woman *wanted* to be caught in a compromising situation with Mr. Studly. Enter the enraged, armed papa. Fade to commercial.

"*Please* don't take off your clothes." He sounded more nervous than he had when she'd threatened to shoot him.

No commercial, Caro, this is real life.

"Fair's fair." Then the woman chuckled. "At least now I know what all the women in town are dying for a glimpse of."

His thighs? His flexing calves? His arms, which looked strong enough to carry a woman to the nearest flat surface and make love to her from here to Sunday? All of the above?

Most especially that hard, sweetly curved rear that cried out to be caressed, held, stroked and clenched in mind-numbing passion? Caro gulped as her nervous habit kicked in: she started to hum the theme song from *Sex in the City*.

"Who would've thought those little black points were the tips of his ears?"

It took a second for Caro to understand what the woman meant. Then she leaned in farther, blinking off the haze of lust to take a really good look at the man. That was when Caro noticed what was *above* his perfect, hard, finger-licking-good backside.

A tattoo. A sexy, wicked, playful tattoo. It told a story that revealed quite a lot about the man it adorned.

Part of it, the little creature in the small of his back, riding just above his right cheek, made her pause. Because it looked familiar. Very familiar.

"Impossible," she whispered, not believing her own eyes. She studied it, blinking a few times, wondering if she was really seeing what she thought she was seeing.

It was a lamb. A cute little furry white lamb, as incongruous as it was adorable when decorating this hunky man's body. "Crazy," she called herself, knowing there were millions of men in the world who had millions of tattoos.

Maybe some *other* hunk had decided to put a cute little lamb on his backside in honor of some *other* woman whose last name was the same as hers. Maybe that other hunk had called that other girl a sweet little lamb the first time they'd been introduced.

Or maybe she'd wronged someone in another life and karma was getting even. That was the only explanation about how fate could be cruel enough to bring *him* back into her world.

"Please, no," she whispered. But even as she did so, she knew it was futile. Somehow, Caroline *knew* this particular tattoo belonged to only one particular man. "Lord help me."

"Okay, Louise, this is getting ridiculous. And I'm getting cold," the man drawled.

This time, because she was listening for it, she did, indeed, recognize the voice.

Mick Winchester. Good God, it was him. She hadn't seen the man for eight years and already he had her down on her hands and knees, playing Peeping Tom. In two minutes flat, he'd turned her into a mindless, brainless female. Just like she'd been during the crazy, passionate year of their relationship.

She couldn't help staring at him again, gobbling him up with her eyes, knowing that once his face was turned to hers, she wouldn't be able to look her fill. Because he'd be watching her, laughing at her, knowing how she reacted to him.

Always had. Probably always would. Dammit all to hell.

In the office, Louise said, "It's good you keep your tattoo covered."

Remembering the tattoo, Caroline stared at it again, studying the whole image. The old tattoo was now part of a bigger picture. The glimpse of the lamb had made her cringe at the thought of facing Mick again. But studying the whole thing and assessing its meaning made her want to punch his lights out.

Because the louse had gone and ruined it.

"That'd just feed the gossip mill, wouldn't it?" Louise said. "They already think you're a horny, hungry devil."

A horny, hungry devil. How appropriate for this horny, hungry, insatiable, exasperating man.

Her teeth clenched and her eyes narrowed as she stared at what the creep had done to the poor little lamb on his hip. Directly across from it, extending from the base of his spine and down over part of his taut left cheek, was a cartoon character. With gaping jaws, a wicked twinkle in its eye and very sharp teeth.

She recognized the character instantly. From the spiky black fur, and the two pointed ears that might, indeed, peek out from a pair of low-riding jeans, to the glistening, salacious smile, the Big Bad Wolf sat silently on this man's body like a predator watching for some tempting prey.

And he had some. Lamb chops *en brochette*.

It was funny. Comical. But intensely sexual. A literal warning to any lamb to be wary of wolves with big smiles and knowing eyes. She didn't know whether to drool or kick him.

But what really made her react with gut fury was the realization that *her* little lamb—the one Mick had gotten during his junior year of college in honor of their first anniversary—was no longer alone. A miniature herd of the furry little beasts marched across his back, waiting for their turn to run willingly into the Big Bad Wolf's waiting mouth.

And Caroline Lamb had led the way.

She simply couldn't help herself. With a strangled cry of fury, she half stood and launched herself into the room.

"Do the women of the world a favor and shoot the bastard," she snarled at Louise.

Then she promptly ruined her grand entrance by losing her battle with gravity and falling flat on her face.

MICK DIDN'T KNOW who the woman lying on the floor was, or why she'd stumbled in just in time to prevent him from trying to physically wrest the gun from Louise Flanagan.

He did know, however, that she looked damned sexy, face-down, with her short white skirt riding up high enough to show him the hem of her filmy white panties.

As for why she'd want to shoot him, well, there could be any number of reasons. The first one that came to mind was that he *did* know her. The legs certainly looked familiar. Then again, any gorgeous legs looked familiar to a leg man.

"Louise, I think you've done enough for this morning," he said, reluctantly, but necessarily, focused on the woman with the gun, not the woman with the silky underwear. Because as much as he'd prefer not to be the only naked one in the room, he had the feeling the likelihood of the gun *going* off was better than the likelihood of the brunette's panties *coming* off.

"Your plan obviously isn't going to work if your father shows up and sees another woman here. Knowing him, it'll just reinforce his already bad opinion of me. He'll think I was trying to draw you into something terribly...unsavory."

Her face flushed and her mouth dropped into an *O* shape. "He wouldn't think I'd do something like that!"

"He might. So maybe you should go now," he told her. Despite everything, he felt touched that she cared enough to try to save his reputation. Even if she'd had to shoot him to do it. Somehow, that made about as much sense as anything else in Derryville.

"We'll forget this ever happened. Go home." Then he said, "Leave the gun." The prankster and movie lover in him almost added "Take the cannoli," but he doubted either of the women in the room would appreciate the *Godfather* reference.

"I…I would never want my daddy to think such a thing," Louise said, lost in thought, her voice sounding shocked. Her trembling hand dropped to her side, leaving the gun dangling there, pointing at the floor.

Speaking of dangling… "Can I please get dressed now?" he asked no one in particular.

The prone woman in the short white skirt, who'd been pounding her fist on the floor and muttering the word "no" over and over into the carpet, finally looked up at that one.

Looked up. Direct line of sight. Got an eyeful.

Then he recognized her face and the bottom dropped out of his gut. "Caroline."

"Mick."

Louise stared at them both. "You two know each other?"

Know each other. Knew each other. Oh, yeah. A lifetime ago.

"Go, Louise." Mick's voice was thick, his throat tight.

Caroline Lamb. Here. In his office. Jesus.

He yanked his khaki pants off the floor and pulled them up over his hips, more to stall for time and regain his suddenly questionable sanity than anything else. It wasn't like he was covering up something Caroline hadn't already seen a number of times. Up close. And personal.

He began to sweat. Caroline slowly rose to her feet, watching his every move. Louise didn't budge an inch.

"I can't believe you did it," Caroline said, glaring toward his half-covered body.

"She was holding a gun on me," he replied in self-defense.

"Not that," she said with derision. Brushing past the wide-eyed Louise, she stalked to stand toe-to-toe with him. Mick felt her anger wash over him as tangibly as a blast of heat. Caroline had always blown over him like a blast of heat. Always. Whether she'd been in a rage, laughing, teasing him or kissing him like they needed each other's breath to survive.

"I can't believe you had that…obscene representation of your own shortcomings tattooed onto your back."

He almost grinned, suddenly knowing why she was so ticked off. Then his grin faded. No, Caroline wouldn't like what he'd done with "her" lamb. But he'd had to do it, had to try to make their relationship mean nothing, seem like nothing. Because it had, once upon a time, meant too damn much.

"Okay, I guess you two do know each other," Louise finally said as she inched toward the door, probably seeing by the fury in Caroline's eyes that an assault was, indeed, about to take place here. But instead of defending him, Louise looked ready to leave him to his fate. She also looked amused.

"The gun, Louise," Mick said, unable to keep his stare from drifting back to the face he'd never thought he'd see again.

He heard a thud, and assumed the gun had dropped to the carpeted floor, but he couldn't look away from that amazing familiar face long enough to make sure. Then the door clicked shut, leaving him alone in his office with Caroline Lamb.

She'd changed. Matured. Oh, she was still a knockout, but she'd lost that small-town-girl look that used to make her eyes a little brighter and her smile a little sunnier than anyone else's. Not that she was smiling now.

"Great entrance," he murmured. "Graceful as always."

She merely closed her eyes and sucked in a deep breath as they both struggled to regain their composure.

She was really here. In the flesh. Very nice flesh.

While she got a grip on herself, he took a moment to devour her with his eyes, noting the things that had changed over time and those that had remained the same. It was easy to tell—her image had been burned into his brain since the day they'd met.

He studied the way her new, chin-length haircut accentuated the sweet curve of her face and the vulnerable delicacy of her neck. Her makeup was designed to accentuate the alluring, vivid blue of her eyes. God, those eyes, such a stunning contrast to her thick, dark hair.

She wasn't quite as slender as she'd been in college, but the curves were in all the right places. His college girl had grown into quite a woman. From the top of her chestnut-brown hair, to the tips of her expensive shoes, she screamed totally-in-control female.

But she wasn't. Not by a long shot.

"Yeah, well, I see you haven't changed much either," she finally said with a falsely sweet smile. "Why am I not surprised to bump into you after eight years and find you with a woman, naked and displaying your best side?"

His eyes narrowed. "Used to be you thought my front was my best side."

She raked a thorough look across his bare chest and arms, his stomach, the unfastened waist of his slacks.

Everywhere her gaze touched, his body tightened and grew hot. His reaction to her was instinctive, and had been since the minute he'd met her in his sophomore year of college.

Somehow she managed to look as though she'd studied him and found him lacking. Which was, he knew, total bullshit. The flush on her cheeks and the way she couldn't quite control her deep breathing told him her dismissing look was as fake as her perfectly manicured nails.

Caroline was a nail biter. A blusher. And a heavy breather.

But she gave it her best shot. Crossing her arms, she managed what would probably pass for a pitying smile. "That was before I got to know you. I'm all grown-up and I've figured out that the rear is always the best side of a horse's ass. The better to watch him walk away."

He grinned, unable to help it. Damn, the woman always had been able to throw a good insult. Her prickliness had been one of the things that had so fascinated him in the old days. Because it came in the sweetest, most adorably sexy package.

"So what are you doing here, Caroline?" he asked, struggling to remain casual and calm, as if his world hadn't rolled over the minute he'd seen her face.

She ignored his question. "Are you going to call 9-1-1?"

He raised a curious brow.

"A woman just threatened to shoot you."

"Yeah, but I don't want you to end up in jail so soon. I mean, we just met again. We haven't had time to catch up yet."

Her eyes narrowed as she tapped her fingers on the top of his desk, near the gun Louise had dropped. "I'm talking about your big friend."

"Louise? She's harmless."

She gaped. "She had you at gunpoint."

"Right."

"She made you take off all your clothes."

"She didn't really *make* me," he explained in his own

defense, not wanting Caroline to think he was a pansy-ass who'd let a woman—even an armed one—make him do anything he didn't want to do.

"Oh, so you just decided it was too warm in here this morning and decided to strip down to nothing to get some fresh air?"

"No."

She tapped the tip of her fingertip on her cheek. "Let's see, you've become a nudist since the last time I saw you?"

"Not exactly."

"So, she was right? You consider yourself hot enough that she'd fall over in a faint when she saw your manly magnificence?"

"Something like that," he replied with a long, low chuckle.

She rolled her eyes. "You're not all *that,* Mick."

He raised a challenging brow, daring her to be honest. Once upon a time, he'd been all that and a lot more to this woman.

No, Caroline hadn't exactly fainted away the first time she'd seen him naked. But she had dropped to the nearest flat surface pretty damn quick.

"She's a nice, misguided lady, who I don't think has ever had a date in her life," he explained, recognizing that Caroline really did think he should call the police on poor, sad Louise. "So, yeah, I somehow thought I might be able to scare her off."

"But you're no *Buddy.*"

He remembered Louise's comments about her daddy's prize bull, who was famous in these parts. "Ahh, you were eavesdropping for quite a while, hmm?"

She pinkened. "Just…scouting out the situation before I decided what to do. I wasn't sure whether I'd interrupted some lovers' tryst, a robbery or a bizarre sex crime."

Mick pulled his shirt on, tucked it in, then refastened his belt. It was easier to deal with Caroline when fully dressed. Half-naked felt too damned vulnerable. "So, what would you have done if it were a lovers' tryst?"

"Backed out gracefully."

"Bizarre sex crime?"

She didn't hesitate. "Called the police."

"And since it was neither," he said suggestively, "you just decided to, uh…watch."

She straightened her back, looking so stiff he thought she might break in two. "I did no such thing."

"You were out there a long time," he countered, keeping his voice at the level of a purr. "Staring at the… scenery."

"The only scenery I was staring at was the nightmare on your butt."

He couldn't prevent a triumphant smile for getting her to admit she'd been staring at his naked body.

"I was trying to figure out what kind of man would shout his true nature to the world. 'I am dog, hear me roar.'"

Tsking, he clarified, "It's a wolf."

"Same species."

He shook his head. "Actually, no. But same genus, I think."

She let out a soft groan, and he knew he was driving her crazy. He'd always been able to drive her crazy, just like this. A highly emotional person—easily swinging from the highest highs to the lowest lows—Caroline had been a perfect foil for someone like Mick, who was so difficult to rile he'd been accused of having no heart at all.

She'd been the one to accuse him of that, come to think of it. Then she'd stormed out, missing the damage Mick was capable of when his emotions *really* got the better of him.

"Want to sit down? You look flushed," he said, thinking she was doing a good job getting riled up all on her own this time.

Ignoring the offer, she shook her head and walked across the office, leaving them separated by a few feet and an ocean's worth of emotional baggage. "You haven't changed a bit."

She was wrong there. He *had* changed. Not that she'd see it, not that he'd admit it out loud. But he wasn't the same guy she'd known.

Actually, he wasn't sure who Mick Winchester was these days. But that was okay. Because nobody else was quite sure who he was, either, other than the black sheep of the Winchester family. The playboy of Derryville. The tattooed bad boy who was much more often found playing poker with the guys on a Sunday than having a weekly after-church gathering with family.

"Still Mr. Cool, aren't you?" Caroline said. "Still trying to pretend you're untouchable."

Untouchable. Perhaps, but only in the emotional sense.

Caroline wasn't the only one to accuse him of hiding his emotions behind an easy laugh and a charming grin. His little sister, Sophie, had told him more than once he was an emotional teakettle, at full rolling boil just beneath a calm, smooth surface.

Sophie was probably right. No one had ever been able to get Mick to completely lose his control and erupt. Except once. With the woman standing right in front of him.

Of course, Caroline hadn't been around to see. That had been after she'd left. After she'd waltzed out of his life, accusing him, judging him, sentencing him and walking away without even giving him a chance to defend himself. Hell, he hadn't even *done* anything. He'd been guilty of what he *might* do in the future, and that was enough for her.

Such trust from the girl he'd asked to marry him.

That was the only time Mick had ever lost himself to anger. He still had the scars on his knuckles from where he'd broken several fingers punching holes in the wall of his room.

Not that her lack of trust and his perceived inability to commit were the only things to break them up. There had also been geography. She wanted west. L.A. Big city, bright lights. All that star-studded stuff a lot of college girls seemed to want. Mick had never been able to picture anything but what he'd always known. Small-town life. Home.

So she'd taken off. He'd torn apart his dorm room and gotten kicked out of school. End of story. Until now.

"Why are you here?" he finally asked again, unable to keep baiting her when he simply felt weary and off balance. "Why after eight years did you track me down?"

"I *didn't* track you down. I'm your appointment."

He simply stared, not sure what she meant.

"Your renter."

His renter. One of the studio executives looking for a place to rent in Derryville for a month.

Caroline Lamb was moving here? To this tiny town where they'd be running into each other all the time?

His dismay must have shown in his expression, because for the first time since she'd stumbled into the office, a genuine smile brightened her face. "Doesn't that just make your day?"

He couldn't even fathom what life would be like if he had to get used to Caroline being back in his world. The thought of having his youthful stupidity and heartbreak thrown into his face on a daily basis was more than he could stand.

Striding out of his office, he nearly tripped on something, but kicked it out of the way. He continued down the darkened hallway, reached the front door and yanked it open.

"Louise," he bellowed into the street. "Get back here and shoot me!"

CHAPTER THREE

"SO TELL ME, what is this rumor I've heard about you renting a room to one of these TV people?"

Sophie Winchester smothered a groan as her peaceful Monday morning was interrupted immediately after she'd stepped into the church office. There was no mistaking that voice. It was Miss Hester, sister of Pastor Bob, her boss at the First Methodist Church of Derryville. Miss Hester's sweet tones—so often heard dispensing wisdom, advice and fortitude to the congregational flock—usually spewed criticism and gossip in private.

"Is it true?" Miss Hester shut the door and turned around. "I heard the rumor yesterday."

So much for keeping her plans a secret. Criminy, she'd only told her brother, Mick, two days ago that she wanted to rent out her house while it was up for sale. And already, the grapevine had gift-wrapped and hand-delivered the rumor to the proprietress of all things proper and good in Derryville, Hester Tomlinson. The one who'd been preaching from her own bully pulpit against allowing any Hollywood types near Derryville.

"Where did you hear that?" she asked, knowing Miss Hester wasn't going to move her considerable girth out of the way to let her go to her desk until Sophie had spilled her guts.

"Tell me it's not true. You, a respectable church sec-retary, are not opening your doors to a Hollywood gigolo who'll ruin your reputation, destroy your en-gagement to Chief Fletcher and make a mockery of everything my dear brother preaches each Sunday."

Oh. So, Miss Hester didn't have the entire story straight. She thought Sophie was going to be *rooming* with some TV people. When she learned the truth—that Sophie was—*gasp*—going to live in sin with her fiancé for a couple of months—she'd shit bricks. Church sec-retaries simply didn't do such things.

Not that Sophie was much of a church secretary. That was just the public life she'd lived for the past few years in order to keep her private one a secret. The pub-lic job wasn't going to be hers much longer. She'd al-ready been planning to resign. When Miss Hester learned she planned to give up her house to live with her fiancé, Daniel Fletcher, it'd be imperative.

"Everyone is talking about making it rich by renting out rooms to those...those Hollywood *lowlifes*." Miss Hester sounded as if she was talking about insects, rather than human beings.

"Yes," Sophie admitted, "it's true. I'm going to rent out my house. I plan to sell it when Daniel and I get mar-ried, anyway."

Miss Hester moved away, shutting the door behind her and striding toward Pastor Bob's private inner of-fice. "Come with me," she said, her authoritative tone allowing for no argument.

Sophie began to smile, almost relieved that things were coming to a head. It looked like she might be quit-ting her job sooner rather than later. That meant she could unglue her tongue from the back of her teeth and tell the old battle-ax what she could do with her stupid job and her stupid rules and her stupid nosiness and her stupid self.

Once Sophie got into the other office, Miss Hester crossed her arms over her massive chest and frowned. "Your wedding's not until October. Halloween, as I recall, as if anyone could forget a bride choosing such an unholy day for her sacred nuptials."

When the truth came out about who Sophie was, and what she *really* did for a living, the wedding date might make sense.

"Actually, I'm going to go ahead and move out now."

She felt relieved it was going to be over soon. She wanted it done, wanted to stop living a lie. She had her letter of resignation ready, though she'd planned to give it to Pastor Bob. But if Miss Hester pushed too hard, the letter would be hitting her so fast she'd think she'd missed someone yelling "fore."

"Whoever rents the house would be there alone," she added.

"Oh," the woman said. "That's better, at least." The woman sounded approving. Sophie recognized the tone. Miss Hester used it on everyone, trying to convince most residents in Derryville that she really was the kindly hostess of her widowed pastor brother, rather than just a small-minded woman who lived on gossip and titillation. "Where do you plan to live in the meantime, dear?"

Sophie didn't fall for the softened tone or the endearment.

"Are you staying with your parents?"

"No," Sophie said, waiting for the right moment to tell Miss Hester that sweet little Sophie Winchester was going to be shacking up with the new police chief.

Before she could continue, Miss Hester was distracted by the ringing of her phone. Since Sophie wasn't out in the reception area, the woman had to answer it herself, leaving Sophie to work up the right words that would mean, basically, take this job and shove it, but wouldn't sound quite so truck driver-ish.

Not that Miss Hester didn't deserve such language. The woman was like a scouring pad pretending to be a cotton ball. But Sophie had been directly in contact with the steel wool these days and knew there was nothing cottony soft about the woman.

Which made it awfully easy to picture killing the old broad. Killing. Mutilating. Maiming. Burying. Oh, yeah, Sophie had done it all in her mind. Not as herself, of course, but as her alter ego, R. F. Colt. The hottest horror fiction writer around today.

There was the main reason for quitting her job. Heaven knew she had enough work to do on her novels without living a secret life as a small-town church secretary. But, even though Daniel had convinced her people liked her for who she really was—not who she pretended to be— she had her doubts. Her family? Yes. Daniel? Yes. A few close friends and associates? Absolutely.

But if she told Miss Hester? The woman who'd pray for her poor, sorry soul and preach to her about the evils of a dissolute mind and a wicked imagination? No way. Not a chance. She'd only planned to reveal her secret once she was ready to whip out that resignation letter and switch to another church on Sundays. Which appeared to be right about now.

Miss Hester finally finished her phone call and turned her attention back to Sophie. "So, where *will* you be living?"

"I didn't see the point in missing the summer real estate season, so I'm going to put the house on the market right away and rent it out in the meantime. It doesn't make sense to wait until October." Offering the other woman a tiny smile, Sophie added, "So I'm just going to move in with Daniel now."

Miss Hester gasped. "You can't. You simply can't."

"It's not that big a deal."

"It's a disgrace. I've worked too hard to let you *ruin* things." The woman's voice rose to a near shout. "If you do this, don't bother to come back the next day."

Sophie shrugged. "You got it. I quit."

Miss Hester's jaw fell open, setting a few of her chins a-wiggling. "You ungrateful, miserable little sneak."

Hmm…Miss Hester looked pretty ferocious when she was pissed off. Maybe the next time she included the woman as a character in one of her books, she'd make her the villain instead of just a comic relief secondary character or a gruesomely murdered victim.

"You're as shameless as that no-good brother of yours."

She'd brought Mick into this? Low. Very low. "I should defend Mick, but *I* mind my own business and leave *my* brother alone." *Let her stew on that.*

Miss Hester did, quickly realizing the insult. "You are no longer welcome in this office." Then, as if she had a direct line to God and could issue his invitations, she added, "Or in this church."

Sophie shrugged. "There are other churches." Just to be evil, she added, "I've been wanting to check out the synagogue, anyway. Or maybe that Buddhist temple up in Chicago."

Miss Hester clutched a hand to her heart. "You wicked girl."

Sophie wasn't listening. She'd already turned toward the door, giving one last mutter. "Oh, drop dead."

Feeling damn good, Sophie breezed into the reception area.

It was then that she noticed the crowd. The one who'd been listening to every nasty word. Mrs. Carlton who had an appointment with Miss Hester this morning. Dr. Ogilvie, a local dentist, who headed up the food-for-the-needy program. A red-faced Louise Flanagan. Darla from the nail salon. Every last one staring at her.

Damn, when she burst out of the closet, she did it in a big way. Giving them all a bright smile, she murmured, "Good morning," then walked out the door into the sunshine.

EARLY THAT AFTERNOON, trapped inside a car with the most exasperating man she'd ever known, Caro was on the verge of a meltdown. Every rental in Derryville had something wrong with it. Either the owners were old, loud and nosy or young, loud and obnoxious. Or the rental room was painted a garish Day-Glo green. Or the chain-smoking owner had created a lot of fragrant memories.

Nothing suited her. Least of all the man showing her place after place, a faint smile always evident on his lips. That smile told her more than his silence ever could.

"You're enjoying this," she said, watching him wave to yet another local on the streets of Derryville.

He gave her an innocent look. "Enjoying what?"

"Enjoying watching me sweat."

"I've always enjoyed watching you sweat," he replied, completely unrepentant. "Does you good to get a little worked up once in a while. You look so…" He gestured toward her pressed linen suit, the stylish linen jacket and short white skirt, as if he found the latest fashion lacking.

"So what?"

"So buttoned-up."

"Professional, I think is the word you want."

"I was thinking more like cold."

Cold? He thought she was cold? Good grief, one of the most difficult things she'd overcome when arriving in Hollywood was the impression that she was an innocent young girl, big of heart, warm of spirit, always ready to listen to a sob story. Impressionable, exuberant, naive but clever, they'd called her.

Now Mick was calling her cold. It shouldn't have bothered her, but, deep down, it did.

"Let's stick to the subject—finding me a place to live."

"You're the one who's being picky. I've shown you four reasonable places."

"Ugh. Reasonable?"

"You didn't have better luck on your own," he reminded her.

No, she hadn't. Not that the jerk had to bring up the fact that she'd tried. This morning, after their initial run-in in his office, she'd stormed off, determined to find someplace to live without his help. She'd been back an hour later, disheartened and frustrated. The local paper hadn't listed one single rental. Nor would any of the people with For Rent signs in their yards agree to let her come through without a Realtor.

"Are you the only Realtor in Derryville?" she asked.

He shrugged. "Nah. I have two associates working with me."

Her spirits perked up at that. Then he dashed her hopes. "But they're both off this weekend."

She groaned and stared out the window. "How is it that the only hotel in this town looks like it rents by the hour?"

"Because it does."

"Yeah, well, I guess you'd know."

"I'm sure Hollywood doesn't have such sordid goings-on."

She couldn't hide a smile. "Okay, you got me on that one."

The tension seemed to ease somewhat, probably because she'd finally lightened up. Mick had always been able to lighten her mood. Heck, Mick had always been able to make anybody feel better. It was impossible to be down with someone who was always *up*.

"Tell me about this TV show," he said, obviously trying to keep the conversation friendly and impersonal. They both seemed to have reached the same silent conclusion that the past was better left undiscussed, at least for now. "Why'd you decide to film it here? Why the Little Bohemie Inn?"

Safe ground. They could talk business without Caro feeling the urge to reach over and play with his earlobe. Either that or give his hair a good yank because he'd made her so angry every time she'd thought about him over the years. "We're always on the lookout for new shows. Reality TV had been really hot the last few years."

He sighed. "Yeah. I was wondering when they'd start the live execution show. Or 'Who Wants to Let Their Dog Marry a Millionaire's Dog?'."

She laughed, unable to help it. Because what he described wasn't so far off the mark. She felt pretty sure that, somewhere, a desperate Hollywood down-and-outer had thought of just such an idea as a way to try to get back in. "This isn't going to be anything quite as gratuitous. Actually, the owner of the inn gave us the idea for the show, herself. Gwen…um…."

"Winchester." He didn't so much as crack a smile, but she heard the amusement in his voice.

She sighed heavily. "Don't tell me…"

"She married my cousin last spring."

Another Winchester. Oh, joy. Another wonderful day-to-day reminder of the only guy she'd ever loved. Her trip to Derryville should be renamed a visit to purgatory.

"So how'd Gwen give you the show idea?"

"A review of the inn in a Chicago paper mentioned they were doing in-character murder mystery weekends. Someone at the network saw it, thought it would be an interesting concept and came up with *Killing Time in a Small Town*."

Mick nodded. "Those in-character weekends at the Little Bohemie Inn are something else. And you should probably thank my cousin, Jared, for inspiring the idea." He wore a secretive look, as though he had a story to tell, but instead kept the conversation away from personal matters. "I'd heard it was a murder mystery show. I don't suppose society has fallen quite so low as to have real murders for our viewing pleasure?"

"Only on cable. Not on one of the big three networks."

He gave her a sideways glance, nodding his appreciation of her humor. Where that humor had come from, she couldn't say. Her mind told her she was still mad at him, still hurt by him, still insane to spend even one minute alone with him.

But her body, her spirit, her long-dormant sunny, open, good nature, reminded her that she'd always liked being around this guy. He'd always been able to make her laugh, make her give in to crazy impulses and live for the moment.

That thought doused the good humor. She'd stopped living for the moment a long time ago. Judging by the fact that some local woman had thought she needed to "save" Mick from himself, he hadn't.

He hadn't stopped being the kind of impulsive person who did what he wanted, when he wanted, with whom he wanted. He was still self-indulgent, still a creature of his senses, still a walking testament to living life for fun and pleasure. Exactly the kind of man she'd predicted he'd be. Exactly the kind of man she'd decided to exclude from her life. No matter how much it hurt.

"How does the show work?"

She cleared her throat, trying to regain her better mood. "It's supposed to walk the line between reality TV shows and the scripted variety. It's like that old party game, where one person is a killer and nobody knows who it is until they get 'winked' at. Then they are murdered and out of the game."

He nodded absently. "So the contestants aren't taking part in challenges to see who wins. They could actually get outwitted and killed?"

"They take part in challenges to try to figure out who, among them, is the killer. And also to earn exemptions on murder nights."

"Are they actors, playing roles?"

She shook her head. "Nope. Real people, not actors. Playing themselves, but always 'in character.'"

Mick gave her a questioning look as he directed the car off the main street through town and turned toward another subdivision with another rental possibility. "Meaning?"

"Meaning, they will have to do *some* acting because they're supposed to behave from day one as if they're really registering at a spooky, possibly haunted inn, and suddenly murder and mayhem erupt in the town around them."

And that was the tricky part of this entire reality show adventure. Because the contestants couldn't just be themselves. To make the show a success, the cast had to act as if everything—every murder, every drop of blood, fingerprint, mysterious stranger and unexplained noise in the night—was real.

Unfortunately, she imagined the closest some of them had ever come to acting was faking the occasional orgasm.

He nodded. "An in-character reality TV cast. That's not so unusual, I guess. I mean, aren't a lot of the contestants of these reality shows acting like sweet, marriageable girls when they're really foot fetish models or all-around bitches?"

She chuckled. "Right."

"Do they have to follow a script or something?"

She shook her head. "Nothing that happens is scripted beyond outlines of where they all need to go every day and the locations and descriptions of the murders. And the murder plot. We've set up the first few victims of the 'Derryville Demon,' but as for who dies after that, it's anyone's guess."

Before Caroline could continue, she saw that an attractive woman was placing a "For Rent" sign in front of the pretty house that had caught her eye. Her spirits lifted. "Is this it?"

Mick glanced over, gave a surprised look, then shook his head. "No, this isn't the one."

"Stop anyway," she urged, liking the profusion of flowers beside the front porch, and the way the big maple tree out front shaded the windows of the lovely yellow house.

"You wouldn't be interested in that one."

"Who says? Stop the car."

"She's renting the whole house, Caroline."

"It's Caro."

"Caro's syrup. It's not a name, it's something you put on pancakes," he muttered.

"No, maple syrup's what you put on pancakes. Caro's—oh, would you just stop?"

He pulled the car up to the curb of the house. The woman, who'd just finished placing the sign, instantly straightened.

"This isn't a good idea," he said softly.

But Caro was already stepping out of the car, smiling at the homeowner. Mick might think she was a big-city snob now, but frankly, Caro couldn't think of a lovelier place to stay during her upcoming weeks in Derryville. The house was small, a one-story cottage with a freestanding one-car garage. With the quiet street, well-kept yard and friendly appearance of the owner, she felt sure this was going to be the place.

It was only when Mick brushed past her, striding over to the small brunette, that Caro realized she might be wrong.

Then she noticed the woman looked upset. "Hey, what's wrong?" Mick asked as he tenderly touched the woman's cheek.

Caro swallowed hard, suddenly remembering the kindness of which this man was capable. Yes, Mick had always been a flirt, a rogue, a…dog. But he'd also always been a sucker for someone in distress. Especially if that someone was a female.

The woman didn't respond in words. Instead, she threw her arms around Mick's neck and hugged him tight.

Oh, but it hurt to see that. Obviously the reason Mick hadn't wanted to stop at this particular house was because its owner was his current...*whatever.* He'd tried to stop her. It was her own fault she had to witness yet another moment with Mick and another female. Kinda like the one that had broken them up.

Well, no way was she going to let him see she was the least bit bothered by that idea. While Mick and the woman talked quietly in the yard, Caro wandered up to the porch, noticing how fragrant the flowers beside it smelled.

"I'm so sorry," a woman's voice said. "You guys caught me at the wrong moment."

"Right moment," Mick said, his arm draped casually over the other woman's shoulders as they walked up to join Caro. "It's not every day you get fired."

"Fired?" Caro frowned. "I'm so sorry to hear that."

The woman shrugged. "I didn't get fired. I quit. Sort of. It was kind of mutual." Then a frown pulled the woman's pretty brow down. "I just wish half the town hadn't heard it."

"You're exaggerating, honey," Mick murmured.

Honey. Ouch.

"Anyway," the woman said, extending her hand toward Caro, "welcome. I'm glad you might be interested in the house. I'm anxious to move, especially now that I don't have to worry about how it will affect my job. My name's Sophie Winchester."

Good Lord. Winchester. Had she been stricken so

numb at seeing Mick again that she hadn't even noticed a gold band on his left hand? Then she remembered something. Her instant relief surprised her. "Sophie. You're Mick's baby sister, right?"

The woman looked surprised. "Yes. How did you know that?"

Caro felt heat rise into her cheeks as Mick watched, an obvious grin on his face. He was enjoying this, enjoying watching her sweat as she tried to explain to his sister that she and Mick had once been *very* close. Often close enough that not a thing had come between them— including clothes. "Mick and I were college friends," she said. "I remember him mentioning you."

"Small world." Sophie graciously dropped the subject as if she read Caro's discomfort. "Come on inside."

Ten minutes later, after touring the house with Sophie, who was both funny and charming, Caro had reached two conclusions. First, the house was perfect for her.

And second, it would never, never work.

Because Sophie had a cat. A big fat cat who reacted as every cat did when Caro came in contact with one. As if knowing which people either didn't like or were *allergic* to them, felines always curled around her, purring and wanting to be petted.

Just breathing the air in the house was clogging up her throat. Petting Mugs, as Sophie called him, could put Caro in the hospital. There was no way she could live here, even with a thorough cleaning. Caro's allergies were simply too severe.

Which left her stuck, again, in two ways. First, she still had no place to live. Second, and even worse, she had to get back in the car to do more house-hunting with Mick Winchester.

MICK SHOULD HAVE known better than to take the side streets back to downtown Derryville to his office. He should have stuck to the main road, getting Caroline to her car and out of his life as soon as possible. He should have done everything in his power to bring their inter-action to an end, letting her figure out on her own where she was going to live.

He'd done none of the above. Instead, some demon deep inside him made him cut through a quiet neigh-borhood with which he was *very* familiar. He told him-self it was shorter. That was bullshit.

The truth was, he was still ticked at her. Still affected by her. Still wanting her gone but not wanting her to leave.

Still stunned that she was here.

Caroline Lamb, right back in the center of his world, and sending it as crazily off balance as she always had. Things had never been peaceful and calm with them. They'd struck sparks off each other from the time they'd met, and Caro had always known how to push his buttons.

Like today. The never-ending house hunt was pure Caroline Lamb. Okay, so old man Snorkle was a heavy smoker and every surface in the house was a sickly beige nicotine color. And yeah, Mrs. Spencer was color blind and the spare room in her house would have been perfect for a patriotic leprechaun. And right, the McKen-zies were old and deaf but refused to use hearing aids so their conversations were at the decibel level of a jackhammer.

Picky, picky.

The fact that she'd refused Sophie's place had really ticked him off. It would have been perfect for her, and would have helped out Sophie. Not that Sophie needed

the money. He almost chuckled at that one, remembering how shocked he'd been to learn his bratty kid sister
was a famous hack-'em-up horror novelist. So successful she could probably buy and sell him ten times over.

But it would have helped her out to know that someone quiet, respectable and responsible was taking care
of her house while she was living with her fiancé.

His jaw tightened at the thought of Sophie living
with a man. Then he eased up. Divorce was so common,
he'd rather Sophie and Daniel give things a try now
than have regrets later.

But Caroline hadn't wanted Sophie's house. When
he'd accused her of rejecting it to try to avoid him, she
hadn't denied it.

So, she wanted to avoid him. Huh. That'd be a trick
in Derryville.

What really bugged him was the evidence that Caroline had turned into such a coward. The girl he'd
known back in college wouldn't have given a damn
where he went, what he thought or what he did. Caroline had been all fire and energy, a whirling ball of excitement, always up for adventure, whether it was going
four-wheeling up in the mountains in a borrowed Jeep
or taking a spontaneous twenty-hour road trip to the
beach one weekend.

That girl was gone. Long gone. Not at all in evidence in the tight-lipped, tight-formed woman sitting in
his car.

So he couldn't really say what had made him choose
this particular street—his anger, his sense of adventure
or his need to once again see Caroline Lamb sweat.
Probably all of the above.

"Stop!" She pointed. "There, that one."

He knew which house she was pointing to. The one on the corner. The big old two-story with the nicely treed lot and the driveway that circled around the front.

"There's a Room For Rent sign."

Yeah, there was. "Not this house, Caroline."

"You only have one sister." She reached for the door handle. "Don't tell me another one of your family members lives here."

He shook his head. "Nope, I'm not telling you that."

Then, because Mick just could never resist giving someone enough rope to hang themselves with, he let Caroline get out of the car and walk toward the house. He followed her, coming close to telling her the truth, but deciding against it.

Caroline went to the sign and pulled out a flyer. Her eyes sparked with indignation. "You have this place listed for rent."

"Yep."

"So why didn't you tell me about it?"

Because I'm not a freakin' lunatic?

"I didn't think it would suit," he replied, wondering why the hell he didn't just admit the truth so they could get out of here. Somehow, though, he was starting to have a little fun.

Caroline kept reading. "It has an in-law suite and there's only one resident. How bad could that be? I mean, there's no ax murderer or psychopath living here, is there?"

"Not as far as I know," he said with a chuckle, "but you can never be too sure about some people."

As if on cue, the front door to the house opened and a very familiar older woman walked out. Mick smothered a sigh, having no doubt what she had been doing inside. *Baking.*

Caroline shot him a glare as she saw the older woman, complete with iron-gray hair, a pair of wire-framed glasses and a brightly colored dress. "Oh, I'm shaking in my shoes," Caroline muttered, sotto voce. "I won't sleep a wink wondering if she's going to have a raunchy sex party."

He gulped at that image. Then he gave her a bit more rope…because she deserved it for bringing up the word sex when that was about all he'd been thinking about since he'd laid eyes on her again.

Sex. With her. Lots of it. The kind they used to have when they were young and hungry, when every cell in his body had contained a raging hormone and every one of them had been screaming her name.

"I can't believe you didn't mention this place. Did you intentionally make me suffer with all those other ones this morning? Was this some kind of ploy to get even because I dumped you back in college?"

Talk about déjà vu. They'd been in each other's company only a few hours and once again she was accusing him when he hadn't done a thing to deserve it. Just like she had when they'd broken up, when she'd thrown ugly words like playboy, irresponsible and "unable to be faithful" at his face. All because she'd seen a questionable moment and chosen to believe the worst.

"The rent *is* very reasonable," he replied evenly, not responding to her barb.

The older woman walked down off the porch and finally noticed them standing on the front walk. "Oh, you caught me," she said, giving Mick a guilty-looking smile. "I just took a pie out of the oven and left it to cool on the counter."

Caroline extended her hand. "Hello, I'm Caro Lamb."

"Caro..lan? How nice to meet you, dear."

"Uh, Lamb. That is…never mind. It's nice to meet you, too. I'm interested in the room for rent."

Mick suffered under a ten-second stare from a pair of eyes that had been able to make him spill his guts with just a glance from the time he'd been a kid. "She's with the reality show and needs a place to stay for a few weeks." One fine gray brow arched a bit. "I've shown her every rental in town," he added.

Those stiffened shoulders eased a bit. "Well then, how wonderful. I'm sure you'll love it. I have a hair appointment, so I'll get out of your way and let you go look."

Mick watched her leave, then turned his attention to Caroline. She went up to the porch, gave the two-person swing a little push and stood up on tiptoe to sniff at a flowering plant hanging by the door. Her smile was evident from down here on the lawn. She suddenly looked much more like the girl he'd known, which didn't make him feel one bit better.

She even sat down on the swing, setting it in motion with a kick and wiggling to make herself more comfortable while she waited for him to open the house.

"This is wonderful," she murmured.

She liked the place. Damn, why did that hurt so much?

"I want to see the inside. If it's as perfect as the outside, then I think I've found where I want to live."

"You're making a mistake…"

"No, I'm not," she said, rising from the swing and staring down at him from three steps above. "Stop telling me what I want and what I don't, Mick. I would have thought you'd learned a long time ago that I don't take well to that kind of thing."

He stiffened. Like he'd needed a reminder of how

she'd reacted when he'd tried to insist she didn't *really* want to move out to L.A. That her future was with *him*.

The anger in her voice and condemnation in her eyes was the last straw. He didn't protest as she looked at the house. As predicted, she loved it. She really went crazy over the rec room with the amazing TV setup. Caroline was ready to move full speed ahead and sign a lease on the spare suite of rooms.

So be it.

An hour later, after she'd signed the papers and paid the full four weeks' rent in advance, he watched her pull away from his office without a backwards glance.

"You made your bed, babe. Now you can lie in it."

He just couldn't wait to see what she said when she found out that bed was in *his* house.

CHAPTER FOUR

"So, TELL ME ABOUT this Caro Lamb."

Great. Just the person Mick didn't want to talk about. And just the person he didn't want to talk about her with—his mother—who'd beelined for his table at Ed's Café the minute she'd entered. So much for his nice, quiet Friday morning breakfast. "Her name's Caroline. And there's nothing to tell."

His mother sniffed, knowing better. Mick watched, amused, while the very predictable Marnie Winchester picked up a napkin, wiped off the seat and made a har-rumphing sound as crumbs floated to the floor. She sat across from him, keeping her purse in her lap, hands folded neatly on top of it. He knew darn well she'd ask the waitress to wipe off the table before she ate a thing.

"Sophie seems to think you knew her before."

Sophie, you're a dead woman.

He merely shrugged, neither confirming nor denying, hoping his mother had lost that whole mind-reading ability once her kids were out of the house. But he doubted it.

"Well?" she persisted, not at all put off by his signals.

She'd been relentless about Caroline since the after-noon when they'd bumped into her coming out of his house. She'd been there baking him a nice homemade pie. Why? Because his mother was convinced he hadn't eaten a decent meal or a good wholesome home-cooked treat since leaving home ten years ago.

"I've told you, she's a producer with the TV show," he said.

"The TV show?" Tina Laudermilk, who was sitting at the next booth listening to every word they said, turned around and gave Mick a good-morning smile. "I hear they've started to arrive."

From behind him, Mick heard a man's voice. "I saw a bunch of trucks at the inn yesterday when I was making my deliveries." It was Earl Donovan, the UPS guy, and an aspiring actor who'd been following the TV show goings-on with avid interest.

Earl and Tina began a conversation right over Mick's and his mother's heads, talking back and forth as if the other booth was not between them. "I stopped by the trailer and picked up the paperwork to be an extra."

"Is it true they're going to do scenes here?" Tina asked.

Ed, the owner and cook, popped his head up from behind the half wall separating the kitchen and the counter. "Yep. And they're paying me, too."

"Better save the money for future food poisoning claims," Mick muttered.

Judging by the way his mother's lips twitched, she'd heard.

"I saw the director fellow in the drug store yesterday," Tina said. She made a gooey-eyed face that told Mick what she'd thought of the man. "And did you hear the host is going to be Joshua Charmagne, from that cop show? What a dream."

The whole thing was more like a nightmare to Mick.

"He's a flamer." This from Donnie Jordan, a truck

driver who ran diesel throughout the state. He swiveled on his stool and jumped into the conversation. "No real man wears purple shirts like he did."

"He's no such thing," Tina retorted. "He was a gentleman detective and back then in Miami men did wear purple shirts and white suits. I bet he doesn't wear purple shirts in real life."

Donnie was not convinced. "Nope. Probably wears those rainbow ones to show his *pride*."

Before Tina could launch herself across the table to tackle Donnie for casting doubts on the manhood of her favorite has-been TV star, Mick figured he'd make his getaway.

"Check, please!" Mick hoped to pay his tab and escape while his mother was distracted by the conversation that had erupted around them. That was typical. Everywhere he went these days, the topic of conversation surrounded *Killing Time in a Small Town*.

His mother wasn't distracted. "She was very pretty."

"Who?"

She just smirked. Yeah, she still had that mind-reading thing going on. Caroline hadn't left his thoughts for a minute.

And his mother was right. Caroline was beyond pretty. She was damned beautiful. Thank God there was no way she'd really move in with him when she arrived for her month-long stay. "Was she? I didn't notice." He dropped his napkin onto his plate, trying to make eye contact with the waitress as he feigned indifference.

He should have known better. "Who are you, and what have you done with my son?" She reached over and put her hand on his forehead, like she used to whenever he tried to fake sickness to get out of going to school.

"Am I feverish?"

"Delirious."

His mother's droll tone made him laugh and drop the pretense. "Okay, yes, she was very pretty. But not my type."

"Is there such a thing?" This came not from his piercing-eyed mother, but from Deedee Packalotte, his regular waitress.

Deedee had been trying to rekindle an affair with him for years. Not that an affair was what he'd call the three or four afternoons they'd shared in her parents' basement, back when he'd been delivering papers and she'd been a teenager going to beauty school. She'd dropped out. Which would be pretty obvious to anyone who took one good look at her hair.

No, he and Deedee had had more like a Mrs. Robinson thing. She'd been the older woman—though only by four years—who'd taught him how to last longer than sixty-five seconds in the sack. Or, rather, on top of the washing machine, or the nearest flat surface they could find in the basement. He wondered if Deedee would be surprised to know he'd once gone sixty-five *minutes*. Not counting the foreplay.

"I'll have coffee." His mother frowned at Deedee for interrupting. "And, dear, would you get a rag and touch up this table?"

God love her.

Mick used her distraction to firm his resolve against talking about Caroline to his mother. His sister had been bad enough. It was hard to keep anything from Sophie. She was an observant person who hadn't been put off by his claims that Caroline had been a casual friend. Luckily, since Sophie had moved in with Daniel and begun telling people her real identity, she had enough to focus on without worrying about his love life. Or, past love life.

Not present. Caroline was definitely *not* part of his present.

"So you're going to rent out a room in your house. I still can't understand why you didn't just tell us if you needed help making the mortgage."

An old story. His parents were always trying to help, whether it was popping by to cook enough food for a battalion or offering him money. No matter how many times he'd told them he didn't *need* their help, they never stopped offering. Sophie suffered the same endless good will.

"I don't need help making the mortgage." True. He *was* fine, at least until the slow winter season came. That was the worst time of year in his business. So he'd thought he'd rent out a room in his big house—which he'd bought at auction and fixed up over the past two years—to fill in some. Of all the bad ideas he'd ever had...

"And this Caro, she's going to be living in your house, but you still say she's not your type?"

"She's not going to live in my house," he insisted as he sipped his rapidly cooling coffee, inhaling its aroma. Ed's served good coffee. Good thing, since the food sucked.

"What do you mean?"

He sipped again. *I mean the minute she finds out she's signed a lease to room with the big bad wolf, a Day-Glo green room or a little cigarette smoke ain't gonna seem so bad.*

"She'll make other arrangements when she arrives Sunday."

In fact, he was going to make damn sure of it. He was ninety-nine percent sure Caroline would storm out on her own the minute she found out she'd rented a room in his house. And he'd give her every penny of her money back. The look on her face would be payment enough.

But just in case, in the slim event that she liked his house enough to overlook the company, he'd developed a plan to help...uh...convince her.

He wasn't sure how yet, but one thing was definite. When Caroline Lamb arrived in Derryville, she was going to find a welcoming committee she'd never forget.

CARO HATED FLYING. It seemed unnatural that something so big should stay in the air, defying gravity. If humans were meant to ride in airplanes, they'd be born with a frequent flier card and an airsick bag.

Unfortunately, her job sometimes required long-distance travel. Like today. But, for once, landing didn't seem much better than flying, which said a lot about how little she wanted to arrive at her eventual destination.

"Derryville, Illinois," she muttered. "How on earth could I have forgotten the name of Mick's hometown?"

She quickly put him out of her mind. Unfortunately, as had been the case for the past three weeks—not to mention the past eight years—he was never completely gone.

She killed time in the usual way during the flight. And, as usual, she drew a few sidelong looks from her seat-mates and the passing flight attendant. Because she was singing.

Oh, she tried not to, tried to do it just in her head, but she couldn't help it. When Caro was nervous she couldn't stop herself from breaking into song in a low, quavering voice. This time as she sang, she pictured Tootie and Blair and the gang.

The woman next to her shot her a puzzled look. Caro almost identified the song as coming from *The Facts of Life*. Then she realized the woman probably wasn't curious about the song. More about the wacky singer.

Okay, so she was a professional twenty-eight-year-old woman with a great hairstyle, perfect makeup, wearing a thousand dollar Donna Karan suit and carrying a leather briefcase that had cost more than her first junker car.

And she sang TV jingles under her breath.

Sue me.

Everyone had their quirks, didn't they? At least she wasn't clicking her teeth or cracking her knuckles or blowing her nose into a tissue and then peeking at the goods like other people she'd sat next to on airplanes.

All in all, her nervous habit seemed pretty innocuous. It was just the TV part that made it look weird. If she'd been humming the latest Alanis Morissette song, nobody would have looked twice.

But Caro's nervous singing habit stuck strictly to her childhood repertoire of TV theme songs and jingles. Like a gambler might only play at a particular table, or an athlete wear a particular pair of socks, Caro relied on her old standby for good luck in avoiding things like midair collisions: television.

It had been her baby-sitter, then best friend and closest companion throughout her childhood. She'd needed somewhere to lose herself with two parents who worked all the time and either fought like cats and dogs or went at it like bunnies—depending on their moods—when they were home. Either way, she'd learned to keep the TV turned up as a kid. Loud—to block out the sounds.

So loud that she could swear she *still* sometimes heard the tune the Huxtables had danced to in 1983 or every note from the *Family Ties* ditty.

Family Ties or *The Cosby Show* her family definitely was *not*.

From the seat in front of her, a man began to hum the song from *Cheers*. Funny how everybody responded to TV. Like it or not—and Caro *liked* it—television was as intrinsic to American culture as a Big Mac. It sparked water cooler debates, show-watching parties, betting pools and hairstyles.

It was also good for airline small talk. Caro strictly avoided weather chats on airplanes, because of the whole lightning, burning, crashing thing. She stuck to TV. She just had to be sure she didn't talk about any disaster movies of the week. Sitcoms were safe. Soaps were right out.

This wasn't the first time Caro had gotten distracted from her fear of flying by getting into a discussion of how the dancing midget had been the beginning of the end for *Twin Peaks*, or how lame the last season of *Roseanne* had been.

Or this. "Mikey from the Life commercials did *not* die of a Pop Rocks and Pepsi eruption," she said to the older woman sitting across the aisle. Caro was in the biz. She knew the urban legends.

"Well, I heard he did." The woman sniffed and turned away.

The one beside her in the center seat continued to feign sleep, probably wondering why she always ended up beside the psychos on airplanes. Caro didn't mind seeming psycho. It kept her distracted from the flying. Or, rather, the crashing. That was the part about flying that she really didn't like—the crashing part. She wasn't *MacGyver*, who'd crashed with four teenage gang kids and survived by making stuff out of other stuff.

"Another one down," she whispered after the plane landed.

"Next time take a sleeping pill," she heard. Turning, she saw her seat mate. The woman smiled. "I do. It works every time."

"Thanks." Caro could have been put out with general anesthesia and she didn't think that'd relieve the anxiety. Frankly, she'd rather be conscious and alert in the last few minutes before her death, if she really was going to do the crashing and burning thing.

"Crash and burn," she muttered. Funny, that's pretty much what had happened on her first ever plane trip. Okay, not *on* her first plane trip, but rather right before it.

She and Mick had crashed and burned right before she'd dropped out of college and flown out west, needing to make a fresh start somewhere where she wouldn't hear rumors about his latest escapades or run into him with his latest girlfriend. A distinct probability since the first couple of times she'd met Mick had been when he was with his girlfriend of the week.

She'd heard the stories from the time she'd started school. Mick was the guy who'd climbed down a third-floor drainpipe to avoid being caught with someone in an on-campus sorority house. The charmer who'd somehow managed to get Hootie and the Blowfish to play at the homecoming dance. The prankster who'd rigged the electronic scoreboard at the football field to flash the answers to an upcoming midterm exam in a tough sociology class. The one who'd drawn over a thousand bucks in a charity bachelor auction…from the ex-wife of one of the professors, no less.

The one she'd found hiding in the storage room of her dorm, trying to avoid the two girls he was dating at the same time.

God, what a dog. And she'd been crazy about him. Crazy about him for a year, up until the day she'd realized being crazy about a bad boy was a much different thing from being in *love* with one.

Crazy was cool. Crazy was just fine for a college kid. But in love? Even worse, in love with Mick Winchester? Insanity.

Exiting the plane, she got her bags and the rental car the studio had reserved. Then she hit the road to Derryville.

By the time she arrived, it was full dark, a lovely September night with a sky full of stars and a huge watery moon. Too perfect a sky to be over a place Caro had begun thinking of as her personal hell.

All except the house. Inside the pretty house was a lovely mother-in-law suite, waiting just for her. With antique furniture, a four-poster queen-size bed, an old-fashioned claw-foot tub. Plus a huge window overlooking the kind of neighborhood the Huxtable or Keaton kids would have lived in.

Not the trailer park where Caro had grown up. Not the high-rise where she paid a fortune for her own small apartment now.

All she could think about was arriving at the little oasis in Derryville. The lovely home with the nice, quiet old landlady on the nice, quiet old street. The house would be her home base, a place to escape from the frenzy that always erupted on a reality television show set.

Best of all, the landlady would give her a physical barrier. She'd be a perfect chaperone in case Caroline lapsed into momentary insanity and lusted for Mick Winchester.

No. No lust. No stroll down a mind-numbingly hot memory lane with a guy who'd always been able to fry her circuits with a smile or have her flat on her back with a touch of his hand.

Damn. No woman should ever be unlucky enough to have a Mick Winchester as her first lover. Starting out with the best meant everything else was downhill from there. And it had been, until it got to the point where she hardly found sex worth it anymore.

Another reason to hate the bastard. He'd ruined her sex life.

When she arrived at the house, she parked in the driveway, surprised to note there were five or six cars parked on the street in front of the house. "Sewing circle night," she mused aloud. "Or maybe a bake sale meeting."

Though she was tired, this would be a perfect time to meet some of the matriarchs of Derryville. With the production schedule set up by the studio, she had to get the cooperation of the townspeople as quickly as possible. The crew was arriving today and tomorrow, the cast at the end of the week. All the extras had to be screened and signed, the locations set, the schedule firmed. They needed the residents on board from day one.

Swinging her soft carry-on bag over her shoulder, she left her other luggage in the trunk of the car. She wanted to sit down and have a nice hot cup of tea. Maybe some cucumber sandwiches or whatever small-town ladies served at Ladies' Guild-type meetings.

The front door was wide open, the screen propped as well, propped by a small refrigerator sitting on the porch. It was probably filled with lemonade, or raspberry iced tea. Buttermilk.

"Okay, this isn't *Seventh Heaven*," she muttered, forcing the images of small-town family dramas out of her mind.

This was real. Not TV.

She raised her hand to knock, then noticed something funny. The noises coming from inside the house didn't sound like a Ladies' Guild meeting.

Another indication that she wasn't going to be walking into a room full of nice gentle ladies was the smoke. Thick. Spicy. Obviously from a cigar. Or ten.

She froze, focused on the sounds. Male laughter. Deep. Raucous. Obviously from a man. Or ten.

Holding her breath, she entered the house, instinctively keeping on her toes to prevent her heels from striking the hardwood floors. She followed the noise, the laughter and a loud stereo playing some deafening music.

And suddenly found herself in a room full of testosterone.

Ten. Yep. That's about what it looked like, though a quick count told her there were really only five.

Five men. Five big, laughing, smoking, drinking, scratching, snorting, belching, card-playing men. They were gathered around a card table that had been set up in the middle of what she remembered was the rec room.

It looked wrecked, all right. Male paraphernalia covered every flat surface. Overflowing ashtrays. Empty beer bottles. A half-empty bottle of Jim Beam and a three-quarters empty one of Crown Royal. Empty glasses. Chip bags. Remnants of pizza in some large boxes littering the floor. Cards. Gambling chips.

And right there in the middle of it, staring at her with a big ol' shit-eating grin, sat a sexy-as-sin Mick Winchester.

MICK HAD KNOWN she was there the minute Caroline walked into the room. Even if he hadn't been expecting her he'd have noticed the change in the air. Female molecules, scents and energy stood out in this place. Especially when they were such attractive molecules, intoxicating scents and seductive energies.

He was the only one who saw her at first as she stood there, clad in another one of those power suits tailored to fit perfectly against her curvy little body. And another pair of wickedly high-heeled shoes that accentuated the long, soft legs he remembered.

Forcing his mind out of his crotch, he continued to wait, keeping a casual eye on his cards, the other on her.

Caroline looked shocked. Confused. Ready to faint. Then, ready to kill. She'd obviously seen him.

"Hey, Caroline!" he called, keeping his teeth clamped on the soggy end of a half-smoked cigar.

All the men at the table, his card-playing baseball team buddies, glanced around to follow his stare. He should have told them about her, or at least prepared himself for their reactions. That may have prevented his fists from tightening as Ty Taylor made a soft wolf whistle and Ty's twin brother, Eddie, muttered something mildly obscene under his breath.

Why he'd want to smash in the teeth of one of his long-time buddies, he really couldn't say. But he gave Eddie a warning look that instantly shut the other man up.

"What is going on?" Her voice was thready and shaking.

"Poker night. Five card stud. Ten dollar max bid," Mick explained. "And Jimmy here is kicking our asses."

She clutched her bag. "I mean, why...why are you *here?*"

He ignored the question. He also ignored his own slight tinge of remorse for planning this outrageous welcoming party for Caroline. He could have just called her and told her the truth any time over the past few weeks. But her snippy, impersonal little e-mails and faxed messages had kept him from doing it.

"Guys, this is Caroline Lamb. She's the producer for the new TV show being shot up at the old Marsden place."

Though he would have sworn not one of the men in the room would have held a door for his own mother after two hours of bourbon, cigars, raunchy talk and cards, each of them stood up and nodded to Caroline. Mick rose as well, acknowledging what he'd always known about Caroline. She brought out a basic male instinct from any man she came across. The good, the bad and the ugly. "The ugly" might have accounted for this whole welcoming reception, which had seemed like such a fine idea the other night over a few beers at the Mainline Tavern, but was making him feel a bit small now.

He shrugged off the feeling, remembering that Caroline was a champion at making people feel small.

"Nice to meet you," Ty said. His greeting was echoed by the other card players.

Mick quickly went around the table, introducing them all. Caroline remained silent until he reached the last name.

Then she just stared, waiting for the punchline. So he gave it to her. "Caroline's my new roommate. How are you doing, roomie? Have a good flight?"

He almost heard her back crack as she straightened it in a stiff stance a Master Sergeant would envy. "This is your house?" Her voice didn't so much as quiver.

"Yep." He sat back down, throwing his cards face-down onto the pile in the center of the table. "Damn."

"This is *your house?*" she repeated.

He looked up. "Uh-huh."

Her already creamy face went a shade paler and her lips trembled a little bit. He wasn't sure whether that was fury or dismay and had to gulp down another bit of unfamiliar guilt.

"Who was the woman? That day. Who was the older lady I met here, the one who baked the pie?"

"My mom."

The guys, who'd slowly retaken their seats around the table, snorted. Then Jimmy said, "You need to change your locks." He gave Caroline a glance and wagged his eyebrows at Mick. "Never know when she's going to walk in on something, uh…personal."

"Hey, she make you any of her chocolate chip cookies lately?" Eddie asked. Mick ignored him.

"You let me think…" she began.

He shrugged. "I tried to tell you this wouldn't suit you."

"I thought this was *her* house," she said, not seeming to care that she was basically repeating herself.

"I never said she was the landlady. And you never asked." Chuckling, he leaned back in his seat, kicking his feet out in front of him and crossing his hands behind his head. "Hope you don't leave panty hose and women's crap all over the bathroom."

"You're a dead man."

Mick shrugged, reached over and picked up the new hand of cards that Ty had dealt. The other guys just watched. Considering how wildly unpredictable Caroline had been in the old days, he couldn't have warned them what they might expect. She could turn and stalk out, not even giving him a chance to laugh and tell her he'd arranged for her to stay at Sophie's place…and that he'd give her back every penny of her rent.

Or she could pick up the nearest object—even the shoe off her foot—and lob it at his head.

Instead, she shocked even him. Shrugging off the suit jacket in a smooth, feminine move that made her silky blouse pull tight against her curvy body, she kicked off her shoes and strode over.

"Deal me in."

IN HER SMALL room in her brother's rectory, Hester Tomlinson sat on her narrow bed. She stared at her black-and-white television as a commercial for *Killing Time in a Small Town* came on. She recognized the street scene, seeing familiar buildings as a man's voice talked about bucolic small-town life.

"Some heavenly place," she said with a snort.

The fellow doing the voice-over made Derryville sound like some Norman Rockwell painting. It wasn't, as Hester knew better than anyone. "This town has secrets," she mumbled, keeping her voice quiet since Bob was praying in the next room.

Praying for her, most likely, as he'd undoubtedly done every day of the nine hundred and sixty-two days since she'd come to live under his roof. Not that she was counting or anything.

She'd been doing some praying of her own lately. She prayed for practical things. A decent steak for once. A big fat emerald necklace that would look much too gaudy for a God-fearing woman.

And she prayed for more secrets. For the power that came with those secrets. For the money that came with the power of those secrets. Yes, indeed, she knew all about secrets, how to spot them, how to figure them out and how to benefit from them.

Hester considered herself a fine judge of character, in spite of her brief lapse in figuring out what was going on with that trashy Winchester girl. "Spiteful, ungrateful little wretch."

The idea that Sophie Winchester had said what she'd said…had done what she'd *done*…had given Hester more than a few sleepless nights lately. Because if she could so completely misread a mealymouthed girl like that, what else might she have overlooked going on right beneath her nose here in Derryville?

A lot. Perhaps a *profitable* amount.

All that seemed somehow unimportant now. She turned her eyes to the TV again, unable to stop the dart of fear that made her quiver in her 3X cotton high-necked Sears nightie—the one she'd had to order from the catalogue since this lousy little town didn't even have a decent department store. One more example that she was the queen fly on a dung heap.

But it was better than being queen of nothing.

Coming here to live with her younger brother after his spineless wife had died three years ago had given Hester something she'd never had before. Status. Respect. A position of authority. She wanted to keep it. So the minute she'd heard TV people were coming to town, she'd begun to panic. Bob had worried, too. The two of them had done what they could—him preaching in the pulpit, and her working the more insidious gossip lines.

It had happened anyway, thanks mostly to those Winchesters. That was one family even the powerful standing of the first lady of the local church couldn't touch, as Sophie Winchester had already proved. No matter what Hester had done to spread rumors about the girl living in sin with the police chief, the thrown mud had slid off her like butter off Teflon.

Sometimes there was no justice. Sophie got away with her disrespect. Her brother Mick...well, he was fine to look at, Hester wasn't too old to note that. But he was a sinner. One had only to look at him, at the way he smiled at women, at the way he wore his pants and the way he walked. Wicked.

Not that it mattered, because now the town was going to be filling up with wicked people. Those Hollywood types, with their prying eyes and their prying cameras. People who liked to learn secrets, just like Hester.

What if one of these sneaky newcomers, by remote chance, recognized her? It seemed doubtful. She'd changed in the past thirty years, Lord knew. But it wasn't impossible.

And that was the only thing in the world that scared Miss Hester Tomlinson.

Exposure.

CHAPTER FIVE

CAROLINE HAD LEARNED how to play poker from her Uncle Louie, who was almost as much of a no-gooder as her own father. Uncle Louie had finally settled down and married Aunt Luanne; they were now affectionately called Loulou by everyone who knew them. He'd become a perfectly content husband, unlike her father, who was living someplace in Florida with his third wife.

One thing was sure. Uncle Louie had been a good teacher, beating Caroline out of every last penny in her piggy bank whenever he came to visit.

Thank you, Uncle Louie. She just loved being able to kick ass at cards. One ass, in particular, Mick's.

"Hell, Caroline, if I'd known you were a card shark I would've charged you higher rent," he muttered as he threw down another hand in disgust two hours later.

She shot him a disbelieving look, amazed that he had the nerve to bring up the subject of rent and renters. That conversation was coming, no doubt about it. But not now, not in front of witnesses who could be used to testify against her in the trial: the one she anticipated after she killed the guy.

She sipped at her now very watery scotch on the rocks, staring at her cards and humming the *Alias* theme under her breath. Kick-butt woman. That was appropriate tonight. Because she was going to kick Mick's butt all over the place once they were alone.

But it's such a nice butt.

No. No thinking of how Mick had looked while naked in his office a few weeks ago. Even as she ordered herself to get him out of her head, however, she knew she'd be unable to do it. The picture of Mick had remained in her brain every minute of every day since she'd seen him again.

The other men in the room were wonderfully good-natured about losing their money to her. Which was a good thing, since two of them were going to be extras on *Killing Time in a Small Town*. Finally, when the eleven o'clock news came on in the background, the one named Eddie leaned back in his chair and gave an exaggerated stretch. "Workday for me tomorrow."

Yes, it was, even for her. Unfortunately, she still had no idea where she was going to sleep tonight. But it was worth it to see the way Mick was squirming, wondering when she was going to erupt, and how she would handle her rooming situation.

She knew the answer to both questions: when they were alone, and, at the rent-by-the-hour no-tell motel out by the interstate.

"It was grand, boys," she said as she accepted her pile of money and tossed her final hand toward Mick. "I think I've earned back a week's worth of the rent this snake slimed out of me."

Mick sipped his water. She'd noted he'd switched to nonalcoholic drinks after Caro had announced she was staying. Probably for the same reason Caro had nursed just one scotch all evening. She needed all her wits about her. Not so much for the game, because Mick's friends, while they might have been all-stars on the baseball field, really stank at cards. But no, she needed to keep clearheaded to deal with Mick once they were alone.

Which looked like it was going to be very soon.

"'Night, Caroline," Eddie, a thick-waisted Italian guy with a shaggy mustache, said.

"It's Caro," she murmured.

"Like the pancake syrup?"

She shot Mick a glare as she heard him chuckle.

"Welcome to town," said Eddie's brother, Ty, who looked just like him except for the absence of about forty pounds. She liked Ty. He hadn't tried to suck up to her by letting her win the first round or two, like the other guys had. He'd gone right for the gut. She liked a man who wasn't intimidated by a strong woman.

Like Mick. He hadn't cut her any slack either. It had been a real pleasure to cut his jacks-over-eights full house out from under him with a royal flush.

If only he didn't look so darn cute. So male, so king of his domainish. She couldn't imagine why she had ever thought this house belonged to the nice old lady— his *mother,* for heaven's sake. Because while it was old, and tastefully decorated with antiques, it did scream male inhabitant.

The rec room with the completely drool-worthy forty-three-inch flat-screen TV and the five-speaker sur-round-sound system should have been a tip-off. Little old ladies didn't usually watch their *Matlock* or *Murder She Wrote* reruns in such high-tech surroundings. Caro had just been too deep in lust with the TV setup to question it.

The rest of the house had held similar hints. From the paneled office with the cherry desk—which she'd orig-

inally thought might have belonged to the nonland-
lady's late husband—to the overstuffed leather furniture
in the living room, she should have expected this. Well,
not *this*. Not Mick. But she should have at least considered the possibility that the woman she'd met was not
the owner of the house.

When they were finally alone, Mick walked over to
plop on the recliner facing the TV. Following him, Caro
found the remote and clicked the off switch. Nothing
happened. Spying another remote, she grabbed that one
and tried again. Still nothing. "Do you not have batter-
ies in this town?"

He didn't even look around. "The little one's for the
stereo. The silver one for the CD player. The fat black
one works the DVD and the really long one runs everything else."

Great. A remote-inept roommate. "Ever heard of universal?" she asked, digging into the sofa cushions for
the long "everything else" one.

Mick wasn't helping. "Can never figure out how to
get the damn things to work. The one time I tried it, it
kept turning on my coffeepot. I thought I'd end up burning my house down."

She saw a nearly hidden smile. "You're so full of it."

"And so are you. You know damn well you're not
planning on staying here. Why didn't you slap my
face and walk out the minute you realized what I'd
done to you?"

He gave her one of those lopsided, cocky grins, as if
daring her to get close enough to slap his face. She didn't
take the dare. Stepping close to Mick would make her
hand itch to do something far removed from slapping.

She already wanted to touch him. Had wanted to touch

him since that first moment in his office. But that was a dangerous, slippery road, one she couldn't afford to travel. She took one tiny, nearly imperceptible step back.

"So tell me," he said, apparently not noticing the sudden flush in her cheeks, "why haven't you left yet?"

She crossed her arms in front of her chest, still standing over him. "Where, exactly, do you suggest I go?"

"So you definitely don't want to be roomies?"

"Not even if you've turned into Tom Hanks from *Bosom Buddies.*"

He rolled his eyes. "Still living life as a sitcom, huh?"

She glanced around the dirty room, which still held a hazy cloud of smoke and a strong smell of liquor. "Still living life as a frat boy, hmm?"

He chuckled. "Christ, how did I survive eight years without hearing those smart-ass comebacks?"

That made her catch her breath, and Mick instantly seemed sorry to have said it. He stared at her, their eyes meeting and exchanging a long, unspoken conversation. *Where has the time gone? Where have you been? How has life treated you? What brought us together and what was it, really, that tore us apart?*

None of the questions were asked. Much less answered.

Instead, Caroline voiced another one. "Why'd you do it? Why'd you set me up like this?" She instantly regretted it, especially when she heard the note of vulnerability in her own voice. Dammit, she'd pulled off strong and in-control all evening. Why'd she have to go and turn into a girl now when they were alone?

He met her stare unflinchingly. "Because I was mad at you and I was being a mean-spirited shit." He rose from his chair and stepped closer, sending prickles of awareness throughout her body. "I'm sorry."

Mick had never been a liar—as someone who reveled in his badness, why would he ever need to be? So Caro knew he was telling the truth now.

"I was going to tell you earlier—before you thoroughly trounced me at cards—that I've arranged for you to have Sophie's house. It's vacant. And I'll give you back all your rent money."

She shook her head. "I can't. I can't live in Sophie's house."

"Oh, for God's sake, Caroline, is a clean, vacant, pretty little house worse than living here with someone you despise?"

She thought about it. He looked slightly insulted that it took her so long to answer, probably because he'd been angling for a protestation that she didn't despise him. He wasn't getting one.

"I can't live in Sophie's house, Mick, because of my allergies."

He quirked up one brow.

"Cats. Remember?"

"What about them?"

"I'm allergic."

"The house has been thoroughly cleaned."

"You don't get it," she replied, breathing an exasperated sigh as she dropped to the sofa and waited for him to sit opposite her. After he did, she continued. "I have major allergies. Those few minutes I spent in her house nearly made me break out in hives. No matter how much it's cleaned, unless the place has been HEPA-vacuumed and recarpeted, I can't spend more than a half hour in there or I'll end up in the hospital."

He looked stymied. "Have you always been allergic to cats?"

She nodded, crossing her arms. "Don't you remember Coolie? My hairless? I had pictures of him all over my dorm room."

Mick frowned. "I always thought he was a rat."

She picked up a pillow and threw it at him.

"So, Sophie's place is out." He looked sheepish. "Damn, I really am sorry."

Caro recognized the look. Mick was a notorious prankster, a joke-player, but whenever one of his harmless pranks turned out to be a little less than harmless, he'd always been the first to apologize and try to make things right.

She didn't let him off the hook that easily. "You should be."

Mick leaned forward and dropped his elbows onto his jean-clad knees. Caro followed his every movement with her eyes, wondering why eight years hadn't been enough to make Mick Winchester look old and unattractive. She didn't know that eighty years could.

He might still be a ruthless prankster, but he had definitely changed physically. Seeing him naked that morning a few weeks ago had proved that. Seeing him now, in his threadbare, stone-washed jeans and tight cotton T-shirt reminded her again.

As a young college guy he'd been a long, lean stud. Now he was thicker, filled out, bulkier and harder, with the kind of solid, muscular arms that said he did more than work in an office all day. His face had matured, too, losing its cute boyishness and gaining a heart-stopping male maturity that a lot of guys in Hollywood would have loved to have. But that grin, and that twinkle in his vivid green eyes was the same.

She drew in a shuddery sigh, forcing herself to pull

her attention off his body and back on his rotten practical joke. "I guess I'd better get out of here."

He instantly stood. "Where are you going?"

"I plan to go stay at the motel on the interstate for the night, even if I do have to pay by the hour."

"You can't."

For a second, she thought Mick was being protective. Then he added, "The county fair is in town this week and that place is sold out."

So much for tender and considerate. She scowled. "This is your fault."

He nodded. "I know. So I guess you're going to have to live with Day-Glo green. I think that's the only rental one of your Hollywood buddies didn't snatch up, so that's your only choice. I'll call the owner right now." He gave her another apologetic look. "And I'll pick up the rent."

Her only choice? Not quite. Before she had a second to think about it, she replied, "I do have a lease, you know."

He just stared.

"You rented me a room in your house and money exchanged hands. You can't throw me out."

This time his jaw dropped. "You can't really live *here*."

"Why can't I? I'm legally entitled." Knowing that Mick was appalled at the idea of having her under his roof for four weeks made Caro start to appreciate the merits of her impetuous idea. The more she thought about it, the more she liked it. "I have been looking forward to a nice, quiet room in this lovely old house, and you rented it to me. Unless you want the studio to sue for breach of contract."

He thrust his hands through his thick, wavy hair, sending a few strands sticking out in a boyish tumble. For an insane moment, she thought about walking over and straightening it. Her fingertips rubbed against each other as if remembering the feel of that hair against her skin.

"This is impossible."

Crossing her arms and feigning a calm she really didn't feel, she leaned back into the couch, making herself right at home. "You made this bed." She let a Cheshire cat grin cross her lips. "Now I get to sleep in it."

MICK FINALLY AGREED that Caroline could spend the night, at least *one* night, while they figured out what to do. Caroline kept insisting, right up until the minute she shut the door to the spare room in his face, that she was staying put for the length of her lease.

"Staying put, my ass," he said as he stood in the hall staring at the closed door. A door—such a minor thing standing between him and Caroline. Not even half a continent had been enough to get her out of his brain for the past eight years.

"Your tattooed ass!" he heard from within the room.

He muttered a quieter curse, but as he walked away, Mick was unable to resist breaking into a smile.

Who would have imagined an evening like this? A *month* like this? Caroline, back in his life, sleeping in his bed—okay, not the same one *he* was sleeping in—but a bed he owned, nonetheless. And that he'd be smiling.

He should have been throwing things. Cursing. Getting into his car and driving away from her, from the memories, from the thought of what an immature jerk he'd once been and what a scared brat she'd been.

"Well, hell, who said twenty-one-year-olds know anything?" he said aloud as he walked into his own bedroom and kicked the door shut behind him.

Especially not *him* at twenty-one. Christ, he couldn't figure himself out *now,* at twenty-nine. So how could he have thought, as a college junior, that he knew what love was? Knew enough to propose to a girl?

"Propose." He shuddered, the word tasting strange in his mouth. He hadn't thought about getting married since that one crazy spring break when he and Caroline had taken a road trip up to Canada. He'd asked her to marry him while the two of them had frozen their asses off under a thin blanket and an endless midnight sky.

She'd said yes. Then a week later, she'd said a re-sounding no. All because Mick had never lost that need to charm, to flirt, to get his way in the same manner he'd *always* gotten his way: with a grin, a wink, an irre-sistible laugh, a little flattery.

He'd been using that technique ever since he was old enough to figure out his place in the large Winchester family. The Winchesters were to Derryville what the Kennedys were to Massachusetts. He'd been raised with cousins as siblings, grandparents up the block or in the kitchen, and various great-aunts, uncles and their kids perfectly willing to comment on everything he did from the time he was old enough to talk.

Probably that old-enough-to-talk thing was what had done him in. His first word had been cookie. And, ac-cording to family legend, it had been accompanied by such an adorable two-toothed smile that every woman he said it to would present him with exactly the treat he'd asked for.

Many women had lined up to give him their cookies over the years.

That was okay. Randy little flirt seemed as good a po-sition in his family as anything else. His cousin, Jared, had already nailed down the role of smart and serious one, and Jared's older sister—now living in Florida—claimed the role as oldest and boss-of-the-world. His own sister, Sophie, was the baby doll who hid a will of steel behind her sweet blue eyes.

So Mick was the prankster. The kid with the toothy grin who'd broken windows with baseballs but always gotten invited in for lemonade when he went to fess up. The one who made enough in tip money to buy a new bike just because the ladies on his paper route thought he was the cutest little thing in town.

He was the first one to admit he'd cruised through life. He'd found his place, settled into it and hadn't bothered challenging himself too much in an effort for more. It hadn't seemed worth the bother when no one in this town would ever see him as anything more than he'd always been.

Going away to college had been his first hint that he *could* be more than he'd always been. Being with Caroline had given him a real taste of adulthood, of a different kind of future. He'd had juvenile dreams of the two of them coming back to Derryville and creating the most respectable, responsible, warm and friendly family anyone had ever known.

"Gag me," he muttered as he yanked his T-shirt off his body and shucked off his jeans.

Warm and friendly? Yeah. That was good. Respectable, responsible? "Gag me *twice*."

Caroline had realized before him that he'd wanted what he wanted for all the wrong reasons. She wanted to go west, to L.A., to live a big life, take chances, be young and wild.

He'd wanted to go home. To…to… "To show

them," he murmured as he sat naked on the edge of his bed.

Yeah. He'd wanted to show them. To show the world that Jared wasn't the only straight-up, all-around-great-guy, destined-for-success Winchester in town.

"How stupid was that?"

Very.

He tried lying down but that just kept him thinking about the stupid mistakes he'd made in his life. Being so rigid with Caroline about what he wanted to do once they got married. Letting his anger with her push him into a risky situation with another girl…who'd been after him for months. No, nothing had *happened* in that situation, but Caroline hadn't believed that. Hadn't trusted him. Had accused him, found him guilty and dumped his ass, all in a five-minute time span.

All because she'd wanted to live, and he'd wanted to prove something.

Finally, sick of calling himself a bunch of names in his head, he got up and pulled his jeans back on over his naked body. Though the evening was slightly chilly, he didn't bother with a shirt. It had been a while since he'd heard any noises coming from Caroline's room, which was separated from his by only one thin wall—wasn't that thrilling.

Going downstairs in the darkness, he made his way to the rec room, still cluttered with overflowing ashtrays and half-filled glasses, and plopped down on the leather recliner. He dug around, came up with the universal remote he'd lied to Caroline about not having, and flipped on his TV.

He'd done about three minutes of serious channel surfing when the air suddenly changed. His body reacted to Caroline's scent before his mind even registered that she was there. He grew tense, aware. He sat up straighter in his chair, not turning around, not needing to see her to know she stood there.

Caroline had always worn sweet, flowery perfumes when they'd dated. The college girl had been stuck in her Southern roots, with a tiny bit of a twang in her accent and a bit of steel in her spine. But since going west, she'd lost not only the accent, but also the light fragrance. Now her skin was perfumed with something headier. Warmer. A fragrance that had driven him crazy that day a few weeks back when they'd been sequestered in his car, looking for a place for her to live.

It wasn't just her scent. He could swear he heard her breathing, felt her warm breaths touching the bare skin on his shoulders as she stood behind him.

He knew why she'd come downstairs. Knew it without a doubt. He'd seen the look on her face the day she'd come to Derryville and he'd shown her this place for the first time. She'd been waiting for her chance, for *this* moment.

Caroline had deep urges and there were a few things that would always arouse her deepest desires. One of them was right here in this room.

Finally, unable to take the silent, heady tension anymore, he murmured, "I knew you couldn't resist."

She didn't deny it. "No, I couldn't."

"I saw the lust in your eyes that first day."

She edged closer. "You know me too well."

"You want it bad," he murmured.

"I do," she admitted with a deep sigh. "*So* bad."

He nodded, still not turning around. He just stared at the giant TV screen and fingered the buttons of the remote, taunting her, building her tension.

"I believe you rented one room of my house. You think that entitles you to roam around late at night, dressed…" He cast one quick look over his shoulder, seeing her dressed in a pair of silky short pajamas that hugged those fine hips, emphasized her small waist, and revealed almost every inch of those sweet, long legs of hers. He gulped. "Dressed, like that?"

"Your flyer said house privileges."

Run of the house. Yeah, that's what it had said. "You've been lying up there waiting for your chance, right? Waiting until I got tired and relaxed so you could make your move."

"Uh-huh."

"You haven't changed a bit."

She stepped closer, until her hip was about even with the back of his reclining chair. He looked up and saw her staring, not at him, but at the irresistible force that had drawn her from her room. "It's a high-definition plasma, right?"

He nodded. "With Pure Cinema II 3:2 film correction."

She moaned softly. "Like being in a theater. You were lying about the remote, of course."

"Of course."

Both of them continued to stare at the TV, the one thing in his house he knew damn well she'd be unable to resist.

Caroline was a TV junkie. And his was top of the line.

"Sound?"

"Bose."

This time, her moan turned into a whimper. "Loaded?"

"Oh, yeah. DVD, CD, CDR, CD-RW, MP3, Digital 5.1 decoding."

She grabbed at his chair, swaying on her feet. Almost not seeming to realize she was doing it, she lowered herself to the padded armrest, scooting his arm out of the way to make room for her pretty little behind. "I hate you."

He merely grinned. "You'd sleep with me for this setup."

"I have slept with you. Will that get me a *Friends* rerun at least?"

He swallowed. Hard. Suddenly the playful repartee with sensual undertones had gone more sensual than playful. Memories of the intensely physical relationship they'd once shared filled his brain.

He pushed the thoughts away. "Well, I suppose since you're leaving tomorrow you should get your shot."

She didn't argue the point, though he knew she was disagreeing in her mind.

Somehow—though she'd been torturing him for hours with her mere presence in his house—he couldn't resist her when her guard was down and she was sleepy and tousled, looking with lust at something of his. Okay, it wasn't something on his body. But he loved his home theater almost as much as his own limbs.

"*The Philadelphia Story* is on one of the movie channels."

"Ooooh," she moaned. "The original?"

Hearing the hopeful tone in her voice, he gave her one short nod, then scooted over on the chair.

As if it was the most natural thing in the world, Caroline slid down to sit beside him, curling up against his body, never taking her eyes from the screen as he flipped to the movie.

And that's the way they fell asleep.

SOPHIE COULDN'T quite get used to sharing a bed with someone other than Mugs, her cat, but by now, at the end of her first week as Daniel's roommate, she'd decided it had its perks. Like at this very moment, when they'd finished making delicious love, and she lay curled in his strong arms, looking at the shadowed corners of the room and plotting murder.

"Stop it."

"I can't," she whispered, smiling to herself in the darkness. "I'm so comfortable and safe with you."

"Safe enough to figure out how to dismember someone in under five minutes?"

Daniel knew the story she was working on.

"My editor wants the proposal by next week."

It still amazed her that everything had happened the way it had. She'd met Daniel Fletcher, the new police chief of Derryville, just months ago. Yet he'd become the most important part of her life. The first man she'd ever known who'd seen past the sweet Sophie facade she'd used to hide her true self from the world for so long. And he'd liked the real Sophie. Wanted her, grisly imagination and all.

The two of them had had a marvelous time exploring everything there was to know about one another.

"You know, most guys might not take it the right way if their fiancées got off on thinking about blood and gore right after...well...getting off."

She snickered. "That was lame." Pressing back against him even tighter, she said, "Besides, you're not most guys." She turned around to meet his dark-eyed stare and gently kissed his lips. "Thank heaven."

He kissed her in return, once, twice, then lazily scratched her hip and curled his hand over her backside.

"So, you're sure you're ready for Derryville—and the world—to find out you're R. F. Colt?"

She frowned. "Did you really have to bring that up?"

"Sophie, you're scheduled to do an interview on the *Chicago Morning Show* in a couple of weeks. Word'll be spread through the Derryville grapevine before you've had your coffee that morning."

She puffed out her cheeks and blew out a weary breath. "True."

"For what it's worth, I'm glad you agreed to do it. And there was certainly nothing stopping you once your job situation was taken care of."

She nodded. "I know, I'm glad, too. I just wish I'd stopped to think for a minute about this particular book I'm promoting."

"Why?"

She nibbled the corner of her lip. "Well, Miss Hester does make an appearance. And it's a particularly gruesome one."

He barked a laugh, well used to her habit of writing fictional death scenes for people who really bugged her. She'd once written a fictional character based on Mrs. Newman—who always had dozens of items in the ten-item-only lane at the grocery store—and had her die by choking on a Twinkie.

"Do you think anyone will realize it's her?" she asked, hearing the note of dread in her own voice.

"I'm sure they won't."

He was an angel for saying so. But she had the feeling he was wrong.

Which meant Derryville was about to find out Sophie had fantasized about shooting Miss Hester and leaving her fat bloated corpse stuck in a too-small bathtub.

Gee. It looked like her Sweet Sophie days were really about to come to an end.

CHAPTER SIX

SHE STAYED. Mick couldn't believe it, but Caroline stayed. In his guest suite. In his house. In his thoughts, his brain, his guts, his life.

Damn.

The one thing he'd thought for sure she wouldn't do was exactly what she'd done. Probably his own fault for letting her curl up with him and watch his pride and joy that first night. He'd set himself up for it by making the prize all the sweeter to a woman as determined and hardheaded as he knew Caroline to be.

So far, the first few days of her residency had been pure hell. Oh, not because they couldn't get along. Truth be told, they barely saw each other. They hadn't agreed to stay apart, but that's what had happened. Waking up together in his lounge chair the morning after her arrival had shocked them both. They'd become uneasy, uncomfortable with one another, each recognizing some unseen boundary they'd accidentally crossed. And they had both apparently decided never to cross it again.

He stayed busy with work, trying to broker a deal with a Chicago development company to bring a large shopping complex to the Derryville area. And Caroline spent fourteen-hour days on the set at the Little Bohemie Inn. She apparently ate her meals there, slipping into the house and straight up into her room at night, so there were days when they never even saw each other.

But he heard her. Oh, yes, indeed, he heard her very well.

Their rooms butted up to one another upstairs, and he could sometimes hear her moving around. He heard her alarm go off in the morning, heard her muttering because she'd apparently never lost her dislike of waking up early. He heard the click of her lamp going on, her hiss when she got out from under the covers in the cool September morning air, her footsteps on the wood floor. Heard her breaths. Heard her thoughts. Heard her heart beating.

Okay, maybe he didn't really hear all that. But his brain thought he did. He'd had several long, sleepless nights this week while he'd lain, breathless in his bed, listening for her slightest movement, wondering where she was, what she wore, how she looked. Wondering if he'd hear her creep down the stairs for yet another irresistible late-night TV binge.

She never did. If she had, he wouldn't have gone downstairs, wouldn't have risked another intimate night like the first one. Mick wasn't that strong a guy. And revisiting that particular period of his life was a bad idea. A really bad idea.

But that didn't mean he didn't fantasize it. Every single night. It was pure sensual torture as only Caroline Lamb had ever been able to dish out.

"This is friggin' ridiculous."

"What is?"

He hadn't even realized his cousin had entered his office until he heard him speak. Looking up, he saw Jared leaning indolently against his desk, his arms crossed, a look of amusement on his face.

"The way you dress," Mick replied with a forced smirk. "Still haven't gotten out of your undertaker phase, I see."

Jared liked to wear black. Always had. Mick used to think it was because his cousin liked looking spooky and mysterious, since he'd once been an FBI agent and now wrote gory true-crime novels. Now he just knew it was because Jared couldn't be bothered matching up anything with color. The man was always too intent on his latest project or deadline to think of clothes.

"Everything goes with black," Jared said with a shrug. The twinkle in his eye and the grin on his mouth were evidence that he was not at all fooled by Mick's flip response.

"Yeah. Casket. Hearse. Corpse."

Jared took a seat at the chair across from his desk, moving nearly silently, as always, as smooth as a cat. "I hear you're living with our intrepid TV producer."

Mick grew wary. "*Our* producer?"

Jared nodded. "Ms. Caroline Lamb. And why do I suspect she's the one who has you looking all tied up in knots?"

"Because you're a writer and you have a vivid imagination?"

"I write nonfiction."

"Because you're a member of my family, which means you're privy to the ridiculous speculations of my mother and sister?"

Jared nodded. "True. So, are the speculations correct?"

Mick trusted Jared like he trusted no one else in the world. But he wasn't ready to go there. He'd never told anyone the full story of his relationship with Caroline and he wasn't about to now that she was back in his life. "No comment."

Jared didn't press. "Just for the record, if there is any truth in the rumors, I happen to like her. She's the only sane one in the asylum."

"That bad?"

Jared rolled his eyes and drew in a long breath. "How the hell Gwen and I ever let Hildy talk us into allowing this TV show to film at the inn, I'll never know."

"She can be pretty persuasive," Mick said, thinking about Gwen's elderly relative who had a will of steel and the wardrobe of a twenty-year-old. "She even got Grandpa to start wearing sandals."

Jared visibly shuddered. Neither of them were sad to see their grandfather so happily involved in an autumn years romance. But Hildy…well, she certainly wasn't much like their late grandmother. Still, everyone adored her, quirky habits, ghosts and all. "Next thing you know she'll have the *Queer Eye* guys over to redo his house."

Mick snickered, then asked, "So tell me how it's going." He was curious in spite of himself. "I've heard tons of gossip but none that sounded reliable."

"The gossip's true. Hollywood is every bit as nutty as you've ever imagined it was."

"Example."

Jared leaned forward. "Remember the huge old tree in the backyard, on the east side of the house?"

Mick snickered. "You mean the one you tried to climb even though you're afraid of heights?"

He should have known better than to bring up that subject. Jared shot him a look that would freeze lava, still blaming Mick for his role in the Halloween mix-up last year.

"Sorry. Sore subject."

Jared relented. "Aww, hell, it brought me Gwen."

So it had. Jared had met Gwen last year, after receiving Mick's invitation to an in-character Halloween party. Jared had shown up at the Little Bohemie Inn as Miles Stone, a tree-climbing secret agent. Luckily, Gwen had been a woman who liked secret agents.

"So I'm forgiven for not telling you you *weren't* a superspy?"

"Didn't you realize you were forgiven when I asked you to be my best man?"

Mick gave him a wicked grin. "I figured you asked me because you have no other friends."

Jared shot right back. "Who said you were my friend?"

"Asshole."

The two of them burst into laughter, well used to the back and forth insults they'd lobbed at one another all their lives. Though a cousin, Jared was as close to Mick as a brother. He, Jared and Sophie had grown up like siblings.

Remembering what Jared had been saying, Mick asked, "So what's this about the tree?"

Jared groaned. "This director, Renauld Watson, is a lunatic."

"I'd heard rumors about that. He got his way on having Decatur Street shut down all day this coming Saturday, in spite of people's protests, didn't he?"

Nodding, Jared said, "He thinks it's still too summery for the place to look spooky. Wants that Halloween feel for the show."

Considering it was only early September, and the days still warmed up to nearly eighty degrees, that was going to be a trick. After Mick said so, Jared continued. "Right. So, to get that autumn look, he decides to paint the tree in the backyard."

Mick's jaw dropped. "I get the feeling you're not

talking about a nice watercolor landscape for over your mantel."

"No." Jared shook his head. "Gwen came home yesterday and found the tech guys on ladders, spray painting individual leaves yellow and orange."

Mick raised a hand to his eyes, shaking his head in disbelief. Where else but Hollywood?

"I thought Gwen was going to shoot them. She was furious."

Gwen was a sweet, beautiful little blonde, but Mick knew from experience that she could be ferocious when protecting someone—or *something*—she cared about. "What happened?"

"Your Caro came to the rescue and smoothed everything out."

"She's not Caro. Caro's pancake syrup."

"No, Caro's what you use in pecan pie."

Mick rolled his eyes. "How the hell do you know that?"

"I like pecan pie," Jared explained with a shrug. "Hildy makes a very good one."

Mick ignored the pie reference and went back to Jared's other ridiculous comment about "his" Caro. "And she's not mine."

"Hildy?"

The twinkle in his cousin's eye said he knew full well who Mick meant. Jared was a wicked tease in his own right. He just preferred to be all serene and conservative while doing it.

"Don't you have somewhere to go?"

"Only back to the inn, which will soon be accommodating the cast of this insane television program. I can live without being there to see their inglorious arrival."

The arrival of the cast. Hmm…he wondered how

Caroline was going to deal with a bunch of nonacting actors, all hungry for the big cash prize and their shot at fame.

"Funny," he said as he rose from his desk, "for the first time, it sounds like something that interests me. I think I'll go up there and check things out."

CARO HAD NEARLY reached her breaking point and the cast for *Killing Time in a Small Town* hadn't even arrived yet.

Between an impossible director, a flamboyant, arrogant, hard-to-please show host, techies incapable of independent thought, an aloof lead camera operator and her own personal hell of living in the same house as Mick Winchester, she felt on the verge of a meltdown. Only Charlie, the on-site tech director, had made an effort to be cooperative. Of course, that was because he was a tired old guy who was close to retirement and just didn't care to argue anymore. But nice was nice. She'd take it.

Overall, things sucked. She'd had one of those back-of-the-head faint headaches for almost two days now and no amount of caffeine or aspirin was making it go away.

"You look like you need a drink."

Caro glanced up from her cluttered desk inside the cramped on-site production trailer, and saw Hildy Compton. The old woman's outrageous outfit—screaming pink leggings, knee-high boots, and a filmy peasant blouse—gave Caro her first smile of the day. "It's only 11:00 a.m.," she replied. "But thanks for the thought."

Hildy shrugged and shut the door to the trailer. "I once knew a Joe who kept a bottle of moonshine in his bathroom to brush his teeth every morning. Said it stuck to them all day and he could lick it when he needed a jolt."

Caro had already become accustomed to Hildy's frequent reminiscences about her gangster gal past.

"That Mr. Watson needs more than a drink. He needs estrogen," Hildy said with a harrumph. "That man's got some wild mood swings for a fella that old."

Caro smiled faintly, somehow feeling a little better because of the outrageous old lady. She was right. The director—with whom she'd never before worked and hoped never to again—had had a serious case of PMS ever since Caro had ordered the crew to stop painting leaves on the trees and putting cheap, fake-looking spiderwebs in every room of the inn.

After shoving a stack of folders out of the way, Hildy settled onto the tiny love seat. "So how are you getting along living with that rascal Mick Winchester?"

"Rascal? I don't know what you mean."

The old lady snorted. "Ha! Unless you got male gear hidden under those tight skirts of yours, you know what I mean. Not a woman alive who can resist that boy when he sets his mind to her."

"Well, lucky for me, he hasn't 'set his mind' to me."

Yeah. Lucky for her. Very lucky, considering she'd felt her resolve and animosity toward Mick melting away through the nights she'd slept under his roof.

God, it was agonizing. She hadn't realized just how thin the walls might be in his old house. Thin enough that she heard—or thought she heard—every move he made, all night long. The picture of him lying there, naked, uncovered by his sheets, like he used to sleep in the old days, had tormented her for hours each night.

Bad enough if she'd had to rely on memories from years ago when her mind betrayed her and drifted to the image of him naked. No, she still had the full glorious Technicolor picture of that day in his office on her mind.

Bad bad mind.

Mick, bed and naked were three words she shouldn't associate with one another. But they were all she thought about when she was in his house, which was why she tried to avoid being there. She'd even considered crashing here in the trailer. Unfortunately, as usual, the on-site production trailer had turned from her private office into a catch-all storage closet for the entire crew.

Heaven help her when the cast arrived. Then they'd be in here at all hours, complaining about the director, their rooms, each other or the game. She didn't know if she was going to survive it.

"That Charmagne fella is a Nancy-boy, isn't he? I can always tell. He wears eyeliner even when he's not on camera, trying to look like he's twenty years younger than he is."

Caro coughed away a laugh, hiding it behind her fist. God love her, Hildy always told it like it was, with no thought for cultural sensitivity or political correctness. Joshua Charmagne would have a fit if he knew his sexuality was being discussed, since it was supposedly such a big, dark secret.

Before Caro could reply, the door opened. Though she didn't even turn to see who it was, she somehow knew. Her skin prickled. Her breath caught. Her nipples hardened.

Only one man had ever caused that reaction.

"Mr. Winchester," Hildy said, confirming her suspicion. "What brings you out here?" She cast a quick look at Caro. "As if I didn't know."

How on earth the old woman knew there was something between Caro and Mick, she had no idea. But there definitely *was* something between them. Something ancient and deep, unattainable but unforgettable. Call it attraction, fate, pheromones. Whatever the case, Mick had an effect on her that Caro didn't appreciate and didn't want. He tempted her like David had tempted Maddie on *Moonlighting*. And look what a disaster their eventual union had meant—cancellation!

Finally turning to face the man in the doorway, she ignored the slight hitch in her heart as she saw the way the afternoon sunlight caught the hints of gold in his light brown hair. His green eyes twinkled as he gave Hildy one of those lopsided, sexy-as-sin grins. "How can I resist a visit with the hottest woman in Derryville? Boy, if I didn't love my grandpa so much, I'd be giving him a run for his money."

Hildy preened for a moment, then walked over to Mick and pinched his cheek. "Boy, you couldn't handle this much woman."

Mick somehow managed to look both chastised and flirtatious. "Oh, but wouldn't I like to try?"

Hildy appeared to be as helpless against his charm as every other female. "You're a naughty one," she said when Mick gave her one of those come-try-me grins. "I'm going to pray for you."

Mick raised a brow. "And where are you going to do that?"

Hildy frowned, her old lady lips puckering out and her forehead descending over her eyebrows. "Don't remind me."

Caro met Mick's eye over the old lady's head. "Problems?"

"Hildy isn't a favorite of Miss Hester's at the local church." Then Mick gently put his arm across her shoulders for a quick hug. "That's okay, some of my favorite people have been kicked out of that church, my sister included."

Remembering how Sophie had recently been fired and/or quit from her job, and having heard the rumors about the pastor's sister trying to make trouble for the TV shoot, Caro nodded. "I know what happened with your sister. But I'm sure she's still welcome at the church. Isn't everyone?"

"Except me," Hildy said with a snort. "Miss Hester needs to brighten up. Take a chili powder. Or a Viagra."

Mick chuckled. "Uh, I think you mean lighten up and take a chill pill. Or a Valium." Then he plopped down on the arm of the sofa. "Although, maybe a Viagra would improve her mood, too."

"I don't understand that Viagra stuff," Hildy said. "Back in my younger years, any man who'd admit to needin' it wouldn't ever have the opportunity to use it again once his gang found out. He'd die of embarrassment—if they didn't pump his Nancy guts full'a lead first." She shook her index finger toward Mick. "I bet you never needed it. Or so everyone in this town says."

Caro couldn't help it. She stiffened.

"No, I've never needed it," he murmured, meeting Caro's stare over the old lady's head. His eyes held something hot and personal, and Caro quickly tried to think of anything but Mick and sex in the same sentence.

Hildy cast Caro an apologetic glance and changed the subject. "Well, as for Miss Hester, she just needs to get a sense of humor."

"I agree," Mick concurred. "I almost fell face-first into my spaghetti dinner from laughing. I certainly wasn't offended by what you said."

"That's not saying much, boy, since I don't imagine you'd be offended if someone told you you were as randy as an alley cat."

He paused, then baldly stated, "You're right. I wasn't."

Hildy chortled a bit. And Caro couldn't help asking, "So, what was it you said that got you in trouble with the pastor's sister?"

Hildy harrumphed at the memory, then explained. "At the annual spaghetti dinner at the church a few months ago I told Miss Hester I was hungry. That's all."

Mick cleared his throat.

Hildy shot him a glare, then grudgingly added, "Very hungry."

As if knowing the woman wasn't about to tell the whole story, Mick continued. "She told the whole congregation that she was hungry enough to eat the leg off the lamb of God."

Caro sucked her lips between her teeth to bite back a laugh. There was something to look forward to in old age—being able to get away with being absolutely outrageous.

Hildy shook her head in sorrow. "I knew I shouldn'ta. I shoulda said the *first* thing that came to my head, which was that I was hungry enough to eat the bum off a low-flying duck." She lowered her voice and leaned closer to whisper, "But I didn't think bum was appropriate to say in a church-type setting."

This time, Caro couldn't hold the laugh in.

"See? *She* can take a joke. She has a sense of humor. Now, you rascal, you've made fun of me enough for today. Be good or I'll sick Moe on you."

"I thought Moe never left the property." He glanced at Caro. "Moe's the ghost of a mobster. He lives in the inn."

"I've heard about the ghosts," Caro said. "But we've yet to see any. We're hoping they'll show up during the shoot."

"Somehow, I have the feeling Moe "Six Fingers" Marcini and his pals are only around when Hildy needs someone to get her out of trouble."

Hildy tsked. "Making fun again…well, mock if you will. One of these nights I'll have Moe go visit your bedroom and see if you're really all the stories say you are."

Caro could have answered that question. *Yes, he is.* But she kept her mouth shut.

Finally, Hildy sauntered out of the trailer, leaving Caro alone with a laughing Mick.

"What a character," Caroline said.

"You can't begin to imagine. Gwen and Jared love her to pieces. We all do."

Caro liked that about Mick. She'd never seen him interact with people outside his own circle before. Mainly, *women* in his circle. But seeing his tenderness, his good humor, the care with which he'd hugged her and his playful relationship with a woman old enough to be his grandmother somehow surprised her. It wasn't the type of friendship a no-good playboy would cultivate. Was it?

"So, what are you doing here?" she asked once Mick had closed the door firmly behind Hildy.

Without waiting for an invitation, he took Hildy's recently vacated spot on the love seat. He crossed his long, khaki-clad legs and gave the trailer a once-over. "I figured it was time to check out the madhouse. I've been hearing stories."

"Stories?" she asked, instantly worried.

"Nothing too dramatic." He grinned. "Yet."

"Just wait 'til this afternoon when the cast gets here,"

she mumbled, wearily brushing a lone strand of hair off her forehead and tucking it behind her ear.

His voice lowered. "You look tired."

"I'm fine."

"You sleeping okay?"

In my big lonely bed?

She choked down the question, wondering where it had come from. She did *not* want to share a bed with Mick Winchester. Been there. Done that. Never gonna happen again.

Yes, it had been good enough to almost make her have an orgasm sitting here thinking about it, but that was way in the past. Way, way, way in the past.

Probably he wasn't that good anymore, anyway. Probably he'd grown older and boring and wouldn't spend hours kissing, licking and stroking every inch of her skin. Probably he wouldn't still be able to torment her by bringing her to the very brink of climax over and over again until she would sob and beg him to take her over the edge. Probably he couldn't take her over that edge a half dozen times in one night.

Probably she should kill herself right now before she started moaning just sitting here thinking about what it had been like to make love to this man.

"You okay, Caroline?"

"Fine." Whose weak, breathy voice was that? Not hers, not the strong assistant producer who'd all week been barking orders and soothing feathers ruffled by Renauld Watson.

God, Mick reduced her to a sighing girl merely by sitting in the same room. She stiffened in her chair. "You shouldn't be here."

"I'm family."

Not her family. But he'd almost been, hadn't he? If she'd gone through with it and decided to marry a man who was destined to break her heart over and over again, yes, he would have been.

The thought hurt her so much she had to drop her hands to her lap and press them against her suddenly tight and aching stomach. That was as close to her tight and aching heart as she could get without him suspecting how much he affected her.

"You do remember that Jared's my cousin, don't you? As a matter of fact, I'm pretty much responsible for him and Gwen hooking up." He gave her a secretive smile that invited her to ask him to share a good story.

She didn't ask. "Right. So feel free to visit your family in the inn. This is the production trailer. Essentially, my office." Now she'd nailed the voice. The prissy, snotty, "get outta my life" voice she'd been going for.

But it didn't even phase him. He looked around and gave her a mournful shake of the head. "As far as offices go, this one pretty well sucks, doesn't it?"

She almost laughed but held it in and kept a straight face. "It'll do." Then she ran another weary hand over her face. "At least until the cast gets here later today and the door becomes a revolving one for them to come in here and kvetch."

"High-maintenance, the contestants on these shows?"

"Oh, yeah."

The very thought made her niggling headache grow stronger, until her temple began to throb and the back of her neck to ache. She dropped her head forward and stretched side to side, trying to straighten out the tightened muscles.

Mick was still sitting there when she raised her head.

Looking at him, just looking at his face, her lips twitched, wanting to smile at the sight of him. In spite of her headache, her job, her stress level, she wanted to bask in that good humor of his, be destressed by one of his wicked jokes and soak up more of his smiles.

The man was born to make a woman smile. And say yes.

Not this woman.

"You should go."

He didn't move. "Caro, what's going on?"

And suddenly, maybe because he'd called her Caro, not Caroline. Maybe because his expression was so concerned and tender, or maybe because she was overemotional, overtired, overstressed and oversensitive, she told him.

"This is a nightmare. The writers keep faxing changes. As of this morning I still don't know who the killer is and I have to brief that person on their means, motive and opportunity tomorrow morning." She paused for breath, then rushed on. "The lead camera operator looks like she stepped out of a Goth movie and I don't know whether she wants to get a good shot or suck somebody's blood."

Now she was on a roll. "The director is absolutely impossible to deal with, and he's flirting with the mayor's wife. The host is flirting with the mayor. The ghosts won't come out. The trees are too green. The inn is too clean. The mystery is too simple. The rules don't make sense. And I've been sleeping lousy knowing you're on the other side of the wall and wondering who I wronged in my last life to be tortured like this on my first big production."

Mick didn't say a word, didn't smile at her confession, didn't frown at her frustration, just watched her suck in a few deep breaths as she realized what she'd allowed to spill from her traitorous mouth.

"Finished?"

She nodded miserably.

Finally, he stood up and stepped closer. "You need a distraction."

He grabbed her hands off her lap and pulled her to her feet, until they stood nearly toe-to-toe. Every inch of her body reacted, sparking to life, remembering what it was like to be a mere whisper away from this man, anticipating a kiss, a touch, an embrace. A long, exquisite night of passion. "What'd you have in mind?" she managed to ask, unable to help it as her mind filled with the amazing ways Mick could distract her.

"Turn around."

The two words scraped across her skin like the touch of a man's roughened fingertip. Arousing her. Promising something indefinable and incredibly desirable. She almost whimpered.

"Turn around, Caroline."

His words weren't a request and she couldn't resist doing as he said. She closed her eyes, waiting, wondering what he intended. When she felt his big, strong hands on her shoulders, felt him begin to stroke, squeeze and knead the stiff muscles there, she gave a nearly inaudible sigh of pleasure.

"You're tight."

Yes.

"Wound like a spring."

"Umm-hmm," she mumbled, dropping her head to the side and closing her eyes as he continued to knead and work on the knots that had once been her muscles and were now quickly turning into lumps of jelly. She could feel the transformation as he eased out every bit of stress tension in her body.

Only to replace it with tension of a different kind.

"Your skin is still so incredibly soft."

His words were spoken softly, nearly whispered, but Caro heard them, inhaled them, let them wash over her, causing as much warmth as his touch.

She should protest. She should step away, throw up a physical barrier or at least a verbal one. But she couldn't move, other than to shiver. Couldn't speak other than to sigh.

She'd waited eight years to have this man's hands on her again. Eight long years when no one else's touch could ever really reach that place deep inside her that had always reacted to Mick.

He lifted her hair away from her neck and she felt his breath touch her skin, bringing prickles of sensation. He moved even closer, filling in that nearly imperceptible gap until his front touched her back, from shoulder to hip. And lower.

She caught her breath, held it, not moving as he continued to knead her muscles and breathe lightly against her neck.

One small shift, a lift of her chin, a turn of her head, and that beautiful, perfect male mouth would be on her lips.

She wanted that kiss more than she'd ever wanted anything.

"Too bad that love seat is so small," he murmured with a deep chuckle.

Perhaps a *wolfish* chuckle? She stiffened. *Dammit.*

"Get your hands off me." She whirled around, nearly

smacking his forehead with hers. "Try your tricks on someone who's a lot more susceptible to them."

He raised an innocent hand to his chest and gave her a silent "Who, me?" look.

"God, you're good," she said, knowing he could tell by her tone that her words were no compliment. "You're so smooth, so assured. I can't *believe* I started to fall for it."

He gave her a reproachful look. "I was trying to help. You looked ready to explode."

Explode, yeah. A few more touches, maybe even just that one kiss, and she would have. Only not the way he meant.

"Sure you were. Help me get flat on my back on that love seat."

He didn't so much as look away out of guilt as he quirked one amused brow. "Actually, I wanted you flat on your front."

Oh, good Lord, the wicked thoughts that put into her head. She gulped. "You're sick."

He tsked. "And you've got a naughty mind."

She paused, not sure what he meant.

"You thought I wanted a bigger sofa so I could, what, make love to you right here in your office where anyone could walk in? Tempt you into doing something so dangerous, so incredibly erotic, strip off that silky blouse, tug down that tight skirt, get you naked and moaning where we could be caught by anyone from your boss to a man with a camera?"

Well, yeah. That's what she'd thought, only not quite in those graphic and—heaven help her—delicious terms.

"Yes."

He frowned, looking disappointed in her. "I just

meant if you had somewhere flat to lie down I could give you a full back rub. It's hard to do this standing up."

A full back rub. He'd been intending only to help, not to seduce? He hadn't been affected by the close proximity of their bodies? She wasn't sure she believed him. Oh, yes, he looked both reproachful and saddened. But this *was* Mick, after all.

He turned and walked to the door, his shoulders slightly slumped, his head shaking back and forth in an almost imperceptible motion. Caro bit her lip, feeling like a total heel. Mick wasn't some horny college guy on the make. He was a grown man who'd kept his hands off her and given her plenty of space since she'd been living in his house. He hadn't made one inappropriate suggestion, dropped one naughty little word—which had really begun to tick her off for some totally twisted reason.

He'd been nothing but considerate and concerned the few times she'd interacted with him this week. And she'd practically gone and accused him of being a lech.

"Mick, wait," she said as he reached for the door handle.

He paused and slowly turned his head to look over his shoulder. He met her stare through partly lowered lashes. That was when she noticed the grin. A purely evil, "gotcha" grin that told her she hadn't imagined a thing.

The wolf had meant exactly what she'd *thought* he'd meant.

Her jaw dropped. But before she could say a single word, he walked out the door.

All Caroline could do was shake her head in disbelief. Then she started to laugh in the empty trailer. Finally, she muttered, "Damn, you are *good*."

CHAPTER SEVEN

JACEY TURNER had been on the set of *Killing Time in a Small Town* for less than a week but it seemed like ten. Though young, she already had a lot of experience as a TV camera operator, and she'd worked on a lot of shows. It wasn't hard to sum up how this experience was going to go down. In a freakin' ball of flames.

The director was a butt-wipe. The celebrity host was an arrogant S.O.B. who looked at her like she was something he'd scraped off the bottom of his Andre Benninis. Derryville was a pit. And the cast was a bunch of greedy morons who didn't know which they wanted more—their fifteen minutes of fame or the million bucks that went to the winner.

But hell, she was a studio ho. She went where they sent her. Since she was lead on the camera crew—her first shot at lead—she knew she had to keep her mouth shut and her lens cap off.

The only decent one on the scene was the one she usually hated the most—the pencil-pushing, budget-conscious assistant producer. Yeah, this always perfectly dressed woman had first looked at Jacey's black hair, black clothes, piercings and heavy makeup with a cautious glance, but she'd at least been cordial.

And she'd totally backed Jacey up on this latest idea.

"Does the camera really add ten pounds?" This came from a busty redhead riding across from Jacey in the stretch limo. The redhead was perky and as chirpy as a squirrel, obviously hoping the hot-looking fireman dude sitting next to her would reply that she had nothing to worry about.

She did. Those curves would turn to fat in five years. Push out a puppy or two and it'd be less than that. Just to be a bitch, Jacey said, "Twenty, at least."

Redhead shot her a glare, which was the first time she'd looked her way since the sixteen contestants had boarded the two limos back in Chicago. The rest of the time she'd just been chattering a mile a minute, making inane observations and giving Jacey a headache.

Red sat up straighter so her tight white dress didn't show that slight little roll around her middle. "Really?"

"You don't have anything to worry about."

Fireman dude to the rescue. So he was a gentleman. She made a mental note.

"Will the cameras really be watching our every move?"

Jacey turned toward the worried-looking young woman on the other side of the fireman. The girl was thin, blond, washed out and had her hands clasped in her lap. Pressing the zoom button on the tiny camera hidden in the lapel of her black overcoat, Jacey winked. "Not when we're in the bathroom, I hope."

Washed-out went ten shades paler and her mouth fell open in dismay. Redhead sniffed, too refined to ever *go* to the bathroom, she imagined, much less talk about it. Another mental note: Redhead wanted to look good all the time and stick-thin would die before embarrassing herself on camera.

All this was coming in handy, as she'd known it would

when she'd pitched the idea of posing as a contestant for the ride from Chicago to the inn. What better way to get to know the real personalities of their contestants than by going undercover as one of them? She had a firsthand glimpse as early alliances were formed, personalities tested, strengths and weaknesses displayed.

The director, being a butt-wipe, had shot her down. So Jacey had gone straight to the producer. Luckily, Caro had some concept of creative thinking and had told her to go for it.

She'd been at the Chicago hotel first thing this morning, wired up with a minicam. The other car was wired, as well. She didn't feel bad about it. Everyone on this crazy show had given permission to be filmed anytime, anywhere once they arrived. And Jacey considered the limo to be part of that arrival.

"I bet I know who the killer is already," Redhead said.

Ginger. That was her name. Like the pouty-mouthed actress on that old show, *Gilligan's Island,* which Jacey sometimes watched on *Nick at Night.* There was the ultimate reality show idea...dump off a bunch of these idiots on a desert island and leave them there. Come back four weeks later, see who was still alive, figure out who'd killed off Ginger and give *that* guy a million bucks just for shutting her up.

"I bet it's that guy who quotes Shakespeare. Nobody could have that personality for real."

"That *was* his real personality," Jacey said, having spent a few minutes talking to the professor, Nigel Whittington. "He teaches English at some college."

Ginger shot her a look that told her to mind her own business. "That could be a cover story." She shivered delicately and oozed closer to the fireman. "I'm so glad he ended up going in the other car. He might kill someone off before we even get to the inn."

Ginger obviously hadn't read the background documents on the show. Or else she was forgetful. Or just stupid. "Nobody knows who the killer is," the fireman said, sounding not a bit impatient as the women on either side of him kept their rapt attention on his face. "To keep it as fair as possible, the killer won't find out he's the one until everyone is on site."

They nearly melted at the display of manly wisdom. For a brief second, Jacey couldn't blame them. He had some face. Some body, too. But he was so completely not her type.

"Not even the killer knows he or she is the killer yet," said the fireman, who Jacey finally remembered was named Digg. She shouldn't have forgotten such an unusual name.

The washed-out blonde, who'd introduced herself as Mona, a florist from Virginia, nodded in agreement. Jacey had a feeling, judging by the worshipful look on her face, that Mona would agree if Digg said Columbus was wrong and if you sailed too far you'd fall off the edge of the world into a dragon's mouth.

Jacey swallowed a grunt of disgust. A stud on the set was never a great idea. There were sure to be catfights. Then she smiled inwardly. Maybe on a regular TV set catfights were to be avoided. But on a reality show? "Perfect," she whispered.

"Excuse me?" Digg asked, turning the full onslaught of his attention on her.

Jacey could handle him. She'd been handling smooth-talking men half her life. "What's your story? Digg's an unusual name."

"Short for Diego," he replied, his name rolling off his tongue with the rhythmic cadence of someone who fluently spoke another language. Likely Spanish.

Mona and Ginger nearly swooned. Not surprising since they so obviously dug Digg.

"And I have no story to speak of," he continued. "I'm a fireman at a station in Queens." He kept those big brown eyes of his focused entirely on her. He didn't frown, didn't look away, didn't react at all to her unorthodox appearance. *A gentleman,* she reminded herself. And apparently more, judging by the small, discreet Remember 9/11 pin on his collar.

She wondered if he'd been there, telling herself she was only interested because of its historical significance, and because of how it would play out on camera when somebody ended up making a movie about it. Which they would. She couldn't really admit, not even to herself, that seeing that pin had suddenly made her wonder if he was the kind of man she'd only ever read about or seen on TV.

A hero.

"What's *your* story?" he asked.

Jacey ignored the question. She wasn't about to let these three, or the five other people sitting in this stretch limo, know that she was part of the crew of *Killing Time.*

Won't they be surprised.

"What would you do with that much money?" This came from a burly guy in a dingy T-shirt and jeans, one who'd given the redhead a visible leer when they'd entered the limo this morning. Willie Packard, Jacey recalled. She'd easily remembered that one because of an old joke from her childhood. *Willie P or won't he?*

"I'd quit my job," Ginger said, "and travel the world."

Fireman Digg merely nodded.

"I'd help the poor." Mona watched for Digg's reaction.

Again, he responded with just a nod, even as Jacey rolled her eyes. He turned his attention toward her just in time to catch the exasperated sigh she couldn't contain. They exchanged a long look. He revealed nothing in his stoic expression, the same one he'd been wearing since they'd entered the limo.

Tilting her head back in challenge, Jacey declared, "I'd buy a bad-ass house, and a bad-ass car and a bad-ass man to take care of my every bad-ass need."

The two women tsked and frowned. Jacey met fireman Digg's stare, held it, dared him to give her one of his nice, polite nods like he had the other women.

He didn't. Instead, Digg smiled. A *real* smile, just for her. His wide, sexy grin revealed perfect white teeth, and two dimples deep enough for a woman to swim in. Genuine amusement and a certain acknowledgment that she'd scored a hit sparkled in his dark eyes.

Jacey didn't quite recognize the sensation washing through her. She didn't know why her hand suddenly wanted to smooth her hair in place, or why she instinctively sat up straighter. Or what the absurd fluttering in her stomach was all about, unless the Chicago hotel had laced her eggs with salmonella.

Then she recognized the unfamiliar feeling. *Attraction.*

God, she was attracted to the clean-cut, gentlemanly fireman with a hero complex and the stupid name of Digg.

She should be screaming or slitting her wrists. But funny…suddenly, keeping a close, camera's-eye view on the thick-chested, dark-haired guy didn't look to be much of a hardship.

No, not a hardship at all.

SURPRISINGLY, no one in the cast—or the crew—was killed on the set of the reality show the first day. Even more surprisingly, Mick wasn't either.

He'd expected Caroline to come after him with both barrels—or a meat cleaver—after his parting shot in her trailer that morning. He still didn't know what impulse had made him give her that salacious look as he'd left her so-called office.

Because she thought the worst.

Yeah, that was probably it. Because, just like in the past, she'd accused and found him guilty in one snap judgment. So he'd let her think his comment about the couch was a come-on. It hadn't been. At least, he thought it hadn't been. But considering his brain had been pretty mushy since Caroline's surprise return to his life, he couldn't be entirely sure. Could be the big bad wolf on his ass had been in control of that conversation.

Tonight, when Caroline had returned from the Little Bohemie Inn a few hours earlier than she had all week, he was prepared for fireworks. But she seemed to have forgotten all about what had happened this morning. One glimpse of her pinched, weary-looking face, and he knew the arrival of the cast had been less than auspicious.

"Beer," she said the minute she closed the front door and dropped her briefcase on the floor in the foyer.

"Porch," he replied, just as succinctly.

She turned right around, and yanked the door open again. Somehow she managed to kick off both her high-heeled shoes midstep as she walked onto the porch. He heard the fridge open and close, then the hiss of a bottle being uncapped. She was pulling a deep draught of it by the time she walked back into the house. "Good," she said, wiping off her lips with the back of her hand.

Totally non-Caroline. Somebody had had a bad day.

"I wasn't expecting you so early." He didn't approach her, never leaving the kitchen counter where he'd been chopping up some veggies for dinner. He'd planned a dinner for one, since she had never returned from the set before 9:00 p.m. this week. Without asking, he grabbed another handful of mixed vegetables and tossed them in the colander.

She walked toward him down the narrow hallway, then through the archway into the kitchen. "Food."

Amused by her one word grunts, he replied, "Ugh. Hunting not good today, Captain Caveman."

She didn't even react to the joke.

"I'd give my Vera Wang gown—the one I bought for last year's Emmy's by taking out a second mortgage on my condo—to be sitting in a mud bath at the Casa de Helena spa in San Diego."

He glanced toward the back door. "It hasn't rained for a few days, but the garden might still be a little muddy."

"Oh, don't I know that it hasn't rained," she said, taking a seat at the kitchen table. She sipped again from her bottle. "Renauld was cursing Mother Nature all afternoon."

Without being asked, he scooped up a big bowlful of tossed salad and walked it over to her.

"Bless you."

Remembering it was her favorite, he grabbed a bottle of French dressing from the fridge and put it beside her salad. Then he returned to chopping vegetables. "Why did he want it to rain?"

"Atmosphere. He wanted a rainy, gray day when the contestants arrived. Forecast called for it today, which is why he brought them in instead of waiting until tomorrow, when they were supposed to come. Everything was thrown off to take advantage of the rain."

Mick tossed the vegetables into a pan to stir-fry them, distributing them over the hot surface. "But the rain didn't show?"

"Right."

Remembering the leaf-painting issue, Mick asked, "Tell me he didn't try to create rain."

"Okay, I won't tell you."

"Is this guy a moron or what? How does he keep his job?"

Caroline shoved a big mouthful of salad in her mouth, cooed a little, then dug in again before answering. "He's been around *forever.* I think he must have something on the head of the studio. They keep him busy, but always *away* from L.A. where they don't have to deal with him."

"So how'd he make rain?"

She ate a few more bites before answering. Then, with a roll of the eyes, she explained, "He had the crew pull a tight shot of each person getting out of the limo and doused them with a sprinkler."

He grinned, picturing the scene.

"Only, he didn't know the hose was hooked to a well."

Mick knew where this was going. "Oooh, Derryville well water always smells like rotten eggs."

She nodded. "Yep. The first woman who got out, a redhead in a white dress, started shrieking first about her clothes, then about the smell of the water."

Mick wondered where Jared had been during this

whole fiasco. Or Gwen's Aunt Hildy. The old woman had been front row center, he'd lay money on that. If there was excitement to be found anywhere near the inn, she was sure to be part of it.

"He had one of the sound guys flipping a big piece of flat aluminum to make storm sounds, but the aluminum got slippery from the sprinkler, flew out of the sound guy's hands, and nearly decapitated another contestant."

This time Mick snickered out loud. She shot him a look that said she didn't appreciate his laughter.

"Come on, Caroline, you gotta admit it sounds pretty funny."

She shook her head. "Yeah, so funny that one of the other contestants burst into laughter. Which made the nearly decapitated one shove him. And, since the ground was wet…"

Trying to keep a straight face, Mick said, "He fell?"

"Oh, he completely wiped out. We're talking early Jim Carrey stuff here."

Mick bit the inside of his cheek this time.

"He took out four other people along with him, until nearly a carful of our enthusiastic, energetic contestants were throwing mud into each other's faces." She finished off her beer in one long pull. "My God, if they'd been naked we could have charged money and sold drinks."

"Mud wrestling usually just involves girls."

She grunted. "I guess you'd know."

"I'm not a big fan of mud wrestling," he said, not rising to the bait of her casually tossed-out insult. "I prefer the good old standard wet T-shirt contest. Much less messy."

"The only good thing," she continued, not rising to

his bait, either, "was that the camera operator we'd had ride undercover in the limo didn't get caught in the mud battle, so that's one less thing she can hate me for."

Finishing off the vegetable stir-fry, he added some ginger and a few other spices, then spooned it over two plates of rice. He carried them over to the table and sat next to Caroline.

"She hates you?"

"Everybody except Charlie hates me. But he's an all-around nice old guy who likes everybody."

"Charlie?"

"Addison. He's the tech director. He rented a room from you."

"Oh, yeah," Mick said, suddenly remembering the man. "He likes a good cigar. The smoke from the Snorkle house wasn't a problem." He chuckled as she wrinkled up her nose. "I took him to see rentals the same day you showed back up in my life."

She merely shrugged, her shoulders still slumped, her lips pulled down in a frown as she began to nibble on the vegetables.

"Caroline, you're incredibly likable," he said, remembering her earlier comment.

"Oh, it's not me they hate," she said, admitting it grudgingly. "It's my title. I don't take it personally. Everybody always hates the assistant producer because we tighten the purse strings whenever the studio says to."

He suddenly sympathized with her, being surrounded by hostile co-workers. "Why do you do it?"

"I love it."

"Oh, that makes a lot of sense," he said, meaning exactly the opposite. "You love working with people who don't like you."

"Like I said, it's not me, personally, they don't like," she said. "It's the job. We're the narcs on the set, the penny-pinching critics who report every single thing back to California and try to rein in impossible directors."

"What fun," he mumbled as he sipped his beer.

"I know it sounds bad," she admitted. "But it's not. Besides it's just a stepping stone to where I really want to be."

"Director?"

She rolled her eyes. "Puh-lease. Why would you think that?"

"Doesn't everyone in Hollywood want to direct?"

"Just actors. I'm aiming for producer of an in-studio cop show the network is considering for a replacement slot in February."

She sounded vehement, determined to make her dream come true. Not the first time he'd heard that tone in Caroline's voice. She'd always gotten what she went after with that fire and enthusiasm.

Even if it meant leaving other things—other *people*—to eat her dust.

He stood abruptly, taking his plate to the sink.

"Mick?"

When he glanced over at her, he saw by the look on her face that she didn't understand his quick mood change. He wasn't entirely sure he understood it himself. But something instinctive and deep-rooted had sparked a flash of anger that had been buried for eight long years.

"Thanks for dinner," she murmured.

"You're welcome," he replied. "Good night." He walked out of the room, hoping she'd have the good sense to realize he'd been about as cordial and friendly as he could manage for one day and still stay sane. Apparently she'd lost some of her women's intuition, because she followed him into the rec room.

"I'm going to watch a movie."

"Oh, good," she said, plopping down on the love seat, curling her stockinged legs under her cute little bottom.

No, no, no, no. No movie evening. No chance of waking up and finding her in his arms again, as he had the other morning. That was not on the agenda, not now, not *any* night while she remained in Derryville.

He could leave, say he'd changed his mind, developed a splitting headache, had a night out planned with the guys. He couldn't say it was a night in, because then she'd just stay again. Then he paused, thinking about it. Why should he leave?

Hell, it's my house. It's my damn TV.

He opened the video cabinet, spied a rackful of movies, and began to smile.

"What are we watching? No tear-jerkers, okay?"

He almost snickered. This one had jerking. But not of tears. He didn't give it another thought, just dove into the crazy idea that was sure to scare her off.

"So, you want straight-up? You're not into anything in particular, are you?" he asked, making an extreme effort to sound blasé.

"Huh?"

Good start. She looked completely confused.

"I mean, I don't remember you being into any fetishes or real kink or anything like that. So, is straight-up boy-girl-girl-girl stuff okay?"

She stood, stepped closer, and looked over his shoulder. He remained squatting, resisting the insane urge to turn his head and come eye level with the hem of her short, fitted little skirt. With those thighs he'd dreamed about every night since she'd come back. With that sweet, wet place where he'd lost himself for almost a full year of his life.

He gave his head a shake and reached into the video cabinet, which was stacked high with videos and DVDs. He retrieved one particular movie from one particular stack and waited for her reaction. He knew he'd gotten it when she gasped out loud. She'd apparently gotten a peek at the title. *Raunchy Redheads in Reno.*

"You think…you expect…you want to watch…?"

He finally looked up, almost laughing at the sound of horror in her voice. She met his eyes and Mick gave her the same challenging look he'd given her the night she'd walked in on his card game. Daring her. Taunting her. Throwing down a gauntlet.

But this time, she wouldn't pick it up. There was no way Caroline would sit here and watch a porn movie with him.

If she did? Well, he'd just have to go jump off a bridge or something. Because there was no way in hell *he* could sit here and watch a sexy video with *her*, either. Not when he'd been able to think of nothing else but Caroline, naked and in his arms, since the day she'd come back. Particularly today, when he'd been so close to her, when her shoulder muscles had grown loose and pliable beneath his hands. When her back, her hips, her thighs, had been separated from his by nothing more than their clothing. Her sighs of pleasure had jump-started every male molecule in his body. They still snapped and sparked, making him aware of each slight shift she made, each breath she took. Heat, raw and intense, roared again, deep within him.

"You're sick."

So much for heat. She was ice-frigging-cold. *Good*, he told himself. She wasn't meeting the challenge. That was exactly what he'd wanted.

But a wicked, wolfish part inside him wondered what might have been.

"My God, do you have stock in a basement studio?" she asked, staring wide-eyed at the stack of X-rated movies in his video cabinet. "Who needs *that* many dirty movies? Can't you have the decency to hide them in the garage or attic? Or how about putting them inside another case no one would ever look at, like an exercise video. That's what a normal person does!" She stepped back, shaking her head, but not removing her eyes from the cabinet.

She didn't stare too closely. If she had, she would probably have noticed that ninety-five percent of the films were still wrapped in plastic. Unopened.

He could have explained. He could have told her that his friends had always given him crap about how he had missed his true calling and he should have just had sex for a living because women were always after him. So every time they came over for a poker night, they all brought him movies. The cheesier, nastier and ranker the better.

"I take it you're not up for it?" he asked, raising an innocent brow.

"No, I certainly am not."

"Suit yourself," he said with a shrug as he stood, video still in hand.

He didn't even turn around. He didn't have to. He heard every one of her angry steps as she exited the room and marched up the stairs. The slam of her bedroom door probably knocked a few pictures off the wall, and it rang in his ears in the silent room for several moments after she'd left.

That was the right thing to do. The last thing he needed was another warm and cozy evening with Caroline Lamb—in his home, the one she might have shared if she hadn't run away back in college.

Christ, it was going to be hard enough watching her walk right back out of his life in a few weeks. He didn't have to make it any harder on himself by letting them get too close in the meantime. They could be cordial, and he'd wave goodbye when she shimmied on out of Derryville.

But my oh my, what a shimmy. He went all shaky just thinking about the way Caroline's hips had probably swayed as she'd stormed out of the room. Hell, he'd been going all shaky thinking about her for weeks.

No one else had come close to getting his attention for ages—even before Caroline had come to town. His last relationship, if you could call it that, had been almost a year ago with a doctor who'd been in town for a few days. They'd kept in touch briefly, but long-distance things usually didn't work out. That one hadn't either.

Somehow, after that, he'd gotten distracted by other things—his house, his business, his family—until months had gone by and he hadn't so much as kissed a woman.

"Get laid," he told himself. That's all he needed to get over this stupid mental thing he had going on with Caroline. *Find someone else and take care of the urge.*

Even as he said it, he knew it wouldn't work. He liked sex, liked it a *lot*. But in spite of what others might think, Mick knew he couldn't just take what he needed from any warm, willing body. He was totally, one hundred percent focused on Caroline. No one else interested him right now. No one else challenged him, aroused him, made him hot and hard every time he thought about her.

"So sleep with her and get it out of your system, jackass," he muttered.

The idea had merit. Then again, the idea of pushing the *Titanic* a little faster had had merit, too. And look how that had ended up.

He couldn't sleep with Caroline and then watch her walk away. First of all, because sex had never been just sex between them. Secondly because if he seduced her—which he knew he could—she'd never forgive him. And third because damned if he'd be used as a distraction while she killed time here in Derryville.

Mick liked distractions. But he didn't want to *be* one.

He was still wondering over the whole matter when he fell asleep in front of the TV.

Watching a basketball game.

CAROLINE TRIED to read but could only fume. She then tried to relax in the bath but instead only fumed some more. She fumed as she brushed out her hair, fumed as she brushed her teeth, fumed as she put on her pj's and got into bed.

Then she realized something. She wasn't only fuming. She was also fantasizing. "No," she whispered as she lay in her bed. "He's a jerk."

A jerk she wanted to have sex with.

That about summed it up. She'd been pushing the thought aside for weeks. Okay, *years*. But it wouldn't die. She wanted Mick like the devil wanted sinners. Like a woman with PMS wanted chocolate.

Like a woman who'd had sex with Mick Winchester. And wanted to again...

Uhh, yeah. That'd be her. She wanted him bad. Hot. Powerful. Wanted him strong. Naked. Seductive. Everything she remembered, everything she'd fantasized about. It had been eight years and they'd both been practically kids. And the sex had still rocked her world. "Good God, what might he be like now?"

Even though she told herself she'd come back to town on Sunday with absolutely no intention of hooking back up with Mick, she had to acknowledge the truth: her pasta-straining diaphragm had hit the trash can as soon as she'd returned to California. It had been replaced by a box of nice, discreet patches. Today, after he'd left her office, hadn't been the first time she'd thought about how glad she was to have them.

As for tonight…. "Porn movies. Disgusting," she whispered, trying to build up her righteous indignation again.

But somehow, instead of indignant, she felt a little…strange. Unsettled. Itchy and uncertain. Aware and tense.

No, she did not want to watch other people having sex on film. Particularly not women with huge boobs and teeny brains, or men with huge…well, huge men.

It was the thought, though, that was driving her out of her mind. The thought of sex, down and hungry, sultry and pounding, that had made her run from the rec room tonight. She couldn't watch someone else having sex when she wanted it so badly herself. So how could *he?*

That, she realized, was what was really keeping her awake. How could Mick have been so close to her earlier that day, touching her with such sultry skill and pleasure, looking ready to gobble her up like the wolf he was, then watch sexy movies alone in his house while she lay right upstairs?

Unless he was completely unaffected by her. Unless that little smile he'd given her when he'd left the trailer today *hadn't* meant what she'd thought it had meant.

There was really only one way to find out. Not entirely sure what she meant to do, Caro slipped out of bed and made her way through the upstairs hallway. She avoided the creaky spots on the wooden floor, and stepped over the second step from the top on the staircase, which also creaked.

She approached the rec room, lit only by the flickering light of the television. Closing her eyes and taking a deep breath to prepare herself for the worst—the worst probably being seeing Mick enraptured by six triple-D breasts filling up his TV screen—and walked up behind him.

She cast one quick glance at his form on the recliner, quick enough to see he was asleep.

How jaded must a man be to fall asleep during a porno?

Then she took a closer look at the TV, and recognized a familiar toothpaste commercial. The unopened movie box was on the floor, over by the entertainment center where he'd been squatting when she'd left.

He'd tricked her. Played a wicked prank to get her to leave him alone with his big beautiful TV. He hadn't watched any porno movie. As the commercial faded, she realized he'd been watching a basketball game.

Sneaky rat. Even as she thought it, though, a part of her was glad he hadn't watched the movie while she was upstairs in bed. That would have bothered her. Tremendously. Still, that didn't let him off the hook for stealing her TV time.

She instantly thought of a way to get even. Knowing Mick, remembering his intensely sexual nature, she knew exactly what to do to make him crazy when he woke from a light sleep probably full of the horny dreams men like him always had. Yeah, she knew what to do.

Give him exactly what he'd asked for.

CHAPTER EIGHT

LIKE THAT FIRST NIGHT, Mick knew the moment Caroline entered the room. He'd been dozing, bored by the game. He'd drifted off thinking about their shared dinner, wondering what *she* was thinking up in her room. Wondering if their thoughts had been the same.

Doubtful. Not unless she'd developed a thing for silk scarves and edible body paints. Somehow, his traitorous brain hadn't gone for the simple sex scenario. It'd gone straight to usual third date stuff—light bondage, amazing oral sex. Headboard slamming and loud screams of pleasure.

Damn, this would never do. He was getting hard again, sitting here in his chair, while she crept around like a sneaky little mouse, launching her silent attack on his TV.

He half thought she was about to start flipping channels and steal a quick *Dharma and Greg* rerun while he was asleep. So her next move really startled him.

She picked up the video box. She opened it. She took out the tape and popped it into the VCR.

He gulped, almost unable to watch.

Then she did it. The little witch pushed play.

No. No, no, no way in hell was she gonna get away with sneaking down here to watch his bad porn. If she'd wanted to get off like that, she could have snuck the tape back up to her own room, where there was a perfectly adequate small TV.

As he continued to watch through half-lowered lashes, Caroline hit the fast forward button until the screen filled with bodies in various states of dress. Not that he was looking. Not that he cared. Mick had never cared for X-rated movies, never needed them, truth be told. That was why the majority of the ones in his entertainment center were unopened.

But, oh, God, did they bring to mind real sex. Right now. Sex with *her*, the woman standing here, backing quietly away from the television as she dropped the empty video box to the floor.

So much for keeping his mind off the things they'd done together. It was hard enough trying to forget the way he'd once been able to make her come just by cupping her through her jeans and sucking deeply on those sensitive, perfect nipples. He'd been remembering, thinking about it every day when he watched her leave in the morning and come back at night. So how the hell could he *not* think about it now, when the room was full of sex and lust and moaning people writhing in pleasure?

He wanted to be one of them. Ached to be one of them. Just as she'd damn well known he would when she turned on the tape.

She turned around just as the *boom-chock-a-wangwang* music got into full swing. Their eyes met and her hand instantly rose to her throat. "I thought you were asleep."

"I wasn't."

She edged around the chair, keeping well out of distance as she tried to ease out of the room.

"Sorry to disturb you."

He shook his head, tsking as she tried to turn and walk out. "Leaving so soon?" he asked, hearing the low rumble of intensity in his own voice.

She nodded. "I, uh, forgot something."

He paused for the length of one heartbeat. "Your vibrator?"

Even in the darkness he could see her blush. "I *never…*"

"You should. You need to get off, babe. You need it badly. I can see it in your eyes."

She looked away. "You're delusional."

He laughed softly. "Right."

"I told you I forgot something."

"Forgot to turn yourself invisible while you snuck down here to get a porn fix?"

Her mouth fell open. "I was not!"

"Then what *were* you doing, Caroline?"

She glanced around helplessly, taking one more step toward the door. "I…um…nothing."

"You could have done nothing up in your room."

She crossed her arms and tilted her head back in false bravado. "I thought I heard a noise."

He hit the mute button on the TV remote. The silence was louder than the movie had been. Then he whispered, "What kind of noise? Moaning? Screaming? Panting?"

Her bottom lip disappeared into her mouth and she proceeded to chew a hole in it.

"What did you hear, Caroline?" Keeping his voice silky smooth, almost hypnotic, he rose to his feet and stood beside her. "Helpless whimpers? Soft sighs of pleasure? Sweet whispers or the slick sound of skin sliding against skin?"

"Stop it." Her voice was weaker than her protest.

"How about wet kissing?" He stepped closer, until their bodies were separated a distance no wider than a lock of her beautiful chestnut brown hair. As he spoke, his breath touched her face. He saw tiny goose bumps arise on her skin and her eyes drifted closed.

"Cries for more?" He raised his hand and ran the tip of his finger, only that and nothing more, along the collar of her pajamas. "The tearing off of clothes? A woman's voice *begging* for release?"

She whimpered, low and soft, deep in her throat. Mick knew he should stop. *Knew* it. But he couldn't. "That deep moan a woman makes when she's finally filled to the hilt by a thick, hard cock?"

"Oh, God. Please stop."

Though his words were inflaming him as much as they were her, Mick *couldn't* stop. "What's wrong? You want to see it, but you don't like somebody saying it?"

She shook her head mindlessly, her eyes still closed. "I don't want to see it."

"Oh," he said as he ran his hands down her arms, pulling her even closer until their bodies brushed against one another with pure electricity. "You don't want to see it. Don't want to talk about it. You must just want to *do* it."

Her reply was mumbled, unintelligible.

"Admit what you were doing down here."

He waited for a moment, not stepping back, letting her continue to feel his breath, his presence, the warmth of his body so very close to hers.

Finally she did. "I was going to put the movie on and leave, letting you wake up to see it. To, uh…"

"Torment me?"

She nodded. Then, finally opening her eyes, she took a step back. He let her go. For now.

"What makes you think that would have tormented me?"

Her eyes shifted to the screen, then immediately back again, obviously shocked by what the man and woman on the screen were doing now. "It was a stupid idea."

She continued to move, to try to slide sideways out of the room, away from the power and heat that had flared between them. But she wasn't going to get away that easily. Moving so quickly she didn't have time to react, he took hold of her arm. Her mouth fell open but he didn't give her a chance to resist.

"You can't leave without getting what you came for." Tugging her with him, he sat down in the chaise again and pulled her onto his lap. "You wanted to torment me. To make me watch this so I'd sit here and think of you upstairs. Think of us and the things we used to do to one another."

She tried to stand up. He held her firmly around the waist, keeping her hips against his groin, and her bottom firmly on his lap. On his erection, which she undoubtedly felt.

"Mick…" His name ended on a moan as she pressed against him in a helpless, ancient invitation of woman to man.

"Shh." He took her chin and turned her face toward the TV screen.

Caroline didn't want to watch, had no interest in watching. What appeared on the screen was nothing compared to what was happening here, now, in Mick's arms, against his body.

He felt divine. Hard and hot and perfect, just like he had years ago. But now he was stronger, maybe a tiny bit dangerous. Not the good-natured young guy, but a man in full control. A man who knew how to make a woman lose her mind.

"Are you watching?" he whispered, his words only slightly louder than the crazy beating of her own heart.

She shook her head.

"Look," he ordered.

She obeyed, unable to resist. Glancing at the screen she saw a flash of intimacy that made her shake in his lap. A man's head between a woman's pale white thighs. Kissing her, licking her.

She jerked, unable to prevent her body's response to the shockingly sexual image, and got a sultry, wicked laugh in return. He knew what he was doing to her. Knew it. Loved it.

"I really do hate you," she mumbled, nearly incoherent.

"I know. This is just about the TV again, right? You're only here because of my TV."

"Uh-huh."

Then she couldn't say anything else. She closed her eyes again, focused only on what was happening here and now, not on the big screen. Mick was doing the most delightful things with his mouth. His whispers caressed her neck, his lips so close they brushed the skin there, and when his tongue slid out to flick at the pulse point, she writhed against him.

His hands moved across her, lightly, letting the silk fabric of her pajamas create incredible friction against her skin. His touch varied, a quick stroke of the thigh, a leisurely hand curving around her waist. And all the while he continued to whisper, to kiss her neck, her jaw, her throat.

She turned to give him better access, still never opening her eyes, not until his mouth moved to hers. They exchanged a deep, slow kiss and when she tasted his tongue for the first time in years, she gave a long, shuddery moan of pleasure. He captured it with his mouth as they shared breaths and wet, deep tongue thrusts.

Mick's kiss had always made her weak in the knees. Now it made her weak in her entire body. So weak she sagged against him, which made it that much easier for him to continue the lethargic caresses.

"You're still so beautiful," he murmured as he moved his mouth down to her throat again. His fingers were working the buttons of her pajama top, but she had no will to resist. When it fell away, she opened her eyes to watch Mick lower his lips to her breast. He kissed, nibbled and stroked her until she was ready to scream at him to take her in his mouth.

She pushed against him in silent demand, and his laughter only inflamed her more. "Please, Mick."

Instead of giving her what she wanted, he went for the death stroke. His other wicked, naughty hand slid up under the opening of her pajama shorts and cupped her between her legs. She jerked against him as his palm created instant delight where it rubbed against her.

"Oh, God, yes," she said on a moan as waves of pleasure built inside her.

Then he moved his lips to one nipple and sucked deeply and she gave herself over to it, willing her explosive climax to carry her over the edge.

But before she reached that peak, Mick gently pushed her off his lap and stood. She stared at him, dazed, confused, wanting more. He bent down and she reached up, ready to wrap her arms around his neck so he could carry her up to bed. It was crazy and dangerous but she wanted him. Now.

He didn't pick her up. Instead, he brushed one light kiss along her hairline. "Caroline?"

"Umm-hmm?" was the best she could manage.

His whisper was soft and barely penetrated the haze of lust in her brain. "I think you'd better invest in a vibrator."

Then he walked out of the room.

HESTER TOMLINSON hated everything to do with the reality TV show invading Derryville. But that didn't mean she was any less curious than everyone else in town. Especially on Saturday, the official kick-off day of shooting.

"I didn't think the president himself could get Decatur Street shut down. How'd these folks manage to do it?"

The question was asked by Maxine MacDonald, one of the wealthy matriarchs of Derryville. And, unfortunately, a reality TV show junkie. Hester had criticized the show to Maxine once. Only once. She knew well enough not to bite the hand that donated to her.

"I imagine if you have enough money, you can buy anyone," Hester replied, knowing Maxine was too dotty to recognize a backhanded insult.

She and Maxine stood by the front window of Darlene's Dresses and More, watching the crowd scurrying around outside. There were cameras set up at either end of the intersection, a mobile home parked in the parking lot of the post office and people yelling their fool heads off all over the place.

"Are you sure this color looks all right?" Maxine said, sounding anxious. "It won't look too cheap on TV?"

Hester, who couldn't believe someone with Maxine's money and standing would want to be seen on a cheesy television show, gave her a supportive smile. "You're fine. And classy." She cast a quick look outside and frowned. "Unlike most of these other fools."

Everyone in downtown Derryville, it seemed, had put on their Sunday finest for today's show. Women were wearing Easter dresses complete with flowered hats. Ellen Snipes was wearing her grandmother's wedding dress—aged lace, moth-holes and all.

She even swore she saw Ed Racine, who owned the diner, dressed in a black suit that looked suspiciously like his ancient tux. The one he'd been wearing during his wedding to Louisa Jean Mayfair, who'd up and left him with a stack of bills and the diner so she could go off to the big city and become a famous hair salon owner. Ed had been pretty far away, though, so she couldn't tell for sure.

Nitwits. A bunch of nitwits. Most of them didn't seem to care that they were wasting an entire Saturday, just for a chance to get on TV.

She hated that they were all obsessed. She hated more that she had no part in it. Everyone seemed to have forgotten how things were supposed to be done around here.

It was while staring into a crowd of people gathered outside the bank that she saw a face she recognized. She froze, certain she was imagining things. Then she inched closer to the window, leaning toward the glass to get a better look.

The crowd shifted, moved, parted. And she saw the face again.

"Impossible," she whispered, wondering frantically if the group was cast or crew, onlookers or journalists.

"What?"

She didn't even respond to Maxine, because she'd suddenly begun to shiver. *Of all places, of all people.*

A cold finger of fear curved up her back. Fear of her past. Fear for her future. Fear of that person—someone who had no business being here.

Slowly, quietly, not even caring that Maxine might think her rude, Hester slipped away from the window, through the store and out the back door. It was all she could do to remain calm as she walked away, through the alley toward the church. She kept looking over her shoulder, thinking, wondering.

I might not be recognized. Of course I wouldn't.

But what if she were? What if she hadn't changed enough, hadn't gone far enough? Heaven help her if that was the case.

Because being recognized might very well cost her her life.

"I THINK THE COOK from the diner dug up his dead grandfather to get that suit."

Caro whirled around from the small desk where she'd been sitting and saw Jacey Turner, the lead camera operator, wearing a look of bemusement. Following the young woman's stare out the window of the RV— which they'd moved downtown for today's shoot—Caro saw the diner owner in question. He was wearing an ancient-looking tux with a yellowed dress shirt. The pants were a few inches too short, the jacket much too tight. "I don't know," she replied. "I'd say he fits in just as well as everyone else here."

Jacey probably heard the note of resignation in her voice. Caro couldn't help it. Resigned to lunacy. Lunacy on the set. Lunacy in her private life. Lunacy all around.

"Why on earth did all these people show up dressed like this?"

"I have no idea. Renauld is having a hysterical fit right now over by the fountain. Not only is it supposed to be sometime near Halloween, it's also supposed to be this century."

Jacey snorted a laugh. When she did so, her face softened, making her look much more the early-twenties young woman Caro knew her to be. And less the vampire wannabe.

When she smiled, Jacey was very pretty. Not that the girl would appreciate hearing it. Aside from being a kick-ass camera operator, Jacey was known for one other thing: her attitude.

"So you've finished your meetings with all the cast members?"

Caro nodded. She'd been holding half-hour meetings with all sixteen of the starting cast members for *Killing Time in a Small Town* since yesterday. During one of those sessions, she'd told the killer—who was from now on to be called the Derryville Demon—about being chosen.

"How do you feel about the choice for the Demon?" Jacey wasn't the type to nose around for information— she just seemed interested in knowing how Caro felt about it. That made sense. Jacey would want to know things were going in the right direction, even though she and the rest of the crew would know nothing about the identity of the killer until at least the final round.

"I was surprised at first when I finally found out yesterday. But when I looked over the test scores, and the personality profile, it did make sense."

Jacey nodded. "Good." Then she grinned. "Don't suppose you'd want to give me a hint about who it is?"

"Nope. The studio wants to retain that fresh, unexpected feel. That means no advance notice to the crew. Sorry."

"I thought not. But it was worth a shot," Jacey replied, her voice still laced with good humor.

"So you're all ready?"

"You bet," Jacey said. "We've got dedicated crews for the four teams going out today."

Caro nodded, pleased that Jacey, at least, was living up to her reputation for professionalism. It would make things easier if she didn't have to supervise every little piece of this production.

She thought again of today's schedule. The sixteen contestants on *Killing Time* would be divided into four teams after a group lunch at the diner and an introductory "walk through Derryville." Each team would receive different clues that would lead them throughout the town, as if they were on a treasure hunt. They'd actually be on a *clue* hunt. Eventually, if they figured everything out just right, they'd make their way to the crime scene. There they'd find the first set of victims.

The *last* team to make it to the scene became the *first* whose heads would go on the block. Three of those four people would be gone by tomorrow. Leaving the cast members to the perfect total of thirteen.

"They weren't too thrilled to find out you were undercover during that limo ride, were they?" Caro asked, remembering with amusement the looks Jacey had gotten from some of the players when they'd arrived at the Little Bohemie Inn. Jacey had instantly gone for a camera and they'd watched, mouths hanging open.

"Nope. Though it didn't seem to phase one or two of them."

Caro heard a different note in the young woman's voice, as if she were standing here, but her thoughts were a million miles away. But before she could ask her about it, Jacey changed the subject. "So, who's Mick Winchester?"

Shocked, Caro could only stare. "What?"

Jacey pointed to a piece of paper on the small, cramped desk in the RV, which Caro had been using during her meetings with the cast members this morning. Following the girl's stare, Caro saw the piece of paper, on which she'd been scribbling "I hate Mick Winchester" over and over and over again.

"Nobody."

"Somebody," Jacey said. "As in *some body.* I met him this morning."

"So why'd you ask who he was?"

"I wanted to see your ears turn red."

The cheeky response was good-natured, and Caro realized Jacey was teasing her. "He's off-limits in conversation."

And in real life.

Jacey shrugged and promptly said goodbye, leaving Caro alone in the trailer.

Mick was definitely off limits. Nonexistent. An invisible person who accidentally shared her airspace in his house—the one she'd be vacating the very second she found someplace else to go. At this point, suffocating at Sophie's place by inhaling cat dander seemed preferable to having to face Mick again.

She couldn't get over what he'd done to her two nights ago. Without apology, without regret, without a backward glance, he'd toyed with her, aroused her to insanity, then walked out.

Isn't that what you intended to do to him?

She told her inner voice to shut up. Having him wake up to a porn movie was *not* the same thing as physical contact. Not anywhere near the same thing.

And oh, that physical contact. She shook just thinking about it. His hands, those glorious hands, and his mouth…what incredible things he could do with them. As well as with other things.

That was the thought that had kept her from going after him the night before with a meat cleaver or a fireplace poker. She hadn't been the only one affected by their interlude. His interest had been noticeable. Very noticeable, God help her, since she'd been sitting on his lap.

He'd definitely had a lapful.

Yet he'd gotten up and walked away when he was in just as aroused a condition as she. Mick had never been *that* strong a man. Which meant he must really, *really* have bad feelings toward her. He had brought them both to the edge of the cliff, then had walked away without letting either of them go over.

He hates me.

"Well, good. Because I hate him too."

"You hate who?" a male voice intruded.

She jerked around. "Charlie," she said with a shaky smile. "Good morning. You doing okay?"

The older man nodded. "Got the sound check done in the diner and in the library. But we got a problem. I just talked to Jacey about it and she's going over to check for herself."

Caro began to shake her head. "No problems, please."

"Sorry. The staircase leading up to the apartment where the bodies are supposed to be discovered is too narrow for a full pan. Jacey's team can do tight shots from the bedroom as the cast comes in. But nothing going up or down the stairs."

Damn. Renauld was going to have a fit. "Anything else?"

Charlie gave her an apologetic shrug. "Yeah, uh, the guy who lives there?"

"Yes?"

"He did some redecorating."

"Oh, God."

"I think he likes the color green."

"How green?"

"Think two tons of strained peas sprayed on four walls. It ain't pretty."

Double damn. Before Caro could go on a rant about how the man had signed a contract agreeing not to make any principal changes to his home before the shoot, Charlie continued, "And, there's these…things everywhere."

"Things?"

"Yeah. Little ceramic stuff. I guess maybe his mother or girlfriend makes it. There's all this crap on every surface in the place, complete with price tags and the logo for a local store that sells them."

This time, the four-letter word that spilled out of her mouth didn't start with the letter "d."

CHAPTER NINE

MICK TRIED HARD to ignore the throng of people as he headed downtown to mail a package at the post office Saturday morning. The crowd was gathered on Decatur Street, listening to some guy with a megaphone calling out instructions. He'd just about made it past the insanity when he felt someone grab his arm. "This! This is what I want!"

He gave the guy who grabbed him a "hands off, buddy" stare.

The man was dressed straight off the pages of *GQ*, and had a balding head which probably reached Mick's chin. He still ignored Mick's frown. "You see? Appropriate look for a man on the street, in the daytime, in the fall." He shot Mick a look. "But go put on a jacket. It's supposed to be October."

Mick shook his head. "You got the wrong guy, mister."

"I am not a mere *mister*," the man replied with an offended sniff. "I'm Renauld Watson, the director of this production. If you want to double your twenty dollars extra pay, help me get these sheep back in their pens to remove their spring wool."

Sheep. Spring wool. Mick looked around, confused as hell by this man who talked a mile a minute and sniffed in a peculiar watery way every third word. "Like

I said. You got the wrong guy. I'm just going to the post office."

"You're not an extra?"

Mick shook his head.

"Then what are you doing on my set?"

"I believe this is called a public street."

Mr. Watson crossed his arms. "And I own it for the day."

Before Mick could reply, he heard Police Chief Daniel Fletcher. "Uh, you bought the right to close the street to automobile traffic, Mr. Watson. This is a living, breathing town. You've got no say about who walks on the sidewalk."

Watson looked ready to argue, but before he could do so, something on the corner crossed his eye. "No, no, no! No advertisements in the store windows." He stalked off to deal with some poor merchant who'd apparently tried to capitalize on the TV crew by putting up a huge banner with the name and address of his store.

"This is a madhouse," Mick said, shaking his head in disbelief.

"Yeah, definitely. Sophie's loving it."

Mick exchanged an amused look with his future brother-in-law. He wasn't surprised Sophie would enjoy this. Since his little sister had begun to emerge from her cocoon, she was turning into one bloodthirsty little butterfly.

"You look like shit," Daniel said in a matter-of-fact manner.

"Oh, thanks."

It was true. Probably because he felt like shit, and had been sleeping like shit. Ever since Thursday night when he'd walked out on Caroline, he'd been restless and uptight, stressed and confused.

He'd done the right thing. Dammit, she would have hated his guts even more the next morning if he'd taken what she was offering. At least, he *thought* she would. He hadn't intended to set her up like that, or to punish her or anything. After all, he'd certainly been punished, too. They'd just gotten carried away, fallen into something neither of them had been ready for and both would have regretted.

His parting shot had been meant to turn her from melting seductress to furious virago. It'd obviously worked. She hadn't even looked in his direction since then.

Before Daniel could say anything more, Mick saw the very person he'd been thinking about. He knew it was Caroline—the sun caught the highlights in her dark brown hair so that even from here he wanted to sink his hands in it.

She looked weary and frustrated as she talked with a couple of techie-looking guys. Mick couldn't help stiffening when one of them put a familiar hand on her shoulder.

"God, man, have *you* got a case."

He looked at Fletcher. "What are you talking about?"

Daniel merely laughed.

Not wanting to hear any more b.s. about Caroline, Mick quickly changed the subject. "I saw the chipmunks on my way over here." He was referring to the two young deputies, cousins who were often mistaken for twins. "Chip and Dale."

"Skip and Chuck," Daniel corrected him with a distinct roll of the eyes.

"Whatever."

Looking almost afraid to ask, Daniel said, "Were they still directing traffic at the corner of Young and Vine?"

Mick shook his head, enjoying the moment.

"Tell me."

"I think they wanna star in a remake of *Lethal Weapon*."

"Tell me they haven't shot anybody."

Mick merely smiled. "Not yet. But I think they were about to handcuff the mayor's wife because she's insisting on driving her Cadillac down Decatur so all the envious people out in TV land can see her shiny new car. They told her they'd shoot out the tires if she tried to go around the roadblock."

Daniel visibly shuddered, shook his head and hurried away. As he did so, Mick heard him mutter, "This department doesn't need a chief, it needs a damn baby-sitter."

Standing alone in the middle of the crowd, Mick couldn't stop his gaze from returning to Caroline. Suddenly, she glanced up and met his stare. Even from several yards away, he saw the way she stiffened and her face grew slightly pink.

Still pissed. No doubt about it.

If only she knew he'd hurt himself far more than he'd hurt her the other night. Yeah, he'd left her high and dry—that is, he remembered with a pleasurable smile, high and *wet*. But he'd also left himself *hard* and dry. Rock hard, hungry and insane with need to finish what he'd so stupidly started. With her.

His own hand hadn't done a thing to help, not in the long run. Nor, he knew, would another woman. It was Caroline or nothing. Just like it had been when they'd met.

It was darn near impossible to do much of anything with a 24/7 hard-on, as he'd discovered. There was only one way it was going away. And that didn't look to happen anytime soon because the only woman he wanted had been ignoring him while mumbling, "I hate you Mick Winchester" under her breath for thirty-six hours.

That woman finally seemed to make up her mind about something. Mick was shocked to see her stride toward him, her steps purposeful and her expression stern.

Here it comes. He braced himself to hear, "I hate you Mick Winchester."

"I need you, Mick."

Well, praise the Lord and pass the ammunition. "Finally realized that, did you?"

She shot him a glare. "I mean, I need to talk to you. Walk with me."

She stepped away, in long, even strides that ate up the sidewalk and dared him to keep up.

He hurried to do so. "Are we talking again? I thought you were just going to keep giving me those 'stay back, peasant' looks until you moved out."

"I can't imagine what you're talking about."

Before he could reply, he noticed Caroline had stopped moving and was staring ahead, a wary look on her face. He followed her glance, and realized why.

"Hi, Louise," he said.

The woman gave them both a nervous, apologetic smile. "Hi there."

"Are you armed?" Caroline asked, taking a tiny step back.

Louise shook her head. "I'm awful sorry about that. I've realized how stupid I was that day. My pastor's been helping me find better ways to direct my need to help people," she said with a self-deprecating smile.

Mick chuckled softly. "Forgiven."

"Thanks, Mick." Louise gave him a look of gratitude and he was pleased to notice she didn't look all worshipful as she had the last time he'd seen her. Good. Hopefully she'd come to her senses. Pastor Bob was a nice guy, in spite of his mean-spirited sister, and he'd probably be very helpful to Louise.

"Well, I have to go," Louise said. "I'm an extra." She rolled her eyes. "And so are my brothers. I have to make sure they're not up to any...mischief."

Knowing her brothers, they'd probably already tied up the camera crew and taken the production trailer for a joyride.

"Have fun," Caroline mumbled. Then she added, low and under her breath so only Mick could hear, "Try not to kill anyone for real on the set."

Louise nodded. "Thanks. Bye!"

The other woman walked away, leaving Caroline staring at him, looking bemused. "You just let her get away with it and that's that?"

"Uh-huh."

"In other places what she did might be called assault with a deadly weapon."

He shrugged. "This is Derryville."

As if that explained everything—and really, it did—she nodded in understanding. Then she started walking again, the purposeful, busy executive. Her cell phone, which was clipped to her purse strap, began to ring. She glanced down at it, frowned when she read the number, then proceeded to ignore it.

As he walked along with her, he could see Caroline looked frazzled and frenzied. He didn't like the look. What she needed was to be kidnapped for a day of fun and relaxation. Not that she'd appreciate it. Not that she'd probably ever be alone with him in private again after what he'd done to her Thursday night.

He was about to mention it, to try to apologize somehow without really saying he was sorry—because that would be a lie, since he wasn't so much sorry as he was regretful—when they were interrupted. One of the girls who usually waited on him at the bank approached from the other direction. She gave Caro a quick, dismissive glance, then Mick a much more friendly one. "Hi, Mick. When you going to come make your next deposit?"

He gave her a noncommittal smile, nodded hello and continued walking.

Caro had grown a few degrees cooler.

"She works at my bank," he explained.

"Isn't the bank closed on Saturday?"

Cooler? That was pure ice. That voice could put Frigidaire out of business. "You wanted to talk to me?"

But before she could say another word, Diane, who cut his hair for him, stepped up onto the sidewalk in front of them. "Hiya, Mick. Aren't you due to visit me soon?" She reached up and playfully tugged his hair, which was almost brushing the collar of his shirt. "You need me, honey."

He would have groaned, wondering what Caroline made of this. "Sure, I'll call."

"Be sure you do," she said with a wave as she sauntered away, her swing a little more exaggerated than usual.

No, he'd never asked her out. No, he'd never even been tempted. And maybe he had a chance of making Caroline believe that. Maybe he'd also have a chance of hitching a ride with the fat guy in the red suit come Christmas, too.

"Caroline?"

God, if her spine were any stiffer, her neck would break. "Forget it."

He wasn't forgetting anything. "You said you needed to talk."

This time, they were interrupted by one of his second cousins, Maureen, who'd bought a house from him a few days ago. "Hey, Mick. I'm so glad I ran into you. I need you to come over to my house and check out my pipes."

This time, he was pretty sure he *heard* the temperature drop even more. They'd passed the ice stage and moved right on to frozen carbon dioxide.

"Okay, I'll call you Monday," Mick replied.

"Gotta run, I'm going to be an extra!"

As Maureen walked away, Caroline swung around and stuck her index finger in his face. "If one more woman stops to talk to you, I'm pushing you in front of the next tractor-trailer."

Without missing a beat, he replied, "The street's closed to traffic."

Her mouth opened. Closed. Then she let out a muffled groanlike sound, planted both hands on his chest and shoved. He stumbled back off the sidewalk, into the street and stood there, looking at her because she'd turned into some kind of madwoman. A jealous madwoman. That wasn't such a bad thing, was it? That proved something, didn't it?

Proved that he'd gotten her interested the other night, that was sure. But it didn't prove much else.

"I guess you don't need me very much after all," he called out, ready to walk away.

Caroline took three steps, her shoulders square, her dark hair swinging and bouncing as she tried to march in righteous indignation. Then she stopped and slowly turned around. As if each word were dragged from her throat with a crowbar, she admitted, "I need Sophie's house."

He sucked in a shocked breath. She was leaving? He'd scared her off for good? That should have made him feel better, should have offered some relief. But the thought of going home to an empty house again, not hearing her stirring around in her bed or humming jingles from commercials in the shower, left him feeling empty inside.

"Your allergies…"

"I'll take some Benadryl."

"You gonna take it intravenously every hour for the next three weeks?" he asked, raising a skeptical brow as he stepped back up onto the sidewalk.

She shook her head, explaining, "I'm not going to *live* there."

He wondered if she could read the expression of relief he couldn't hide. "Oh."

"I need to know if it's available, and, if so, I need you to come over there with me."

"Armed with Benadryl?"

"Yes. And a butcher knife. I'm about to kill someone in your sister's house."

Mick could only hope it wasn't him.

HESTER HAD FRETTED and stewed most of the morning about the face she'd seen among the TV people. A face that instantly brought up long-buried memories of another life, another time. And made her quiver with the kind of fear she hadn't felt in a few decades.

By late afternoon, however, she'd realized something. She was a different person now. A strong person. A clever one and certainly a more self-reliant one.

Hadn't she proved that, right here in town, fooling the world with one public face and successfully hiding her more private one? Even her own brother didn't *really* know her. No one did.

Finally she had reason to be thankful for packing on a hundred pounds or so in the past thirty years. "I won't be recognized. People see only what they want to see."

That was true. People looked at her and saw the devoted first lady of the church. The one who looked after her poor, sweet, wonderful younger brother who was so beloved by the town. Miss Hester the miserable old spinster whose only role in life was to play the martyr, that's what they saw.

Only a few—the few whose secrets she'd learned and exploited since arriving in Derryville—knew the real woman.

And now the biggest, most profitable secret of all had landed here in her own backyard. "It might even be enough to get me out of here for good."

Taking a nondescript piece of white paper and a standard black ink pen, she sat down at her small writing table, where she so often tweaked and edited her brother's sermons.

She wrote down two words as she pictured a face from her past. Two simple, nearly forgotten, but very valuable words.

"Victoria Lynn."

THE ONE GOOD THING about having the network already deeply committed to this project was that they had writers on call. And Caro took full advantage, paging and faxing several of them for their immediate assistance.

"You talked to your sister?" she asked Mick as

they stood on the back porch of Sophie Winchester's small house.

He nodded. "She agreed. Have them fax you a contract and she'll sign it."

Caro drew in a deep, relieved breath. God, she hated having to rely on him, having to ask for his help. One more thing to be under his thumb for. First sex, now the show.

She'd almost been under a lot more than his thumb the other night. Closing her eyes, she shook off the memory. "At least she won't have time to paint it pea-green," she mumbled, trying to fill the silence, to make him think she was focused strictly on business when the truth was far from that.

"That's why you needed to move the location of the shoot here?"

Caro nodded, briefly explaining their troubles with the owner of the downtown apartment, which was originally supposed to be the crime scene. "So," she said, "I immediately thought of this place. It's perfect, even though I can't be inside for more than a few minutes at a time."

He gave her a worried look, probably noting her red-rimmed eyes and puffy cheeks. "Are you going to be all right?"

She nodded. "I'm not inside much, and the Benadryl is helping. And this house is absolutely perfect. Enough light, big enough for a full camera crew. Vacant but still partially furnished. We just need to change the final clues for each team, so they're led here instead of downtown."

"That's where I come in?"

She nodded. "You have to talk to the writers on my cell and give them enough information to make sure a newcomer to town would find this place."

"Can do," he said.

He was being extremely accommodating. But was the least he could do, she reminded herself, considering he owed her. Big time. He now officially owed her several nights' sleep—which he'd ruined. As well as a few damn good orgasms, which he'd silently promised and hadn't delivered.

Though, she had the feeling neither the sleep nor the orgasms were going to show up in her near future. Not unless she took his suggestion and invested in a vibrator. Because after what he'd done to her Thursday night, there was no way she was ever letting him touch her again.

Even though having Mick touch her was about the most perfect thing she'd ever experienced.

The jerk. Just when she'd convinced herself he couldn't possibly be as good as she remembered, he'd gone and shown her he was better. Oh, Lord, was he better. And that was only just the slow buildup part. She couldn't begin to imagine what the finale might have been like.

Luckily, before Mick could turn around and ask her why she had such a stupid, lustful look on her face, Charlie and a couple of the other techs stepped out of the bedroom, where they'd been measuring and setting up.

"Hey there, Mr. Winchester," he said, "be sure to tell your sister how much we appreciate this, okay? She's a lifesaver." He turned to Caro. "This place is perfect, much better than the apartment. You still want one stiff in the kitchen and two on the floor in the bedroom?"

She nodded. "Props knows to come here right?"

Charlie nodded. "And Jacey's heading here right after the contestants split up into groups of four from the diner." Charlie snickered. "That is, if they ever split up considering they can't nail the shot. Seems the chef has decided he's an opera singer this morning. And the waitress is dressed like one of Charlie's Angels. And the ladies in the place are acting like they're eating cucumber sandwiches rather than greasy burgers and fries."

Mick snorted a laugh. Caro could only sigh.

But that was Renauld's problem for today. She was too busy putting out this fire to deal with that one. Let him douse the flames at the diner.

JACEY WAS THE FIRST one to see the fire.

Shooting had finally gotten underway, after the extras had finally changed their clothes, lowered their tea-party pinkies and nearly forgotten they were going to be on television.

Even the owner of the diner, Ed, had been persuaded to remove his tux, put on an apron, and stop singing an aria from some fat-people opera while he fried up the onion rings. Unfortunately, it didn't stop him from trying to show off his skill with those onion rings. And that was when the trouble started.

"So how do you like our fair town?" said one of the extras, a guy in a cop uniform who looked like a kid playing dress-up with his father's clothes. Jacey had already dubbed the two officers—who were inseparable—Thing One and Thing Two. They looked just as alike and caused about as much trouble.

"It's lovely," said Ginger, who was, as expected, the first one to take to the camera. Jacey had to hand it to her, twenty pounds or not, Ginger looked pretty good on tape.

Not to be outdone, the extremely pompous college

professor—Whittington—added, "This country air would inspire the bard to write another *Hamlet*."

Just what the world needs, Jacey thought, remembering her high school Shakespeare. *Another play that makes you want to slit your wrists.* She kept her camera on Whittington. Something about the guy rang very phony to her. Or else he just creeped her out by being obsessed with a dead writer.

Before anyone else could say a word, Jacey caught a movement through the pass-through into the kitchen. The cook, Ed, was flipping onion rings out of the fryer, one at a time, and attempting to catch them on a long skewer. For some reason, Jacey pulled her camera off the cast, knowing her team had them covered from three other angles in the diner. She zoomed in through the pass-through, catching the cook's act.

He flung another ring. This one landed in a pot of chili on the stove. Then again—this one bounced through the pass-through, hitting the buxom waitress in the back of the head. The woman swung around to see what had hit her. Jacey wondered if the woman had thought, "big freakin' cockroach," since that seemed a probable explanation in this place. But she just shrugged and didn't say anything. Meanwhile Ed continued his acrobatic show.

Or, at least, he continued to *try.* Flip, miss. Flip, miss. Flip, another one in the chili pot.

Then, finally, because even a broken clock is right twice a day, he got one. Jacey almost wanted to clap for the guy. Almost. Because her second impulse was to warn him that the onion ring had to be pretty stinkin' hot.

Apparently, it was.

"Ow!" he shrieked as the ring slid down the metal

skewer and landed on his fisted hand. His yelp wasn't loud enough to drown out one of the contestants who was singing the praises of the cool days of autumn. *That* guy deserved an Emmy since they were all dripping sweat in this cramped diner on an unseasonably hot September day.

Nobody else seemed to notice the cook's dilemma, but Jacey gave him a sympathetic look as she contin-ued to shoot. The moment he'd gotten burned, he'd flung his skewer—not to mention the winning onion ring—away. He'd grabbed a big hunk of butter and started spreading it on his wrist, which made Jacey cringe from here. Butter on a burn—did people still do that? Good grief, during the two or three Girl Scout meetings she'd attended as a kid—before getting kicked out for punching another little girl—she'd learned bet-ter than that! Some people should have to get a license to walk out their front doors every day.

It was while tsking over the bad butter move that Jacey noticed the smoke. And heard the pop. And saw the tipped-over deep fryer—which the cook's arm-wav-ing appeared to have caused—lying on the stove. Boil-ing hot grease slid across the huge flat surface, which was still coated with burger guts and pieces of burnt chicken.

Whoosh.

Flames shot up from the cooktop. Ed's eyes widened to almost comical proportions. Mr. Whittington droned on about dead poets. The camera crew and director ig-nored everything but the set.

And Jacey watched the kitchen go up in flames. "Umm…"

Before she could say another word, she realized she

wasn't the only one who'd witnessed the catastrophe. Digg shot up out of his chair, pushed past the waitress who'd been putting her boobs as close to his arm as she could get while taking his order earlier, and sprinted toward the kitchen. He somehow did a move Jacey had only ever seen in movies, never real life. He didn't even break stride as he reached the breakfast counter. Throwing one palm flat on the counter he launched his whole big, yummy self over it in one leap.

Jacey never took the camera off him.

"Back up!" Digg yelled to the cook, who still watched slack-jawed as the onion ring nightmare began to consume even more of his kitchen.

The rest of the people in the diner finally noticed. Renauld started to wail about the interruption. The celebrity host, Joshua Charmagne, darted for the door. She wondered what the fans of his old cop show, *Southern Heat,* would think of their tough-guy hero now.

The contestants all jumped to their feet, and the townspeople began to yell for the fire department. And, per their good training, the other camera operators immediately panned to the action in the kitchen. She would've wrung their necks if they'd dropped the cameras to go help put out the fire. Probably pretty twisted. But hey, she was a camera junkie.

Besides, Digg seemed fully capable. Though she half hoped he'd whip off his tight black T-shirt and try extinguishing the flames with the cloth, he instead beelined for an industrial-size fire extinguisher on the wall of the kitchen. He had it off the wall and in operation within about fifty seconds of leaving his seat.

The fire was out a few seconds later, leaving him, unfortunately, fully clothed, but also a savior. Everyone froze for one long moment after the fire was out. Then activity erupted. Everyone clapped, cheered and poured into the kitchen. Ed grabbed Digg's hand and kissed it. The buxom waitress threw her arms around his neck. Ginger and Mona shoved her out of the way and hugged him themselves.

And Jacey watched through the camera.

Finally, after the excitement died down and Renauld called for everyone to go back to their places, Digg edged closer and closer, until he stood right beside her. "You catch the whole thing?"

"Uh-huh."

"Would you have stopped shooting if my clothes had caught on fire?"

"Huh-uh."

He tsked. "Very nice."

"At least not if it was your shirt," Jacey admitted. "If that was coming off, I would definitely have wanted to get it on tape." Then, to make sure he didn't get the wrong idea, she added, "For our female viewers."

She wondered if he heard the note of blasé amusement she'd been going for in her voice, or if he'd zeroed directly in to the attraction she was trying so desperately to hide.

"Ahh."

Just that and she knew he'd heard the attraction. The interest. The surprising desire she felt for this most unlikely of guys. Unlikely, at least, for her, whose taste ran more to the motorcycle-riding, black-leather-wearing bad boys she'd grown up with in the poor part of L.A. Not serious-looking, thoughtful, intense do-gooders.

"Do you *ever* come out from behind that camera? Or do you only live life through it?" His voice was slightly challenging.

Jacey gritted her teeth to avoid letting him know that he'd scored a hit. One of the big arguments she'd had with her father was over Jacey's desire to watch the world, not live in it.

"Why don't you get back over there to your adoring public?"

"Why don't you answer the question?"

As usual, when Jacey was challenged she reacted with her typical defense. An aggressive offense. "Go on, Meat, you're the entertainment. I'm the crew. Get back to your job so I can do mine."

He didn't reply for a long moment as Jacey held her breath. Finally, unable to help it, she pulled her attention away from the ruckus in the diner, away from her camera lens, and turned her head slightly to look at Digg.

He was just staring with those deep, knowing brown eyes, giving her one of those tiny, precious smiles. And looking as if he knew her, *really* knew her, like no one ever had.

"I'll get you out from behind that camera one of these days, Jacey Turner." His words were a promise more than a threat.

"You can try." Damn, her voice had cracked. She stiffened her jaw.

"Oh, I will," he said softly. "Wait and see."

CHAPTER TEN

"DON'T YOU THINK I should act out my death scene?"

Caro smothered an impatient sigh. "No, I don't."

Five seconds went by. Then the plea came again. "But I really think…"

You're not being paid to think.

"You're just supposed to be dead, okay, Mr. Smithback?"

Caro had been having this same argument with Eldon Smithback for a half hour here in Sophie Winchester's house where they were setting up for the first murder scene. Eldon wanted to go out with glory. Caro just wanted him dead on the floor. God, extras were going to be the death of her. If the cast wasn't first. Not to mention her allergies.

No, strike that. *First* would be the man standing in the kitchen, watching the madness as the crew got ready for the arrival of the cast of sleuths. Mick. Watching all, seeing all. Laughing silently in the background while he observed the mania Caro had become well used to in the TV business. Mania like people hired to play corpses who decided they wanted to do a *Sopranos*-type death scene instead.

Renauld owed her big-time for leaving her here to sort this out. Dealing with discontented extras wasn't her job.

"I could surprise the intruder after my wife and son have been killed."

Caro continued reading the messages she'd just received on her alphanumeric pager. Messages from the four runners she'd sent out to plant the replacement clues. The writers had come through big-time on that. Thirty seconds after the new clues had come off the fax machine, she'd had the techs racing out to place them at the four locations. They'd just paged to let her know everything was a go.

"I did a play once in high school and the schoolmarm said I was the best George Washington she ever saw."

Considering how old the guy was, the schoolmarm had probably known the real one. She'd had enough. "Look, you're dead, okay? Just…dead. If you surprise the intruder, well, your face might give something away to the audience."

Instead of being dissuaded, he puffed up a little more. "That'd be great. A clue. I could be the first clue!"

Arggh! "You're not supposed to be a clue. You're supposed to be a corpse."

The old man wouldn't be put off. As if auditioning, possibly for the play he'd done in high school, he froze, let out a bloodcurdling scream, clutched his hands to his chest and proceeded to stagger all over Sophie Winchester's former bedroom. Caro watched impassively, waiting for the guy to finish. It took a while before he clunked to the ground and twitched around a bit.

"See?" he said hopefully after he'd gasped and moaned his last.

"No," she bit out between clenched teeth, even as another sneezing fit threatened to force her out of the house. "You. Are. A. Corpse."

He was going to be a real corpse, soon, if he didn't leave her alone.

"Maybe I can help."

Mick. That silky-smooth, reasonable voice could belong to no one else. She really didn't want his help. Actually, she didn't want him around at all, but since he'd provided some real assistance with his sister—and the writers—this morning, she couldn't very well order him out.

"Do you have any tranquilizer darts, like the ones they use on rampaging elephants?" she asked. "I think that's what it's going to take to keep him down."

Mick chuckled, then walked over to Mr. Smithback, who was standing up, saying something about how much more action there would be if he wrestled with the killer and tried to take the knife.

"You're not killed with a knife, your son is," Caro muttered, not even really paying attention. "Your wife is strangled and you get shot."

Then she turned her attention to Charlie and Joc, who had just completed a sound check and finished setting up lights to capture the cast as they entered the foyer. By the time she turned back around, Smithback was nodding at Mick. He looked quiet, chastened and, amazingly, cooperative.

"How's this?" he asked Caro.

Before she could answer, he flopped over onto his belly, sprawled his arms and legs in different directions, and buried his face in the carpet.

"Good," she murmured, silently counting the seconds he remained totally still.

One. Two. Ten. Thirty.

"Um…can you breathe?"

"He can breathe," Mick said.

"That'll do, Mr. Smithback."

The man continued his carpet dive.

"Okay, Eldon. I think she's got it," Mick said, raising his voice a few levels. Then he glanced at Caro. "He wears his hearing aid in the right ear, the one closest to the wall. Couldn't hear you."

Mr. Smithback sat up, sucked in a few deep breaths and gave Caro a hopeful look.

"That was fine, Mr. Smithback," Caro said. Then she whispered, "My God, would he have suffocated himself if you weren't here to tell him to stop?"

Mick merely shrugged.

"What'd you say to him to get him to drop the idea of dying on camera, anyway?"

"I reminded him of what happened during his Moose Club trip to Las Vegas three years ago. He might not want his, uh, weekend *wife* seeing him on TV and recognizing him."

Caro grinned, acknowledging not for the first time just how good Mick was with people. He'd basically blackmailed Mr. Smithback into behaving, but the man looked at Mick like he was a hero.

That was a gift. One that had both attracted her and concerned her back in the old days. It was too easy for Mick to make people like him. People? Okay, *women.* That was the part that had bothered her in the old days.

But not anymore. Because, after all, after Thursday night, she hated the bastard, she really did.

He walked over to help deal with the old lady extra, who was being slightly hysterical about having to lie on the floor in her lovely new dress. Caro didn't want to think of what the woman was going to say when she found out how much fake blood was soon going to be scattered all over the other two victims. As the one strangled, the female extra should've been grateful.

Mick gave her a quick grin and a wink as he got the woman calmed down within ten seconds. And Caro had to admit, hate him or not, Mick was proving to be a godsend.

"All right," she called, watching the makeup people finish putting the fake knife and gore on the chest of the third extra. "Let's practice some dying!"

ONCE THAT FIRST DAY was over with, things actually started to go well on the set. Jacey told herself it was just because she could spot a hit when she worked on one. In truth, she was enjoying watching this microcosm of society—the cast—begin to team up and draw lines, to find their place in the show, and to form alliances.

It was always the same. Whether the show was a *Survivor* type, or a manhunt, or a lust fest, the people competing reacted in the same, predictable manner.

Ginger had come out a lot stronger than first impressions had led Jacey to believe, and Mona absolutely as weak. Professor Whittington got on everyone's nerves, and Willie the truck driver just wanted to get laid. Jacey would lay money that the schoolteacher from Des Moines, Deanna, had already hooked up with James, a store owner from Baltimore. That didn't seem to sit well with Logan, a computer geek from Chicago.

As for the others—well, Frank from Fresno was a freaking loser who always wanted his way and wasn't above whining to get it. Jacey really wished somebody would shove a handful of glue into his mouth one of these days. There were one or two more men, and the other women hadn't impressed her enough for her to even remember their names.

That could also be because they, like Ginger and Mona, always seemed to be hovering around everyone's favorite contestant. Mr. Popular. Mr. Stud. Mr. Hero.

The guy walking toward her.

"Hey, Jacey."

"Digg," she replied with a nod, turning her attention back to the breakfast soufflé she was consuming in the nearly deserted dining room of the Little Bohemie Inn very early Sunday morning.

"Wow, I can actually see your face. No camera in front of it."

She deliberately raised a big forkful of her food and stuck it in her mouth. He didn't get the silent message.

"I didn't think you guys ever turned the cameras off."

She finished chewing. "Who says they're off?"

He gave a quick look around but didn't ask about the placement of hidden cameras in the room. Everyone knew they were there. Sometimes it was best not to think about it, even for Jacey and the crew.

Digg crossed his arms and sat back in his chair, staring at her, studying her face so hard she suddenly felt uncomfortable. "You're not wearing your Bride of Frankenstein look this morning."

She shot him a glare.

"I can actually see a little color in your cheeks. Amazing."

"I thought I could eat in peace so I didn't bother putting on my makeup. Speaking of being in peace, why aren't you upstairs in your room resting up for today's round of clue-hunting? The next quiz is coming up. You don't wanna be one of the ones locked out with the Derryville Demon during the second episode, do you?"

He shrugged, looking unconcerned. Then he reached for the coffeepot and poured himself a cup. "I feel pretty comfortable. I paid attention yesterday. For instance," he said, leaning closer and resting his elbows on the table, "I noticed that your black sweater actually had a little pink in it. And I'm almost certain I saw you wearing a pair of yellow shorts when you took off early Friday morning."

God, he was observant! She'd slipped out of the inn before dawn Friday and yesterday, as usual, needing to get some exercise and fresh air. She'd gone for a long run at the state park she'd found the first day here and been back at the inn before the first guest had come down.

"So what does that prove, beyond the fact that you're not color blind?"

He smiled a tiny bit. "Just that you're changing. Relaxing, maybe? Dropping some of the defensive attitude you usually have. I mean it's pretty obvious your appearance is meant to scare people off."

"Thanks Dr. Phil," she muttered, reaching for her cup again.

"Where do you go?"

"What?"

"Where do you go so early in the morning? Do you get outside for a little exercise?" He rolled his shoulders and stretched his neck, obviously one of those guys who always needed to be moving.

I could definitely help you move, Mr. Hero. She told the voice in her head to be quiet, and forced her attention back on his words. Not on his big, hard body.

"That's one drawback to small-town inn life," he continued, "there are no gyms within thirty miles."

She sipped her cooling coffee again. "Right."

"And since none of the guests are allowed to leave without a member of the crew, not that we could if we wanted to since we don't have cars…"

His unmistakable hint hung there in the air between them. Digg wanted to share her workout time. As if he didn't have enough women here at the inn who'd give up every pair of shoes they owned to get him alone for five minutes.

A part of her instantly reacted. Her heart sped up a little, and though she hated it, she could feel warmth rising in her face.

Digg just stared, implacable, watching as he always did. Then, when she didn't respond with an immediate invitation, he took the initiative. "Can I hitch a ride with you some morning? I could use a break from this place." He looked at her camera case, which she never left without. "And from the cameras."

No, no, say no.

The words came to her mouth, hung onto the tip of her lips, but got stuck there, somehow. Finally Jacey nodded weakly. "Okay."

"Great." He looked genuinely appreciative, a man who accepted every little kindness or good deed in life and didn't keep count.

Jacey couldn't help adding, "And, uh, you don't have to worry about the camera. I'd never let it be turned on when I'm wearing anything as hideous as yellow shorts."

This time, when he smiled, she couldn't resist smiling back.

BY THE END of that weekend, Mick had revised his opinion about Caroline's job. He'd originally thought it had to be about glamour and power. Now he knew it was about baby-sitting and putting out fires. Sometimes literally, given what he'd heard had happened at the diner. He had to hand it to her, she'd kept her temper and her cool a lot longer than most people would have been able to.

"So, that's over with," he said Sunday evening as they stood in his kitchen, alone for the first time since Thursday night. They were sharing a pint of Ben & Jerry's Chunky Monkey, eating right out of the container with two big spoons.

It had been that kind of weekend. No sleep. No real meals. Tons of stress. Actually, he'd kind of liked it.

She ruefully shook her head, licking off the spoon, her little pink tongue creating streaks in the ice cream— and a blast of heat in Mick's body. So much for going back to a cordial relationship. Right now, he wanted to dribble Chunky Monkey all over Caroline's naked body, watch it melt and then lick off every bit of it.

"Just beginning," she said. "But at least we're on our way. The show will have a dynamite opening with the triple homicide."

"Who's the killer?"

She shook her head. "Can't tell."

"I'd originally thought it was going to be that guy with the Southern accent who said he's a farmer. His fingernails were too long to be a farmer."

"Well, it's obviously not him since he's been bumped out."

Bumped out, bumped off. Whatever. The farmer, along with two other people from his four member team, had been eliminated from the game since they were the last to find the three bodies in Sophie's house. Only

Whittington, the college professor, had survived from that foursome because he'd solved the most clues during the day. That hadn't surprised him too much. He'd thought from the moment he'd met him that there was more to the man than met the eye.

Caroline continued to lick her ice cream, her visible appreciation for it almost making her look like she was having incredible sex. Or he could just be seeing incredible sex because that's what he'd been thinking about nonstop for days.

"So, are we going to talk about it?" she asked, continuing to lick her ice cream, but now staring at him over the spoon. Her eyes were knowing, as if she could read what he'd been thinking. And had been thinking it, too.

"Talk about it?"

She nodded. "I spent all day Friday hating you. But I have to admit it, Mick, if you hadn't been there on the set yesterday and today, things would have been a lot more difficult."

That was an understatement. For some reason, it pleased him to know that Caroline had admitted she needed him. If only to help the writers get the layout of the town. Or to blackmail extras into behaving. Or, as he had this morning, to get on the horn and have the local shipping company open up on a Sunday so Caroline could get some much-needed packages delivered.

Yeah. She'd needed him. For more than just what she'd needed from him Thursday night.

"So, I figure we'd better clear the air about what happened the other night. Because I have a proposition for you."

His mind instantly went into the gutter. "A proposition?"

She tsked but didn't look offended. "Not that kind of proposition. I want you to work with us while we're here in Derryville. Be a sort of…liaison to the town. But that'll only work if you and I can come to some sort of peaceful arrangement."

"We've been peaceful."

"Okay, how about *cordial* arrangement? Not going from lust to hate and back again every other hour."

He couldn't keep the intensity from his voice as he replied, "I've never hated you."

She slowly lowered her spoon, leaving it sticking out of the ice cream container on the counter. "Not even when you had your back tattooed…for the *second* time?"

Knowing Caroline as he did, he figured she'd resent it if he acknowledged that hint of hurt in her voice. He didn't know which surprised him more—that he heard that note of vulnerability, or that he'd ever had the power to hurt her to begin with. But apparently, he had. He'd hurt her long after she'd left, when he'd tried to remove her importance from his life by removing her significance on his body.

"I didn't hate you," he finally said. "Some people cauterize their wounds. I tried to get rid of mine with needles and ink."

Her eyes widened. Without saying so, it was clear she understood what he meant. That she'd wounded him. Something she'd probably never believed she could do.

Treading even deeper into dangerous territory, she asked, "What did you do after I left, Mick? I know you didn't graduate. What happened?"

The ice cream was feeling heavy in his stomach. Or maybe that was his past causing the discomfort. In any case, he didn't particularly want to discuss it. Instead he said, "About the other night…you really think we can work together, live together and, uh, forget about what happened?"

She shook her head. "No, I don't."

He gave her a triumphant smile.

"So obviously we need to agree to stop these silly revenge games, and keep our interactions and relationship cordial and professional. Not personal."

He stepped closer, unable to help it. Damned if he'd be reduced to being Caroline's associate. He'd rather be her enemy.

Bullshit. He wanted to be the man who shared her bed.

He shrugged off the thought. He could have been. Could have done that easily Thursday night, with a flick of a few buttons and some maneuvering on the couch. But he hadn't. And it was too late to do anything about that now.

"You really think we can be business associates? Keep it professional and nothing else?" he asked, his voice low and intense with knowledge that what she suggested was impossible.

She cleared her throat. "Yes, I do."

"You're delusional, Caroline."

"Why? People do it every day. Just because we share a past doesn't mean we have to let it determine our future."

She sounded so reasonable, like she was laying out a perfect argument to her boss at the studio, or someone on the set of her show. Which really torqued him off.

He stepped close, crowding her, putting both hands on the counter behind her until she was caught between his arms. "We can never be just associates. And even though we were once friends, we can't go back to that either." He stepped closer, wanting her to admit the truth. "We're *lovers,* Caroline. We always have been. We can't be anything else. Whether we're making love these days or not, that's the only word to describe our relationship."

Color rose in her cheeks and she parted her lips, which still had the tiniest bit of ice cream in the corner. He wanted to taste it. Wanted to sample its flavor combined with the taste of Caroline's mouth. So he dipped down, kissed it off, licked it away.

She remained frozen, not moving a muscle. But he'd swear he heard a soft, helpless whimper in her throat as he ended the brief kiss and looked down at her. "We're lovers, Caroline."

She shook her head.

He lowered his mouth to hers again in another soft, intimate kiss. This time he stepped closer, until their bodies met. He brushed against her in a deliberate, seductive invitation. She answered it with a deep, throaty moan.

Then he lifted his head, held her chin in his hand to force her to look at him and whispered, *"Lovers."*

Something flashed in her eyes. "Then why didn't you make love to me Thursday night?" She instantly bit her lip, as if cursing herself for saying that out loud.

He'd been asking himself the same thing for days. How could he explain that he'd been trying to protect them both? Would she appreciate him trying to prevent them from falling back into the same pattern: her not trusting him and not being satisfied with the world he wanted? And him watching her walk out of his life again?

Somehow, though, resisting her now seemed harder than it had Thursday night when he'd been going crazy with lust for her. Because tonight had suddenly flamed with more than lust. It now involved something he'd almost forgotten about. *Emotion*. He'd admitted she'd wounded him. And she'd visibly displayed her hurt. They had begun to open the floodgates on emotion and he wondered if they'd ever be able to be closed again.

But he had to try. "I'm not going to be a diversion for you," he finally replied, keeping his voice as even as he could given the storm of intensity raging inside him. "I can't be a distraction for you while you're in town."

Her jaw dropped. "Funny, that sounds like just the kind of thing you would have liked, once upon a time."

He didn't even try to deny it. "Exactly. And if I didn't give a damn, if I *only* wanted you for sex, then we wouldn't have left my bedroom since Thursday night." He knew his tone held supreme confidence, almost arrogance, but it was merely the truth.

She rolled her eyes, which made him tense with the need to prove it to her, even if only with his words.

"I'd have made love to you dozens of times." He stepped closer again, crowding her back against the counter. "I'd have loved you once for each birthday I've missed. Once for every Christmas Eve I didn't spend with you." His voice grew husky. "I'd have made up for all the mornings I didn't wake up with you next to me and all the nights I was in bed with someone else, wishing she was you."

She drew a shaky hand to her heart, obviously shocked, but Mick couldn't stop his mouth. "I'd have licked every bit of your body to remind myself that nothing ever tasted as good as you. And I'd have buried my cock inside you as often as I could just so I could lose myself, remembering how tight and hot and perfect you always felt. I'd be insane and inside out and helpless and stupid."

True. All of it true. But so was this. "And so would *you*, Caroline. So would you."

She said nothing. There was no response she could make when they both knew he was right. They both continued to breathe raggedly, a sea of unspoken words churning in the few inches between them. All one of them had to do was keep talking.

The silence stretched on. Finally, Mick took a mental step back, then a physical one. Lifting his shoulders in a helpless shrug, he said, "But I can't do it. I can't be casual about you. About this." Turning slightly away, he put his spoon in the sink, and the ice cream container back in the freezer. "Hell, maybe I'm finally growing up."

She lifted her hand, as if reaching out to touch him, but Mick wasn't in the mood for a comforting word or a tender touch. He hadn't liked what he'd said, hadn't enjoyed admitting that he was still vulnerable to her. What man would? With some women, the weapon he'd just handed over could be deadly.

"You'd better go upstairs," he said, his words almost a growl as he fought an inner battle with a sudden, unexpected anger.

She didn't move, merely looked at him, waiting for him to continue. But he had nothing else to say. They'd reached no agreement because there was none that could be reached.

She wanted him to be something he couldn't. And he wasn't willing to *prove* to her that he was right about the constant nature of their relationship. That they were lovers. Only that, and could never be something more simple or basic. It was taking every bit of control he had to stick to the decision he knew was the right one. To stay away from her, emotionally, physically, in every way possible. Even though she lived under his roof, he didn't have to put himself under her thumb.

But damn, it was hard. Those brief touches of her lips, the look in her eyes, the way her soft shirt brushed against those sweet curves of hers, the spicy, womanly smell of her body. He wanted her more now than he'd ever wanted a woman in his life.

And he'd wanted a lot of women in his life.

Never like this.

Which was why he had to be strong. If she stepped one bit closer, raised those perfect lips of hers or studied him too intently with those beautiful eyes, he'd be a lost cause. Right here in the kitchen, he'd show her what they were to each other, in deed as well as word. *Lovers.*

"Good night," he said, turning away and walking toward the rec room. In his mind he screamed, *Go, go, go now.*

He heard her drop her spoon to the counter. Then heard her sweep it to the floor. "Goddammit," she snarled, "if I have a lover why the hell haven't I had a real orgasm in two years?"

He froze and turned around, not sure if she meant what he thought she meant. That she'd had no one—no sexual involvement—in that long. Cursing himself for pausing, he couldn't help but state, "You must have had some lousy partners."

He silently urged her to admit the truth. He should have known she'd never do it.

"Yeah. A whoooooole lot of them." Without another word, she swung around and stalked out of the kitchen.

A whole lot. He felt like he'd taken a punch to the gut. He had absolutely no reason to question whatever choices she'd made. Just because he'd been her *first* didn't mean he was entitled to be her *only*. Though, that didn't mean he wouldn't cheerfully consign any man she'd been with to the pits of hell in a heartbeat.

A whole lot. Jesus, he flinched just thinking about it.

Unable to help it, he turned and followed her. "How many is a whole lot?"

She never broke stride. "None of your business."

"Caroline…"

"Leave me alone."

He couldn't. Anger and attraction and emotion and curiosity and, damn it, lust, were clouding his head, making him react from his gut instead of his brain. "Tell me."

She stopped in the hall. Her expression was both angry and challenging. "Too many to count," she said with a flick of her hand, dismissing the subject. Then she walked away again. "Maybe I'll just pull one of your tricks to solve my little problem. Don't have sex with my *lover,*" she said, emphasizing the word with derision, "but find somebody else to *distract* me while I'm in town."

That image flooded his brain, made his blood get hot and his pulse pound wildly. He'd meant to keep them from making a mistake with each other, not to push her into making one with someone else.

"Like hell you will," he yelled, stalking after her. He reached the foyer just as she'd started up the stairs. "I'm not finished with you."

She stopped and looked over her shoulder. "Apparently you are."

"You're not falling into bed with anyone else while you're living in my house. In my town."

"You know what? It's none of your business what I do, Mr. Landlord. You're not my friend. You're not my colleague. You're not my *lover,* or whatever you think you are to me."

"I'm serious, Caroline." He started up the stairs after her, slowly, one deliberate step at a time. "You get involved with someone else while you're here and you're going to have a fact-based reality murder show."

She turned around to look down at him, her eyes widening in apprehension. Then she moved one foot up and back, climbing one step higher. "Was that a threat?"

He stepped up, following her, until his eyes were level with her chin. "More like a promise. Any man you set eyes on is going to have to go through me first."

She stepped up again. "You're crazy."

He followed. "Yeah, maybe I am. You accuse me of being too laid-back, of not reacting. You want to see a reaction, you just think about letting some other man give you what you've been *begging* for since the minute you hit town."

Her jaw dropped. She stepped down, pushing him back as she stuck her index finger in his face. "Begging for? You're psychotic!" Then she dropped her hand. "Besides, what would you care, anyway? I'll bet you moved on two hours after I left back in college."

More like two *years.* It had taken him two years to touch another woman. But he wouldn't tell her that.

"Don't push me. You don't want to see the kind of emotion I'm capable of. It'd make you run away and hide. As usual."

She groaned in fury, her mouth working but no sounds coming out. Electric heat, sharp and dangerous, snapped between them, as real and tangible as a frayed wire. "Leave me alone, Mick. You made your point. You don't want me, so just leave me alone."

And while she stared at him, enraged, aware, furious, Mick clenched his teeth, wondering how she could know him so well and not know him at all.

"I can't do that. This ends here. Now." He grasped her arm and held her eyes with his, wondering if she could see the storm of emotion raging behind them. "Right *now*."

CHAPTER ELEVEN

CARO SENSED that something had changed between the kitchen and here. Her confrontation with Mick in the other room had still held some of that playful teasing.

Now there was none of that.

This wasn't play. It wasn't teasing. It was elemental truth. Something was happening. Something she felt powerless to control. Mick was almost someone she didn't recognize.

"Let me go," she murmured, not sure whether she wanted him to comply or not. She stepped up and back again, feeling her way to the next step with her heel, pulling herself away from him with every ounce of strength she possessed.

He shook his head. "It's too late."

Part of her knew immediately what he meant. It was far too late to let him go. On the other hand, he was far too late to take what she'd offered Thursday night. The pride in her wouldn't allow that. "I don't want you," she said, lying through her teeth and knowing it.

He knew it, too. "Liar."

She stepped again, but this time her heel caught the edge of the step. She stumbled a bit, fell to her butt and landed on the step above him.

He didn't hesitate. Before she could think, could

breathe, could decide anything, he was kneeling one step down, his body between her thighs, his chest in line with hers. "You're not going to sleep with anyone else here in Derryville, Caroline."

"You can't tell me what to do."

"I can and I am. Now lie back," he bit out.

"No."

"Lie back." He pushed closer, until the hard, thick ridge of him pressed against the seam of her pants and his chest touched hers from collarbone to tummy.

God, he felt delicious. Hard and solid. Warm and complete. Like only Mick had ever felt.

She laid back.

"You make me crazy," he growled as he bent low and nipped at her neck. "So crazy, I can't be noble even when I want to." His hands instantly moved to tug her cotton shirt out from the waist of her pants. "If you need it so bad, I'll be the man to give it to you."

She didn't even think to demur, to admit that she'd lied. About wanting anyone else. About having anyone else. There'd been no one, not in a long time. But she wasn't going to tell him that, didn't want to hand him that ammunition.

"I'll take you places no other man could ever dream of taking you."

Reason struggled to prevail against sensation. She slid up one step, guiding her body up, trying to get away from his sensual words, his hot, hard body and his heated touches. "No."

He followed. "Yes."

Then his hands were working her shirt up and over her head, tossing it away as he looked down and his eyes feasted on her body. Caro was caught someplace between anger and insanity, knowing she was a fool to let this happen but dying for it anyway.

But it was only when he paused, looked down at her and said, "Yes?" so obviously giving her a chance to say "no"—and *mean* it—that she knew for sure what she was going to do.

"Oh, yes."

Once Caro made the decision to do what she'd been wanting to do since she'd first seen Mick weeks ago, she suddenly felt ravenous. She reached for the collar of his shirt, yanking it open, not caring that buttons went flying.

"I have to touch you," she murmured, knowing the physical need was audible in her voice.

He didn't protest, instead shrugging the shirt off and tossing it away. She could only look up at him, at the hard planes and shadows of his body. God, his chest was impossibly big, hard and broad. So strong she wanted to bite it and stroke it and sleep on it and wake up on it.

She couldn't resist leaning up and running her tongue and her teeth on his collarbone, then sucking his sweat-moistened skin. "You taste so good, Mick."

He did. Her own senses fell into memory and she inhaled his scent, his taste, the feel of him against her. Everything was as perfect as she remembered. More so, because the passion was more intense, more adult than it had been when they'd been two horny kids impatiently exploring.

Oh, they were impatient now. But it was a different kind of impatience. This was teasing and hungry. Each caress was deliberate and provocative, made more so because they knew what was to come.

"Tell me you were lying about taking up with some other man while you're in town," he whispered as he ran his tongue down her front. He worked open the buttons of her blouse with his teeth. His breath touched her skin along with those perfect lips and she shivered and grew weak beneath them.

"You know I wouldn't have."

Another button popped. Then he made quick work of unfastening the front of her bra with one easy snap of his fingers. Her breasts exposed to his gaze, she opened her eyes, wanting to see him looking at her.

His eyes glowed with heat and intensity and pure, visual desire that rocked her where she lay. God, to be looked at that way by such a man. It was every woman's fantasy.

And hers for the taking.

She reached for him, pulled him down, wanting his mouth on her. She tangled her fingers in his hair.

"You were just tormenting me."

She nodded, arching up, silently answering while silently begging, *More. Now. Everything. Please.*

His hands worked her shirt completely off. It went flying over his shoulder, probably joining his at the bottom of the stairs. "We should go to bed," he murmured.

She shook her head. "I can't wait."

"Neither can I. But in spite of what some people may think, I don't go around carrying condoms in my pocket."

She shook her head dismissively and stroked his hip, teasingly moving lower, beneath his pants and briefs. He hissed in response. "I'm covered."

"Thank God." Without another word, he moved his hands to the waist of her jeans. She reached for his as well, wanting nothing between them—not their pants, not even the air.

Somehow their clothes disappeared and Caro nearly cooed at how good his lean naked hips felt between her legs.

"Say it," he urged her, dropping his mouth to her throat where he pressed a hot, moist kiss.

"We're lovers," she admitted. He growled deep in his throat. Then he moved lower, sampling her skin, his slightly grizzled cheeks creating a delicious friction everywhere he touched.

She writhed and twisted, wanting his mouth on her breast, his hips between her thighs, but he tortured her, touching, kissing, stroking everywhere but where she most wanted him.

"Please, Mick," she said with a whimper, lying back on the carpeted step. She raised one leg, curling it around his hard butt, tugging him close, so close to where she wanted him.

Then, finally he caught her mouth in a deep, wet kiss and slowly sunk into her body. "Oh, yes," she moaned, unable to believe how good, how utterly good he felt inside her.

He didn't plunge hard, merely teasing her with ever deepening strokes until she thought she'd go out of her mind with want. "Please."

"Slow down," he whispered. "Don't you remember how very much I like to go slow?"

She whimpered and shifted on the carpeted step, trying to pull him with her legs. "You go too slow and we're both going to go tumbling down these stairs when I smack you for tormenting me like this."

He stroked again, then kissed her cheek, licked her earlobe and nibbled on her jaw.

"Mick," she moaned, starting to shake with the ten-

An Important Message from the Editors

Dear Reader,

Because you've chosen to read one of our fine romance novels, we'd like to say "thank you!" And, as a **special** way to thank you, we've selected <u>two more</u> of the books you love so well **plus** an exciting Mystery Gift to send you — absolutely <u>FREE</u>!

Please enjoy them with our compliments...

Pam Powers

Lift here

Peel off seal and place inside...

How to validate your Editor's
"Thank You"
FREE GIFT

1. Peel off gift seal from front cover. Place it in space provided at right. This automatically entitles you to receive 2 FREE BOOKS and a fabulous mystery gift.

2. Send back this card and you'll get 2 brand-new *Romance* novels. These books have a cover price of $5.99 or more each in the U.S. and $6.99 or more each in Canada, but they are yours to keep absolutely free.

3. There's no catch. You're under no obligation to buy anything. We charge nothing—ZERO—for your first shipment. And you don't have to make any minimum number of purchases—not even one!

4. The fact is, thousands of readers enjoy receiving their books by mail from The Reader Service. They enjoy the convenience of home delivery...they like getting the best new novels at discount prices BEFORE they're available in stores... and they love their Heart to Heart subscriber newsletter featuring author news, horoscopes, recipes, book reviews and much more!

5. We hope that after receiving your free books you'll want to remain a subscriber. But the choice is yours— to continue or cancel, any time at all! So why not take us up on our invitation, with no risk of any kind. You'll be glad you did!

GET A *Free* MYSTERY GIFT...

SURPRISE MYSTERY GIFT COULD BE YOURS **FREE** AS A SPECIAL "THANK YOU" FROM THE EDITORS

The Editor's "Thank You" Free Gifts Include:

● *Two BRAND-NEW Romance novels!*
● *An exciting mystery gift!*

The Reader Service — Here's How It Works:

Accepting your 2 free books and gift places you under no obligation to buy anything. You may keep the books and gift and return the shipping statement marked "cancel." If you do not cancel, about a month later we'll send you 3 additional books and bill you just $4.74 each in the U.S., or $5.24 each in Canada, plus 25¢ shipping & handling per book and applicable taxes if any.* That's the complete price and — compared to cover prices starting from $5.99 each in the U.S. and $6.99 each in Canada — it's quite a bargain! You may cancel at any time, but if you choose to continue, every month we'll send you 3 more books, which you may either purchase at the discount price or return to us and cancel your subscription.

*Terms and prices subject to change without notice. Sales tax applicable in N.Y. Canadian residents will be charged applicable provincial taxes and GST.

sion of having him half inside her body. "Fill me up or I'm taking over."

He chuckled. "I'd like to see you try that in this position."

She pushed, shoving against his chest, forcing him to roll over until he was half-reclining on the step and she just above him. She met his beautiful green eyes, giving him one second's warning that she was about to take what she wanted. His cocky smile told her to go right ahead.

So she took. She plunged down, filling herself to the brim with Mick. Filling her body with him, filling her eyes with the perfect sight of him, her ears with his groan of pleasure, she was surrounded by his masculine scent.

She was completely filled—in every way—for the first time in years.

She rode him, slowly, deliberately, without any of the awkwardness their long separation should have inspired. They fell into perfect sync, as if they'd never been apart.

But when she started to move faster, Mick grabbed her hips, slowing her down. "When did you get so impatient?" he asked, leaning his head to capture one sensitive nipple in his mouth. That sent another shock of sensation down to her lower body, where she and Mick were joined, and she felt her first orgasm begin to build.

"I'm just…taking what you didn't…give me Thursday night," she replied brokenly. Then she couldn't talk at all, she could only urge him with moans and sighs, until he reached down and plucked the sensitive skin at the apex of her thighs with his fingertips, bringing her to the edge and sending her screaming over it.

When she finally could breathe again, she opened her

eyes and looked at him, seeing the look of pleasure he didn't try to hide. He liked bringing her to climax. Over and over again. He always had. And that was way back when he wasn't as controlled and patient as now.

This was shaping up to be one of the most amazing nights of her life.

"Bed," he ordered, not waiting for her to agree.

He held her around the waist as he stood up and urged her to wrap her legs around his hips. They were still deeply joined and as he walked up the stairs, Caro dropped her head back, reveling in the movements of their bodies. "Oh, God, yes."

They reached the top of the stairs and he stopped, backing her against the wall, as if unable to help himself. "You drive me to the brink of insanity," he growled, plunging into her three or four mind-blowing times. The wall scraped her back, but it was a delicious roughness. She responded by digging her nails into his shoulders, demanding more, taking all he had.

Then he walked again, kissing her, deeply and powerfully, as they finally reached his room and fell onto the bed.

"Caroline, now that we've evened the score for Thursday night, we're doing things *my* way," he said as he pulled out of her. "And my way means backing up to cover all the steps we just skipped."

"I don't remember skipping any steps," she teased. "I think we covered that stairwell from bottom to top."

He gave her a cocky, Mick-like grin. "My way means now I'm going to cover *you* from bottom to top."

Before she realized what he meant, he was moving down, lowering his mouth, down her body in a never-ending line of kisses, licks and tastes.

Her last coherent thought was that his way was pretty damn good, too.

MICK WOKE UP first Monday morning, hearing the trash truck cruise down the street and the slam of the back door of his neighbor's house. Mr. Tyler was letting Buddy, his chocolate lab, out into the backyard. In ten minutes the door would open again. Buddy would gallop back across the lawn into the kitchen where the kids ate breakfast and prepared for another school day, wondering why the long, glorious summer days had come to an end so quickly.

Across the street, the Wilson boy would be delivering papers. Mrs. Larson would be sipping tea on her front porch, watching the world come to life on another cool, sunny morning. The day would stretch out, seeming long and endless as Indian summer days tend to do. As if there was all the time in the world to visit with a neighbor or have a beer with a buddy after work.

Small towns stretched time somehow. They didn't go by the regular clock. And while on some days the pace, the routine, the *sameness* of it all threatened to send him screaming out of his mind, on mornings like this he remembered what he loved about it.

He turned toward Caroline in the bed in the semi-shadowed bedroom, listening to her breathe. Sharing the air. Reliving the night. And wondering what the hell he'd done.

Because she didn't love *anything* about this life. Not its people. Not its pace. Not the attitude it engendered. Not the kind of man it had made him become.

Mick's casual familiarity with anyone had been considered friendliness in a town like Derryville, where

there was all the time in the world to cultivate relationships. But in Caroline's world it had meant something
else. A lack of commitment. A lack of seriousness. A
laziness toward his emotional responsibilities. He was
very much afraid Caroline viewed it as the inability to
be serious and faithful and all the other things she'd
thought she wanted because of the way her lousy old
man had been.

She'd painted him with that brush before. And nothing had changed, in spite of last night. She was the
same. He was the same. The geography still sucked.

So why the hell was he doing this again? Getting involved with Caroline was the last thing he'd planned on
doing. Christ, it had taken him years to get over her the
last time.

That had been back when he'd been a stupid kid.
Now he was a grown man. So what had he let himself
in for this time? A lifetime of wondering if he should
have asked her to stay—which he wouldn't, knowing
how much she loved her life? Or wondering if he should
have gone with her, which—on a morning such as
this—seemed as foreign to him as the idea of relocat-
ing to the moon?

Besides, she'd never suggested it. Never asked him
to come with her all those years ago. She'd simply
walked out after throwing accusations in his face. If she
had asked, well, there had been *other* days when the
idea of starting something fresh and new in a fast-paced
world appealed to him tremendously.

Too late. Much too late now with them both estab-
lished in their separate worlds.

And now he'd been stupid enough to go and sleep

with her again. Let her fill his head and consume his body and make his heart do stupid things it had no business doing. Like caring too much. *Asshole.*

"Mmm, good morning," she said softly, burrowing under his comforter as if she missed his body heat.

It was tempting to give it to her, but Mick still had some sense of self-preservation left. He slid out of the bed, walking naked over to the window to stare down in the backyard. Just in time to see Buddy respond to his owner's whistle, tearing toward the back door of his neighbor's house. Like clockwork.

"What time is it?"

He glanced at the clock. "Seven."

She sat up in the bed, letting the covers fall to her lap. Then she blinked a few times and shook her head slightly. She looked around. At the room. At a few pieces of their clothing tangled on the floor. At him.

Color rose in her cheeks and she pulled the covers up.

"Don't worry. Nothing has changed," he muttered, knowing what was going through her head.

She was having regrets. Already wondering how to save face, to salvage their ridiculous "roommate" situation now that they'd gone and given in to their attraction to each other.

"How do you figure that?" she asked, her voice thick with sleep and confusion. "I'd say something has definitely changed here."

"Well, we'll just change it back." He pulled a pair of jeans out of a drawer and drew them on, covering his naked body.

Caroline watched him, drawing the blankets around her as she rubbed the sleep out of her eyes. "Change it back. There's a trick." She sounded more annoyed now, even though he'd given her what he thought she wanted: a graceful way out of this situation.

"I mean…look, we went a little crazy. We should probably just forget it ever happened."

Her jaw dropped and she gave him an incredulous look. "Oh, so now it didn't happen. You did *not* make love to me three times last night." She rose to her knees on the bed, growing visibly angry. "You *didn't* whisper those things to me, you *aren't* insane for me, you really *would* have survived if you couldn't bury your cock in me until the rest of the world didn't exist?"

He flinched. Somehow the heated words they'd exchanged in the night didn't sound quite the same in the light of day. "That's a low blow."

"We didn't even get to the blowing," she snapped, her expression taunting. "Guess we never will now." She hopped out of the bed, taking the sheet with her.

"You're angry."

"You think? God, even in California they wait until after coffee before giving the old heave-ho 'catchya later, babe.'"

He grabbed her arm, forcing her to meet his eyes. "That's not what this is. I didn't plan last night and neither did you. What happened was more about stress and anger and a lot of years' worth of memories that needed to be revisited. By both of us. It didn't change the world."

It certainly hadn't changed *their* world.

She yanked her arm away, bent over and scrounged around for some clothes, looking both furious and adorable, sexy and sweet. She finally found one of Mick's shirts and pulled it on, probably needing the defense of clothing so she wouldn't feel so vulnerable. Exposed.

Like he'd been feeling a few minutes ago, before she'd woken up.

"Okay, let me see if I follow. We got mad, we fought, we had sex, it's out of our systems and now we forget it ever happened?"

"No, we won't forget. But I meant what I said last week. We've been down this road before. We go crazy for each other, have incredible sex. Then something happens to piss you off—"

"Like now," she interjected.

He continued as if she hadn't spoken. "You doubt me and you walk away. The only thing that's different this time is that you have a set date and a set location for the walking away part. Two weeks. And California."

Her eyes shone with some unvoiced emotion and he saw the tiniest quiver in her lips. God, he'd totally screwed this up. She'd gone from sleepily seductive, to angry, to hurt, all in about two minutes. He stepped close and reached out a hand.

She thrust it away. "Okay, I guess we're clear."

"Caroline, I'm sorry…I *don't* regret last night." Then he ran a weary hand through his hair. "But I still can't be your diversion while you're in town."

"You don't have to say anything else. Because you're right. This was a mistake. A bad one. I'm on the job— we know it can't go anywhere. It would only hurt us both more in the end."

She was right. She was voicing exactly the same words that had been swimming in his head for the past half hour. Somehow, however, they hurt a lot more when she said them. "If we could change things…"

She cut him off. "We can't. We already know that. Now, if you'll excuse me, I have to get ready for work."

She walked toward the door, her spine straight. "Thanks for helping me...blow off some steam last night."

After she left, he stared at the closed door, listened to her enter her room, slamming the door behind her. Within a minute or two he heard what sounded like a mournful little cry.

Mick stood there for a long time, wondering if he'd just saved himself some serious heartache. Or if he'd just made the biggest mistake of his life.

"HESTER, have you been out again so early?"

Hester froze in the kitchen as she was locking the back door early Monday morning. She took a few quick breaths, trying to hide her frustration that her brother was up at this hour. Bob usually never got up until 8:00 a.m., which was why Hester ran her more secretive errands so early.

Turning around, she gave him her usual, comforting smile. "Oh, I hope I didn't wake you. Where are your slippers? The floor is much too cold for you to walk around in bare feet."

Her brother wasn't distracted. "Where have you been? You're going out a lot lately." He gave her a conspiratorial look. "Is it possible you've...well, have you met someone?"

Met? As in met a *man?* Hester nearly barked a laugh at that idea. Bad enough to have to put up with any male. At least living with her younger brother she could come and go as she pleased. And she certainly wasn't interested in any physical goings-on with a man. She'd had enough of that nastiness.

"I'm just taking lots of walks," she finally explained, knowing Bob was too honest and good-hearted to doubt her words.

Thank goodness he had her in his life. That honesty and good-heartedness meant someone could easily take advantage of him if she wasn't around to keep him safe.

He gave her a pat on the shoulder. "I'm so happy to see you taking better care of yourself. Would you like me to make you a fruit plate for breakfast?"

"No, thank you, I'll make us some pancakes in a little while, all right? Why don't you go back upstairs for an hour while I get cleaned up? I didn't mean to disturb you."

He gave her a brotherly kiss on her forehead, and her heart tightened a little. Bob had been very good to her. Better than she deserved, some would probably say. But she'd certainly been repaying him for the past three years.

Before he walked out the door, Bob looked over his shoulder and cleared his throat. He sounded nervous for some reason. "Oh, by the way, can you set an extra place for dinner tonight? I've invited someone to join us."

Hester lifted a brow. *Someone?*

"Certainly," she finally said, keeping her tone even and patient. "May I ask who?"

"Uh, Miss Flanagan."

Flanagan…Flanagan… She thought frantically, then placed the name. "You mean Louise?"

Bob nodded, and an unusual color pinkened his cheeks. "I've been meeting with her and we've become…friends. I'd like her to share a meal with us, if it's all right with you, Hester."

All right to have some cheap young woman come into her house and eat with her easy-to-fool brother? Hester would sooner sit down and dine with the hobos who lived in big-city parks.

But she couldn't say so. Not if she wanted to keep up appearances. And she had to do that, at least for a lit-

tle while longer. At least until she found out whether the
notes she'd been sending a certain Hollywood type were
going to pay off.

She'd sent three now since Saturday. So she'd soon
find out whether she could pull it off and set herself up
for the rest of her life. No more housekeeping for a
widowed brother. No more scrambling for extra pennies
by ferreting out other people's embarrassing secrets,
and being paid to keep them quiet.

She was going to be out of Derryville so fast Bob
would barely remember her face. Then he could have
all the Louise Flanagans he wanted over to supper.

Only a little longer.

Bob stared at her, waiting for her response, probably
wondering if she'd say something disparaging about
him having a woman twenty years his junior come over
for a social evening.

It was on the tip of her tongue to do just that. Then
she thought better of it. If Hester truly was going to get
her way and get out of town, Louise might be an answer
to a prayer. Not worrying about Bob would sure make
things easier in her new life; he was the one person
who'd been truly good to her in the past thirty years.
Having a wife, instead of a sister, meant he could go on
living his boring, staid life, and she could disappear.

Besides, she just remembered the last time she'd
seen Louise Flanagan. She'd come into the church a few
weeks back, needing someone to talk to about something stupid she'd done at Mick Winchester's real estate
office. She'd hate for anybody to find out that secret.
Probably including Bob, who still didn't know the
whole story.

It wasn't such a bad thing to have something to hold

over a potential sister-in-law. Not a bad thing at all. Especially if the money ran out too quickly.

She gave him a big smile. "I can't wait to have her over. She's a nice girl."

Bob's relief at having her approval was visible. And Hester counted that as her good deed for the day.

CHAPTER TWELVE

CARO WENT A GOOD twenty-four hours before she said another word to Mick. She had to hand it to him, he handled the silent treatment pretty well. Better than most men. He didn't get mad or give her flowers or try to tease her into acknowledging he was in the room. Or do what her father used to do: grab her mother by the arm, drag her into the bedroom and within minutes have her howling loud enough to wake the neighbors. By the time they were done, her mother had forgotten whatever she'd been mad at him about. Until the next time.

Mick wasn't like that, thank God. Well, since sex was the problem anyway, he couldn't very well try to *solve* it with sex. But even if it weren't, she knew him better than that. Mick was a decent guy. Maybe too decent, dammit all, considering the way he'd refused to let them fall into a purely sexual affair.

At this point, a purely sexual affair sounded pretty darn good to her. At least until two weeks from now when she'd have to figure out what to do about this whole mess.

Mick did nothing to make it easier on her. He wasn't trying to solve their situation. He was giving her time to fume, to be mad at him, to give him snotty looks and the cold shoulder. So that's what she did. Even though she knew deep down he'd been right, it was still hard to get over that he didn't want her enough to take a few risks. That was what *really* bugged her. Well, that and the fact that she wanted him again so badly she couldn't sleep at night.

"Coffee," she mumbled Wednesday morning when she stumbled out of bed at the whine of her alarm clock. She'd had yet another sleepless night, listening for the sounds of Mick prowling around the house, as he often did. She'd have loved to just veg out in front of his big-screen downstairs during the night, falling asleep to the familiar sounds of her childhood: canned sitcom laughs. But she couldn't risk it because of her fear that she'd find him down there.

It was early, only six-fifteen and the sky was still mostly dark, not even a hint of light peeking through the partially open drapes. Not bothering with a robe, she sleepwalked out of her room, down the hall past Mick's closed door, and downstairs into the kitchen. She flicked on one light, lifting her toes off the cold tile floor and shifting from foot to foot to try to keep them warm. The mornings were chillier now, a true sign that fall was arriving. "Definitely need coffee," she muttered.

She measured out enough coffee for *one* cup and put it in the coffeemaker. "Make your own coffee, Mr. I-don't-need-sex-like-you-mere-mortals."

It was only when she turned toward the doorway and saw him standing there that she realized he'd heard. "Oh, crap."

"I guess that's better than being ignored," he replied evenly. Then he lowered his gaze, his eyes moving over her skimpy white nightie that barely skimmed the top of her thighs and did little to conceal the tiny matching panties she wore underneath.

Caro forced herself to remain standing straight and ordered her legs not to wobble or melt into jelly even though his stare felt as intimate as a touch. And the silence was heady with the same kind of tension that had erupted between them right here in this kitchen Sunday night.

Then she made the *huge* mistake of looking at him in return.

Mick wore only a white towel slung around his hips. His hair was damp, a few droplets of water riding along the ropes of muscle rippling on his shoulders and chest. More drops swirled in the dark, crisp hair on his chest and glistened on those taut nipples she'd been licking Sunday night. Her gaze followed the path of one lone drop of water as it slid down the long, lean stomach, disappearing into the thin trail of dark hair that led below the low-slung waistband of the towel. She knew where it led. Knew very well.

Caro gulped and closed her eyes, saying a quick silent prayer for strength. *God, don't let me humiliate myself in front of him again. Don't let me beg.*

"You're up early," she finally said.

"I just got out of the shower and thought I'd put some coffee on," he finally said, breaking through the heat that had erupted between them.

"I was making some."

He glanced toward the pot. "Enough for one."

Tilting her head back, she shook off her momentary visit to hornyville and gave him a haughty look. "Doing things alone seems to be the only way to take care of certain *needs* around here."

His jaw stiffened as her jab hit home. Then he shook his head and his lips parted in a rueful smile. "Maybe I was better off with the silent treatment."

She moved to brush past him. "Yes, you probably were."

Before she could leave the kitchen entirely, however, he put one hand up on the wall, blocking her exit with his arm. "By the way, I *am* a mortal."

It took her a second to figure out what he meant by that almost-growled statement. Then she noticed the look on his face, the way he almost couldn't tear his eyes away from her lips. The way his towel didn't fit quite as nice and flat as it did before. And she remembered what she'd been saying when he'd walked into the kitchen.

She drew a shaky hand to her chest and sucked in a deep breath. He still didn't move his arm, that thick, strong arm that had supported her with such exquisite tenderness and raw passion Sunday night.

"Okay," she said, her tone breathy and thin, "you're mortal. You need sex. Just not with *me*."

He slowly shook his head. "Oh, Caroline, you never learn."

Before she could ask what he meant, he'd lifted his other arm and trapped her there, against the wall. Those hard arms were inches from her shoulders. She had a sudden insane urge to turn her head and bite on his wrist to give him both pleasure and pain.

"I want sex with *only* you," he finally said, his voice thick and intense. "But I want a lot more, too."

Then he stepped away and let her go. Caro somehow managed not to look back as she raced back upstairs, wondering the whole time exactly what he wanted from her.

BY MIDNIGHT Thursday night, Mick had had six beers and was working on a nice buzz to dull the ache in his gut and the tension in his brain. That probably explained why he was trying so hard to pick a fight with one of his best friends.

"No, I don't want a rematch," Ty said, putting his pool cue away and walking toward the bar in the Mainline Tavern.

The Mainline was an old standard in Derryville and had been in business during prohibition when it had sold hard cider and mountain stuff out of a back room. It wasn't usually crowded, tonight even less so. The weekend beer drinkers were playing by their wives' rules—staying home during the week in exchange for a no-hassle night with the guys on the weekend.

On a Friday or Saturday, the place would be wall to wall with regulars. Sometimes it drew in the odd highway traveler who wanted to stop for a cold one at a quaint bar that advertised dollar beers, misspelling the word dollar on the sign outside.

Only the pathetic singles—like Mick—or their very understanding friends—like Ty—were here so late on a weeknight.

"Why don't we go out for some late-night breakfast?" Ty asked.

Mick shook his head. "Not interested."

They'd played four sets of pool. Mick had already lost twenty bucks and was determined to win his money back. Actually, he was determined to blow off steam in any way he could. Including trying to get a rise out of Ty, which only showed how tense this week with Caroline had been. "Since when did you turn into the kind of guy who walks out on a betting situation? You afraid?" Even to his own ears, his tone sounded belligerent.

Ty obviously noticed. "Pal, we both know I can't

take you," his friend said, visibly losing his patience, "but I swear to God if you don't get the bug out of your ass, I'll go down swinging and land at least a few good ones before I hit the floor."

Mick raised a brow, impressed in spite of himself. Ty prided himself on being a peacekeeper. He'd been keeping Eddie, his twin brother, out of fights since they'd all met back in first grade at Harding Elementary School. He was the most laid-back guy Mick had ever known— next to himself.

"You're really ready to fight me?" He wondered if Ty heard the surprise in his voice.

You really wanna fight me?

Mick thought about it.

"I mean, if you want some bruises messing up that pretty face of yours, I am eventually going to oblige," Ty said, sounding both resigned and disgusted.

Before Mick could take him up on the offer—and he was stupid drunk enough on beer and emotion that he might have—someone gave him a face full of water.

"What the f—" he sputtered, wiping the icy cold water away with his palm. He swung around, fists clenched, looking for who had doused him.

"If you're finished behaving like a total ass, I'd be happy to take you home."

Jared, staring at him with that quiet, intellectual, assessing gaze that had always made Mick squirm. It was the same look his cousin had had on his face the time Mick had decided to try smoking with his friends in fourth grade and had thrown up all over the dugout in the park where they used to hang out. The same one Jared had worn when he'd come to drive Mick home from college after he'd been cordially invited to leave the campus.

"What are you doing here?" Mick asked, removing a few more droplets of water from his face with the sleeve of his shirt.

"I called for him to come get you outta here before you took somebody on who doesn't know you're drunk and lovesick," Ty said.

Mick glared at his friend, who held his ground and stuck his finger in Mick's face. "There's a reason you don't drink much, my friend. You're a stupid drunk."

Jared nodded. "He's right."

Ty wasn't finished. "Stupid drunk is bad enough. Stupid drunk who uses a few beers as an excuse to get pissed off is trouble in motion."

Jared gave Ty an assessing look. "Correct. I didn't realize your friends knew you that well, Mick."

Mick gaped at his cousin and best friend for a moment, watching them exchange a knowing glance. Then he looked down, not facing either one of them as he gave his head a shake to try to clear his brain and avoid making any more of an ass of himself.

"Let's go," Jared murmured. "This isn't your dorm room."

Those words did a fine job of starting to sober him up. "Shit."

"Yeah," Jared said.

Feeling much less drunk and angry than he had two minutes before, he turned to Ty with a sheepish expression. "I'm a schmuck."

"No, you're just a damn emotional volcano," Ty replied with a resigned shake of his head.

Earl and Freddy, two other occasional friends who sat at the sticky bar, nursing their dollar beers and making flirtatious remarks to the weary-looking waitress, nodded in agreement. "Not good for a man to only get mad once every few years," Earl mumbled. "It causes testicular cancer."

"Colon," said Tommy helpfully. "You don't even want to know what the doctor has to stick inside you to check for that."

Jared just rolled his eyes. "Come on."

With another mumbled apology to Ty, who shrugged it off with a look that said "no problem." Mick followed his cousin out into the cold night, feeling like a younger sibling bailed out by a big brother.

Once in the parking lot, Jared handed him the foam cup he'd been holding. Mick hadn't even noticed it.

"Black. One sugar."

Mick sipped at the coffee gratefully, then nearly spit the mouthful out. "Christ, this tastes like motor oil. No way did you get it from Ed's."

Jared nodded, not even breaking into a grin. "Last cup from the bottom of the pot at the truck stop. Liquid tar. Good for cleaning sewer drains and sobering drunks."

"Thanks. I think I'd prefer to clean the sewer drain than drink any more of this."

"Tough. Drink it or you're not getting in my car."

Mick glanced toward Jared's ride, a sleek black Viper that had been his cousin's number one priority until he'd met Gwen.

"You even *think* you're going to hurl in my car and I'll push you out without slowing down," Jared added.

Mick finished the coffee and sucked in a few deep breaths, clearing away more of the beer-induced cobwebs in his brain. He leaned against Jared's car. As his cousin shook his head, Mick straightened back up. "You're so anal."

Jared didn't miss a beat, replying, "You're so stupid."

"Oh, thanks for the support."

"You want nice and supportive?" Jared reached into his pocket and pulled out his cell phone. "Call your mother."

Mick groaned. "Don't even think about it."

Jared put the phone back into his pocket. Mick watched his cousin from under lowered lashes, for a minute or two, feeling the coffee do its magic and the cold air put a normal thought back into his head. "Thanks for coming down," he finally murmured, able to meet his cousin's unflinching stare.

Jared gave him a brief nod. "I should have let you get your ass kicked as repayment for the whole secret agent thing."

Mick shrugged, knowing Jared didn't mean it. Blood made them cousins. Genuine emotion made them brothers. He trusted Jared more than anyone else in the world.

"Want to talk about it?"

"Talk about what?"

"About why you're in a bar picking fights with your best friends when the woman you're crazy about is alone in your house?"

Mick's jaw dropped.

"You think I don't have eyes? And ears?" Jared's lips curved into a tiny smile. "Or a decent memory? I did see the condition of your dorm room, you know. I remember the name of the girl who inspired your, er, rather memorable reaction."

Mick didn't know of anyone better to share his problem with than Jared, who could be counted on not to repeat a word of anything he was told. His years of training in the FBI and in writing true-crime novels had taught the man how to keep secrets.

"So," Jared said after Mick briefly told him why he was here nursing his sorry-ass wounds with beer, rather than home straightening things out with Caroline, "you *have* become a monk."

Mick rolled his eyes.

"Sorry," Jared said with a laugh. "I guess I'm just not used to Mick Winchester, Derryville's number one player, walking away from a sure thing. You obviously love her."

Mick gaped. He hadn't mentioned that part to Jared.

"Do you think I have gotten as far as I have in my career by not being able to do a bit of deductive reasoning?"

"I guess not," Mick mumbled, wishing Jared didn't have to sound so satisfied about it. What was it with married men that they just couldn't be happy until every freewheeling single guy they knew had also fallen into the sucker pit known as commitment.

"So, your way of trying to get her to see a future for you two is to make her think you don't want her."

Put that way, the plan sounded pretty stupid. "That's not the way it was."

Jared just raised a brow. Typical. Jared always believed in lending lots of nice, silent rope, until the person he was questioning had tied the noose around his own neck and leaped right off the gallows. "I hate that you're always right."

"It's a gift. I can't help it."

"Gwen must have to slap you silly regularly."

"At least she doesn't send strippers to my book signings."

Mick snickered, remembering that particular incident.

"So, any other bright ideas for building a future with Caroline?" Jared asked, not distracted from the subject at hand.

Mick instantly stiffened. Jared's words hit too close to home: he *had* been seeing a future with Caroline, and was angry at himself for falling into that same old bad habit. "Who says I see a future with her?"

"You do, or else you'd just sleep with her and move on in a few weeks when she left." Jared made it sound like a complete no-brainer. It probably was.

"It isn't just geography," Mick said, knowing there were deeper, more serious issues keeping him and Caroline apart. Her lack of trust. His anger at that lack of trust. But he didn't want to get into that part with Jared; it seemed too much of an invasion into Caroline's past to discuss with anyone else her parents fucked-up relationship.

"So, you plan to sit back and watch her go back to California, hoping she'll regret leaving, quit her job and come back here to join the Bunko club and sort your mail for you?"

"No," he replied, not having to give it a moment's thought. "She'd never be happy with that life. Caroline loves what she does. She was smothered, kept in a box disguised as a nineteen-inch television set for the first eighteen years of her life. I'd *never* want to put her back there."

He paused, listening to his own words echo through his brain, wondering why he hadn't realized that before, long, long ago, when he'd been fuming, cursing her, missing and aching for her when she'd first gone away. Too young. Too selfish. Too stupid. Too...whatever.

Jared tilted his head and leveled a steady stare at him. "Then I guess it's you who has to change." He brushed past Mick and unlocked the driver's side door of his car. Once Mick had walked around to the other side and gotten in, Jared added, "It seems to me you can be pretty happy with any life, buddy. You just have to decide whether you want one without her in it."

Somehow Mick didn't even have to think about that one. It was another no-brainer.

CARO HAD NO IDEA where Mick was Thursday evening, and frankly, she didn't care. At least, that's what she told herself. But when she'd flipped the play button on the answering machine and heard not one but two messages from different women—one named Marcie and one named Deedee—she couldn't prevent a hint of annoyance from creeping up her spine.

"How many women does one man need in his life?" she asked herself as she flipped aimlessly around the channels on his big-screen TV. Since it was nearly midnight, she had her choice of late-night talk shows, repeats or old movies. So far, nothing was ringing her bell. But it sure was fun flipping the channels of a TV that cost more than some cars.

She finally found a station playing old *Moonlighting* episodes and got interested in spite of herself. Somehow, she'd always had a thing for the flirtatious playboy type. Huh. Fat lot of good it had done her.

Trying to decide whether Bruce Willis looked better young and with hair than he did now and bald, she didn't even hear the front door open. She had no idea Mick had returned home until he walked into the family room.

She instantly froze and straightened on the sofa. After grabbing the remote from the next cushion, she tried to punch the power button and only succeeded in muting the sound.

"You're up late," he murmured, looking at her from

the entrance to the room. He leaned against the jamb, arms crossed. His legs were crossed, too, the toe of one boot resting on the floor beside his other foot. The position pulled the fabric of his jeans tight against his thighs and hip. And crotch.

Sucker.

"I'll go upstairs," she murmured, dropping the remote and walking toward the door, determined to keep this a strictly roommates 101 interlude. No way was she going to ask about the smell of beer and cigarette smoke on his clothes. Nor did she really want to know why his hair was all messed up. For all she cared, some local dairy queen could have been rolling around with him in a pumpkin patch, and she wouldn't have wanted to know a thing.

But she couldn't pass by without asking about his shirt. "Why are you wet?"

He glanced down, then shrugged his shoulders, not meeting her eye. "It's nothing."

There was more to the story, she knew it, but it wasn't her business. "Hope you had fun," she said, keeping her chin up as she waited for him to get out of the way. "I'm going to—" *not bed, she couldn't say bed to him* "—my room now."

He didn't move out of the way. "Aren't you going to ask where I was? What I was doing?" He leaned closer, until his chest brushed against hers, so close that her pajamas began to soak up the moisture from his wet shirt. She would never admit it, but being so close to him, feeling his heat and his warmth, his breath and his intense stare, and she began to get wet elsewhere. She cleared her throat. "It's none of my business."

His eyes narrowed. "You don't want to know if I was out with another woman?"

God, almighty, if he was she'd find Louise Flanagan's gun and shoot him herself.

"Nope. No concern of mine."

He laughed, a low, wicked laugh. That was when she noticed the slight glassiness in his eyes and the tiny wobble in his legs. "You're drunk." Even as she said it, she could hardly believe it. She'd never known Mick to drink more than a couple of beers, and never once seen him inebriated.

"Nah." The denial was accompanied by a stronger whiff of beer.

"Yes, you are—I can tell." She narrowed her eyes. "Why? You never drink this much."

"Maybe I needed to get my mind off a few things," he replied, his voice tight and measured, suddenly very controlled. So maybe he wasn't completely drunk, after all. But he wasn't completely sober, either.

"Yeah, well…uh…ditto," she replied. The stupid little quiver in her voice needed to be ripped out of her throat and put in front of the firing squad right next to Mick.

She pushed him out of the way, ignoring the heat, the steam, the chemistry that always exploded between them when they were together. Chemistry wasn't enough. They'd proved that more than enough for one lifetime.

But before she could walk away, Mick grabbed her arm, turning her to face him. He stared searchingly into her eyes, opened his mouth to say something, then seemed to reconsider.

"What?" she prompted, her heart picking up its pace, knowing whatever Mick had on his mind, it was important to him. To them.

He shook his head and let go of her arm. She began

to walk away with a disappointed sigh, but as she reached the hall, she heard him ask one question. Very soft. Whispered. Obviously meant for his own ears, not hers.

"Why did you walk out on me?"

She paused at the bottom of the stairs, her hand on the banister. Used to be she thought she knew the answer to that question. But suddenly the reasons she'd used over the past eight years to convince herself didn't seem enough anymore.

She nearly turned back, nearly opened the dialogue that would clear the air for both of them once and for all. Before she could do that, however, she realized something. Until *she* knew the answer to his question, she couldn't even try to explain it to him.

CHAPTER THIRTEEN

THE WEEK HAD BEEN ROUGH for Caro. Professionally taxing, personally draining. She couldn't say she went home and felt better, so her days had stretched longer and longer as the week had progressed.

"Maybe that's because it's not your home," she reminded herself, not for the first time, as she drove to work Friday morning.

Right. This was a temporary situation. In just over two weeks, she'd be going back to California. To her real life. Which meant, once again, leaving Mick behind. After last night's brief conversation, his softly whispered question—which she wasn't ready to answer—she should probably be feeling better about that.

Even aside from her confusion about that question, after what had happened Monday, she should have been delighted about going back to California. It would at least end the heartache of seeing him every day. It had been torture to return to their cordial roommates-only relationship. She was sleeping in his house, separated from him by only one flimsy wall and an ocean of confusion. Their all too brief encounters had been thin on conversation, but oh so heavy on awareness.

And now, all this knowledge was there, too. This sensual memory of the amazing things they'd done together Sunday night. The way he'd made her feel again, like she was alive and a woman for the first time in eight years.

"Dammit, why?" she asked aloud, slamming her hand on the steering wheel of her car.

Why was it *only* Mick?

Because he was her lover. Mick was right about that. She'd had sex with other men over the years, but Mick was the only one she'd ever considered her lover. He was the only man who'd touched her in some intangible place deep inside, where fingers, lips or other body parts couldn't reach.

Someplace like her soul.

She couldn't even claim to be mad at him anymore. Well, not *too* mad. Though she'd been very confused Monday, eventually she'd understood that he'd been right. He'd said exactly what she would have been thinking an hour later, when she wasn't warm in his bed, still glowing from their incredible night.

That should have made everything a-okay. They were both with the program, in the game, on the same path.

And miserable as hell.

Though they were amicable on the set whenever he was around, and quiet but not unfriendly at home, it wouldn't last. Yeah, they'd formed a truce, managed to pull off that next-to-impossible trick of being on good terms with someone after having incredible sex with them. But the tension was building again. It had been since that shared moment Wednesday morning in the kitchen when she'd been in her nightie and he'd been in the towel and they'd both been naked and panting in their minds. Again last night, they'd been reminded of what was at stake.

There'd been such heat. Instant, unrelenting heat. It still made her shake when she thought about how their stares had met, held, asked and answered. *Yes* and *no*. They wanted each other badly, but they weren't going to make the same mistake all over again.

"Yeah, right," she muttered. Mistakes were made to be…well, *made*. Weren't they?

She forced thoughts of Mick and their private life out of her mind as she arrived at the trailer. Jacey was there to greet her. The younger woman looked a little fresher, brighter than usual. And, if Caro wasn't mistaken, she didn't have all that white stuff on her skin or the super black makeup around her eyes. Of course, the short dark hair was still spiked, and her clothes were strictly black on black. But it was a change, at least.

"You're very chipper this morning," Caro said as she got out of her car and walked to the entrance of the trailer.

Jacey shrugged, but wouldn't meet Caro's eye. "Had a good run, that's all."

Surprised, because Jacey looked anything like the health nut type, Caro raised a brow. "Running?"

"Sure."

Just because she had a sneaking suspicion about something, Caro quietly asked, "Alone?"

Bull's-eye. Jacey's face pinkened, making her look even younger than her age, which was already pretty young. So young, Caro had sometimes wondered how the girl had gotten as far as she had in Hollywood. Since she and Jacey seemed to have struck up an odd sort of sorority on the set—because of the good old boys who surrounded them—maybe someday she'd ask her.

"Well…"

"Anybody I know?" Caro asked, opening the door

and leading Jacey into the trailer. She flipped on the light switch, smothered a groan at the pile of faxes that had come in overnight and reached for the coffee machine.

"That's what I wanted to talk to you about."

Surprised, Caro swung around and looked at her. Jacey wanted her romantic advice?

"I hate having to discuss my private business…"

Okay, not a girl gab session. Jacey was obviously concerned about something.

"I've sort of been spending some time with Digg."

Now Caro got it. Jacey had fallen for the handsome, heroic fireman who had all the female contestants—and the male host—oohing and aahing. Hopefully the TV audience would tune in to satisfy their own need to ooh and aah, as well.

Jacey continued. "It's very low key, but someone saw us coming back from running today and I was just afraid there might be trouble. I had a cryptic note shoved under the door to my room."

"Note? What'd it say?"

"Nothing important. I tossed it. But I figured I ought to let you know, get this thing out in the open, in case this creates a problem."

Caro thought about it. "I'm not sure. I mean, we're not *Joe Millionaire,* or *The Bachelor.* None of the women on the set has any right to be jealous—there's no competition for Digg for heaven's sake."

Jacey probably heard Caro's unspoken concern. "But?"

Caro sighed, then leaned her hip against the desk, crossing her arms in front of her chest. "But, you are a member of the crew. If Digg were to be the winner, other cast members could accuse you of helping him because of your status as an employee."

Jacey's jaw clenched and she stiffened. "I don't even know who the killer is."

True. Caro, Renauld, the writers and the killer were the only ones in on the truth.

"I thought for sure it was that slimy car salesman from Pittsburgh," Jacey added. "But when he got murdered at the grain warehouse the other day, that blew my theory."

The car salesman was victim number nine of the Derryville Demon, if you counted the three original fake victims from Sophie's house. The cast was now down to ten. Not as magic as thirteen, but at least becoming more manageable. And another would bite the dust by the end of today.

"I'm not saying you would, or even could, do that, Jacey," Caro said. "I'm just saying it could be perceived that way."

Jacey's shoulders slumped and again, Caro saw a glimpse of a vulnerability she'd never have imagined.

"However," she said, giving in to an impulse she didn't quite understand, "as long as you play by the rules and keep things low-key, I don't suppose there's any harm in you being friendly with any of the contestants. Digg included."

Jacey flashed a bright smile. "You're not so bad for a pencil-pushing tightass."

Caro raised a brow. "Gee, thanks."

"That *was* a compliment."

"I wouldn't have thanked you if I hadn't known that."

Jacey moved to leave the trailer, then paused and turned to face her again. "By the way, would you and that Winchester dude make up already? The two of you are making everyone around here pretty miserable with all your sighs and heartfelt looks."

Before Caro could even express her shock that her feelings had been so easily read, Jacey continued. "You two need to get it on. And soon."

This time Caro's mouth fell open. Then she snapped it closed again. "That's pretty personal."

Jacey plopped onto the sofa and bent over to rest her elbows on her knees. "Got anyone else around to talk to?"

Anyone else. Hmm…there was Renauld, the menopausal director. Joshua Charmagne, the self-absorbed host. The players in the game. And oh, sure, how about Mick's sister, mother, his cousin's wife or her geriatric sexpot great-aunt? Pretty depressing. "Nope."

"I don't go for girl-talk stuff, but I do know how to keep my mouth shut—just in case, I don't know, you feel like getting anything off your chest."

And suddenly Caro was. She started blabbing like a gossipy woman revealing someone else's dirty laundry. She might as well have been Mrs. Kravitz on *Bewitched*.

She didn't go as far as to include Sunday night's events, though she imagined Jacey could read between the lines.

"So, *why* aren't you sleeping with him again?"

Caro sighed. Leave it to Jacey to go to that part. The part she'd tried to omit. "He doesn't want to be used."

This time Jacey responded with a snorty laugh. "All men fantasize about being used for sex."

"Not this one."

Jacey replied with a skeptical lift of her brow. "You sure he's straight?"

This time it was Caro who choked out a laugh, responding with a vehement nod. "Oh, yeah. Very sure."

"Is he into that weird Tantric stuff, self-denial, bizarre things like that?"

Caro had no idea what the young woman was talking about. "Uh, I don't think so. Basically he just doesn't want to be a temporary fling—someone I can kill time with while I'm here before blowing him off to go back to California."

Jacey reclined on the love seat, lifting her boot-clad feet to rest them on the armrest. She put her hands behind her head and lay there, thinking about it. "Wow. A guy who *doesn't* want no-strings sex from a woman he knows won't expect anything more from him in two weeks."

Sounded crazy, given the sex drives of most men Caro had known. Heck, ninety percent of the unmarried male population probably would have leaped on such an opportunity. But Mick had always followed his own beat, walked his own path. She rubbed her aching temples with her fingertips. "He's an unusual man."

Jacey remained silent for a moment, just staring up at the tiled ceiling of the trailer. Caro watched her, wondering what the girl was so interested in, but saw nothing except some mildew spots and dust.

"So why's he so sure you're going to blow him off?" Though her voice was deceptively soft, her tone held a note of sharpness that told Caro the young woman had cut directly to the heart of the matter.

"There's this whole geography issue—"

"That's a lame excuse." Jacey shrugged, not looking apologetic in the least. "I mean, married people commute coast to coast these days."

"His life is here, and this isn't exactly a hot commuting spot," Caro said in self-defense.

Jacey nodded, conceding the point. "And you're certain he wants to stay here? Wants you to give up everything and come to him?"

Caro nibbled her lip. Once again, Jacey had cut right to the point. Because no, she wasn't sure. She'd never asked him. Not now, not way back when. She'd just predicted the way things would go and cut out first before it became too painful to handle.

"Ah, so you *don't* know."

Caro finally shook her head, admitting that much, at least.

"Sounds like a conversation you should have."

Right. If the geography were the only issue, maybe it would be as simple as Jacey seemed to think. But she didn't want to get into those issues with Jacey, including Mick's thing with women and her own self-doubt. There was also the insecurity that she'd grown up with, of knowing she'd never have a normal family or a normal home with people who lived like the families on television. Because she'd always lived *through* them. Not *like* them.

"Well," Jacey said, "I think you've got to give it a shot. If you don't, you'll live the rest of your life wishing you'd risked it."

BY SATURDAY, after his talk with Jared and each of his interactions with Caroline throughout the week, Mick had realized close-but-not-involved just wasn't going to cut it. Not with them. Not with that hurt look in her eyes and the emptiness in his gut. Not with their past and the ever-lurking possibility of their future.

He needed to spend time with her to see if she felt the same way. He suspected she did, judging by the careful way she'd danced around her words in the past few days. Having time alone wasn't easy with Caroline working incredibly long hours. Of course, so was he.

First because of his day job, and now because of his extra duties as volunteer liaison between Hollywood and his hometown.

The job was pretty thankless. So far he'd had three people beg him to give their phone numbers to Joshua Charmagne. They'd all been men, so there was one rumor substantiated. *Score one for* The National Enquirer.

He'd also received a few bribe offers. The editor of the small local paper wanted him to try to snap secret pictures on the set. Several women had offered him everything from a free haircut—Diane—to free checking—the bank teller—to free pie—his own mother—if he could get them special work as a featured extra.

His mother had assured him as she'd handed over the apple pie that she'd make a great corpse. As if that wasn't bad enough, she'd gone on to say she'd be perfectly willing to do it nude if they needed a drowning in the tub or something.

Okay, some things weren't even worth apple pie. After picturing his dead, naked, sixty-two-year-old mother broadcast across the country, he didn't think he'd ever eat pie again—or anything else, considering the sudden nausea. Mick had somehow managed to get away from her without offending her by losing his cookies— not to mention his pie—right there on his front porch.

Realizing that he and Caroline weren't going to have a chance to move forward unless they made an effort, Mick plunged into one of the biggest risks he'd ever taken.

He was kidnapping her.

Well, he wasn't really kidnapping her. But he was strong-arming her into coming away with him Saturday after work.

They'd had a pretty okay day, though they hadn't talked much in the on-site trailer. Mick had hung out there more to be close to her than because he was needed for any Hollywood vs. Small Town interpreter duties. The tentative looks they exchanged—the sentences started but never finished—convinced him she'd reached the same conclusion he had.

That conclusion was, basically, go for it.

Heartache? Okay, possible. Anger? Yeah, that too. A long-distance relationship that didn't last longer than a five-hundred-minute telephone card you could pick up cheap at Wal-Mart? Conceivable.

But, what the hell. If they didn't go for it, they'd never know. So, he decided, they were going to try.

"You really can't just kidnap me, you know," she said with a nervous laugh as they settled into his car. They were heading away from the trailer, where Mick had just made sure Renauld knew Caroline was taking a much-needed night off.

"Yeah, I can. I just did."

She twisted her hands in her lap. "Where are we going?"

"We're going by my place. Pack a bag for overnight."

"Overnight." She drew out the word, giving it an infinite variety of meanings and promises. "So, uh, tell me, what kind of *overnight* trip is this?"

He knew what she was asking. She wanted to know about much more than location or entertainment. She wanted to know what it meant to them, their future. And whether or not they were going to blow each other's minds with some fabulous sex.

Instead of answering directly, he said, "I think we should give it a shot, Caroline."

He heard the breath she sucked in. Then, in a shaky voice, she asked, "Give the weekend a shot?"

He kept his eyes on the road. "More than just the weekend. I mean *us*. I don't think we should worry about next week, or talk about the past or concentrate on the future." He took in a deep breath, then continued. "Let's live in the right now. Okay?"

She didn't speak for a long moment, and he risked a quick glance over at her. Caroline stared out the windshield, a slight smile playing about her lips. Then she finally murmured, "Okay, Mick."

He was so relieved, he closed his eyes and said a quick, silent thanks.

"Eyes on the road, buster, I don't want to give us a try when we're dead."

"I'm surprised I'm not already," he admitted, giving her a teasing look. "I thought you were going to kill me this week."

She pursed her lips. "I am spending my days surrounded by murder and mayhem. I just couldn't decide whether to get you with poison or a raging band of wild dogs."

After their laughter died down, he admitted, "I've been kicking myself all week for Monday morning."

"I wanted to kick you a few more times myself."

Man, that was his Caroline. She just wasn't letting him off the hook. "So, is a simple 'I'm sorry' going to suffice?"

"If it wasn't, I wouldn't be in this car with you right now." She looked at him expectantly.

Nope, she wasn't letting him off the hook until he made it official. You had to love a determined woman. "I'm sorry, Caroline. Really sorry that I was such an ass Monday morning."

She nodded. "Thanks for saying that. And, as twisted as your logic was, I did understand it."

She didn't say anything else for a little while. Neither did he. The silence between them wasn't thick or uneasy. It was charged, expectant, comfortable and excited all at the same time. Then, finally, over the slight hum of the car engine and the sounds of traffic on the road, he began to hear music.

Caroline was humming. It took him a minute, but he finally recognized the tune: the theme song from *Dharma and Greg*. Good choice. Hadn't that TV couple decided to just give it a shot against a lot of odds, too?

Remembering that Caroline usually turned to singing or humming when she was stressed, upset or scared out of her mind about something, he chuckled lightly. "It'll be all right, Caro." She gave him an appreciative look.

Then, feeling better than he had all week, he began to whistle the tune along with her.

ON SATURDAY AFTERNOON, Hester handed the last note over to the teenage boy who'd been helping her deliver them. She'd taken care to make sure the glue was nice and tight on the envelope so he couldn't do any snooping. She'd dropped off the first few notes herself, then passed the task on to Brent to avoid suspicion.

It was an equitable arrangement. He did her the occasional odd job, and she didn't tell his parents—or the police—that she'd caught him cutting school and smoking marijuana behind the church last year.

"You're sure this is it? The *last* one?" Brent said.

He looked around nervously as if someone might spot him at the back door of the rectory after dark. Probably afraid some of his hooligan friends might spot him and accuse him of fearing for his sinning soul.

"Yes," she said. "Take it to the same place you took the one on Wednesday."

He nodded, then squared his shoulders and looked her in the face. "And this is the end. The end of *everything?*"

There was a challenging glint in the boy's eye tonight. Hester had noticed it before, but now it was more prominent. A challenging boy could be an angry boy. And an angry boy could be one who told tattletales.

This resource had just about dried up. Fortunately, since she'd soon be gone, that really didn't matter.

She pasted on a gentle look and patted his shoulder. "Of course, Brent. I think you've learned your lesson, haven't you? That's all I've ever wanted to do, is help you learn your lesson. You needed to learn to mend your ways and now I've helped you do that."

His brow pulled down as he puzzled over that one. Probably wondering how being blackmailed—such an ugly word, that—to do chores for her would teach him not to do drugs. He didn't understand yet. Someday, though, he'd remember and always remind himself of the value of knowing secrets.

She'd probably created a little monster. Not that she really cared.

Before he could question her further, Hester gave him a little push. "Go on now. Good night." She shut the door before he even had time to respond.

After she was alone in the house—Bob having gone off to the diner to visit with some of his friends—Hester sat at her bathroom vanity and stared at herself in the mirror. "Even you wouldn't recognize me, Vicky," she whispered, thinking of her long-dead friend, the party girl known as Victoria Lynn. "No one would recognize the former Esmerelda Devane now," she added, seeing only glimpses of the wild girl she'd once been. The curve of her eyebrows was the same, and the color of her eyes.

She'd been quite a looker once upon a time. She and Vicky had caused a stir wherever they'd went.

But thirty years had taken its toll. Now she was no longer Hester Tomlinson, rebellious daughter of a preacher from Minnesota who'd run off as a teenager, wanting to live a little before she died. Nor was she Esmerelda Devane—who'd lived a *lot*. And she wasn't Miss Hester, the loving, supportive sister who had no life but to serve her brother and his parishioners.

When she left Derryville, she'd be Hester Devane. A wealthy widow. That was the perfect story, and she could play the part well.

"This is meant to be," she told her reflection. She deserved this success, and wouldn't regret the gamble she had taken, the risk she'd put herself in.

She thought about Victoria Lynn, a woman she hadn't seen or thought of in nearly thirty years. A woman no one had seen in thirty years. And never would again.

Victoria Lynn had disappeared into the night, like mist swirling away beneath a streetlight. She'd been a victim of the life she'd gotten caught up in. Now, Vicky's death would at least in some way be avenged.

Even if the vengeance was only through money.

"Money will do," she murmured. "Lots of it."

Lots of money would definitely do.

CHAPTER FOURTEEN

"Where are we going?" Caroline asked as they took off in his car toward the highway. They'd spent only a half hour at his house to pack their overnight bags. They'd packed light, since they wouldn't be able to spend more than tonight and a bit of tomorrow morning out of town. The show was shooting a big party scene the next evening and they'd have to be back for it.

"Far away from *here*," he replied.

"Oh, goody."

Mick reached for her hand, twined his fingers in hers, and pulled them to his lips. He gave her a gentle kiss, then turned her hand over and kissed her palm also. Unable to resist the sweet flavor of her skin, he tasted her pulse point with his tongue, feeling the beating that sped up by the second under his touch.

"You'd better keep your eyes on the road," she reminded him softly, nodding out the window toward passing highway traffic. He gave a disappointed sigh but let go of her hand.

"Where exactly are we going?"

"I'll tell you if you tell me something."

"Okay. But you tell first."

"Chicago," Mick replied.

"Oooh, yummy!" She sounded like a kid being told

she was going to Disney World. Mick couldn't claim any surprise. Caroline was a big-city woman now; he didn't imagine places like Derryville held much charm for her.

Shrugging off the moment's unease about her excitement at leaving, he asked his question. "Okay, my turn. Who's the killer?"

She gave a deep, exaggerated sigh and rolled her eyes. "You know I can't tell you that."

"Oh, sure you can," he said, his tone cajoling. "I can keep a secret."

"A secret? You must be kidding. I don't think there is such a thing in that hometown of yours."

"It isn't *mine,*" he reminded her, again feeling that brief sense of unease. Every time she mentioned his hometown he was reminded that she'd be leaving soon. Much too soon.

"It isn't? I thought you said it was when you ordered me not to sleep with any other men in *your* town."

He shrugged and shook his head. "Oh, I just used the wrong words. I think the exact term I was going for was 'no other men in the known universe.'"

Pleased laughter spilled off her lips. So Caroline liked his brief moment of possessiveness. He wondered how much she'd appreciate knowing he wasn't kidding, that he couldn't stand the thought of her being with anyone else. Ever.

You moron, you're falling for her all over again.

No, he wasn't. Because, as hard as it was to admit, he'd never really gotten *over* her. Which was probably why he'd had a string of fun, casual relationships, but not one serious one since college. Which made this experimental attempt at one with Caroline a lot more important than he wanted her to realize.

"Okay, you can ask me another question since I can't tell you who the Derryville Demon is."

"Can you tell me who it *isn't?* Just tell me for sure that it *isn't* everyone on the set except the cast member over sixty who thinks every conversation should begin with the words 'to be or not to be.'"

She snickered. "Not telling."

"Come on. It's the professor, isn't it?"

"Forget it, you can't make me tell."

He shot her a sideways glance out of the corner of his eye. "I have ways of making you tell."

She nibbled her lip. "Not about this."

"If I weren't behind the wheel of this car I could."

She instinctively scooted away, closer to the window. "Keep your no-good tickling self away from me, Mick Winchester."

"What about my no-good seducing self?"

He saw her shiver in reaction. "Definitely not."

Knowing the way he'd once tickled and then seduced Caroline into making love in an empty classroom on campus, in broad daylight, he figured he had a fair shot at making her spill her guts now.

If only his hands weren't occupied—too busy driving for any tickling—and his mouth wasn't so far away—much too far for the kind of kissing and licking and tasting he'd like to do to make her melt and promise him anything if only he'd give her some satisfaction.

He cleared his throat, willing away the images. "Okay, you don't have to tell me. Let's just play twenty questions for it. Is the killer female?"

"No."

"Was that a no to the female part? Or a no in general to the twenty questions part?"

"No to twenty questions. I'm not telling," she replied primly, folding her hands in her lap and looking straight ahead out the front window.

He sighed heavily. "Oh, you win. But, I know I'm right. It is the professor, isn't it?"

"Not telling."

"He's so full of himself. It's him. Or else it's Mona. You always have to watch out for those quiet, sneaky ones."

She stuck her fingers in her ears and began to hum. He immediately recognized the theme song from *Married With Children*. Geez, she must be desperate to have gone to that one since he knew Caroline had always liked the happy family shows, not the dysfunctional ones.

"Okay, okay," he said with a laugh, pulling one hand down. "No more questions about the killer."

"Good."

Knowing he still had his one question to ask, he thought about it for a few moments. There were so many things he wanted to know, so many conversations they hadn't shared over all these years. There hadn't been much talking since she'd been back. Their time together had been spent either bickering, or dancing around their physical relationship. Their wonderful, hot, sexy, crazy, physical relationship. He shifted in his seat.

Some of the things he wanted to ask her, he couldn't. Not yet. There was, however, one he had to have the answer to right now. "How do you like what you're doing with your life?"

She tilted her head, giving him a quizzical look. "That's your question? How's life?"

He nodded. "Pretty much."

Caroline shrugged and leaned back in the leather passenger seat. She kicked off her shoes and lifted one bare, delicate foot to rest on the console, stretching out for the ride to the city. God, he was lusting after a woman's bare foot. What did that say about him—and how he felt about *her*—that her bare foot made him want to get naked and make love to her here and now, right in the front seat of his car?

"Good."

Yeah, it would be so *good.*

"Mick?"

Giving his head a quick shake, he took his mind off her delicately curved ankle and pretty, pink-tinted toenails. "Sorry."

"I said it's good. Life's good."

"One-word answer, that's the best you can do?"

"You gave a one-word answer—Chicago," she shot back.

"True. But the rest is a surprise."

"Well," she said crossing her arms in front of her chest, "my answer's not exactly a surprise. Life's good. I like my job, I like my condo, even though it's tiny. I have a few good friends who drag me out to clubs occasionally. I run on the beach but never after sundown. I even go on a date once in a blue moon."

His hands tightened on the steering wheel. "Anything serious?"

She shook her head. "Not at all. My job's been my focus for a long time. It wasn't easy breaking in without finishing school first. I finished up my Bachelor's at night during my first couple of years at the studio. I worked as a secretary in the beginning. Got a break— covered the rear end of a studio exec when he'd lost an important treatment—and got a low-level job in production."

"So," he said when she'd finished, "the rest is history?"

"Right. Though, of course, I'm not where I want to be yet."

"I remember. In the studio. Top loony in the loony bin." Flipping his turn signal to pass a slow-moving truck in front of them on the highway, he began to shake his head and chuckle. "Sorry, babe, I just can't picture you having the nerve to spray paint somebody's tree or squirt people with stinky water."

She tsked. "That was the director, remember?"

"And you don't want to direct," he replied, remembering one of their earlier conversations.

"Nope. So, how about you? You happy with the way your life has gone?"

He heard a tiny, breathy hitch in her voice and wondered if the question—and his answer—were as important to her as hers had been to him. "It's…okay."

"Just okay?"

He shrugged, trying to remember why it was just okay when a month ago he would have said everything was great. Why the life he'd always wanted—the one he'd lived since Caroline had walked away—suddenly didn't seem like one he was satisfied with.

"I mean, I own a successful business."

"Real estate. It's so you. Mr. Salesman. You could charm an old granny into buying a G-string."

"Yeah, but I wouldn't want to see Hildy model it," he immediately retorted. Then he continued. "But yes, I seem to do well in sales and marketing. It was real estate or used cars. And you know me and cars."

She snickered, as he'd intended her to, obviously remembering his bad track record with the succession of junker rides he'd had during college.

"By the way," he informed her, figuring she'd find out sooner or later, "you're not the only college dropout who took some night courses."

Her mouth dropped open, then she smiled with pleasure. "Oh, Mick, you did finish school?"

He nodded, as if it had been no big deal, though it was something he was very glad he'd done.

"So, we two college dropouts did pretty well in spite of sabotaging ourselves."

"Sabotaging each other," he muttered, before thinking better of it.

Caroline's smile faded. "Yeah, I guess you're right," she murmured. Mick felt a thin wall of tension between them, when there had been none before. Caroline glanced out the window, suddenly focused on the passing scenery, not on their conversation.

That had been a stupid thing to say—he'd known it as soon as it left his mouth. But it was true. They had sabotaged each other. He with his immaturity, she with her suspicions.

He wasn't entirely sure they'd changed that much. They still had to deal with her ambition, her need to be driven and successful, compared to his own lazy, laid-back life in Small Town, U.S.A. Her reaction to the women Mick saw casually on the street let her know that Caroline still didn't entirely trust him. Perhaps she never would. All of that didn't even take into account the geographical issue.

Things appeared much the same as they had eight years ago. But this time, Mick was determined their story was going to have a very different ending.

Caroline had half expected Mick to pull up in front of a pricey hotel in Chicago for their overnight date. She hadn't been sure what to bring when he'd told her to pack a few things.

She wondered what he'd think when he saw what she pulled out of her little overnight bag. She nearly shivered thinking of the white lace bra and panties with garter set. That and one or two very naughty things that she'd stuffed in her suitcase back in L.A. for some strange reason.

Strange reason? Not likely. It had been the same reason she'd ditched her dusty diaphragm and started using the patch.

Mick.

Even weeks before she'd stopped hating him, she'd known they were much too explosive to stay apart for long. Now she just regretted the time they'd wasted. Two more weeks couldn't possibly be enough to build the kind of memories she wanted to take with her when it was time to leave Mick.

Oh, God, she hated to even think those words together. Leave and Mick.

She knew him well enough to know he wouldn't *want* her to. And she knew herself well enough to know she *had* to. Maybe they could swing something long distance for a while. But only for a while. Because, really, how long would it take for her to go completely mad, wondering how a man like Mick was occupying his time during their long periods apart?

She shook off the thought. Mick had done nothing to deserve it—this time.

"So, now that we're almost to Chicago, are you going to tell me where we're going?"

He glanced over and shook his head. "Not 'til we get there."

Giving him a deliberately pouty look, she said, "Pretty please? Is it shopping? You know how much I love shopping. And I saw some ads for some trendy place called the Red Doors that I'd love to check out."

"They sell fabulous lingerie." Then he snapped his mouth closed, as if realizing he'd said something he shouldn't.

She laughed lightly, forcing the image of Mick buying lingerie for another woman out of her mind with a quick, internal sigh. "Look, we've been apart for eight years. It's not as if I've expected you to be celibate."

"Good."

She glanced out the window. "I mean, it's not like *I've* been."

He stiffened in his seat. "Oh, right, we're back to that whole lot of lovers conversation, are we?"

She shook her head. "No."

"As I recall," he said cutting the car off the interstate and heading toward downtown Chicago, "we never did finish talking about it."

"Nope, we got, um…sidetracked." There was almost a purr in her voice—she heard it herself.

"You were definitely tracked. The wolf tracked you down," he said with a self-satisfied grin.

"Tracked. Huh. More like stalked."

He growled lightly. "He was overwhelmed by your charms and you couldn't deny your womanly urges."

"Ugh. You should've quit while you were ahead."

They laughed together as he drove toward downtown, and all the while, Caro kept remembering the way they'd been before. Just like this. With laughter and teasing and great sex.

She just hoped they weren't heading down exactly the same path. The one that had led to years of heartbreak and loneliness. She'd do just about anything to change things this time.

"We're here," he said, interrupting her unpleasant thoughts.

Expecting a hotel, she was surprised when instead Mick pulled up to a huge, familiar-looking building on a Chicago street. "The Art Institute?"

He nodded and parked the car in an employees-only lot, not offering any explanation.

"Mick, the museum is closed. It's late."

"Don't you worry about that." He gave a suggestive lift of his eyebrows. "I have ways."

She didn't hide her skepticism. "Of breaking and entering?"

He shook his head and got out of the car, coming around to open her door. "Let's go."

"This is silly."

"Come on."

He wasn't taking no for an answer, and reached down to take her arm and help her out. Walking with him, Caroline nearly accused him of just using the nearly empty lot for free parking while they went somewhere else nearby. But he headed straight for a back entrance to the building, marked Staff Entrance.

"Mick?"

"We're right on time." He pulled his cell phone out of his pocket, punched in a few numbers and held it up to his ear. "Hey, we're outside." He nodded. "Great, thanks." Then he turned off the phone and dropped it back into his pocket.

Caro could only shake her head, wrapping her jacket tighter around herself in the cool evening air. "No way. There's no way you're getting us into the closed art museum."

"Oh, ye of little faith."

Caro rolled her eyes, watching the door, almost holding her breath. To visit the institute during the day, when the museum was open, had been one of her major thrills back in her college days. She'd minored in art appreciation and had loved nothing more than spending rainy weekend afternoons inside the quiet building, standing in awe before some of her favorite paintings.

In those days, Mick had usually been at a basketball game or a guys-drinking-beer-in-the-woods kind of thing.

When no one came to the door, she blew out a disappointed breath and glared at him. "Okay, ha ha, I almost fell for it. It's too late for practical jokes."

"It's never too late for practical jokes," he replied. "Not that this *is* one."

"Come on, where are we really going?"

"Trust me," he said, stepping closer to put his arm around her shoulders and hugging her tight. He didn't say another word, just watched the door with that sexy, confident little grin of his.

Then, to her complete and utter surprise, it opened. Caroline watched in shock as a heavily pregnant young brunette opened the door and beckoned them inside.

"Mick, you came!"

She had her arms around his shoulders and her big belly against his flat one not ten seconds after they entered the building. Mick hugged her back and Caro felt her spine stiffen the tiniest bit. Then she gave herself a mental kick. Old habits died hard, but the one of her not trusting Mick around other women really had to go and she knew it. Besides, this very pregnant woman appeared to have a very big ring on her finger and a happy, contented smile on her face.

"I can't believe you managed to get him here," the woman said to Caro. "I've offered so many times and sent invites to all the openings and parties and he's never come."

"That's because the people that come to those things are the walking dead types who actually *like* art openings and the opera and stuff."

"Invite him to a bikini contest and he'll be first in line," Caro said, extending her hand.

Mick stepped back and slid his arm casually around Caro's waist. "Caroline, this is Maddy Josephson." He pointed to the woman's stomach. "And that is my goddaughter, Michaela."

Maddy rolled her eyes as she said hello to Caro. Then she added, "We don't even know if it's a girl."

"I like girls," he said.

"No kidding," she said with a droll laugh. Then she continued, "And if it is a girl, her name will *not* be Michaela."

He didn't give up. "Micki's cute for a girl."

"Just because you don't ever plan to settle down and have kids doesn't mean we have to name our kids after you." Then, apparently realizing she'd said something insensitive, Maddy flushed a little. "Sorry," she said to Caroline. "That was Mick's attitude in the *old* days."

"Which is why you never went out with me after our first date," he told the pretty, pregnant woman.

Sheesh. An evening with another of Mick's exes.

"Will we be running into anyone you *haven't* dated during this visit?" she couldn't help asking. "Because I don't think traffic is banned on Michigan Avenue and there are always big trucks around."

He laughed, obviously remembering her threat in Derryville last Saturday.

"Don't worry," Maddy said, playfully punching Mick on the upper arm. "We were just friends. He set me up with his best friend, Sam." She gestured to her stomach. "And the rest is history. Mick was even our best man."

Caro gave the woman a big smile, somehow relaxing in her chatterbox company. "So I guess Mick *is* partially responsible for the conception of little, uh... Michele?"

Maddy thought it over, then nodded. "I guess he is."

"Oh, please, don't let the word get out, it'll ruin my reputation," Mick said, looking offended. "As if I could ever have anything to do with procreation that didn't involve...well...the act that procreates."

Maddy giggled. "Okay, enough, you fiend. Are you two ready for your tour?"

Caro couldn't believe this was happening, but it looked like they were, indeed, about to get a private tour of this incredible place. Stunned, she grabbed Mick's hand. Her mouth opened, but she didn't really know what to say.

"What?" he asked, obviously knowing what she was thinking. "You think I can't remember what you like to do? You've been working hard. You needed some downtime."

"But this...good Lord, I expected a movie. A Cubs game or something."

Mick's face suddenly appeared woeful. "I tried but my buddy was using his box seats tonight. This was definitely my second choice. Make sure you wake me up if I fall asleep in front of some picture of white-haired dead guys."

She giggled, knowing he was pulling her leg. "Cretin."

"Remember," Maddy said, watching them with an interested expression on her pretty face, "I have to stay with you, but you're welcome to visit any public area you like."

Caro nearly shook with anticipation. Beside her, Mick drew in a long, resigned breath. "Okay, let's go. It's gotta beat the black velvet Elvis collection in Ed's Diner."

"Caveman." This time the insult came from Maddy.

As they walked toward the first gallery, Mick dropped his arm across Caro's shoulders. "I have only one request. Can we start with the guy who painted all the naked women?"

Caro and Maddy exchanged a look. *Men.*

"Fine with me," Caro said. "To the naked women wing."

Maddy gave her a conspiratorial look. "Oh, I think I have just the artist. He'll really appeal to Mick's taste in women."

Mick grinned. "Sounds good."

"Right this way," Maddy said, "to the Rubens area."

Caro snickered and Mick whistled as they made their way through the silent building. With each step, Caro stayed close by his side, feeling happier than she had in a long, *long* time.

JACEY BELIEVED she and Digg had done a pretty good job of hiding the fact that they were becoming…friends.

Friends, that's all. They ran together, they talked, end of story. No physical contact had happened whatsoever.

Which totally sucks.

No, it didn't. She didn't need to go getting involved in a relationship with Mr. Perfect. Not only did he live on the opposite side of the continent, but he was all wrong for her.

Digg was clean, neat, respectful and polite. Jacey didn't care how she dressed or what her apartment looked like—unless her mother was coming over, in which case she threw away the mountain of Thai carry-out boxes. She'd never been accused of being respectful, and politeness didn't get you ahead in Hollywood.

Politeness sure hadn't earned her her first shot. No, that had been pure blackmail. "Thanks, Dad," she muttered.

Once she'd found out who her real father was, she'd shown up on his doorstep and asked for a job in lieu of seventeen years of child support. Hadn't he been surprised. She had to hand it to him—he'd come through, and not just to avoid child support. She believed him when he said he'd never known about her and would have gladly supported her growing up.

Burt Mueller, her dear old daddy, *liked* having his unacknowledged daughter around, so he'd helped her get her first job. And she'd proved her worth, operating on several of his TV shoots.

Killing Time in a Small Town was the first time she was working with someone else. She found she was liking it—but she missed her eccentric—aww, hell, *crazy*—father.

"Here all alone?" a woman's voice said, interrupting her quiet moment in the parlor of the inn Saturday night. She looked up and saw Mona. The woman gave her a smile, then quickly glanced around the room. "You're not, uh, with someone?"

"Who would I be with?"

Mona gave a delicate shrug then sat down on an empty chair. "Well, you seem to be spending a lot of time with Digg."

Jacey stiffened. "We've gone running a few times."

"Running," Mona said with a slow nod. "I see."

The mousy female wasn't looking so mousy now. Instead, she looked rather catlike as she considered her next words. "You know, there's been some talk. About you, a member of the crew, possibly helping someone figure out this mystery."

Jacey stiffened. "That's bullshit."

Mona immediately nodded in agreement. "Oh, of course it is. Digg is much too honorable to cheat. And he's much too old-fashioned a guy to take up with someone…with someone…."

Someone who was one step away from a gang as a kid, who had street smarts but no real education, and was the bastard child of a man loved by much of TV-watching America?

"Someone from Hollywood," Mona finished.

Same difference.

Though Jacey already knew she and Digg were worlds apart, Mona's words still stung. "You're imagining things."

Mona's smug smile never faded. "Well, I wanted to warn you, for your own good. Some of the other players aren't as understanding. There have been grumblings. I'd hate for Digg to lose his chance at winning all because of you."

She turned and walked toward the door. "Good night,

Jacey. Hope the Derryville Demon doesn't get you in your sleep."

No, but Jacey wouldn't mind if he got Mona.

CHAPTER FIFTEEN

MICK HAD HAD A few good ideas in his time. Sending a drag queen to perform at his high school principal's retirement party came to mind. But tonight had to rank right up there among the best.

Caroline absolutely glowed. She spent every minute of their time in the museum looking thoroughly happy. And he had to admit it, even he hadn't been bored, though he'd had fun pretending he was.

She'd finally forced him to admit he was having a great time. He'd never imagined how much he'd get out of the cool eeriness of an enormous building, empty but for walls filled with priceless art. Silent but for the sounds of their own footsteps echoing in room after room. He knew there had been other people around—he'd spotted two security guards, after all. But even with Maddy acting as tour guide and chaperone, he and Caroline had shared some pretty special hours. Hours he hoped she'd remember whenever she started hating him again. Or leaving him. Somehow it always seemed like they went down that road.

He shook off that unpleasant thought as the two of them arrived in their hotel room late that night. They'd grabbed a quick dinner after spending a few hours in the museum and were now fully alone in one of the city's more upscale hotels.

"I really like that guy who paints with the dots. I think I saw that painting in *War Games*," he said.

"*Ferris Bueller's Day Off*," Caroline explained as they dropped their overnight bags on the bed.

"You sure?"

She raised a droll brow. "Remember who you're talking to here."

"Ahh, yes," he replied, sliding his arms around her waist, "the girl who drew me the character connection chart for *Beverly Hills 90210*."

She nodded her head slightly, taking a modest bow. "And how wonderful to be appreciated by the man who used to think Homer Simpson was the greatest philoso pher of our time."

He hugged her tighter, liking the laughter on her lips and the warmth in her beautiful blue eyes. She slipped her arms around his waist, never breaking their stare, then gave him a sweet, warm little kiss of infinite tenderness.

"Mick, I can't begin to tell you how much tonight meant to me. It was beyond anything I've ever imagined. I need Maddy's address because I plan to send her a big bouquet of flowers."

"And you can pay me back the next time the Cubs are in town."

She nibbled her lip. "Sorry, I've never dated anyone who might be able to get us into the dugout." Then her smile brightened. "But I could probably get you into the Emmy Awards."

"Cast of *Friends* usually there?"

"Yes."

"You're on."

She grinned then gave him a coy look out of the corner of her eye. "Jen usually brings her hubby."

He frowned and shook his head, trying hard to look jealous, though he knew she wasn't serious. "Better stay away from Brad Pitt. I don't think your heart could take it. Maybe we should sit with the *Frasier* crowd."

"Oooh, that Niles, he makes me shiver," she said with a deep sigh.

"Wench. You're just determined to pay me back for knowing so many women."

"Knowing? No. Sleeping with? Maybe."

He grew serious, cupping her chin in his hand, knowing it was time to set that particular record straight. "There haven't been as many as people think."

She nibbled her lip. "I wasn't asking for explanations."

"I'm not offering any. Just telling you the truth. I like women, I like being around them, I like dating and having fun. As for sexual relationships, well, let's just say that part of my reputation has been a little exaggerated, mainly by women who *expected* me to sleep with them and didn't want to lose face when I didn't."

She tilted her head and smiled slightly. "So that means you've been a monk for the past eight years?"

"Are we talking *Monk* on the TV show?"

Laughing, she shook her head. "No. Your neuroses aren't *quite* that bad."

"Thanks…I think. No, I haven't been a monk. But I haven't been a gigolo either. Just a *normal* man."

He could see her working things out in her head, sorting through his reputation and his past, the rumors and the lies. The evidence she'd seen since she'd been back in town—good and bad.

She finally appeared to reach a conclusion. "You're far from normal, Mick Winchester. And I'm very, very glad."

She stood up on her toes and tightened her arms

around his neck. This time her kiss was warm and womanly. Her lips parted, her tongue sliding out to lazily engage his in a sweetly intoxicating dance that was more about emotion than sensuality.

Emotion and sensuality. A potent combination. They swirled together in his brain, making him both weak and strong, vulnerable and powerful. Completely and thoroughly entranced.

"I'm glad you came back," he admitted once their lips drew apart.

"So am I."

Mick spied the bottle of champagne chilling on a table by the bed, exactly as he'd requested. "Thirsty?"

She followed his glance, pulling away, but remaining close enough that he could feel her warmth. Their playful teasing had dissipated during their kiss. They were both fully aware that they were alone again. They were away from the real world and had plenty of time. No pressure, no TV show, no room for rent. Just a lovely big bed and a bottle of champagne in a beautiful highrise Chicago hotel.

She nodded. "Yes, please." Then she glanced at her own hands. "Give me a few minutes to freshen up, all right?"

While she grabbed her bag and headed for the bathroom, Mick popped the cork on the champagne. He poured two glasses, sipping at one while he undid his belt and kicked off his shoes.

When Caroline didn't emerge after a few minutes, he grew restless and contemplated going in to see if she was taking a bath. And if she wanted company. He didn't do it, though. Because for some reason, she'd looked tentative, almost shy when she'd left. Hell, that was bizarre considering some of the sultry moments they'd shared in the past week. Still, he had to give her her space.

This wasn't fast and crazy sex on the stairs. Or late-night half-asleep sex in his bed. This was a night of sensuous, deliberate lovemaking.

He only hoped she wanted it as much as he did.

One thing was sure, *he* wasn't shy about it. After unbuttoning his dress shirt, he dropped it on a chair. He undid the waist of his trousers and let them fall slightly, but then paused. If Caroline was feeling some trepidation, the last thing she needed was to walk in here and see him stark naked, dick in hand, ready to dive on her.

Finesse.

With his trousers hanging loosely about his hips, he walked over to the window. When she came out, she wouldn't think he'd had nothing but sex on his mind. He hadn't arranged the museum tour to get some great thank-you sex. He'd wanted to make her happy. That was it.

Probably pretty mind-blowing for most people who knew him. Mick loved his family and had great friends, but he didn't know if there had ever been anyone in his life whom he'd truly just want to make smile.

Except her.

And tonight, he hoped to make her smile a whole lot more.

CAROLINE DEBATED for a full five minutes over which of her sexy outfits to wear back into the bedroom. Her body was screaming at her just to get naked and jump on the gorgeous, amazing man waiting for her in the next room. But tonight she wanted to slow down, to give him something as delightful as he'd given her this evening.

All she had to give him was herself. "And he deserves to have his present wrapped up in a pretty pink bow," she murmured.

Only, she didn't have pink, she had virgin white or hooker red. He'd die if he saw the red. Simply fall flat at her feet at the sexy red bustier and thong.

The white, though…for some reason, the white seemed sultrier. Wicked in its innocence. The kind of underclothes that satisfied propriety while at the same time flouting it.

Kind of like Mick.

Deciding, she drew on the white push-up bra and the silky garter belt. Then came the white lace panties, cut high on the thigh. And finally, white stockings.

"Please don't laugh, please don't laugh," she whispered as she reached for the door handle. Putting on stockings seemed terribly ridiculous at the end of the night.

Gulping for courage, she opened the bathroom door and stepped into the bedroom. At first she didn't see Mick. He wasn't on the bed, nor standing by the champagne bottle. Then a slight movement caught her eye and she glanced toward the window overlooking the downtown street.

Mick stood there, facing away from her, staring down at the twinkling lights of the traffic twenty stories below. His arms were raised above his head, his palms flat on the walls on either side of the window. The soft lighting in the room cast lines and shadows across his thickly muscled arms, his bare shoulders, then down his back and across his lean waist. She closed her eyes and grabbed the door frame, thinking again that she'd never seen a more perfectly made man in her life.

Even those two wicked, tiny pointed ears rising above the low-riding waistband of his pants didn't bother her tonight. They challenged her. They would challenge any woman to step closer, to take on the Big Bad Wolf, right in his own lair, and live to tell the tale.

Oh, she wanted to take him on. She wanted to touch every bit and taste every inch of him. Nibble his hip and run her tongue over those spiked ears.

She crossed silently over the carpet, then slipped her arms around his waist and pressed against his back.

He leaned back, until his head nearly rested on her shoulder and their cheeks touched. "I was wondering if you'd fallen asleep in the tub."

"Just took my time deciding."

"Deciding what?" he asked as he reached back and caught her hand in his. The touch was electric and Caro shook in reaction, which made their bodies come that much closer.

"I was trying to decide," she said, moving back so she could press a moist kiss on the nape of his neck, "where I wanted to kiss you first."

He moaned as she continued her oral exploration of his shoulders, his neck and his spine. "I guess you decided."

"Mmm-hmm," she mumbled as she moved lower, lower, until she was kneeling and kissing the small of his back. Then she moved her mouth over and traced her tongue over those wicked little ear points. "I've grown rather fond of him," she whispered.

She reached around his waist and found the tab of his zipper, drawing it down slowly, letting her hand brush against him through the fabric.

He hissed in response and tried to turn around. Caro wasn't ready for that. The moment he saw her, she knew the focus would change. That was fine with her. But first, she wanted to be in charge. She wanted to be the one making *him* crazy with need.

She tugged the pants down, and with them his boxers, revealing more of the wolf's face, then his wicked, salacious smile. She tasted every bit of the figure, pausing here to nibble Mick's hip, and there to kiss the small of his back again.

His trousers dropped to the floor and she began to rise, kissing her way up his body, loving the hot, salty taste of him as his skin grew slick with sweat.

She'd made him sweat. How utterly perfect.

"You're killing me. Let me turn around."

"Not just yet." When she was standing, she pressed against him again, letting him feel the jut of her nipples against his back. Their skin was separated only by the thinnest wisp of lace. She curved her hips forward in invitation.

Only after he groaned did she reach around his body and begin to caress his chest. His stomach. Lower.

"Oh, my God," he cried when she encircled him in her hand.

He was thick and hard. Caro's mouth grew dry and her breathing rasped. She could feel his pulse throbbing against her, feel his blood roaring through his veins, and she squeezed him tighter. She continued to stroke him, using his body's own moisture to slicken her palm and slide it up and down his shaft while she kept kissing, biting and licking his shoulders and neck.

"I hope to God nobody has a pair of binoculars trained on this window," he muttered, his voice hoarse and thick.

She peeked over his shoulder and saw that yes, they

were fully visible in the high-rise window, their images reflecting in the smoked glass.

She'd never seen a more erotic sight. She couldn't pull her stare away, focused on the reflection of her hand encircling him, stroking back and forth against all that smooth male skin. His head was back, his eyes closed, a look of pure physical pleasure on his face. Then he opened his eyes and met her reflected stare.

She thought there'd never been a more hungry look on Mick's face than the one he wore right now. It made her nearly incoherent with sudden, driving need. Need for more than just her hand surrounding his throbbing erection.

She let him go and stepped back.

He immediately turned around. Another low, guttural groan fell from his lips as he saw her, studied her, inhaled her visually as if he'd never seen her before. "You're stunning. The most beautiful woman I've ever seen."

She knew that wasn't true, but for now, for this moment, she completely believed him. He *made* her believe him. His eyes didn't lie. His voice shook with sincerity. And his hands, when they reached for her, nearly trembled with suppressed tension and undiluted want.

"You like it?" she asked, knowing that he did by his heavy-lidded eyes and the play of clenching muscles beneath all that golden male skin.

But she should have known better than to expect Mick to burst into flames. Oh, no, he was too controlled for that. Too much a creature of sensation, a lover of all things intimate and sultry. He drew her toward him, pulled her in front of the window. And turned her around so her back was to him.

"Mick…"

"Shh," he whispered against her shoulder as he began to kiss her, to taste her, sample her as she had him. "Fair's fair."

"What if someone's watching?" she asked, picturing a thousand faces behind the thousand windows in the surrounding buildings.

"Then they'll think I'm the luckiest bastard in the world."

Then she couldn't speak, couldn't protest, could only drop her head back and moan as he moved his way down her body. He kissed every single tiny bone of her spine, leaving her shaking and weak. The brush of his tongue on the small of her back sent a shock of sensation shooting down her legs.

"Ahh, still sensitive here."

She couldn't respond, could only nod mindlessly, feeling weak.

As if sensing her weakness, he wrapped his big, warm hands around her hips, steadying her, but also stroking her with those strong fingers, so close to where she was throbbing and hungry for him. "Mmm," she moaned.

"You don't have a tattoo. We might need to fix that," he whispered against the elastic waist of her thong panties. "But not a lamb. A sleek, dark cat. Mysterious and sultry. With thick dark hair like yours and amazing eyes that stare right through you."

She could picture it, her mind filling with the images his words painted.

"You wouldn't be allergic to that kind of cat, would you, Caroline?" He kissed her just below her right hip, the same spot where his body held his original little lamb. Then he nibbled there lightly. "I'd love making you purr when I taste that pretty pussycat on your body."

Good Lord. His words were deliberately provocative, making her think of other places he would kiss her. Taste her. She nearly came right then and there. "You are so wicked."

"That's what you love about me."

Yes. She did. She had always loved him and she always would. Because of that wickedness, not in spite of it.

But she couldn't tell him that. Not now, not when her mind was drifting somewhere out of her body. She gave up trying to think. She could focus only on his touch, his lips, his tongue, his warm breath making goose bumps on her flesh. He toyed with the waistband of her thong, tugging it with his teeth and tasting the skin beneath, then nibbled his way across her cheek, until he reached the back of her garter.

God in heaven.

She didn't know of a single man on earth who could unfasten a garter with his mouth, other than Mick. Where most men would have fumbled if they'd even used both hands, he had no such difficulty. He flicked the hook with his tongue and teeth, leaving her bare to his mouth.

Then he finally moved his hands. After deftly undoing the front hook, he cupped one thigh. With slow deliberation, he slid his palms down, bringing the silky stocking along with them, touching every inch of her limb.

Then he repeated his actions on her other leg, until both stockings were puddled on the floor below her feet.

Finally he rose, just as she had, delighting in making her quiver by teasing her with mouth and hands, letting his fingers dip between her thighs and brush her curls, but never touching her as intimately as she desired.

She whimpered, wanting so much more, wanting him *there* and, oh God, *there.*

She thought she'd die when he finally reached a standing position and mimicked her yet again. He pressed against her, his erection resting against her buttocks and thighs, hot and heavy. Then he tilted his hips closer, rocking up as she had against him, mimicking a kind of lovemaking he knew damn well made her turn into a madwoman.

She choked back a helpless sob, unable to help it. "Please, Mick…"

"Almost," he whispered. "One final thing."

She remembered just as he moved his arms around her waist. One of his perfect hands dropped down to her panties and slid beneath them. When he dipped one finger into her moist flesh, she went weak and jerked in response. She had to lean against him, making nearly incoherent cries as he plucked and caressed with lazy circles that brought her higher and higher.

"I've got you. Open your eyes."

She did, watching their shadowy reflection in the window, watching the way his dark hand moved against her soft, pale belly. She couldn't speak as his other hand rose to cup her breast through the bra, tweaking her nipple until the touch merged with the visual and she got lost somewhere in between.

Then, finally, he unfastened her bra and they both watched it fall away. He stared at her reflection, slowly moving his hand up to cup her breast, catch her puckered nipple between his fingers and delicately pluck at the sensitive spot.

She whimpered. The tension rose. And while she loved the way he touched her breasts, and his other hand stroked her hip and thigh, she wanted more. She shifted, arching toward him, wanting to feel some part of him inside her. *Now. Right now.*

He understood and complied. She cried out as his finger dipped into her wet body. Watching the reflection—the movement of his hands, the way his fingers disappeared inside her—was almost as delicious as feeling them. Almost.

"More," he whispered as he finally stepped away. Caro couldn't move, she was hot and mindless, almost unable to remember where they were or who she was or anything except how it felt to be in Mick's arms.

He swept her up into those arms and carried her to the bed, then placed her gently in the center of it. For a moment, he stared down at her, devouring her, his control nearly gone. She could tell by the jagged breaths he drew through parted lips and the dark, heavy-lidded look in his eyes.

"Take me, Mick."

He nodded. But before he joined her, he went back to the window and looked outside. Giving a tiny, mocking bow he whispered to the night, "I think you've seen enough."

Then he closed the drapes and returned to the bed.

MICK WOKE UP slowly Sunday morning, aware of the coolness of the air in the hotel room, not to mention an unusual sensation on his chest. His stomach. His thighs.

Sweet, silky, so soft as it slid down his body, over his morning hard-on. He wondered if Caroline had found a feather, or was scraping her silky panties over him. But no. It was her hair. Caroline's hair was sliding across him as she made an erotic journey down his body.

The covers were gone, the room lit by a sliver of morning light creeping in through the slight part in the drapes.

Not that he could see much with his eyes nearly closed. Not that he could think anything with his mind focused only on what she was doing. Not that he could feel anything other than her mouth, her hands, her tongue…her *tongue*.

"Oh, God," he moaned, wondering how Caroline had the energy to torment him after the long, sensual night they'd just shared.

"Good morning," she whispered as she continued to kiss, taste and lick her way down…down…pressing her lips to that hollow over his pelvic bone, then lower. Her sweet dark hair, so soft and thick, slid across his skin with the sensuality of silk. And her mouth…what her mouth was doing to him could make a grown man beg for mercy.

"Caroline…"

"Shh," she whispered against his thigh. Then she moved over him, took him in her mouth, slowly sucking the length of him until he thought he'd go out of his mind.

Wet. Hot. Tight. So incredibly erotic that it was hard to control his instinctive reaction. His body wanted him to come right then, to give in to the sweet suction and the little coos of delight she made as she pleasured him. She liked driving him crazy like this. She always had. And it had always taken every bit of restraint he had not to explode into her mouth when what he really wanted was to explode deep inside her body.

"Enough," he groaned, grabbing her shoulders to pull her up.

She resisted, taking one or two more mind-blowing tastes of his cock, as if she'd never tasted anything better and didn't want to stop.

"Caroline...."

"Oh, all right," she grumbled, letting him pull her up so she rested on his chest and their eyes met. Hers held a definite twinkle, a bit of mischief. "I was hoping you wouldn't wake up until it was...um...too late."

The mental picture of what she suggested made him lean back his head, close his eyes and groan. He clenched his fists to strive for control. Her words inflamed him as much as her touch.

"You okay?" she whispered, her tone sultry, her lips brushing against his neck.

He thrust up against her, letting her feel just how okay he was. Then, before she had a chance to get away, he grabbed her arms and rolled her over on the bed.

"My turn."

He didn't give her a chance to protest before he traveled the same path she had gone on him. Stopping to taste the indentation of her navel, the curve of her hip. That sweet, tender skin just above the dark curls at the apex of her thighs.

Caroline began to sigh, then to groan and finally to cry out as he brought his mouth to that sweet spot. Her cries sounded as good to his ears as her moisture tasted to his tongue. He sipped, drank her in, making her shake and come in his mouth before he returned up her body to kiss her as she demanded.

"Finish," she ordered, thrusting up in demand.

"Finish?" He chuckled. Then he thrust into that wet place where sanity ended and fantasy began.

"Oh, baby, we're just getting started."

HESTER COULDN'T THINK of a better time to pay a visit to the Little Bohemie Inn than during the ridiculous Halloween party being taped Sunday night. Everyone in town would be there and even if she was noticed, no one would think a thing of it. So it suited her purposes, even though at first she'd been disgusted by the idea. As if the holiday weren't decadent enough, did it really have to be put right into the middle of nice, God-fearing September?

When she arrived at around eight—dark enough to slip in shadows, and late enough for some drinking to have taken place—it looked like half the town was present. Of those, three-quarters had had too much spiked cider, beer or candy. They were high on liquor, sugar and the presence of those all-seeing TV cameras.

That made it ever so easy to slip around the back of the inn, away from those prying eyes and prying lenses. She entered through the mudroom door. Hester had been in this house before, back when it had been an abandoned white elephant, dusty and dour, overlooking Derryville like some horror movie set.

She'd preferred it then. It had some character. And it was good for scaring bratty kids who had the gall to ring her doorbell and run. All she had to do was yell out a threat to chase them up to the Marsden place and that would be the end of that nonsense.

She knew the owners had done some work on the place, but felt pretty certain they wouldn't have changed much of the actual layout. Her first few steps inside confirmed that. Not much had changed, except, of course, there were no cobwebs, drooping wallpaper, mouse turds or moldy stains on the floor.

It surprised her when she saw just how well that nutty Hildy Compton and her niece had fixed up the place. She'd predicted a quick failure back when they'd shown up in town. Obviously, she'd been wrong.

"Well, anybody can be wrong *once*," she muttered, not willing to concede that it had ever happened before. She didn't count her friendship with Victoria Lynn, and the life they'd lived. She hadn't been *wrong*, in that instance. Merely young and misled.

Seeing the antique settee and delicately carved telephone table in a hall alcove, she harrumphed. The Compton women did appear to have some taste.

But she had no time for looking around. Hearing laughing voices in the kitchen next door and from the front hallway, she ducked into a doorway until the coast was clear. Not an easy feat, but the dark shadows aided her effort.

When all was clear, she made her way to a set of back, enclosed stairs, nearly hidden by a small doorway set into the paneling. They'd probably been built for servants during the house's heyday. She remembered them being a bit narrow, and a bit steep. They were still both, as well as dusty. She was out of breath by the time she reached the first landing and almost gasping by the time she reached the second.

But it was worth it. She was coming to the end of her own adventure. Just a few more minutes and she'd be picking up a plain brown bag filled with money. Lots of money. Then this stupid town and her pious brother and his chippy girlfriend could eat her dust as she rode away and never looked back.

CHAPTER SIXTEEN

GETTING OUT of his car in front of the Little Bohemie Inn Sunday night, Mick wondered if he should have accepted Caroline's offer of help from the costume department after all.

Everyone—from cast to crew to all the extras from the town—was dressed in full Halloween regalia. There were wizards and clowns, witches and killers. Old man Shin made an interesting-looking Batman, particularly since his chest sunk in instead of bulging out in the costume. Sid Shepherd, a local accountant, was walking around in a big white diaper, which made Mick wonder what had been in that guy's bottle. And Tim Morrison was dressed in drag, complete with hooker heels and a feather boa.

All in all, the crowd kinda made his simple Zorro mask and cape look bland.

"You made it!"

He glanced up and saw his sister, Sophie, in a Little Bo Peep costume. How completely out of character. Might as well put a Barney suit on Stephen King. Beside her, Daniel, her fiancé, wore a cowboy hat, plaid shirt and a silver badge. A western cop. It worked.

"Are you trying to lure the sheep toward the wolf?" he asked his sister when she stood on tiptoe to kiss his cheek.

"I don't know. Do you have any particular sheep in mind? Just tell me where you'll be."

He laughed in return. His sister knew all about his tattoo.

"As a matter of fact, I do. But I don't need my kid sister's help to lure her. So I guess you'll just have to lead some other poor helpless sheep back home for yourself." He glanced at Daniel.

"Ha ha." Easygoing as always, Daniel didn't appear to take offense. "She's trying to do advance damage control with that sweet little costume, you know, before the interview airs tomorrow. I told her she should just come as Freddy Krueger and get it over with."

Mick knew Daniel was referring to the morning show segment, when Sophie was going to reveal herself as R. F. Colt. "How did the taping go?"

"Fine," Sophie replied. "I autographed so many books afterward that my hand went numb."

She didn't sound displeased about it. Good. It was about time his sister got to take the bows she deserved for breaking out as such a big sensation in the horror fiction world.

"You really think Derryville's ready for their own celebrity psycho?" he asked.

She giggled, then gestured around them to the party underway on the lawn of the inn. "I think I fit right in these days, don't you? Anyone happening along would think we were all a little psycho having a Halloween bash in September."

Before Mick could reply, he felt a familiar tingling sensation which told him one thing. Caroline was nearby. Though it had only been a few hours since he'd dropped her off at the site, his whole body had grown cold, missing her, wanting her. He sucked in the warmth her presence had always provided.

"Hi." Her soft voice washed over him, reminding him of the incredible way they'd spent the night before. And this morning. And this afternoon when they'd arrived back at his house in Derryville. God, would he ever get enough of her?

He smiled. "Hi yourself." Not caring that his sister and Daniel were watching, he turned around and pressed a quick, possessive kiss on Caroline's surprised mouth.

She smiled, then pulled away with a warning look. "No more of that. I'm on the job."

She wasn't in costume, which made her stand out. "I thought you were going to dress up. How come I had to if you didn't?"

"I won't be on camera," she said with a grin as she looked him over from head to toe. He lifted his Zorro mask, which had been dangling from his fingertips, and put it over his eyes to complete his costume.

"Very sexy," she said with a purr.

"You should have come as a devil." His tone was every bit as sultry as hers. "I recall you wearing something red and sinful this morning."

Sophie chuckled. Hell, Mick had almost forgotten his sister was standing there. Color rose in Caroline's cheeks.

"I guess you two have become really *friendly* roomies?" Sophie asked.

"Mind your own beeswax," Mick retorted, the familiar childhood retort coming out of his mouth before he thought about it. He'd said it to her many times over the years. Intuitive, nosy Sophie had always been able to find out anything she wanted to know.

"Anything in particular I should know about tonight? Any specific problems anticipated?" he asked Caroline.

"If you can keep the Civil War soldiers from actually killing each other, I'd consider your job well done tonight."

"Is one of them my grandfather?"

She nodded.

"And the Confederate soldier a man with white hair down to his shoulders, a pair of glasses five inches thick and a layer of spit and denture cream clumped up on his bottom lip?"

"Eww…I didn't notice the denture cream."

"It's usually mostly spit," Sophie offered. "At least it was when he taught my tenth grade Geometry class. Everyone used to race to class to avoid sitting in the front row, within firing range."

Caroline laughed helplessly. "Okay, yes, it was him."

"No problem then," Mick said with a shrug. "He and Grandpa haven't tried to kill each other in a good, oh, twenty…"

"Thirty at least," Sophie said helpfully.

"Yes, thirty years."

Caroline and Daniel exchanged an amused look.

"So, is anyone getting killed tonight?" Sophie asked.

"Oh, it's going to be a bloodbath," Caroline replied. "We're thinning out the cast fast and furiously now."

The four of them walked toward the crowd gathered around the bonfire, the hay ride and the hot-cider stands. On a stone patio set up as a dance floor, a few couples, including some of the contestants, shook to the Monster Mash. Others watched a group of kids bobbing for apples.

"Reminds me of the Halloween parties we used to go to as kids," Sophie said, sounding reminiscent.

Caroline nodded in satisfaction. "It's supposed to. Though, things have changed a little bit since the old days." She shook her head and emitted a heavy sigh. "We've had to replace the apples in the barrel already because some kid kept biting into them, but dropping them back into the water. Another little girl was horrified, saying they would all get streptococcus germs and die if they bit from the same apple."

"Welcome to the twenty-first century, land of ten-year-olds who watch *C.S.I.*"

"Don't go dissing my favorite show," Sophie said, pointing her index finger at Mick.

"Besides," Daniel added, "it's only fair that the kids get into the spirit, right? This is *Killing Time*. Isn't dying the whole point of the thing?"

Caroline shook her head. "No, solving the *mystery* is the whole point of the thing. That, and backstabbing your way to a million dollars and fifteen minutes of fame doing spots on all the morning TV shows when it's over."

"Any frontrunners?" Sophie asked. "I've been hearing the odds at the nail salon are heavily on the fireman. But I have a feeling that's because all the women in the salon are picturing him naked, rolling around in a million one-dollar bills."

"Sticky," said Mick.

Before she could reply, the director of the show, Renauld Watson, approached them. Like Caroline, he wasn't dressed in costume, though his Hollywood designer outfit probably appeared more costume than reality to most of the residents of Derryville. Especially since it probably cost more than the average Derryville resident's car.

"This is perfect," Renauld said, giving them all a

beneficent smile. "Imagine the ratings on Halloween night."

Mick shrugged. "Sorry. I'll be trick-or-treating."

Sophie nodded. "Me, too."

Renauld shot them each an annoyed look. "It's a 9:00 p.m. show. Even *children* will be finished by then."

The guy really got on his nerves, which made it way too tempting to push his buttons. Mick couldn't help saying, "By then I'll be busy with the toilet paper and soap."

"And shaving cream," Sophie piped in.

Renauld shook his head, muttered something and walked away.

"You two are incorrigible," Caro said.

"You should see them when Jared's around," Daniel said with a heavy sigh. "They try so hard to make him stop being serious that they never let up."

"Speaking of which," Mick said, "what's he dressed up as?"

Sophie answered. "I'll give you one guess."

Mick didn't have to think twice. "A secret agent."

"Uh-huh. And Gwen's Madonna. But the real kicker is Hildy."

Sophie nodded toward someone in the crowd, and Mick snorted a laugh. "Good grief, she's dressed up as a little old lady?"

Hildy's costume included a cane, gray wig in a bun, oversized flowered dress and granny glasses.

"She's certainly dressed up as somebody other than herself," Caroline said as she admired the costume.

"Okay," Mick said. "Let's go celebrate Halloween before Watson decides to deck the inn in holly for Christmas."

JACEY DIDN'T HAVE to attend the party in costume. She was working, after all, her camera in hand as she cruised the party, capturing moments, big and small. But for some reason she couldn't explain, she'd given in and looked through the prop room for something. She hadn't had any luck and had given up when she'd run into Gwen Winchester, the owner of the inn. Gwen, who'd been incredibly gracious, had invited Jacey to come up to the attic and search through some old trunks of clothes for a costume. Hence the outfit.

"A flapper?"

The low, deeply timbered voice at her shoulder made Jacey shiver a bit, which even the chill in the night air hadn't been able to manage. She paused her camera—which had been zooming in on Willie P. in a sheikh costume trying to pinch the butt of dancing girl Ginger.

"Well, there's a stretch," she said when she looked at Digg in his fireman costume. He looked good, incredibly good, but then again, he always did.

She told herself she hadn't been looking for him all evening, hadn't been wondering where he was, and with whom. Lots of people had drifted in and out of the party, going inside to get warm, taking hay rides, or visiting the haunted house set up in the garage of the inn. She'd visited all those areas and hadn't seen him once.

"Had to search hard for your costume, hmm?"

He shrugged. "What can I say? Might as well wear what feels good. My gear at home isn't nearly this clean, and it's made of much sturdier fabric." He grinned, his teeth shining white in the semidarkness. "But I liked the fireman's hat."

She laughed, eyeing the hat, which looked like the ones little boys played dress-up with.

"Besides," he added, "it suited my personality."

"I thought the whole point of dressing up for Halloween was to be someone completely different from your personality. To hide who you are."

He looked at her intently, those dark eyes glittering in the dancing light of the bonfire. His gaze slid across her hair, which she'd pouffed up in a bob, to her bare shoulders and the thin black straps of her fringed dress. "You didn't stretch too far, did you?"

Oh, right. L.A. Goth to Charleston-dancing twenties girl.

He probably saw her skepticism. "You look like an incredibly sexy, beautiful woman, which is exactly what you are in real life, isn't it?"

She almost dropped the camera. "Oh, please."

"Please what?"

She wasn't about to be one of those women who turned away compliments just so they'd be repeated. She knew she wasn't beautiful and the last thing she wanted was for him to try to convince her she was. How utterly embarrassing. How…how Ginger-ish.

"Please drop the Latin lover bit. You don't need it with me."

Her jab didn't phase that always calm exterior. "You know me better than that. Actually, you know me quite well, don't you?"

She shook her head but he interrupted her protest. "Oh, you do. You see everything through that camera lens, and the invisible one in your mind. I've seen you watching me since that first ride in the limo. Just as I was watching you."

"Why?" she asked, almost unable to believe this conversation was really happening. "Why me? Why when there are so many other women here, more beautiful, more available, hell, *nicer* women all around you?"

He raised his hand to run a few fingers through a wisp of her hair, tucking it back in place beside her ear, then smoothed one fingertip across her cheekbone. She sighed, her cheek curling helplessly into his hand.

"You're unique. You're wounded. You're funny. You're beautiful."

She shook her head.

"And you're obviously in need of a bad-ass man to take care of your every bad-ass need."

She shook her head as he threw her own words back into her face. "I think you've been drinking too much hard cider."

He held up his fingers in a Scout's honor sign. "Stone sober."

"Halloween dementia."

"Just a little honesty between friends under the stars."

She looked up at those stars, brilliant in the dark blue sky, wondering if this conversation was really happening. If the warmth she felt was merely the weight of her covers as she dreamt this conversation, or if Digg was really here, close and warm and solid. "Please…"

"Please what? Please go back to being the nice jogging partner you've spent this week with? Please be like the rest of the world who sees the tough veneer and ignores the perfect paleness of your skin and the sparkle of your eyes?"

Jacey thought those were the most words she'd heard Digg speak at one time, but she wanted him to stop. She couldn't have this conversation. Hadn't she been avoiding a serious conversation with him from the moment she'd become aware of these powerful sparks between them?

But it appeared Digg wasn't abiding by the rules. Though it wasn't really Halloween, he was honoring the holiday by being daring, risking danger and pushing them both toward a line she'd thought they wouldn't cross.

"You want me to pretend I haven't noticed the curves you hide under your black, shapeless clothes?" He stepped closer, glancing down at her body, separated from his by no more than an inch. Everywhere his eyes caressed her, she reacted, until her legs were shaking and her breasts aching sensitively against the dress.

"You should get back to the party," she said. Even to her own ears, her voice was weak and unconvincing.

"Maybe I'd rather have a more private party."

She tsked. "Smooth lines don't become you."

"It wasn't a line, Jacey. I wasn't talking about sex… although, I want that, too."

Was that an earthquake? She was sure the ground had just shaken, which would explain why her legs felt like jelly and she half stumbled against him. His hands caught her around the waist and he easily braced her against his body.

That big, warm, broad body.

He brushed his lips against her temple, rubbing his skin against her hair. "You can't be surprised that I want you."

She took a deep breath, forcing away a stab of disappointment as she took a tiny step back. Regaining her space. Losing his heat. "Sex, sure, not a surprise. You're a guy. I'm just, well…you've got a lot of women who'd be happy to take care of that for you."

"You didn't let me finish. Yes, I want you—which I

can't say is true about any other woman right now—but I also want you to drop the act, to open up the way you do when we run. To see what's happening here."

"What's happening here?"

"Oh, Jacey," he said softly, sounding almost amused, "you're falling for me."

"What?"

"But that's okay, because I'm falling for you, too. All you have to do is give us a chance to see how far we fall."

The arrogance of the man, assuming she was in any way "falling" for him! They hadn't even kissed, had barely touched. Okay, they'd shared several wonderful, quiet mornings this week, jogging through miles of trail in the early dawn hours, sharing a private time of day that Jacey had never shared with anyone before. But that didn't mean anything, other than that they both liked exercise. Right?

"Stop trying to figure it out. Just put down the camera and let's see what happens." He held out his hand. "Let's dance, Jacey."

She was close, so close her fingers were already moving to the switch on her camera. He leaned in until their lips brushed in a featherlight touch so gentle and intimate she wondered if she imagined it.

But before she could find out, they heard what everyone else did.

A gunshot.

"WHY DIDN'T YOU tell me there was a shooting scene?" Jacey called as she came tearing up the front lawn toward the steps of the inn.

Caro looked over her shoulder, watching the camerawoman hurrying to catch up. Her camera bounced along her hip. Caro would bet it was already taping. "I didn't know."

She'd been as surprised as everyone else when the boom had echoed through the party. It had seemed to come from inside, but with the clear night, it could actually have been from somewhere else. That seemed unlikely, though. She'd given a quick look around, seeing no signs of activity other than the party.

She also hadn't seen Mick, whom she'd instinctively sought out. He'd said something earlier about going to the haunted garage to look for Jared, but had disappeared, along with several other familiar faces. Most of the people still outside braving the rapidly cooling night were the extras who still wanted their few minutes of fame on the show, along with a few townspeople who'd had a little too much of the spiked cider and were now trying to do the Time Warp without breaking their ankles. She didn't see one of the cast members outside, nor any members of the crew, except Jacey, who caught up to her on the porch.

"Do you know where Renauld is?" she asked the young woman, wondering what he was pulling and why he hadn't told her about it.

Jacey shook her head, then reached to pull up the loose strap of her flapper dress. Caro had noticed how attractive the young woman had looked earlier in the evening. Now there was a definite sparkle in her eyes and her cheeks were vivid with color. Not just attractive—Jacey looked downright beautiful. But also very intense, very much a hunter on the scent.

"Damn, I can't believe I got distracted and missed this. If one of my team's not on it, I'm going to shoot myself."

"Well, just use the prop gun. We need you," Caro said with a grin.

When they entered the inn, they found a flurry of people rushing around asking what was going on. A couple of the contestants—who looked like they'd had a few too many glasses of mulled wine—were among them. A few, however, including Ginger, Mona, Whittington, Digg and Willie, were nowhere to be seen.

"I can't believe Renauld would spring something like a shooting without letting me know to have my crew set up," Jacey complained as the two of them stood in the foyer, watching the contestants race around, checking rooms in the inn.

"I know," Caro replied. "To my knowledge, there was supposed to be a poisoned candy apple and a fall onto a pitchfork to eliminate two contestants tonight. Plus the assorted murders of a few extras."

"Weird," Jacey mumbled. "But, maybe Renauld decided one of the extras would be shot."

Right. And Caro had been too busy having incredible sex this weekend to find out about it. Not professional. Not smart.

But oh, God, how could she have resisted?

"Let's check the kitchen," Jacey said, heading away from the common rooms where the contestants were busy trying to outsleuth one another.

They did, but found nothing. Caro and Jacey continued the search, if only so Caro could get an explanation and Jacey could set up her shot ahead of the contestants' arrival. They had no luck after fifteen minutes of searching the huge old house, from the basement through all the common rooms on the first floor.

Then they froze, as did everyone else in sight, when they all heard the same thing. A scream.

"One of the second-floor bedrooms?" Caro asked.

"Yeah."

The two of them headed for the stairs and a few others followed. As they reached the second-floor hallway, they heard another scream from above.

Caro and Jacey's eyes met. "Third floor," they said in unison.

This time, knowing whatever was happening was going on one floor above them, they ran up the stairs, taking them two or three at a time. Jacey even kicked off her high-heeled shoes. She raced barefoot in her flapper costume, swinging her camera up in front of her face as they reached the third-floor hallway.

A crowd was gathering outside one of the two suites. They beelined toward it. Some of the extras were milling about in the hall, looking disappointed that they couldn't get in. Caro pushed past them into a large bedroom suite which, to her knowledge, was where Renauld had been staying during the shoot. He and Professor Whittington were the only ones who'd been rooming on this floor, since Whittington's former roommate had been eliminated last week.

Caro immediately spied the director whispering direction to a member of Jacey's team, whose camera was pointed toward the open bathroom door.

"What the hell's going on? Why wasn't I told of this?" Jacey hissed into the director's face, angry but still conscious of the rolling cameras.

Caro was about to ask the same thing, but before she did, she saw the startled look on Jacey's face. Curiosity made her follow the camerawoman into the large bathroom, where members of the cast stood near the shower or sat on the counter. Willie even reclined on the closed lid of the toilet.

All of them had their sleuth notebooks open. All were taking notes, trying to capture every detail of the scene so they could answer any potential questions on the next elimination quiz.

"She's been shot, that's for sure," one of them muttered.

"Maybe it wasn't a gunshot we heard—maybe it was a car backfiring and we were supposed to think it was a gunshot," said another. "Maybe she just fell in the tub and hit her head."

Professor Whittington puffed out his chest and pointed out, "The wound is on the *front* of her body."

"What about a drowning?" Mona asked.

Whittington gave her a withering look. "There's no water. And she's dressed. And there's blood all over her!"

When Caro finally swung her gaze to look at the victim in the bathtub, she gave thanks that the corpse was not naked, bloody and wet. Because the dead extra was none other than Miss Hester Tomlinson, the pastor's sister. A shot of that particular woman in such a state was not something Caro wanted to contemplate airing.

"How on earth did you get *her* to play an extra?" she asked Renauld, sotto voce, mindful of the cameras. Given the way the woman had protested the show, she couldn't figure out why she'd want to actively participate in it.

He didn't answer, still intent on whispering instructions to the crew, including a lighting tech who was erecting a pole to illuminate the scene from above.

"Let us through," came a voice from the bedroom.

Caro looked up to see two young men dressed as

cops. She recognized them as real police officers from Derryville.

"I sent for them since they were here at the party," Renauld whispered. "Thought it would look very authentic to have the local police involved in this scene."

Caro still hadn't forgiven Renauld for setting up the scene without her, but she did like this cop touch.

The young officers pushed into the bathroom, both growing pale when they saw the corpse in the tub. Even Caro had to admit, it was disturbing. The makeup people had done a good job with this one.

Though the bathroom was full to overflowing, the remainder of the contestants had to get in, so Caro stepped back out, making more room. Jacey, she saw, had climbed up onto the bathroom counter, one foot on the faucet, the other in the sink, and she was capturing every moment.

"What's going on?" a voice asked. Caro instantly recognized Mick, who had entered the room with Hildy.

"An unexpected murder."

"The Derryville Demon strikes again?" This came from Hildy, who tried to peer around the bathroom doorway. Then she cocked her head sideways, and frowned. "Strange."

Mick spied one of the two young officers in the bathroom. "Good grief, you've got the Chipmunks in there? At least call Daniel. Unless you *want* the comic relief of fumbling cops on your show."

That was probably exactly what Renauld wanted, which would explain why he hadn't called for the chief of police to appear in the scene. From what she'd seen of Daniel Fletcher, he seemed sharp-edged, intuitive and very capable. Unlike his two young patrolmen.

Hildy was frowning, the expression accentuating the

wrinkles in her face—both the real ones, and the ones she'd drawn on to accentuate her old granny costume. "Something's not right here," the woman said.

Lots wasn't right here tonight. Starting with how she'd let herself get so distracted by her whirlwind trip to Chicago with Mick that she'd missed a key decision to add a shooting victim in an upstairs bathtub!

She couldn't entirely blame Renauld. She'd been the one who'd gone away, leaving her cell phone and pager behind. Not that she regretted the trip. But she didn't like losing control over her production. Didn't like it one bit.

"So what's wrong?" Mick asked the old woman, apparently not noticing Caro's sudden frown. "Did the ghosts tell you something?"

She shook her head. "Nope. The smell did."

Before Caro could ask the woman about her strange comment, she heard Renauld call, "Cut! The blood, it is drying too quickly. Too sticky and dark. Get makeup to add more."

Caro stepped back into the bathroom as the contestants milled around. She met Jacey's gaze as the young camerawoman continued to shoot. That was Jacey's job, keeping the cameras going, even during the off moments.

Digg apparently noticed, too. Caro saw the two of them exchange a long look.

"Doesn't she want to take a break or something?" Mona asked, looking at the woman in the tub.

"How's she going to get back out of that tub? That's what I'd like to know," whispered Willie.

"Miss Hester?" one of the police officers said, giving the woman's shoulder a little shake. "Ma'am, do you want to sit up? Want a glass of water or something?"

No response. Not a flicker of an eyelid or the twitch of a finger. *She's good.*

"She's in character like a good actress," the other officer said. "That's what actors do—they stay in character. Don't you watch that *Actor's Studio* show with that guy who looks like Guy Smiley from *The Muppets?*"

The other officer frowned. "Guy Smiley doesn't have a beard."

"He doesn't?"

Caro didn't know why she was even listening to these two, who sounded like they were doing a scene from a Nickelodeon kids' show.

The second one replied, "No, he doesn't. But I do know what show you mean. It's on that boring channel. I watch it sometimes, though, because I like the part where he asks the actors to name their favorite swearword."

"Last count, the f-word was in the lead for this season," his partner said with a grin.

Caro just rolled her eyes as the two of them yucked it up, completely forgetting about seeing to the comfort of the dead extra in the bathtub. Who still hadn't moved.

The props person came in, carrying a big bottle of fake blood. She bent close to Miss Hester. "Here you go, sweetie. Don't you worry, we'll have something else for you to wear as soon as we're done."

She liberally poured the blood on the large victim's flowered dress, running a line of it down her arm, which dangled over the side of the claw foot tub. Caro thought the bit of blood dripping off the woman's fingertips and pooling on the linoleum floor was especially effective. A quick glance toward Jacey told her the young woman had already noticed it, and was zooming in.

"Uhh…something's wrong here," a woman's voice said. Caro realized Hildy had entered the bathroom, but she didn't have time to deal with the old woman right now.

"Were there notes on this victim's identity?" Ginger asked. "I don't remember reading about her in this morning's briefing."

"Is this a pop quiz kind of thing?" Mona asked, her eyes widening as her face went pale. "How can we figure out why the Demon killed her if we don't even know who she is?"

"You should have done something about that," Renauld whispered to Caro. She hadn't even heard him come up behind her in the bathroom.

"About what?"

"The notes," he replied. "This was effective, but I don't like being kept in the dark. And the writers should have been notified so they could include this in today's briefing."

Caro wasn't following. For some reason it sounded like Renauld didn't know anything about this, either. But that was impossible.

"You folks have a bigger problem than solving your TV mystery." This time Hildy's voice was loud and unwavering.

Caro cast a quick glance at Mick, still standing out in the bedroom. She gave him a pleading look. "Can you take her out of here?" she mouthed, nodding toward Hildy.

He squeezed into the crowded bathroom, giving her a reassuring smile. "Come on, Hildy darlin', let's leave these bloodthirsty souls to their murder."

She didn't budge. "Murder is right."

Then, leaning close to Miss Hester, still lying silently

in the tub, she poked her with one long finger. She leaned over, sniffed and nodded to herself. Everyone in the bathroom stopped talking, wondering what on earth the old woman was doing.

"Yep. Can't disguise that smell."

"Smell?" one of the officers asked, looking confused.

"Of real blood," Hildy explained matter-of-factly. "Smelled it one too many times in the old days whenever the gangs got riled up and went for their Tommy guns." Hildy never seemed to have any qualms about referring to her colorful past.

Then Caro realized what she'd said. Blood? Real blood? "Hildy, what are you talking about?" Caro asked, even as the truth began to sink in.

"Well," the old woman explained, "this here isn't one of your made-up murders." She shook her head and lifted Miss Hester's hand. When she let go, it plopped heavily onto the woman's pendulous belly. The victim didn't even flinch.

"What you got here is an honest to goodness corpse."

When no one responded right away, Hildy let out an impatient sigh. "Get it? She's really dead!"

Silence greeted the pronouncement. Silence, and the expression of disbelief on the faces of everyone in the room. Disbelief gave way to shock. Then understanding. Then horror.

One of the female contestants, Deanna, fainted dead away, not even caught by the two men who'd been vying for her attention for two weeks. The incident seemed to snap everyone out of their lethargy, because, finally, one of the young policemen shrieked, "She's really dead? But...but I *touched* her!"

He punctuated his shrill remark by going pale. Then

he promptly lost his candy corn and apple cider all over his shoes.

Not to mention all over the victim.

CHAPTER SEVENTEEN

IN THE DAYS following the murder of Miss Hester, everyone in Derryville speculated on who had done it. And why. Mick had heard all kinds of theories.

Miss Hester found out about kinky, evil things going on up at the set and they killed her to shut her up. Miss Hester figured out the fake killer and threatened to tell one of the contestants, so the fictional killer had become a real one, not wanting to lose the million dollars. Miss Hester had discovered a secret affair. Miss Hester had been attacked while praying for the heathens from Hollywood. Miss Hester had startled a thief. Miss Hester had been set on by the ghosts of the Little Bohemie Inn. Miss Hester had been having a fling with the director and he'd killed her in a jealous rage.

Mick found that one especially hard to believe.

But the one he disliked the most was the one that had begun to circulate yesterday.

"Well, she *did* threaten to kill her. Right there in the church office. I heard all about it a few weeks ago."

Mick stiffened, but continued to eavesdrop on the two women speaking in the next aisle in the drugstore.

"And she'd obviously been thinking about it. She had it all worked out in the book."

"In a *bathtub*, no less," the first woman replied.

Mick felt no compunction about listening to the two gossipy women. Because they were talking about his sister, Sophie.

"Anyone with that wicked an imagination is bound to have murder in her soul," a voice continued.

"Poor Miss Hester. She was *so* good."

The first woman tittered. "But it doesn't look like it'll take long for Pastor Bob to replace her."

The women's voices drifted away as they left the aisle. Mick didn't care. He'd overheard enough to make his blood boil. The town suspected Sophie of the murder. "Damn that interview," he muttered. "And double damn that book."

The timing couldn't have been worse. Sophie had taped that morning show interview a week ago, but it had aired the very morning after Miss Hester's murder. The whole world—not to mention the town of Derryville—had discovered that R. F. Colt was living in their midst.

At first they'd been thrilled. They'd barraged her for interviews and autographs. Then they'd driven over to the mall in the next town and bought copies of her newest book. The one with a sanctimonious, heavy, pinch-faced female church deacon who was found murdered in a bathtub.

"Jesus, Sophie," he whispered as he made his way to the checkout. Of all the times for her to come out of her writing closet. It had to be with a book that included a very obvious Miss Hester-like victim.

That would have been bad enough if Miss Hester *hadn't* died. But now, with the murder, the scandal was much more serious. Sophie was under suspicion of homicide.

Hard to fathom, but even the state police had asked to question her, not trusting the locals to do the job. Especially because the chief was the suspect's fiancé.

"Hey," he heard. He glanced up to see his cousin, Jared, standing near the checkout counter. "Your secretary said you were here."

"Have you heard anything?"

"No. I've put in a few calls, though." Jared looked around, as if making sure they weren't overheard. "I've also called in someone I used to work with. He's in business for himself these days. And he's very good at tracking down people's backgrounds."

Mick raised a curious brow.

"It might be a good idea to know more about our victim."

Mick realized that *was* a good idea. Hester wasn't an old-time resident of Derryville. She'd moved here only a few years ago, when Pastor Bob's wife—who'd been loved by the town—had tragically died while only in her forties. Miss Hester, a helpful older sister, had been accepted by one and all due to their love for the pastor. But she'd always remained somewhat private. An enigma. A woman with secrets whose dour demeanor made her look older than her years.

"Let me know what he finds out, okay?"

His cousin nodded.

"Let me know, too."

Neither of them had heard Daniel approach, until he spoke. The chief looked tired and haggard, his brow pulled into a perpetual frown and dark circles under his eyes.

Mick patted his shoulder. "You hanging in?"

Daniel shook his head. "I just officially took a leave of absence."

Jared eyed him. "Bad move. That leaves Chip and Skip in charge."

"Chuck and Skip," Daniel interrupted.

"Whatever," Mick said, knowing where Jared had been headed. "Dumb and dumber are now in charge of a murder investigation? God, didn't Skip do enough damage throwing up all over half the evidence? I can't imagine how the coroner felt about that one. As if the fake blood wasn't bad enough."

Daniel merely shrugged. "I don't even want to hear about it because I can't be unbiased. I won't be part of an investigation that turns its eye toward Sophie. But don't worry, the state guys are taking over the case, not Skip and Chuck."

Jared cocked a brow. "State doesn't usually get involved with local crimes."

"I asked them to." Daniel looked resolute. "They can look for the real killer while I focus on keeping Sophie out of this mess."

Mick nodded in appreciation, but couldn't completely erase his frown of concern. "And while you keep Sophie away from the eye of the police," he said, thinking about Caroline's job, "I'm going to focus on trying to keep Caroline away from whoever the hell killed Miss Hester."

"THEY FOUND THE GUN."

Mick hadn't even heard Caroline enter his office until she spoke. He immediately looked up from the closing documents he was preparing for a sale and dropped his pen onto the pile of papers. "What?"

She shut his office door behind her. "They found the gun they think was used to kill Hester Tomlinson."

Noticing that Caroline looked visibly shaken, Mick stood, walked around his desk and took her hand. He led her to a chair and sat beside her. "Where?"

"There's a small door accessing the attic of the inn hidden in the closet of the room where she was killed. The gun was in the attic, lying in some insulation. There were some pieces of paper with it, but the police didn't say whether they were connected."

He shook his head, wondering how the police could have let the weapon remain hidden for three full days. "Okay, so they found it. Now maybe they can find the real killer."

She nibbled her lip. "Mick, I recognized the gun. It was the one Louise Flanagan was holding on you the first day I came to town."

His jaw dropped. "You gotta be kidding! Are you saying you think Louise did it?"

She ran a weary, shaking hand over her brow. "I don't know. All I know is, it *looked* like the same gun. I was so shocked, and the policeman noticed, so he questioned me about it."

Mick frowned. "You told them about Louise?"

"I had to, Mick. I hated to do it, but I was worried. Because your fingerprints could very well be on that gun. At least this way, they'll know *why*."

He thought about her words, then stiffened. "Wait a minute, you were up at the Little Bohemie Inn when they found it?"

She nodded.

"Damn, Caroline, I hate you going up there while some psycho killer is on the loose."

She gave him a look that said she appreciated his concern, but also telling him she was a big girl. "There are

security guards all over the place. Nobody goes anywhere alone."

"I thought the inn was off-limits due to the crime
investigation."

"It was. But the chief investigator decided to open
up the bottom two floors of the inn so we can resume
shooting."

Resume shooting. In spite of everything, the network
was going to go ahead with *Killing Time in a Small
Town*. He shouldn't be surprised—he'd half expected it,
after all. But he had been hoping it would take longer.

The longer the show stayed around, the longer Caroline would. Not that he'd admit that aloud, and he'd
certainly never have wanted anyone to die just so she
wouldn't leave. But he wasn't about to question any decision that kept her in his life just a little longer. He was
already dreading the day she'd leave again.

"When's the last time you saw Louise's gun?" she
asked.

Mick shrugged, hardly remembering. "That day.
Here in this office."

"Didn't you pick it up? Remember, you told her to drop
it. That's why I was worried about your fingerprints."

Mick shook his head, wondering how in the hell he
could have overlooked something as big as a pistol on
the floor of his office. Of course, he'd been a little distracted that day. He and Caroline had gone on their
house-hunting trip right after the incident and he hadn't
thought about the gun since. "Sorry. I didn't remember
to look for it. It certainly wasn't lying around for me to
see, and I eventually forgot about it."

"You left a loaded gun on the floor of your office?"
She sounded shocked.

"I don't know if it *was* on the floor. Like I said, it wasn't when I got back, or I'd have seen it. Besides, I'm sure it wasn't loaded. Louise wouldn't have threatened me with a loaded gun."

She frowned. "You sure dropped your pants pretty quick that day, so you must have thought it was at least possible it was loaded."

"I dropped my pants to scare her off."

With a quirked brow and a barely suppressed smile, she said, "I wish I had a tape recorder. You'd have sooner shot yourself than said something like that back in college."

He chuckled with her. "You're probably right."

"Yeah, well, you're lucky your plan didn't backfire and Louise didn't leap on you instead."

"Would you have stormed in and saved me?"

She shook her head. "Nope. I probably would've walked away, thinking you were getting exactly what you deserved."

He grabbed her around the waist and pulled her over to his chair to sit on his lap. "Evil woman."

"Wicked man."

They kissed, long and sweet and wet, as if they hadn't just made love in his bed that morning. When their lips parted, Caroline rested her head on his shoulder. "Someone must have found the gun here on the floor that morning. Do you have any idea who was here?"

He thought about it. "Tons of people came in and out of the office that week. People from the show looking for rooms, a developer I've been working with. Friends. My mom. Sophie."

He stiffened, unable to help it when he thought of the rumors he'd overheard about his kid sister.

"What?" she asked.

He quickly explained the latest speculation on the murderer, not even trying to keep the anger and frustration from his voice.

"That's ridiculous," she said with a disgusted frown.

"Of course it is."

Then she shivered slightly in his arms. "I still can't believe Sophie's R. F. Colt. Those books scare the pants off me."

He responded with a lascivious lift of his brows. "Oh?"

"Don't get any ideas. We're in your office, remember."

"Mmm, office sex. My desk is awfully strong."

"Your front door is awfully unlocked and your assistant is right out in the reception area."

Too bad. Making love with Caroline was probably just about the only thing that could distract him from Sophie's situation.

He still couldn't believe that someone—anyone—could think his kid sister capable of murder. Sophie had been the town sweetheart last week. The nicest, gentlest, friendliest girl from the most respected family in town. And now the piranhas were calling her a murderer, just because they found out she had an imagination and writing talent. "It's so damned unfair."

She gave him a sympathetic look. "Sophie?"

He nodded. "So she had a fight with Miss Hester and happens to write horror fiction. There's no evidence, no real motive, nothing. But the rumor mill has already convicted her."

He didn't say it aloud, but the idea of being judged and found immediately guilty made him think of his past with Caroline.

"If everyone who fantasized about killing their boss was accused of murder, a lot of us would be in jail right now," Caroline said. "Heaven knows I've been tempted. Especially today, with the pressure."

Her voice had softened and she looked away, not meeting his eyes anymore. He had the feeling he wasn't going to like whatever she was about to tell him.

"Pressure?"

She nodded, then got up from his lap. In a stall for time, she wandered over to his desk, straightening some papers, putting a few scattered pens into a cup.

"Tell me."

She turned and leaned her hip against the desk, crossing her arms in front of her chest. "They're elated about the murder."

He shook his head. "Nice."

"Not that somebody's dead, of course, but my God, you should hear the execs and Renauld. They're already filming new commercials tying the real murder into *Killing Time. Inside Edition, Entertainment Tonight* and some other tabloid shows are scheduling on-location interviews and the debut is going to be a two-hour special, instead of one."

"In other words," he said with a distinct frown, "they're going to capitalize on somebody's murder."

She nodded.

Mick stood and faced her beside the desk. Caroline didn't pull away and kept her gaze steadily on him. "How do you feel about that?" he asked, gently brushing a wisp of hair off her cheek and tucking it behind her ear.

"It's horrible, of course."

She said the words, and he knew she meant them. There was something in her voice, though, some measure of excitement, that told him she had more to say. "Be honest with me, Caroline."

She lowered her eyes. "I am being honest. It is awful to exploit someone's tragic death. But…?"

"But?"

Her voice dropped lower. "But I can't help thinking of what it could mean for the show."

With those words, Mick felt a thin veil of something drop between them. Caroline, his Caroline, had become such a Hollywood insider that she didn't mind using someone else's tragedy to get ahead. He took a step away from her, studying her face, her big blue eyes, her beautiful lips, the bottom one trembling slightly.

"Do you think that's easy for me to admit about myself?" she asked. "I know how ugly it is. Logically, I'm disgusted and appalled and know I should take the high road and walk out before I let myself be involved with this."

"So why don't you?" he asked softly, trying hard to keep any hint of condemnation from his voice. In truth, he wasn't condemning her, he just couldn't understand her position.

"I can't. That would be professional suicide."

"There are other studios."

She ran a frustrated hand through her thick, dark hair. "Who'd blackball me in a minute for bailing on a production that is doing exactly what any other network would do—capitalize on publicity any way they could to make a hit."

He could concede that point. Her job meant a lot to her—hadn't she left their relationship behind so she could go out to California and pursue it? But she was a different person now. And he couldn't help wondering—if her career suddenly changed, might *their* future look a little different, too?

"There are plenty of jobs you'd be capable of, Caroline."

"So you think I should quit?"

He didn't answer because he wasn't sure he could answer unselfishly. His logical side understood her goals because he was ambitious enough to know how she felt. His emotional side wanted her to tell them to take the job and shove it. He remained silent.

"The show is good, Mick. It's *really* good. I'm damn proud of it. Do you know how rare it is to be involved in something in L.A. that shines with uniqueness? I don't want to give up my chance to be part of that."

There was no hint of hidden feelings in her expression. She meant what she said. He still didn't agree with what the studio was doing, but he was at least beginning to understand Caroline's dilemma. It would be pure hell to put your heart and soul into something, then have to make a choice to watch your efforts result in something fantastic, or walk away due to your morality code. He didn't know that he'd feel any differently than she did, in the same situation. He finally nodded that understanding. "I do get it."

Relief and gratitude flashed in her eyes.

He quickly added, "But there's one more big problem with you staying on the set."

Her relief faded. "Oh?"

"Yeah. There's the little matter of a killer running around up at the Little Bohemie Inn. I don't want you anywhere near that place."

"Mick, I can't be an on-site producer if I'm not on site."

He gave her a measured look that he hoped convinced her of just how serious he was. "You're spending twelve hours a day with that group of people, any one of whom could have killed Hester Tomlinson. You're telling me you're not the least bit worried?"

"No, I'm not telling you that. I'm scared out of my shoes."

He quirked a grin. "Good thing you have such cute little feet."

She ignored him. "But I swear, nobody's doing anything alone. We're all working in teams."

"What about the lucky person whose teammate is the killer?"

She gave him a look that accused him of being a pessimist, but didn't even try to argue the point.

"Well, there's just no other way around it. I'm going to have to step up my part-time job into a full-time one," he said, leaning over to his desk to gather up the papers he'd been working on. "You have a spare table in that trailer of yours, right?"

"What?" She stared at the papers he was shoving into his briefcase, then at his face. "What are you talking about?"

He shrugged and explained. "Well, if you're spending all your days on the set of *Killing Time in a Small Town,* so am I."

"Ms. WINCHESTER, will you tell us, please, where you were at the time of Hester Tomlinson's shooting?"

Sophie had, of course, anticipated the question and wished she had the kind of answer that could put this whole ridiculous investigation to rest. Unfortunately for her, she didn't.

"You don't have to do this," Daniel murmured.

The investigator from the Illinois Department of Law Enforcement, Detective Willis, shot him a stiff stare.

"She hasn't been charged with anything. We're just asking questions here."

"I know, and I want to be as forthcoming as possible," Sophie said, giving Daniel's hand a reassuring squeeze.

She knew she was lucky they'd allowed him to stay. But since she'd refused to talk to them if he couldn't, they'd really had no choice. She hadn't been charged with anything, hadn't been taken into custody. They were sitting at the kitchen table in Daniel's own house, for heaven's sake. He wasn't going anywhere.

"As I said earlier, I had ripped my costume. Some gracless dancer stepped on my hem."

Daniel didn't even crack a smile though she'd been trying to lighten the moment.

Willis wrote a note on his pad, tapped his pencil, then looked up. The pause was long and deliberate, straight out of mystery novel writing 101. "And you were looking for your cousin's wife to see if she had a needle and thread."

"Exactly," Sophie replied. "Someone told me she was in the kitchen, so I went looking for her. A few people were milling around, but no Gwen."

"Then what happened?"

"I went upstairs to look for her."

"Alone?"

She nodded, wishing she'd just taken off the stupid costume and returned to the party. If she'd been in Daniel's arms when the shot was fired, they wouldn't be asking her these questions. It was like something she'd have written in one of her books—the wrong person being investigated for the crime because he or she was unlucky enough to have no alibi.

"What next?" Willis asked.

She lifted her hand to her face and rubbed her eyes, trying to remember every moment of Sunday night. "I'm thinking."

"You couldn't find your cousin's wife in the kitchen…" Willis prompted.

"Right. So I went to her room, knocked, but no one was there." She cast a quick look at Daniel and winked. "Did you know Gwen and Jared have an enormous waterbed with a mirrored headboard?"

His lips barely twitched.

Willis gave a nearly inaudible sigh of irritation. "Did you go into their room?"

She shook her head. "Just peeked inside, saw it was empty, then decided to go upstairs to one of the guest rooms. Gwen once said they keep sewing kits in the bedside tables of all the rooms."

"You went up the main stairs?"

She shook her head. "No, there's a back stairway off the hall behind the kitchen."

Something sparkled in the investigator's eyes. He shifted his gaze away and exchanged a look with his partner, whose name was Lyons. He hadn't said a word since the questioning had begun.

Willis continued. "Was anyone else on the stairs?"

Sophie shook her head. "Very few people use them. They're horribly dusty. I know about them because I'm friendly with Gwen."

Willis nodded, exchanging one more look with his partner. Sophie didn't have time to wonder about that before he moved on with the questioning. "And then?"

"Then I went to the second floor, knocked on a couple of doors, but didn't get any response. The door to one room was wide open, and it didn't look like it was occupied."

Lyons finally broke in. "I thought *none* of the rooms were occupied because everyone was at the party." He bent over the table, standing over her right shoulder in a pseudo-threatening manner, almost pouncing as if he'd caught her in a lie.

Bad cop.

No way was she falling for that one. A quick glance at Daniel confirmed that he, too, had pegged the game these guys were using. He gave her a reassuring little wink.

"No one answered at any of the rooms, and all the doors were closed. This particular room, I believe it was the Bonnie Parker Boudoir, had an open door. There was no luggage, no unmade bed and no personal items were in evidence. I therefore assumed it was not being occupied by anyone staying at the inn." Sophie almost applauded herself for sounding just like the kind of credible witness she often wrote about in her court scenes.

Lyons conceded the point with a brief nod and stepped back, removing himself from Sophie's personal space. She felt Daniel's hand drop onto her leg under the table. He gave her a reassuring squeeze that both congratulated her and reminded her to keep calm and cool and not get cocky just yet. They weren't through with her, she imagined. Not by a long shot.

"Did you go into the room?" the first officer asked.

"I did. I found the sewing kit in the table, went into the adjoining bathroom and took off my costume to fix it."

"All right. Anything else?"

She nodded. "I was standing in the bathroom in my long underwear, sewing my skirt when I heard the shot."

This time Willis looked slightly confused. Skipping right over the vital "shot" part of Sophie's statement, he asked, "Long underwear? It's only September."

"I was Little Bo Peep," she explained with a simple shrug.

He still looked confused.

Daniel interjected, "Not long johns. Long frilly…female-looking things."

The officer's face pinkened slightly. "Ahh." The second officer—bad cop—merely grunted.

"I had to get dressed again before I could go see what was going on." She got tired just thinking about what a pain in the neck that costume had been.

Then again, it could have been worse. She could have taken Daniel's advice and gone as Freddy Krueger. Wouldn't that have been interesting to the cops?

Their questions continued for another half hour, and Sophie continued to answer as truthfully as possible. She admitted that she'd had a bad relationship with Miss Hester. And yes, she'd created some characters based on the woman in her books. And yes, she had murdered her in those books.

"But I also murdered my piano teacher who used to smack my knuckles with a ruler," she added helpfully.

Lyons pounced again. "Her name and address?"

Sheesh. These guys had no sense of humor at all.

"Okay, gentlemen," said Daniel, "you're grasping at straws." He stood and dropped his hand on Sophie's shoulder. "She's answered your questions. Now I think you should go."

Sophie could have kissed him right then and there, because she'd truly been at the end of her patience. Thank God Daniel knew her so well. He'd recognized that when she started cracking smart-ass jokes, she might go on to say just about anything.

Lyons gave Sophie a piercing look. "We were hoping you'd provide a sample of your handwriting and your fingerprints."

Daniel took the man by the shoulder and ushered him toward the door. "You want fingerprints and handwriting, you charge her. Don't come back without an arrest warrant."

Sophie sucked in a breath, shocked at how quickly Daniel had become angered. After the men left, she asked, "You don't think that went well?"

He shook his head. "I'm afraid not. They have something, some other evidence, and they think it ties back to you."

She thought it over but could think of nothing. In her fiction career, however, she knew the suspect was often blindsided by an unexpected witness or damning bit of testimony.

She was living one of her novels. A sick feeling rolled through her stomach. "Thank you for getting them out of here. I don't think I could have stood much more."

He stepped close and pulled her into his arms, giving her the kind of kiss that had always made her toes curl. When they drew apart, she asked, "You sorry you hooked up with me? Sorry you ever came to my rescue when that dog knocked me over onto the ice last winter?"

Daniel shook his head. "Not one bit. Maybe we should have told them that story."

She raised a questioning brow. "Why?"

"Well, we have reasons to be thankful to Miss Hester, don't we? If she hadn't been such a skinflint, the sidewalk at the church would have been salted, you

wouldn't have fallen and I wouldn't have swooped in
to rescue you."

She gave him a tremulous smile as the weight of
everything began to descend on her shoulders. "You're
exactly right." Then, as nervous tears rose to her eyes,
she added, "So will you testify to that at my trial?"

He drew her tightly in his arms, cradling her head and
whispering sweet murmurs of support as Sophie gave
in and truly cried for the first time all week.

CHAPTER EIGHTEEN

TRUE TO HIS WORD, Mick practically took up residence in the trailer on the set of *Killing Time in a Small Town*. He had a cell phone to keep in touch with his secretary and the other agents from the office. When he had a showing, he scheduled it to coincide with taping, so Caroline wouldn't be by herself.

Renauld Watson had given him a few annoyed looks. The guy had never forgiven him for not being wowed by his celebrity. Mick had simply crossed his arms and raised a brow, daring the cocky little bastard to say one word about him being here, protecting Caroline. Who, he had to admit, didn't seem to need his protection, but did seem to like having him around for occasional shoulder rubs and makeout sessions on the love seat.

"We shouldn't be doing this," she whispered against his lips as they curled up together Thursday morning. "Anyone could come in."

"I know. That's part of the turn-on," he whispered as he teased her into opening her mouth for him to deepen the kiss.

When she did, their tongues met in a slow, lazy dance of warm desire. He'd just made love to her last night, a passionate, frenzied kind of love. But now he wanted her again. Wanted to go slowly, inhale every inch of her soft skin and savor the sounds she made. He loved her little hitchy sigh the best, even better than when she cried out and moaned. The helpless sigh always welcomed him home when he entered her, either in a deep, fast plunge, or a slow, gentle joining.

She wriggled on his lap, upping the pleasure, increasing the heat that had already begun to center there. "Have I told you how much I love your legs?" he asked, sliding his hand under her short skirt to tease the soft skin of her thigh.

"Considering you had a pretty good glimpse of them up my dress the night you hid in the storage closet in the dorm, I had to assume you did."

He chuckled, remembering that long-ago first night when he'd been hiding out from two girls in the dorm. He'd been knocked out by Caroline from the first time they'd met. A goner that night when she'd looked down at him hiding in the closet and called him a dog right to his face. But she hadn't ratted him out.

"I love more than your legs," he said, giving her teasing little kisses on the corner of her lips, then her cheek, chin and, finally, her throat. She moaned softly, and arched farther back to give him access.

"I love your hips," he said as he nibbled just below her ear. He raised his hand higher, cupping her hip, running a teasing finger beneath the elastic edge of her panties. "I love holding your hips to keep you steady when you're on top of me."

A warm flush rose in her cheeks. He laughed at the sign of embarrassment. How on earth she could be embarrassed around him after everything they'd shared, he had no idea. "I'm not teasing you. You're beautiful. That's one of the best views of my life—looking up and seeing that look on your face, your hair wild around you. Watching you touch your own breasts, or lowering them to my mouth."

She shook in his arms, and Mick realized he'd taken this office play session a bit too far. He was hard and hot and ready, wanting nothing more than to flip her skirt up, tear her little panties down and plunge into her, right here, right now.

"We have to stop," she mumbled, pulling away to look down at him with lethargic, lust-glazed eyes.

"That door needs a damn lock."

The minute the words left his mouth, the doorknob turned. Caroline gasped and jumped up as they watched it swing open. Luckily, Renauld was yelling to someone and entered the trailer with his head turned away. Caroline had a few seconds to smooth her skirt. She managed to look calm and professional by the time the director got inside. Mick just stayed seated and willed his dick back into standby mode.

"Have you heard from the people at *Ambush Magazine?*" Renauld snapped to Caroline as he stalked into the trailer.

Caroline cocked her head to the side, looking confused. *"Ambush?"*

Renauld nodded, brushing past her to check the contents of the fax machine bin. "They're sending someone to cover the story."

Oh, great, Mick thought, the tabloids were in on the act. *Ambush* was a newer one that specialized in getting sordid photos of famous people, and digging up dirt wherever they could. If anything could kill a hard-on, it was the thought of those people digging around.

"You can't be serious," Caroline said. "They're the worst kind of trash."

"Publicity," Renauld replied, a hint of impatience in his voice. "Even trash publicity is good publicity for a new television show."

Caroline crossed her arms. "I disagree."

Renauld seemed to hear the note of steel in her voice, a tone Mick had only heard her use on rare occasions. She wasn't backing down. Renauld finally turned and gave her his full attention. Mick leaned back, crossing his arms on the back of the headrest and lacing his fingers together. This was starting to get interesting.

"Now, Caro," the director said, sounding conciliatory, "you know we have to take whatever spotlight we can get before the premiere."

She didn't budge. "I never saw their name on the list of approved media visitors. We don't need that kind of spotlight shining on this production."

Renauld shrugged. "So the magazine appeals to a certain type of audience. That audience does watch television."

She didn't concede the point, though Renauld was probably right. Instead she asked, "Who approved this?"

The cocky little rooster didn't look so cocky now. He gazed away and shrugged. "It's nothing official. So many other newspapers have called, the tabloid shows are here. What's one more? What a story! Horror novelist murders church matron on set of new reality show. What could be better than that?"

Mick sucked in a breath even as Caroline cast him a quick, reassuring glance.

"We're not going down that road."

Renauld merely smiled. "Of course we are. The studio is ecstatic." Then he turned to Mick. "Oh, yes, the author, she is your sister, isn't she? Pity. I liked her books. Do you think she'd have any interest in selling movie rights before she goes to jail?"

Mick launched off the love seat so fast the obnoxious director had no time to react. Mick had pinned him against the wall, one arm tightly clenching his shoulder, the other pressed flat across the man's neck. He leaned close and his voice shook with anger. "You do anything to hurt my sister and you're going to have a hell of a lot more to worry about than ratings."

Caroline grabbed his arm, pulling him away. "Mick, let him go. Don't do this."

Mick dropped his arm and stepped back, noting the paleness of Renauld's face. "Violence runs in your family, I see."

"You wanna see violence…"

Caro tugged at him again. "Stop, please. It isn't going to happen." She glared at Renauld. "No interviews given by anyone on this set will discuss R. F. Colt."

Renauld merely drew in deep breaths and straightened himself up. He backed toward the door, edging along the wall as if afraid to get within five feet of Mick. Before he left, he cast them both an angry glance. "Call the studio and discuss it with them and then we'll talk again." Then he pointed at Mick. "Without *him*. I want him out of this office, now." Then he walked out of the trailer, slamming the door shut behind him.

Once he was gone, Mick drew in a deep breath, trying to slow his racing pulse and let go of his anger. "That guy's a real piece of work."

Caroline nodded in agreement.

"You're going to stop him, right?" he asked, looking

in her eyes. "You won't let them tear Sophie up in the press?"

Caroline didn't hesitate. "I'm absolutely going to stop them. Don't worry, Mick. Renauld has a lot of enemies at the studio, which is why they usually give him these types of assignments, in faraway locations. They won't give in to his stupid demands. The network won't want this kind of trash publicity any more than I do."

He believed she meant every word coming out of her mouth. After drawing her into his arms, he kissed her temple and stroked her hair. Even as she reassured him, however, he couldn't help wondering how the studio would really react.

And how Caroline would respond if they didn't back her up.

SINCE THE BIZARRE crime Sunday night, Jacey hadn't spent much time with Digg. The entire cast and crew had to move out for two nights, filling up every gnarly room at a nasty old motel out by the interstate. Mona and Ginger had had to share a room, and Jacey didn't know who suffered more—Caro Lamb, who had to listen to their complaints, or the roaches, who had to listen to the two women bickering.

But by Thursday, when they were allowed to resume production, she noticed the entire cast and crew were infused with a new energy and excitement about the project.

"Genuine murder must really get the juices flowing," she muttered aloud as she checked her gear to prepare for tonight's elimination quiz. Because of the delay, they were stepping up the pace and three more contestants would be at risk tonight. Two would be gone by tomorrow. They'd be down to four by Sunday when they kicked into high gear to shoot the final two episodes.

She found herself praying that Digg would be among those final four. Not just because she'd be happy if he won but because she wasn't ready for him to leave. Not yet. Not until she figured out what their fast but intense little relationship meant. To both of them.

"You really think the murder has everybody more in the game-playing spirit?"

Jacey didn't turn around, closing her eyes as his familiar voice washed over her in the abandoned parlor of the inn. God, how could she have so missed a man she barely knew? Why did those mornings they spent running in the park seem to have such significance to her? And oh, Lord, why could she touch her fingertips to her lips and almost feel that faint, interrupted kiss from Sunday night?

Finally she turned around to face him. "Good morning."

"No run, I see," he said, noting her work clothes.

She shook her head. "Stricter rules now, because of the, um...situation."

Digg entered the room, closing the French doors behind him. He wore his typical dark jeans, black boots and tight black T-shirt that hugged his taut, trained body. "You never answered my question."

She forced her mind to the present, and off the image of Digg wearing his silly little fireman's hat—*and nothing else*—leaning so close to kiss her that she still almost felt those phantom lips against hers. "What question was that?"

"Do you think everyone's more interested in playing amateur detective because there's a real crime to solve?"

Jacey nodded. "Yeah. I mean, I don't think anybody figures they'll actually solve the thing, but it does up the stakes a little, doesn't it?"

He stepped closer, so close his jeans brushed her long black skirt and she felt his warm, minty breath on her skin. His cheek was freshly shaven, but he'd missed the tiniest bit of shaving cream, up near his earlobe. Unable to resist, she lifted her finger and wiped it away, glad for the opportunity to touch him. That touch was electric, sending warmth through her hand, down her arm and on, until it filled her whole body.

He closed his eyes briefly, then opened them and stared at her as she pulled her hand away. Before she could lower it, he'd grabbed her fingers and pressed them to his mouth. "Oh, Jacey…you had to go and do that. It's too late, now."

"What does that mean?"

He gave her a rueful smile and stepped even closer, until she lost herself in the golden flecks scattered across the dark brown eyes. "It means I can't wait now for a more convenient time. Can't wait until this is all behind us."

Wait? Wait for what?

He answered her unasked question. "I'm just going to have to kiss you now."

She barely had time to absorb his words before his mouth was touching hers, his lips gentle and sweet. She moaned, or he did, or they both did, and the kiss deepened, becoming a living thing between them where there wasn't just Digg, or just Jacey, there was now Digg and Jacey.

It was only much later, after many more kisses and touches that ended with them wrapped in each other's arms on the sofa that they heard the door click.

And realized someone had been watching them.

CARO HAD TO RUN over to the local office supply store to pick up a fresh stack of copy paper Thursday afternoon. Mick had agreed to her request that he go back to his office for the rest of the day. She didn't need any more run-ins with Renauld.

So far, she'd placed three calls to executives back in Hollywood and hadn't gotten any response. She told herself not to worry, that they were on a different schedule. But she couldn't help it—she *was* worried. As much as she hated to admit it, Renauld might be right.

"Don't even think that," she reminded herself as she left the production trailer to run her errand. "Just go and by the time you get back, they'll have called."

They'd run through reams of paper with all the writers' changes, last-minute clues and the twisting turning nature of the show. Just the thought of that twisting turning nature made her smile. *Killing Time* was going better than she'd ever dreamed.

She hadn't been kidding when she'd told Mick she was taking real pride in this project. Personal pride. The kind that came from being responsible for a success, seeing a little dream grow into a thriving, entertaining, genuinely good product. And *Killing Time in a Small Town* had turned out to be just that. It could revive reality TV, could bring back the more strategic programs and maybe push aside some of the cheesier ones.

But she wanted the show to do it on its own. Not because of some vicarious thrills viewers would get due to the scandal. Especially not at the expense of Sophie Winchester.

She pulled her car out of the parking lot, waving at Jacey and Renauld, who stood on the porch of the inn. They looked to be having yet another heated conversation. Not surprising. The two of them didn't get along at all.

She didn't realize it might be more than just another run-in until she got back from her errand to the store and found Jacey walking out the front door of the inn. The young woman's camera bag was slung over one shoulder, and a duffel bag over the other "What's up?"

Jacey shot her a disbelieving glance. "You mean you don't know?"

"Know what?"

"That I've been fired."

Fired? The best member of their crew had been *fired*? "That's not possible."

Jacey gave Caro a searching look, apparently noticing her genuine shock. "You really didn't know? I wondered if that's why you left, so you wouldn't have to be the one to do it. I didn't know whether to thank you— for liking me enough not to have the heart to fire me— or to flip you the bird as you left."

Caro reached out and touched Jacey's hand, wanting to make sure the girl knew she was being totally honest with her. "I knew nothing about any firing. And if I did, I'm certainly not enough of a coward to disappear when there's something unpleasant to take care of."

Jacey nodded, accepting Caro's words. "So it was just the butt-wipe."

"Which one?" Caro retorted before she thought better of it.

"Renauld. He said my personal relationship with one of the contestants made it impossible for me to continue here on the set. He was so damned judgmental, as if I'd destroyed the pristine reputation of Hollywood."

Caro smiled, liking the girl's sharp wit, which didn't fade even under crappy circumstances like these.

Jacey continued, "I wouldn't be surprised if he calls my father."

"Father?"

The camerawoman looked away. "Never mind."

Caro didn't push for an explanation, sensing that would be a long one. "I want you to know, I didn't tell Renauld about you and Digg."

"I know you didn't. That would have been Mona or Ginger or Deanna. Though Deanna's so busy going back and forth between Logan and James, I don't think she'd have cared if she'd walked in on me and Digg, uh…"

Caro couldn't believe it. Jacey was blushing That was definitely color spreading over the girl's ghost-white cheeks. It was attractive, though she sensed Jacey wouldn't agree. "You and Digg…?"

"Forget it. Doesn't matter why. I'm outta here." She looked around. "I just, uh, wish I had a chance to say goodbye to a few people. Charlie. And some others."

Caro knew whom she meant. "Digg and his team are supposed to be holding a strategy meeting in the basement. Go ahead and say goodbye." But before Jacey could go, Caro added, "By the way, don't leave after you see Digg. This isn't over yet."

The camerawoman met her eye, then slowly nodded, reading Caro's silent message. It looked like her battles with Renauld weren't finished for the day. Giving her a grateful look, Jacey turned and went back into the inn, leaving Caro free to go find Renauld and get some things straightened out.

She blew into the trailer, figuring she'd see the

puffed up little rooster ready to regale her with the results of his massacre. But instead of Renauld, she saw Digg, sitting on a chair beside her desk. "Jacey was looking for you," she said. "I told her you were at the meeting."

"I blew it off."

Caro sat opposite him, staring at the young man who held himself tightly in check. "You already heard."

"I heard. You have anything to do with this?"

Caro raised a hand to her heart and the other in the air. "I swear I didn't."

Digg shifted restlessly in his chair. "I figured that. I'll just sit here and wait until I can talk to the person responsible. There's no way I'm going to let Jacey get tossed out for something we both did."

Caro gave him an assessing look wondering just how far this young man would go. Had he really fallen for Jacey so fast? Did he honestly love her, or expect that he could? "What do you plan to say to Renauld?"

Digg's jaw stiffened. "That he's a friggin'—"

Waving her hand, Caro interrupted. "After that part."

Digg's brown eyes flashed with emotion and anger, something she'd never seen before in the calm, reasonable young man. There was usually something very relaxing and comforting about him, as if you could rely on him for always, never doubt him.

Why couldn't she have fallen for such a man?

Maybe because no man like that had ever excited her, driven her out of her mind and made her fall insanely in love. Only Mick. And frankly, thinking of the roller coaster ride their relationship had always been, she preferred it that way. Life with Mick would always be an adventure. Even if the adventure was only going to last another week.

"I'm going to assume full responsibility for what happened. He can take it out on me," Digg said.

Caro leveled an assessing look at the young man. "You know he *can't* do that."

Digg just held her stare. He understood what she was saying. Of all people on the cast, Renauld could *not* afford to let Digg go.

"Maybe it won't be his decision to make," Digg replied steadily.

He sounded like he meant it. This close to the end, with him looking like such a strong contender to win the game on *Killing Time,* he sounded ready to give it all up. For Jacey. "Would you really walk away? From the money, the fame?"

He didn't answer right away and she began to feel a hint of disappointment in him. *So much for true love.*

He sighed and leaned back in his chair, staring up at the ceiling. He and Jacey shared that trait—looking up for answers when they weren't sure what to say—which made her smile.

Finally Digg returned his attention to Caroline. "I'm not the type of man to back away from my responsibilities. I made a commitment. To you, and to the guys at the station."

"The station?"

He shifted uncomfortably, then looked side to side as if to make sure no one else was hiding in the tiny, cluttered trailer. "We have some plans for the money."

She still didn't understand. "We?"

He nodded. "We all knew someone that day." He glanced at his discreet pin, which Caro had noticed before. She instantly knew what he meant, and Digg went up several notches in her estimation. "You're giving all of it away?"

He finally grinned, bringing out two cute little dimples that had probably had Jacey begging from day one. "Well, not *all*."

She laughed with him. From what she'd begun to surmise about Digg, she had a feeling "not all" would mean all but enough for him to do something nice for his family or other people he loved.

In that respect, he was a lot like Mick. That's one thing they had in common—a generosity toward people they loved.

"Okay," Caro said, coming to a decision. "Renauld is king here and I can't force him to change his mind."

Digg's fingers clenched in his lap, and Caro quickly hurried on to add, "But I know people who can, and I've already got calls in to some of them." She swung around in her swivel chair and reached for the phone. "Time to start being a pest and call them all again."

CARO LEARNED two important things about Hollywood over the next twenty-four hours. First, producers would do anything to keep a good thing going, including undercutting the authority of the director if the occasion warranted it. And second, they were scared as hell of the word slander.

Both those things worked in her favor when dealing with Renauld Friday morning. He'd breezed into the office, and she'd hit him with newsflash number one: Jacey was back on the job.

"But, I fired her," he said, looking stunned. "What do you mean she's back?"

"I rehired her."

"On whose authority?"

She picked up the phone. "The studio's. Want to call and double-check?"

He sank to a chair, obviously understanding the implications. He didn't have the power over the little nobody on-site producer that he thought he did. Caro had always known that. This was just the first time she'd had to prove it.

"I don't believe it," he whispered. "They wouldn't interfere with on-set operations. They know we can't have a camerawoman involved with a contestant."

She leveled a steady gaze on him and fudged the truth just a teeny tiny bit. "He threatened to walk."

Renauld just stared.

"Did you hear me?"

Renauld finally got it. "Digg? Threatened to *leave?* Because of *her?*"

Caro didn't answer the question directly, because Digg hadn't threatened directly. But he'd hinted, and that had been good enough for her. She didn't even address the scorn in Renauld's voice when he'd mentioned Jacey. That would just make her angrier, which wasn't going to do her any good in dealing with the director.

"I got on the phone with Mr. Littman."

Renauld looked ready to lose it. "You went to Littman?"

She nodded. "I told him to look up Digg's file, see if he thought we could afford to lose him and then call me back."

"Of course we can't afford to lose him!"

Exactly the point. Which was just what Littman had said when he'd called late yesterday afternoon. So Jacey was back on the job, with the understanding that she and Digg would have no personal interaction for the remainder of the shoot. Since it would all be over within a matter of days, she figured they were in the clear. At least on that issue.

Before she could move on to issue number two— that of the tabloid trash reporters surrounding them— the door to the trailer opened. Mick walked in, carrying a paper bag which looked suspiciously like it held donuts.

The last thing he'd said to her this morning as she'd left for work was that he'd wanted to have breakfast in bed. Powdered sugar donuts that would sprinkle sugar all over her body—so he could lick it off.

She immediately flushed, going warm and liquid inside.

"I ordered *him* off the set," Renauld snapped, looking at Mick. But Caro noticed that, at the same time, he stepped back, closer to the desk.

"You can't order him off this property," Caro said with a satisfied smile. "His cousin and his wife own it and they've given him express permission to access any part of it."

Renauld looked ready to spit.

"Good morning to you, too," Mick said, giving the man a measured nod. Then he put the donut bag on Caro's desk and slid an arm around her waist. "I brought you breakfast." He reached up a hand and touched his fingertip to her lips, letting her taste the tiny bit of powdered sugar on his skin.

Fiend.

Renauld huffed and turned toward the door. Before he could go, Caro delivered the final blow. "By the way,

Littman also said we're giving access only to legitimate news and TV organizations."

He turned to look over his shoulder, his jaw hanging open.

"If anyone says a slanderous word about R. F. Colt, they're to be escorted off the site, immediately." Despite knowing Renauld would think she'd done it all for personal reasons, she still tried to make him understand. "The legal ramifications for slander against a public figure could kill us, Renauld. Littman and the other execs agree. Sophie Winchester hasn't been charged with a crime and she's off-limits in terms of interviews."

The man's jaw snapped shut. Without another word, he stormed out of the trailer.

"Well done," Mick said when they were alone. He lifted his hand again and brushed more powdered sugar on her lips. "Thank you for going to bat for Sophie."

She licked off the sugar and closed her eyes. "Mmm. Tasty. And you're welcome, though I would have done the same for anyone. We don't need a lawsuit."

"Whatever the reason, I'm grateful."

She pulled her wits together enough to give him a warning. "It's taken care of for now. But if she actually gets charged, Mick, I don't know that I can control it."

He met her stare evenly. Caro hoped he understood, hoped he realized how much she was trying to hold everything together. The show, her career, his sister's situation.

And, most of all, *them.*

"Understood." Then he gave her one of those devastating smiles. It was accompanied by a devilish twinkle in his eye. "I have something else I brought for you today."

"Bagels?"

Shaking his head, he reached into his pocket and drew out a padlock and key. Without another word he walked over to the door, drew in a top latch and hooked the lock through it, effectively trapping them inside.

"Privacy," he said. Then he began to walk toward her. Slowly. Deliberately. Like a wolf stalking its prey.

"I'd call it insanity," she said, her voice shaky.

"We're alone…"

She took a step back. "We're a few yards from a dozen other people."

He jiggled the bag and approached again, his smile decidedly wolfish now. "I have donuts with extra powdered sugar."

She backed up again, step by step, until her legs bumped into something and she could go no farther. "I have a brown suit that would show every little *fleck* of powdered sugar."

Wrong thing to say. That was a definite red flag waved before a bull. She knew it as soon as the words left her mouth.

"Well," he said, reaching to pull her into his arms, "we'll have to get that suit off you so it doesn't get messy."

Before she could protest, before she could even *think* to protest, her jacket was coming off, her blouse unbuttoned and her skirt lifted. "Mick…"

"Shh," he said as he reached into the bag and captured some powdered sugar between his fingers. He sprinkled it over her chest, letting it drip down between the curves of her breasts and over her lace-covered nipples. Then he bent down and unfastened the front clasp of her bra with his teeth.

She groaned and gave up all protest. "Oh, God…"

She started to tremble as he began to lick the sugar away. As with every aspect of his lovemaking, he was *very* thorough. His lips and tongue created incredible friction on her breasts until she was practically begging him to take her hard nipple into his mouth. When he finally did, she arched back and savored the strong pulling sensation as he suckled her. "You're so wicked."

He didn't bother to reply, just pulled her skirt higher, grasped between her legs to tug her panties away, then reached for his zipper.

"You want me to stop?" he growled against her throat as he eased between her legs.

"You stop and I'll kill you," she mumbled with her last coherent thought.

Then he was sliding into her, taking her right there in the trailer. He lifted her legs around his hips, cradling her bottom in his big, warm hands. When he'd driven home, she gave a little, helpless sigh, which made him smile broadly. Then he began to move, pulling her with him in a wild tango to their own unheard music.

Outside the voices of the crew carried through the morning air as they set up for the shoot. She didn't care. She cared about nothing except the excitement and the danger and the incredible pleasure of feeling Mick's body joined with hers.

Their rhythm was driving, forceful, unusual for him since he usually liked to draw out the pleasure for hours. They strained and panted and then finally exploded together and fell to the love seat.

When they could breathe again, Mick leaned over and placed a gentle kiss on her lips. "Tomorrow, I'm bringing pancakes."

She gave him a flirtatious look. "With *maple* syrup?"

He shook his head, nuzzling her neck and whispering, "I think I prefer Caro."

She could only shudder in anticipation and draw his mouth up so they could exchange one more long, loving kiss, before they separated to prepare for their day.

CHAPTER NINETEEN

MICK SHOULD HAVE KNOWN that sooner or later the state investigators were going to come knocking on his door. He was just glad they hadn't shown up at the trailer when he'd been nose to nose with Renauld Watson. He might have been questioned this week along with Sophie.

He was also glad they hadn't shown up today when he and Caroline had been, um…having breakfast.

"Mick?" his secretary, Sandy, said after buzzing him at his desk Friday afternoon. "I think you'd better come out here."

He expected exactly what he saw. The two state detectives—who, unfortunately, didn't look nearly as incompetent as Chip and Dale—were talking in quiet tones. "Can I help you?" he asked.

"We'd like to ask you a few questions if we may."

He cast a quick glance at Sandy. "Hold my calls."

"Consider them held," she muttered under her breath. She then gave him a surreptitious thumbs-up as he led the two cops back to his office.

"Can I get you something?" He played host despite knowing these bastards were out to nail a murder on his sister.

"No, thanks," the one officer, Detective Willis, said.

Then he got to the point. "We'd like to ask you about the gun."

The gun. Shit, of course, the gun. It all came back to that, didn't it? "You mean Louise Flanagan's gun, I assume?"

The officer nodded.

Mick quickly affirmed what Caroline had already told them, making light of the whole situation, including making fun of himself for being caught with his pants down.

Willis had a twinkle in his eye. Lyons remained emotionless, standing in the corner of the room, almost out of sight. When Mick had finished, he shrugged and lifted his hands in helpless resignation. "What can I say? I wasn't thinking straight enough to even remember the gun until much later."

"You never picked it up?"

Mick shook his head. "Never touched the thing."

Lyons leaned over the desk, appearing out of the corner so fast Mick hadn't even noticed. "So someone else took the gun out of this office while you were showing Ms. Lamb the property?"

Someone. Sophie. That was the name they wanted him to give. Not that he was going to do it. "A number of people were in and out of the office that day."

The man persisted. "Including your sister."

"I don't recall." He blessed his reputation as being Mr. Cool. Considering the number of times he'd gotten angry recently, he was lucky he didn't let his temper rise with these guys.

Lyons frowned. "She already admitted she was here that day."

"So why'd you ask me?" Mick shot back.

Lyons stepped away and Willis took over again. "Does your sister have a temper? Like you?"

Mick chuckled. "Me? I don't have much of a temper. As most of the town will tell you, I'm a lover not a fighter." His voice continued just the right amount of self-deprecation and charm.

Willis merely tilted his head, looking confused. "Well, that's interesting, considering the incident at your college."

Damn.

"That was a fluke."

"And at the Mainline Tavern last week. A few people said you were looking for trouble."

Damn again.

Mick leaned back in his chair, giving them both a rueful, man-to-man look. "Look, both of those occasions involved woman trouble, and I never laid a hand on anybody. It was me being mad at myself for being a stupid sucker."

They shared a look, one every man on earth knew and had worn in his life. They understood that much. Mick relaxed a bit.

"And you say neither you nor Ms. Lamb touched the gun?"

Mick nodded. "That's correct. Louise was the only one who touched it, so I assume the only fingerprints on it would be hers…and the killer's. Have you already gotten Louise's fingerprints to compare them?"

The detectives exchanged a look. Mick sensed the men were annoyed with one another. "We, uh, will be obtaining Ms. Flanagan's information shortly. She's been sequestered with the victim's brother, helping him through his grief."

Louise and Pastor Bob? He almost laughed, thinking the officers were mistaken. Then he remembered that day on the street when Louise had told him how the pastor was helping her. Maybe helping her by giving her someone else to focus her attention on, once she'd gotten her ridiculous crush on Mick out of the way?

It wasn't out of the question. Louise was a nice, honest young woman. Pastor Bob was only in his forties, and had probably been lonely since the death of his wife. He could think of worse matches.

"So," Mick continued, "as soon as you rule out Louise's prints, and focus on whomever else's are on that gun, you'll be able to eliminate other suspects. Including my sister. Right?"

Lyons responded. "We're not free to discuss the details of the case, Mr. Winchester."

Mick was ready to tell him to stuff the details of the case when they all heard the ring of a cell phone. Lyons answered and spoke quietly, then listened for several long moments. Willis leaned forward in his chair, and Mick had the feeling this phone call was important.

As Lyons finished his call, a smile appeared on his dour face. That was the first one Mick had seen today. After he'd disconnected, he looked at his partner. "It's in."

"And?"

"It's a match."

As soon as Caro heard from Hildy that Sophie Winchester had been taken into custody for questioning in the death of Miss Hester, she raced home to Mick's house. It was late Saturday morning, and the cast and crew were preparing for the second-to-last elimination episode. A big one. Not that she cared. She'd been out of the trailer thirty seconds after Hildy had come in, not even telling anyone she was leaving.

When she arrived, she saw a black sports car in Mick's driveway. Inside, she followed the sound of voices to the rec room and found Mick involved in a discussion with his cousin, Jared, and Jared's wife, Gwen. Mick saw her, stood and gave her a quick hard kiss. "You heard."

She nodded, then extended a big thermos. "Hildy sent this."

"Hildy's coffee," Jared murmured.

Gwen, a pretty woman with waist-length blond hair, laughed lightly. "I think we're going to need it."

Caro sat down and asked Mick for an update.

"She hasn't been charged. Daniel called and said they took her in for questioning. She's at the State Police substation in Margate. He's there now, with Sophie's lawyer and my parents."

Caro had a basic understanding of the law because of all the cop shows she'd watched over the years. "They have to charge her or let her go, right?"

"They can hold her for twenty-four hours. Then, if they don't charge her, yes, they'll have to let her go."

Caro nodded, relieved the police didn't have enough evidence to charge Sophie with a crime. Yet. "So what happens now?"

Mick looked at his cousin. "Jared was just about to fill us in on some details about the victim."

Gwen, who'd been in the kitchen getting cups for the coffee, returned in time to overhear. "Please tell me there's another suspect somewhere. I hate to think of Sophie in that place."

Jared leaned forward on the sofa, dropping his elbows on his knees, staring at Mick. His brow furrowed, his dark eyes grew intense. "Miss Hester has a very secretive past. She disappeared for a long time during her early twenties. When she came back to her family, she was using the name Esmerelda Devane."

Esmerelda? *That* wasn't a name she'd picture for the woman.

Mick also looked puzzled, tilting his head. "Something about that name sounds familiar."

"Apparently Esmerelda was her middle name. She was married briefly to someone named Devane out in California," Jared explained. "I have my investigator looking into those missing years. But until we know more, we have to look at other options."

"Local options," Gwen said, looking thoughtful.

Mick nodded. "Jared's not the only one with friends. An old friend of mine works as a clerk in the Margate substation." He cast a quick glance at Caro, but she didn't so much as flinch, despite being certain Mick was referring to a former girlfriend.

He continued. "She says the notes found with the gun mention a woman's name. And they set up a time and place for a meeting."

"Was Esmerelda the name? Maybe Miss Hester was being blackmailed," Caro said.

He shook his head. "No, the name was Victoria Lynn. And my friend tells me the reason Sophie's being questioned is because a note with the same name, found in another part of the house, has both Sophie's and Miss Hester's fingerprints on it."

Caro sucked in a shocked breath. That was pretty damning.

"How'd they get Sophie's fingerprints?" Jared asked,

looking surprised. "I know Daniel wouldn't have let her give them voluntarily, and they didn't bring her in until this morning."

Gwen had the answer. "She told me months ago she took a fingerprinting class to be sure she could get the details right in her books. Every student was fingerprinted for practice."

"And the police could have subpoenaed those prints," Mick said, shaking his head in disgust. "Too bad Sophie was such a detail-oriented writer."

This was looking worse and worse for Sophie. Caro didn't know her that well, she'd only met her a few times, but she still had trouble believing the woman could hurt a fly, no matter what she did in her imagination. But, if it were anyone else, she'd at least be wondering because of the evidence mounting up against her.

"Have they matched her prints to the gun?" Caro asked.

Mick shook his head. "No, they haven't, according to my source. So far, the victim's are the only prints they've officially identified on the gun."

"Interesting," Jared mused. Then he furrowed his brow, sitting back in the chair and rubbing the corners of his eyes with his thumb and forefinger. Gwen watched him, as did Mick. They seemed familiar with this deep-thinking mode. Caro fell silent, too, interested in the criminologist's viewpoint.

Finally Jared murmured, "How do you know Louise left the gun in your office that day?"

Caro and Mick exchanged a look. Obviously Mick had filled his cousin in on the entire story before her arrival. "You told her to drop it," she said.

"I heard a thump."

Then they both looked at Jared, who was shaking his

head, looking disgusted with himself. "Don't you see? There's another explanation. There's another way someone could have gotten hold of that gun."

He paused, and Caro couldn't help inserting a little mental *Columbo* music during the heavy pause. "Louise never dropped the gun," he finally concluded.

Mick and Caro looked at each other again, both trying hard to remember every detail of that day in his office. Finally, Mick nodded slowly. "You could be right. She might not have. In which case, we need to find out what happened to it after she left."

Gwen cleared her throat and everyone turned their attention toward her. "I've heard rumors that Louise and Pastor Bob are an item. Is it possible Miss Hester didn't approve, and Louise, um, wanted her out of the way?"

That was one of Caro's first thoughts. But the two men in the room looked doubtful. "You don't know Louise," Jared said, dismissing the idea.

Mick appeared to agree. "If she was going to commit murder, I'm sure she would have done in her rotten hooligan little brothers sometime over the years."

Caro and Gwen exchanged a look, neither convinced.

"I'm going to try to do some more background checking on Esmerelda Devane," Jared said. He stood and reached out a hand to Gwen.

His wife nodded, a determined look on her face. "Drop me off downtown on your way home," she told Jared. "I have a feeling the rumor mill in Derryville might come in handy." She looked at Mick. "If there's any secret to be found about Miss Hester I'll hear about it at the Hair and There Salon."

Her husband ran his fingers through a long strand of

her golden-blond hair. "Don't you dare let Pammy Morrison lay one finger on your hair."

Gwen laughed softly and looked at Caro. "She's been after me to get a bob."

Jared visibly shuddered.

"While you two are at that," Mick said, "I'm going to talk to Louise."

Caro instantly rose to her feet. "Not alone you're not."

"You don't have to come."

"Oh, yes, I do. The last time you were alone with that woman, she held a gun on you. And no matter what you say about how nice she is, I still think she's nutty. So I'm coming along."

He gave her one of those devastatingly sexy smiles, which made her relax in spite of the circumstances. "To protect my body?"

More to protect her own heart, since Caro couldn't imagine what she'd do if anything happened to Mick. But now wasn't the time or place to admit such a thing. So she merely smirked. "Damn right. And you'd better get used to it."

As MICK AND CAROLINE drove over to the church to track down Louise, Mick couldn't stop running the details over in his mind. Sophie in jail. Unbelievable. A murder in Derryville. Also unbelievable.

And those names. Something about those names…

"What are you thinking?" Caroline asked.

He glanced over to see her staring at him with tender concern. "Just going through it all in my mind. There's something there. Something I'm missing."

"Do you really think Louise will be honest about what happened?" Caro asked.

Mick nodded. "Look, it's just as impossible for me to believe that Louise had anything to do with this as it is for me to think of Sophie as a murderer."

"Okay. If you're sure," she said.

He heard the doubtful tone in her voice and wasn't surprised. And yet even with those doubts about Louise, she'd wanted to come along. To protect him.

"Mick, you do understand that with Sophie being taken into custody, this changes things."

His hands tightened on the steering wheel. She didn't even have to say what she meant. "You're talking about the show. The press."

"Yes. When the word gets out—"

"The studio won't be so scared of slander, because now it's official that she's a suspect."

He looked over at Caroline. She nodded, watching him with wide eyes, waiting for his reaction. He honestly didn't know how to react. In one moment, the woman was ready to face down a possible murderess to protect him. In the next, she'd admitted that her company might engage in a smear campaign against his sister.

"That puts you in a tough position," he murmured, wanting to know what she was feeling. "What are you going to do?"

What would she do, if it came down to it? Would she leave Sophie out there, free for the cast and crew of *Killing Time* to crucify in upcoming television interviews? Or would she take a stand?

"I don't know," she finally said, shaking her head as she stared out the window. "I honestly don't know."

A stab of disappointment raced through him. He didn't know what he'd expected. Maybe for Caroline to say she'd walk out, quit her job, stick to her principles?

And stay with him.

Before they had time to discuss it further, they reached the church and parked outside the pastor's residence. "Let me do the talking, okay?" he said as they got out of the car.

She nodded, still quiet after their conversation. A conversation they'd have to continue later.

Louise answered the door within a few moments of their knock. "Mick!" She stepped out, threw her arms around him and gave him a big hug. "How sweet of you to drop by. Bob will be so glad." Then she turned to Caroline and gave her a pleasant, if sheepish, smile.

Louise looked different. Though weary, her face was pretty and soft, with a hint of makeup that he'd never seen her wear before. She also wore a dress instead of her usual overalls.

Somehow, she fit very well in the church residence. All the rumors about her relationship with Pastor Bob seemed to be true.

"Louise, can you talk to us for a few minutes?"

She looked confused, then shrugged and nodded. "Yes, of course, but can we step outside? Bob's lying down. He's having such a hard time dealing with this."

Of course he would be. Mick couldn't even imagine losing his sister. To death. Or to prison.

They stepped onto the porch, and Mick wondered exactly how to broach the topic. But he didn't have to. Caro charged right in. "Louise, have the police questioned you about the gun yet?"

So much for letting him do the talking.

Louise's eyes widened and she shook her head. "The gun? What gun?"

Mick cast a stern look at Caroline. She winced, and bit her lip. "The gun used to kill Miss Hester," Mick explained. "It appears it was the one you brought to my office…that day."

Every bit of color drained out of Louise Flanagan's face. She went as pale as a bowl of Ed's tasteless grits down at the diner.

Right then and there, Mick knew without a doubt that she'd had nothing to do with the murder, not that he'd ever thought she had. But there was no way she could feign such shock.

Caroline also seemed to notice Louise's distress. She put her hand on the other woman's shoulder and grabbed her arm, lending support. Knowing Louise probably had sixty pounds on Caroline, he grabbed the other arm.

"You didn't know?" Caroline asked.

Louise just shook her head. "Bob…what will I say to Bob?"

She looked dazed, and Mick hadn't even gotten to the most important part yet.

"I can't believe the police haven't questioned you yet," Caro said, sounding confused.

"They tried calling yesterday, but I'd gone out."

Yesterday. After they'd questioned Mick in his office. Christ, the cops hadn't even confirmed the story of the gun with the woman who'd been carrying it! They'd just accepted Caro's and Mick's statements as fact.

Now it was time to get the *real* facts. "What did you do with the gun that day?"

She blinked a few times, looked back and forth between Mick and Caroline. She suddenly seemed less dazed, but now a puzzled frown pulled at her brow. Finally she explained. "I came right here to the church. I wanted to see Pastor Bob, to talk to him, but he wasn't in." She looked at Caro. "We were just friends then, and he was the nicest man I knew. I figured he'd understand."

"But he wasn't here?" Caro prompted.

"Right. I was standing in the reception area with some others. We all heard Sophie," she glanced at Mick, the color returning to her face, "your sister, arguing with Miss Hester. Then she left. And I waited until Miss Hester was alone, so I could ask her about Pastor Bob."

Mick was beginning to understand what Louise was telling them. He almost knew what she was going to say before she said it. "You were alone with Miss Hester?"

Louise nodded, tears rising in her eyes. "I was so embarrassed, Mick, so horribly embarrassed. Miss Hester made me realize it wasn't a good idea to tell Pastor Bob what a fool I'd been. She offered to help."

Of course she did. And Mick suddenly knew exactly how Pastor Bob's sister had offered to help. Louise's words confirmed it.

"Miss Hester took the gun."

JACEY HAD BEEN LOOKING for Caro all afternoon, but couldn't find her. She needed to talk to the woman, needed to get her alone to try to find out how the heck she'd pulled off the miracle of getting Jacey's job back.

She knew damn well Renauld hadn't done it out of the goodness of his heart. He'd acted that way, of course, when he and Caro had called Jacey to the production trailer and told her she'd been rehired. But Jacey had known Caro was responsible.

She was thankful. But also unhappy with the one stipulation: that she stay away from Digg.

"I guess he didn't care so much," she muttered aloud as she stood in her room at the Little Bohemie Inn. Digg hadn't sought her out at all, not even when he'd thought she'd been fired.

So much for Mr. Hero. Once their friendship had been exposed, he'd covered himself, making sure he didn't get ejected from the game by steering clear of Jacey. She didn't know whether she was more disappointed or heartbroken.

Heartbroken would involve her heart. So she refused to think that, even though in her deepest thoughts, she suspected that's what this ache, this emptiness, meant.

It was dinnertime and the rest of the cast and crew were downstairs eating a meal the studio had had brought in. They couldn't take a long break tonight because they'd be taping well into the evening.

Tonight would determine the final four—the four contestants who would go on to the last episode of *Killing Time*. The last one standing that final night would walk away with a cool million. Either the killer, who'd fooled and killed off all the other players in the game. Or else one of the contestants, who'd survived long enough to finger the Derryville Demon during the last, dramatic confrontation.

One of the four would be eliminated after the final quiz during the last episode. Then the last three would face off, questioning each other, going over the case, trying to figure out the killer while also trying to trick the other players into naming the wrong person.

If both players guessed wrong, the killer won the prize. If a player named the killer, however, and put all the pieces of the entire puzzling case together, that person would get the money. It couldn't just be guesswork.

The winner had to actually have figured out the means, motive and opportunity for every crime.

She wondered how Digg would fare, if he'd survive, if he'd come out of this adventure a millionaire. If he'd give her a second thought once he was gone. "Probably not. I'll be a distant memory chalked up as a notch on the new fireman's hose he'll buy with the million bucks."

"Actually," a voice said from the doorway, "there will be a new fireman's hose if I win. I plan to help refurbish the station. But if anyone cut a notch in it, it wouldn't be much good at putting out fires, would it?"

Jacey closed her eyes, wondering why Digg was here, entering her room, closing the door behind him. But oh, so very glad he was.

"What are you doing? You know we can't be alone together."

Digg shrugged. "Everyone's at dinner. And I assume the crew's rooms aren't wired?"

Jacey shook her head, thankful for that much. This was one room in the inn where they actually could talk in private.

"I've been trying to get a minute alone with you since Thursday." He stepped closer, running the backs of his fingers over her cheeks. Damn, if there were tearstains there, she'd just have to jump off a bridge or something.

"Jacey, I'm so sorry about what happened."

"You are?" Her voice shook. She couldn't help it. "I wasn't even sure you knew. Or cared."

He pulled her into his arms and kissed her temple. "You really need to work on your self-confidence issues."

Her jaw dropped. "Me? I don't have issues. I'm a ball-breaker, not scared of anything."

He smiled slightly. "Except genuine emotion. A real relationship. The possibility that nice guys do exist and the tough girl can fall in love."

She tried hard to hold herself stiff, though her entire body wanted to melt against him. "You think I'm in love with you?"

He nodded, kissing her cheek, then her nose, then the corner of her mouth. "I know you are." Then, before he moved his lips over hers, he murmured, "Because I love you, too."

Then he was kissing her, touching her with his mouth and body, even as he'd touched her with his words. Jacey wrapped her arms around his neck, holding him tight, kissing him unreservedly, with all the emotion she'd kept locked up inside herself forever.

When the kiss finally ended, she looked up at him, losing herself again in his serious brown eyes. "You could have waited and told me this after the show. I hate that you're risking yourself for me."

He shrugged, completely unconcerned. "You're worth any risk, Jacey. And they know if you go, I'll go too." Then he gave her a cocky smile and lifted a teasing brow. "And I *definitely* cannot go."

She tilted her head in confusion. "If I go, you...?" Then the truth started to dawn. "Oh, my God, you're the reason they brought me back. You threatened to quit."

"Something like that, but not in so many words. Caro went over Watson's head."

As she'd suspected, Caro had been involved. But she'd never imagined Digg had.

He'd stood up for her. In all her life, Jacey had never had anyone stand up for her, want to fight for her, to be a hero for her. She stood up on tiptoes and kissed him again, thanking him without words for his trust, his support. And his love.

"Can we really make this work?" she asked, a bit of self-doubt creeping in. "In the real world?"

"They have firemen in L.A., don't they?" he asked.

His supreme confidence renewed her own. "And they have studios in New York," she answered with a big grin.

Suddenly, everything seemed possible. The future rolled out in front of them, endless and unexplored. "When do we go?"

"Wednesday morning," he replied without hesitation.

She nibbled her lip. "We can leave now. Just so, you know, if you ever doubted why I stayed, if you thought it had to do with the money you might win..."

"I *can't* leave." He chuckled. "Besides, I haven't won yet."

"I won't care if you don't."

"Good. Because if I do, a lot of it's going to charity."

Perfect. Just perfect. "I'm glad."

That sparkle appeared in his eye, a boyish excitement that hinted at a secret. He hadn't told her everything. She thought about his words. How the studio couldn't let him quit. How he *couldn't*. "Wait a minute. You *can't* leave?"

He simply watched her, that twinkle in his eye confirming what she'd just realized. He brought his finger to his lips and winked. "Shh."

She threw her arms around his neck and hugged him tight. "I won't tell a soul."

No, she wouldn't reveal the truth to anyone.

Digg was the Derryville Demon.

CHAPTER TWENTY

THOUGH SHE HAD no desire to be away from Mick, Caro had to get back to work on the set Sunday. The pivotal final episode was to be taped this evening. She couldn't bail on her responsibilities, though it killed her to leave Mick alone for the first time since yesterday. He said he planned to meet his parents for lunch, and would come by the set later.

Maybe it was just as well. She didn't necessarily want their first impression of her to be as the predator whose TV show might kick their daughter when she was already down. And it didn't look good for her. Even though Louise had gone to the police and told them that she had not left the gun in Mick's office, they hadn't released Sophie.

They still had the note. And they found it just as easy to believe Sophie could have gone back to the church office and gotten it later. She did have the keys, after all, since she'd been the secretary.

When Caro arrived on the set, she realized that exactly what she'd feared was going to happen *had* happened. The media had heard about Sophie being taken into custody yesterday. Though she still hadn't been charged, that was enough scandal to get the bloodhounds baying. And they were all over the story, digging up everything they could on the famous young author.

Caro was in the production trailer, answering the questions of a hungry reporter from *Entertainment News,* when Mick showed up. He walked in just in time to hear her try to deflect a question about R. F. Colt. "We can't comment on an ongoing police investigation," she said, sounding stiff even to her own ears.

"Everyone else is commenting," the reporter said. "They say the author, Sophie Winchester, used the cover of the Halloween party you were taping for your reality show to lure the woman she loathed to the inn."

Caro just shook her head. "Again, I'm not going to speculate on a murder case. If you'd like to talk about the fictional one on the set of *Killing Time in a Small Town,* I'd be happy to oblige you." She gave a soft, deliberate laugh designed to encourage the reporter's curiosity. "We have quite an amazing drama playing out here. Bodies and clues everywhere. The stage is set for tonight's grand finale."

The reporter took the bait, finally asking some questions about the show. Caro answered them with all the enthusiasm she could muster. She even managed not to flinch when she looked up in time to see Mick leave the trailer. His expression had been unreadable, his body stiffly held.

God, she'd hoped it wouldn't come to this. Hoped Sophie would be cleared so Caro wouldn't be put in this horrible position—firmly between her job and the man she loved.

Oh, yeah, she loved him. There wasn't any doubt about that. She'd lied to herself about it for a long time. Years. But now, she couldn't lie anymore. Mick had stolen her heart back in college and he'd never really let go.

It just remained to be seen if he felt the same way—

which she suspected he did. And what they were going to do about it—which was anyone's guess.

The interview ended soon, and she found Mick fifteen minutes later, in the kitchen of the inn. "We knew this might happen," she said softly as she joined him.

He nodded, sipping at a steaming cup of coffee. Caro helped herself to some, then sat down with him at the table. "Mick, talk to me."

He finally met her eye. "I liked your answers."

"You did?"

"Caroline, you sounded like the cool, professional studio executive you are. You're doing exactly what you were meant to do." He reached across the table and took her hand, bringing her fingers up to his lips. "You're damn good at your job."

Relief flooded through her. He understood. He wasn't going to condemn her, or encourage her to make some kind of difficult choice. She might still have to make one. But at least she knew Mick trusted her enough to make it on her own.

"That doesn't mean I haven't heard what some of the other people on site are saying about Sophie." He didn't ask, didn't try to convince her to do something, but she knew that's what he was hoping she'd do. If she could.

"I don't know if I can stop that. It's public now—it's out in the open and the studio is going to want to milk it."

His mouth narrowed, but he nodded, apparently understanding. "I know. And I know you'd change that if you could."

"You're right." She was warmed by his trust, even though she sensed his disappointment. He deserved to have that trust repaid. There was only one thing, one final truth, that she could offer him to prove that trust. She wanted him to know how she felt about him. "Mick, I..."

"Well, Miss Hester seems to have had a *few* enemies in this town," a woman's voice said from the back door of the kitchen.

They hadn't realized Gwen was entering until she strode in, her face flushed, her hair windblown. She looked very excited as she pulled up a chair at the table.

Caro smothered a frustrated sigh at the lost moment. She'd been ready, so ready, to start trying to make things work between them. But what she had to tell Mick wouldn't change. She had time to tell him she loved him, because that emotion wasn't going to change for the rest of her life.

"Is that Hildy's coffee?" Gwen asked.

"Jared's," Mick said.

"I'll pass."

"What'd you find out?" Caro asked, driven by the excitement in Gwen's face. "I heard you struck out yesterday at the beauty parlor."

Gwen nodded. "That's right. This line of gossip ran a little bit deeper than the curler and hair dye set. I had to go right to the source." She fell silent, building the anticipation.

Caro couldn't stand the tension. "Well?"

"I went to church this morning."

Caro almost laughed. Gwen made it sound as though she'd ventured into the hideout for the Hell's Angels.

"It's amazing how people loosened up and started talking afterward, especially since Pastor Bob wasn't there to deliver the service." She shook her head, tsking. "Poor man. He really loved his sister, whether she deserved it or not."

That sounded interesting.

"I can't be sure, mind you, not sure enough to go to the police. But it appears Miss Hester might have been in the habit of finding out personal, perhaps embarrassing, information about people, and profiting by it."

Caro's mouth dropped open, and Mick's eyes widened.

"You mean she was blackmailing people?" she asked.

Gwen nodded, then rose, went to the fridge and got herself a bottled water. She took a few deep sips from it. Obviously gossip gathering was very thirsty work. "So says the very deepest, darkest part of the Derryville rumor mill," she finally replied, "the group that sticks it out until the last donut is eaten in the social hall of the First Methodist Church of Derryville."

"The upstanding matron of our town a blackmailer." Mick shook his head, not even looking surprised. "Small towns. No wonder they're perfect for bizarre reality shows."

Caro shot him a frown. "Hey, no cracks about my show."

"Sorry."

"I have two sources," Gwen continued, ignoring their spat. "Both were secondhand, both saying they knew someone else who'd paid Miss Hester off either with money or favors. One of them was a teenage girl who said her boyfriend had been under Miss Hester's thumb for months."

Caro just shook her head, unable to believe someone would stoop low enough to blackmailing a kid. This murder victim sounded less and less like a poor innocent.

Mick, Gwen and Caro stared at each other for a minute in the silent kitchen, thinking over the ramifications. Before they could discuss it further, Jared walked in, interrupting the charged moment. Gwen got up, put her arms around him and told him what she'd learned.

"So," he said when she'd finished, "Miss Hester has a history of collecting secrets. She had the gun. She'd touched at least one note mentioning a strange woman's name, and giving a time and place for a meeting." Jared looked at them all expectantly, waiting for them to catch up.

Caro finally put the pieces together. So did Mick. They looked at each other and said, in unison, "Miss Hester was killed by someone she was blackmailing."

Gwen looked disappointed that they'd beat her to the conclusion as Jared nodded in approval. "I believe so. And it's very possible the person she was targeting was someone she knew in California back in the early seventies. My P.I. says Hester Esmerelda Tomlinson Devane was somehow involved in show business, but he doesn't yet know how."

Mick narrowed his eyes, muttering, "Esmerelda. Esmerelda…" Then he sucked in a shocked breath. He shot to his feet, pushing his chair back so hard it fell to the floor with a crash. "Son of a bitch!"

Caro, Jared and Gwen gave him their full attention.

"Esmerelda Devane and Victoria Lynn. I've finally remembered why the names sound so familiar." He grabbed Caro's hand and dragged her toward the door. "Come on, I need your help."

"Hey, what about us?" Gwen said.

"I'll let you know if my hunch is right," Mick said over his shoulder. "Jared, keep your guy in California nosing around until I get back. Caroline and I are going to be busy for a few hours."

"Busy doing what?" Caroline asked.

But he didn't reply. She sensed that he kept silent because she wasn't going to like the answer. When they arrived back at his house, he beelined right for the TV room and the cabinet where he kept his stash of movies.

"Tell me."

"It'll sound too crazy."

"Crazier than a blackmailing church matron found dead in a bathtub on the set of a reality show?"

He laughed out loud and she did too, both of them badly needing the levity. She didn't know quite how much she'd be needing the lightened moment, until she saw exactly which movies he was sorting through. "You must be kidding."

Caro stared at Mick, not believing what she saw. He was kneeling in front of his entertainment center, digging through piles of videos. *Those* videos.

"I'm not kidding."

"Mick, this is no time for us to watch dirty movies! Remember what happened the last time?"

He looked up and gave her a decidedly lascivious look. "Oh, yeah, I remember."

Heat rose to her cheeks. "I still haven't forgiven you for that night."

"I bought you a present to make up for it."

"You did?"

He nodded. The evil look in his eye should have warned her. "It's a vibrator."

She grabbed a pillow from the sofa and hurled it at his head. He easily deflected it, laughter on his lips. Then he returned to his task.

Finally, just when Caro thought she couldn't stand the suspense anymore, she heard him make a satisfied sound.

"What?" she asked, almost afraid to know.

He turned toward her, a confident look on his face as he held up a video box. "Bingo."

IT WAS CRUNCH TIME, time to start taping the final episode of *Killing Time in a Small Town*, and the on-site producer was nowhere to be seen. Jacey appeared to be the only one who noticed. Everyone else was too keyed up, too excited. Finally, the mystery would be solved. Cast and crew would learn who the killer was, who would walk away a millionaire and who would leave empty-handed.

Jacey hated the suspense. Knowing that Digg was the killer made it that much tougher.

The four finalists entered the parlor of the Little Bohemie Inn to discuss the last murder. It had come down to Digg, James, Logan and Whittington. Mona, thank God, had been among the casualties the night before, as had Ginger. Jacey had been glad as hell to see Mona go since she was nearly certain she was the one who'd been spying on Jacey and Digg the other day. But she actually kind of missed Ginger, who'd been damn good at the game until she got tripped up over the murder in the public library.

Joshua Charmagne tapped a spoon against his wineglass to get the attention of the contestants. He'd settled pretty well into his role as host and innkeeper, once he'd realized he wasn't going to find a playmate on the set.

"We've come to our last night," he announced, looking carefully at each of the final four. "If we don't find out who the killer is, he will be free to wreak havoc on Derryville during the biggest social event of the season—the Christmas ball."

Leave it to Renauld to throw another holiday into the mix. God help them, if he decided to shoot some extra scenes with a September Christmas tree, Jacey was totally out of here.

Well, no she wasn't. Not until Digg was out of here with her.

She put her attention back where it belonged. On her camera. On the scene. On the quiz.

They began. The four contestants each sat in a corner of the room, answering two dozen questions related to the Derryville Demon case. They had to have been paying attention all along the way. The questions dated back to that first killing, in Sophie Winchester's house. One misstep would lead to sudden elimination.

They wouldn't use all this footage, of course. The editors would trim down a thirty-minute quiz to about five, with close-ups on the contestants. The sweat breaking out on James's upper lip. The way Logan's eyes were narrowed in concentration. The nervous pencil tapping Whittington couldn't contain. And Digg, watching them all with his standard, impassive, unreadable expression.

He didn't dare look at Jacey. She'd known he wouldn't.

Finally, the tests were collected and taken away to be graded while the cast and crew took a brief break. It seemed to take forever before Joshua Charmagne returned to the parlor to announce tonight's first big loser.

"I'm sorry to say farewell," he said once the cameras were back on and the cast members assembled, "to Professor Whittington."

"YOU CANNOT BE SERIOUS."

Dead serious, Mick replied, meeting Caroline's gaze, not flinching, though the words coming out of his mouth sounded unbelievable, even to his own ears. "Look for yourself." He held out the proof he'd found, moments before, in his video cabinet.

She took the video box. A tape still wrapped in plastic, unopened, from Mick's collection. He heard her tiny gasp when she read the names of the stars of *Psychedelic Sex Dreams*.

"Esmerelda Devane and Victoria Lynn."

Right. That's why he'd recognized the names when Jared had first mentioned them. Individually, they'd have been unusual enough. Together, they were incontrovertible. At least to him.

"Miss Hester made porn flicks?"

Mick nodded.

"Eeew." She dropped the box.

"I need to find all I have with those two in them," he replied, turning his attention back to the stack of films in the cabinet.

Caro didn't say anything, just kept looking stunned and wrinkling her nose in distaste as if visualizing the whole thing.

That's what he'd been doing mentally since the second he'd recognized Miss Hester's former name. Eeew was right.

He began sifting through the movies, looking for the older ones that Earl was so fond of bringing to him on poker night…just so he could crack up about how the women might look thirty years later. That brought Miss Hester right back to the forefront of his mind. Earl had been on to something.

"Wait, I don't understand," Caro said. "Doesn't this make it look like Miss Hester was the one being blackmailed?"

He nodded, having already considered that. "Yeah. I'm sure she didn't want this getting out."

It would almost be divine retribution. The hypocritical blackmailer being blackmailed.

"So she *wasn't* the blackmailer after all?"

"I don't know. Either way is possible. But I honestly have to think she was the one who spotted someone from the past and exploited the situation. Because I just can't see anyone from her past seeing her now and—" he held up the video box showing a buxom blonde "—*recognizing* her."

Caro nodded. "True."

"Either way, whether she was blackmailer or victim, I think we're going to find that the person who killed her is someone involved with the reality show."

Caroline didn't even try to argue. "I suppose it makes sense, given her past."

"And it explains why she fought so hard to keep *Killing Time* from coming here to begin with."

He returned to his task, finding another, and then a third video with the name Esmerelda Devane on the box. Victoria Lynn was on both as well.

They were in for a long evening.

"We just have to find out who on the set of *Killing Time* might have known Hester in her wicked old days," Mick said. "I'm laying money on that bastard Watson."

Caro didn't respond, knowing Mick's feelings toward her director. "Okay, I get what you're saying, but I still don't see how. I mean, don't we have to leave it to Jared's investigator? Tell him to look into the porn industry of the '70s and see what connections he can find?"

Mick shook his head, waiting for her to figure out where he was going. "There's a much quicker way."

She looked at him, then at the boxes surrounding him on the floor. She began to shake her head as it sunk in.

"Huh-uh. You can't be serious."

"I'm serious."

"I'm not watching porn tapes with you."

"It'll be for research purposes only."

"Yeah, right. Like last time?"

"Last time," he retorted, "I wasn't picturing a dead Miss Hester in the bathtub every time the naked star appeared on the screen."

Her face paled. "Oh, crap, you're not really gonna make me watch Miss Hester pornos are you?"

"Sorry, babe, you're the one most likely to recognize a face."

"Do they show faces in those kinds of movies?"

"Oh, they show lots of heads," he said evilly. "Hopefully one of them will pop out at you."

She threw another pillow. "I'll get you for this."

He grabbed her hand and pulled her down to sit beside him on the floor. "If you help me get my sister cleared of murder, you can get me any way you want me."

They grew quiet, and Mick groaned inwardly at how he'd worded that. The truth was, Caroline could have him any way she wanted him already. He loved her. They were going to be together. No matter what. He just didn't have time to figure out how yet.

After they examined all the tapes, finding four that had Esmerelda Devane's name in the credits, they sorted them out. "Let's eliminate the one that Victoria Lynn wasn't in," Caroline said, "and start with one of the ones she was."

So they did. As painful as it was, they began to watch the cheesy, poor-quality tapes. "Basement stuff," he muttered, glancing over at Caroline and seeing the look of shock on her face.

"Oh, my God," she whispered. Then more bodies filled the screen. Lots of them. At the same time. "Oh, my God!"

She threw her hands over her face, only peeking through and cringing every few moments to try to help him.

He began to fast forward, pausing when someone new entered the frame. The low-grade, drug-era video was almost painful in its cheesiness, complete with mushroom-dream sex sequences where Miss Hester—Esmerelda—was dressed up as a geisha girl.

It made Mick decide then and there to swear off sushi forever.

When the movie ended, he couldn't stop a sigh of disappointment. They hadn't recognized a single person, other than Miss Hester. And he was still getting over the shock of that.

He reached for the next box, removing the plastic wrapping as the first film ended and the credits began to roll. He was about to pop the tape out of the VCR, not wanting to waste the time even to rewind it, when Caroline gasped in shock.

"Pause the tape, Mick." She looked stunned. "Pause it now!"

He did. Then he focused on the screen, wondering what had captured her attention. He read the first name. Then the second.

And then he read the third.

"Oh, my God," he whispered.

"He's still at the inn," Caro replied, her voice also hushed.

Then Mick rose to his feet and held out his hand. "Let's go *get* him."

ONCE WHITTINGTON had been eliminated, the cast and crew took a break from taping to prepare for the final showdown. Jacey met Digg's eye as he, James and Logan were escorted from the parlor. An hour from now they'd return, be given details of the latest murder—that being Whittington—then they'd begin one final group meeting.

That meeting would likely be the key to the whole thing. The three men would be playing a mental game, trying to be absolutely certain who the killer was, while also trying to bluff someone else into voting the wrong way.

That's why Digg had been such a good Derryville Demon. As Caro had said that first day of taping, back before Jacey had known who she was talking about, Digg had the perfect personality type. Stoic, calm, honest, heroic. He'd been everyone's favorite, women and men, cast and crew.

And oh, my God, he's mine.

It seemed impossible to believe, but he really was.

"You do know you won't be doing the taping with the individual finalists," Renauld said. He'd entered the kitchen silently where Jacey had been sitting alone, grabbing a PB&J sandwich for dinner during their brief break.

She glanced up. "I figured as much."

"You might have your job back, but we can't afford to allow you to be alone with any of the final contestants, for fear they might later claim you influenced their choice."

She hated the pissy little director, she really did. But she had to concede that he was right. "I know," she said, giving him as close to a humble look as she could manage. "Charlie said he'd be happy to step in for me."

Renauld nodded. "Good. With his camera experience, he'll do fine at managing the team."

Jacey sipped again, then grudgingly admitted what she'd already realized about *Killing Time*. "The show's going to be a hit. It's really good."

Renauld seemed surprised, then met her eye. "I think you're right. As long as we nail this next hour." He managed a pleasant nod before walking out.

The next hour, yes. The accusation sessions would be particularly critical. Each of the finalists would enter a private booth and vote on the killer. They'd also have to provide the motive and tie the entire case together if they wanted to win the one-million-dollar prize.

All except Digg.

All he had to do was stay cool and hope James and Logan—who'd been competing for Deanna for the past couple of weeks—would turn on each other. Jacey hoped so, too.

She stayed in the kitchen until the end of the break, then returned to the parlor to tape the final discussion meeting between the three men.

As expected, Digg kept cool, James and Logan got in personal jibes wherever possible and each man exited the room looking supremely confident of the outcome.

Now it just remained to wait and see what happened.

CHAPTER TWENTY-ONE

CARO AND MICK arrived back at the Little Bohemie just as the taping of the private booth scenes began. Caro groaned inwardly at first, then realized it was just as well. They'd get the show done, and afterward, once Chief Daniel Fletcher had arrived, get the answers to the rest of their questions.

As they entered the expansive parlor, Caro instantly spied Jared and Gwen, waiting along with everyone else, including a very excited-looking Hildy. Everyone was drinking coffee and pacing around. In spite of what was happening in the real world, Caro felt a thrill of excitement. The expectation in the air was palpable as everyone speculated on who would win and who would walk away with nothing. It felt good to be part of this. She resented the hell out of the person who'd almost spoiled it all by dragging the sordidness of Miss Hester's death into their midst.

That person. She *still* couldn't believe it was true, though she'd seen the evidence with her own eyes.

"Where's Renauld and the rest of the crew?" Mick asked Jared, keeping his voice low.

"Apparently they're taping the final guesses."

"Who lost the last challenge?" Caro asked, dying to know which of the four had been eliminated in the final quiz.

"Whittington."

"Where is he now?"

"Upstairs packing," Jacey said.

Caro hadn't even realized the young woman was in the room. She gave her a quick smile of welcome, then asked, "Is Whittington with an escort?"

"Absolutely."

Caro glanced at Jared and Gwen, who looked curious. "None of the eliminated contestants have been left alone. We don't want them spilling anything to those who remain."

"And hopefully that prevented anybody from stealing our china on the way out, too," Gwen added with a cheeky grin.

"Where is our esteemed celebrity host right now?" Caro asked, wanting to know where everyone was before Daniel arrived.

"Joshua Charmagne? I think he's in his room, as usual," Gwen said, "on the phone with his agent who's supposedly getting him a major movie deal worth ten million."

Right.

"He'll be down soon," Jacey added, "probably just in time to demand a fresh pot of coffee and a freshly baked croissant."

Caro wouldn't be surprised, given the demanding nature of their guest star.

She took Mick's hand, squeezing it, sensing he was every bit as anxious about the delay as she. But there was nothing they could do except wait for the chief of police.

He gave a resigned sigh, then asked, "What's this final showdown?"

Caro quickly explained the procedure.

"So," Mick asked when she'd finished, "they're with Renauld and the camera operators in one of the third-floor suites—I assume it's not the one where the real murder took place?"

"Correct," Caro add, shivering at the thought. "The tech crew is there, too. No one's left the inn today at all." She shot Mick another look that urged him to be patient.

"Uh, no, actually the tech crew's not there," said Jacey. "Renauld's orders—camera operators, contestants and him, that's it. Nobody else."

Caro instantly asked, "So where's Charlie?" Then, before Jacey could answer, Caro realized what *else* was seriously wrong with this picture. "Wait a minute, what are *you* doing here? Why aren't you in on the taping?"

"That's the answer to your first question—Charlie's covering for me. Renauld and I agreed that I should back off at this point. Just in case."

Good grief, Jacey and Renauld had agreed on something, and she hadn't been around to see it. "That was probably a good move."

She felt Mick touch her shoulder. He nodded toward the door. Beside them, Jared and Gwen also watched with interest as Chief Daniel Fletcher entered. He was in full uniform and looked both serious and determined.

He beelined for Mick. "He's here?"

Mick nodded, as did Caro. "Upstairs," they said in unison.

They'd called Daniel the minute after discovering the video connection. He'd made it up here pretty quickly considering he'd had to go to a local judge for a warrant first. When Mick raised a questioning glance at his future brother-in-law, Daniel tapped his pocket. He'd apparently *gotten* the warrant.

"So you're back to work?" Gwen asked. "I thought you went on a leave of absence."

"I came back on the job about an hour ago. Just in time, I think."

Caro couldn't agree more.

Now it just remained to wait here in the parlor until the person they all wanted to speak to came down the stairs.

THOUGH MICK, Caroline and Daniel were the only three in the room who knew exactly how much was at stake tonight, everyone else was just as keyed up. Even though he was completely distracted, wanting to nail the bastard who'd been about to let his sister take the fall for a murder, Mick couldn't help catching the undercurrent of everyone else's excitement.

They'd come to the end of their road and were about to see the culmination of a job well done. Caroline literally sparked with energy and life, and he knew damn well it wasn't just because of what they'd discovered watching *Psychedelic Sex Dreams* back at his place.

She was in her element. Loving every bit of what she did, getting an almost physical charge from it. He liked the look on her face, the tension in her body, the half smile she couldn't contain whenever any of the crew commented on how great this show was going to be.

She'd have her hit. She'd have her success. She'd have her future.

It was about time for him to figure where he was going to fit in it.

"Here they come," someone said.

They—everyone—stood as footsteps approached from upstairs. Renauld Watson entered the room, followed by Digg, Logan and James. The crew reacted instantly, setting up for the final scene, touching up the makeup of the contestants, putting the room back in order.

Renauld spied Caroline. Mick wondered at first if he was going to question her about where she'd been, but the cocky little rooster seemed too excited to care.

"It's perfect," he said, low, to her, though Mick was close enough to overhear.

Caroline met the director's eye and they exchanged a long, comprehending look. Then Caro smiled. But she wouldn't say a word.

"Tell me," he muttered once Renauld had walked away. Mick was caught up in the thrill in spite of himself.

"You'll see."

So he watched, along with everyone else while Joshua Charmagne emerged with three videotapes.

"Now," the host told the three final contestants once the cameras were rolling, "it's time to see how you all explained this mystery, and to determine who is going to walk out of here a millionaire." He paused, the heavy silence ratcheting up the anticipation. "And who is going to leave with…nothing."

He inserted the first tape into a VCR hooked up to a state-of-the-art television. Logan appeared on screen. Everyone leaned forward, watching, hanging on every word as Logan detailed a convincing-sounding scenario. Even Mick bought it and thought they might be listening to tonight's winner. Then Logan fingered the killer: James.

Mick looked at Caroline, trying to gauge her expression. Damn, she had her poker face on. She revealed nothing. Beside her, though, the camerawoman, Jacey, was practically bouncing on her toes.

"Now we'll hear James's solution," Charmagne continued.

In went the second tape. James looked a little less prepared, a little more frantic and fumbling. He rambled and had no real motives for the murders of the first three victims, the ones who "died" back at Sophie's house.

When James named the killer, he did it with a glimmer of spite in his eye. Logan.

Next to him, he heard a tiny gasp. Mick glanced over, knowing Caroline hadn't made the sound, though a tiny grin played on her lips. Beside her, though, Jacey was trying unsuccessfully to hide a joyful look. He had the feeling the noise of elation had come from her.

Then Mick glanced at the final contestant. The fireman. Digg.

"Son of a bitch," Mick whispered under his breath, realizing the implications of what had just happened.

James had accused Logan. Logan had accused James. Neither had claimed responsibility as the killer.

And he suddenly knew the outcome.

"The final accusation," announced Charmagne with his well-known melodramatic flair.

The third tape was put on. Diego Martinez looked at the camera. Then he began to explain in minute, intricate detail every step of the killing. It was an incredible story of greed and extortion, revenge and rage. The plot all tied together so perfectly, so delightfully that Mick felt as if he'd just read a brilliant mystery novel. Maybe one as good as his own sister could have written.

At the end of his monologue, Digg looked at the screen. Smiled. And delivered the death blow.

"The Derryville Demon is…me."

Everyone in the room remained quiet, not bursting out in reaction until the last scene was shot. But the players reacted. James groaned. Logan chuckled a little, looking admiringly at the man who'd just beaten him out of a million bucks.

Neither of them had realized the implication of whose tape would be played last. Of course it had to be the killer's, otherwise the suspense wouldn't have lasted so long or been maintained at such an edge-of-the-seat level.

"Congratulations, Diego, you have successfully eliminated every one of your competitors," Joshua Charmagne said in his smoothest, commercial talk-over voice. "You have won one million dollars by killing time in a small town."

Renauld called cut. And everyone in the room erupted.

THE CELEBRATION lasted for several minutes. Then Daniel, Caro and Mick exchanged one long, knowing look. Caro knew the time had come. The show was over. The fictional murder case solved. Now it was time to resolve the real one.

"You have the tape?" Daniel asked Mick. Mick nodded, taking Caroline's hand. They'd agreed before that she, as the one who knew everyone in the cast and crew, should be the one to approach their suspect.

"You have backup in the kitchen?" Mick asked Daniel, not for the first time. He hadn't liked the idea of Caro spending a moment with a murder suspect, but even he'd agreed it was the best way.

No one wanted to accuse the killer in a room full of people—potential hostages. They needed to get him alone in another part of the house.

Taking a deep breath, Caro made her way through the crowd. She schooled herself to keep the genuine shock and disappointment from her voice as she smiled at the person she believed was responsible for the death of Hester Devane.

"Charlie?"

The old man, the friendly, grizzled tech director who'd been the first to offer a smile on this production, looked up. "Caro! Congratulations!" He threw his arms around her and gave her an exuberant hug. "You did it, kid. You are really on your way. A hit under your belt and the sky's the limit."

Caro's heart broke a little. God, how it hurt to think this man could be a murderer. But it made sense. More than any other possibility, this one made sense.

"Can I talk to you in the kitchen?"

Charlie nodded his gray head, taking her arm and leading her out of the packed room. "I was so glad the fireman took the loot. Logan seemed like a nice enough fellow, but if that James had won it, I think I would have lost all faith in reality TV."

Caro couldn't prevent a tiny chuckle. There was an interesting place to put one's faith.

"What'd you want to see me about?" Charlie asked. But as they entered the kitchen, closing the door behind them, he saw Daniel at the table and his two police officers moving to block both entrances of the room.

His face fell.

"Charlie, the chief would like to speak to you," Caro said softly.

He nodded, suddenly looking older than his years. "Do you mind if I sit? It's been a long couple of weeks."

Daniel held out a chair, remaining silent, assessing

the suspect. "As long as you don't mind if I check your pockets."

The man lifted his arms and spread his legs without demur. One of the officers—*not* the one who'd thrown up on Miss Hester's corpse—patted him down quickly and efficiently. He'd probably learned the technique by watching cop shows. Caro wasn't one to criticize. She'd learned a *bunch* of useful things from television.

The officer stepped away with a nod at the chief, and Daniel gestured toward the chair. "You do know you don't have to talk to us. I'm not arresting you, but I do have a warrant to search your room and belongings."

"I know my rights," the old man replied, sounding more resigned than afraid. "I'm tired and just want this over with. I'm ready to tell you what happened."

Once Charlie sat down, Daniel said, "Are you aware that a suspect is in custody for the murder of Hester Tomlinson?"

To give him credit, Charlie's eyes widened and his mouth dropped open in shock. "No. Who?"

"My sister," Mick bit out from between clenched teeth.

Daniel shot him a glance telling him to stay out of it, as he and Caro had both agreed to do. That was the only way Daniel would let them stay. Silenced, at least for the moment, Mick crossed his arms and leaned against the wall.

Charlie looked around the room at them all, finally resting his gaze on Caro. He looked defeated, sad, even apologetic. Then he spoke to Mick. "Your sister didn't kill the woman…Miss Hester, you say? I didn't know her by that name."

"You knew her as Esmerelda Devane," Daniel said.

Charlie nodded. "I did."

"And you killed her."

"I did not." Charlie's spine stiffened. "She killed herself. It was an accident, but as God is my witness, she was the one who pulled that trigger."

Caro gasped, unable to help it. The junior officers stared at each other, bug-eyed as two cartoon characters.

"Explain. Start with the blackmail," Daniel ordered.

Caro held her breath, waiting to see if Miss Hester had been blackmailer or blackmailed. An innocent or a victim of her own greed.

Charlie set that to rest immediately. "She recognized me from the old days. She thought she had something on me. Something ugly and awful. So she started sending me notes. They came to the Snorkle house, where I've been rooming. Never saw who slid them under the door."

"And they mentioned Victoria Lynn?"

Charlie nodded. "They did."

"Hester's former colleague in the, er, movie business."

Charlie started to rise from his seat. For the first time he looked angry, rather than forlorn.

"Victoria Lynn is my *wife*."

That silenced them all. And they remained silent while Charlie told them his whole sorry story.

THAT NIGHT and the next day, Mick spent a lot of time with his parents and sister. Sophie had been released from jail once Charlie had come forward with the truth of Hester Devane's death. They'd all been a little shocked by the story, but Mick, at least, had no doubt it was true. It wouldn't surprise him at all that Miss Hester would try to blackmail someone who she thought had murdered her best friend and former roommate.

Apparently Hester, as Esmerelda, had fallen in with

a serious drug and porn crowd in California in the early '70s. She and her roommate, Victoria, had starred in a few bad movies.

Then Victoria had disappeared. And Hester had believed that Charlie, a cameraman and Victoria's sometime lover, had been involved in her death.

"She'd heard talk of snuff films and believed that's what happened to Victoria," Mick explained to Jared and Gwen Monday night as they sat on the front porch of his house. His parents had gone home, and Sophie and Daniel had decided to leave town for a few days to get over what had happened. Sophie was already plotting to work in a false murder charge in her next book. "That's what scared her away from California and her secret identity." He shifted on the porch swing. "In reality, Charlie had spirited Vicki away to get her in rehab. He has the pictures and marriage certificate to prove he and Victoria have been married for nearly three decades."

"Why didn't he just tell Miss Hester about his wife?" Gwen asked.

Caroline came out of the house in time to overhear. "He was protecting Victoria. He had no idea who was blackmailing him. At first, he didn't even recognize Miss Hester once he saw her. He wanted more than anything to keep his wife's past a secret from their children and grandchildren."

"Sad," Gwen murmured.

Beside her, Jared appeared unconvinced. "And when he appeared at the drop-off spot, the third-floor suite, he claims Hester was the one with the gun?"

Caroline sat down with Mick on the porch swing, curling up against him for warmth in the cool evening air. Dropping his arm over her shoulders felt as natural as breathing.

"She was," Mick said. "Hester had the gun all along. She'd taken it from Louise."

"Plausible," Jared said, conceding the point as he thought it over. "A blackmailer would want a weapon for defense."

Mick continued to relate the story. "Once he figured out who Hester was, Charlie tried to convince her that Victoria was alive and well, and begged her to leave them alone."

Caroline stepped in. "But she didn't believe him and thought he was trying to distract her and take the gun."

"The old 'they both reached for the gun' defense?" Jared asked.

Mick nodded. "It went off."

"Miss Hester hit the tub," Caro added.

"Charlie panicked, picked up the gun with one of the blackmail notes to keep his fingerprints off, and stuck it in his back pocket."

Jared rolled his eyes. "For someone in a panic, he had the presence of mind to try to avoid prints."

Mick didn't try to convince Jared that his suspicions were wrong. Jared hadn't been there to hear the older man break down. But his words had convinced everyone in that kitchen that he'd been telling the truth. Every one of them would be willing to testify to the emotion of the moment when it came time for trial—if there was one.

"How'd the gun end up in our attic?" Gwen asked with a little shiver.

"It fell out of his pocket, along with the notes, when he climbed through the access door to get away," Mick said. "He'd been spending his days at the inn—he knew the ins and outs, so to speak."

Gwen and Jared exchanged an intimate look and a smile. Mick, remembering that the two of them had first fallen in love at the inn, didn't question it.

"The thing that really damaged Sophie was admitting that she'd gone up the back stairs," Caro said, shaking her head as she thought it over.

Mick squeezed her closer, liking the way she felt against his side. Liking having her here, on his porch, with his family, in his world. "They found her footprints, and Miss Hester's, and read too much into it. Plus Sophie, being the good girl she is, picked up what she thought was a piece of trash off that back stairwell and threw it away in one of the upstairs bedrooms."

"Let me guess," Jared said, "a note Miss Hester had dropped earlier."

"Bingo," Caro and Mick said in unison.

They talked for another hour, discussing Charlie's future, the manslaughter arrest, the pending investigation and trial. Mick felt certain that the man would be okay, as long as the justice system worked. He hoped, in this case, that it would.

Eventually, Gwen and Jared left, leaving Mick and Caro alone on the porch swing.

"You okay?" he asked her softly. They'd had no real alone time since the previous day. God, things had been such a whirlwind, he hadn't even asked her what had happened on the set today.

"I'm fine. Really." Then she laughed softly. "It's amazing how quickly a studio can change its tune when it's one of their own employees involved in a murder investigation, rather than a celebrity."

Mick knew without asking what she meant. The studio was no longer going to be exploiting the real murder, not when they might very well get hit with a lawsuit or something by Miss Hester's next of kin. But he doubted that. Pastor Bob seemed the type who would want to move on and forget the ugliness as soon as possible. Putting it out there for public consumption would mean exposing his sister's past, something no brother would want to do. He seemed content to move on with his life—with Louise Flanagan, who hadn't left his side in days.

"I have to tell you something," she said softly.

His spine straightened. The tone in her voice told him he wasn't going to like what she had to say.

"Yes?"

She drew in a deep breath, then released it. Her warm exhalations caressed his neck and he tightened his embrace.

"I have to leave tomorrow."

Christ. Tomorrow. "So soon? I thought you had until the end of the week."

She dropped her head, looking away. "Things changed because of the case. Now that Charlie's gone, and Jacey quit to take off with Digg, there's nothing left to do here."

"Of course."

They fell silent. Now nothing lay between them—no murders or TV shows. Now there was only their past and their desires, their feelings and their geography.

And one more thing.

"Why did you leave me, Caroline?" he asked, needing to know that before he decided what he was going to do.

Everything hinged on her answer. He'd realized that

days ago, back when he'd been torturing himself by trying to stay away from her when *with* her was the only place he wanted to be.

Because if her distrust of him hadn't changed, then nothing ever would.

"Did you really believe I betrayed you one week after asking you to marry me?" he asked, trying to sound merely curious, and not hurt, though he'd been nursing that wound for a very, very long time. Through other women and relationships. And tattoos.

She didn't answer for a long moment. Then, finally, she tilted her head back and stared at him, her face lit by soft moonlight and her eyes glistening with emotion. "I did."

A part of him died at her answer.

"I don't now."

He nodded, waiting for her to go on.

"Mick, I know now that what I interpreted as your inability to commit, to ever settle down and be faithful, was really my own out clause from our relationship."

"Out clause?"

"I'd built in an easy escape. Deep down I never, *ever* thought I'd be able to hold you. Any more than my mother could hold my father. Or any woman with a lousy outlook on love could hold a man who seemed to love everybody—" she rolled her eyes "—as often as possible."

He laughed, unable to help it, amused by her droll tone. "We've been over that. And for the record, I've only ever *loved* one woman. As I believe I told you one night many years ago."

She sucked her bottom lip between her teeth, but didn't press for more details. There were still words to be said before they could go down that road.

"The point is, I convinced myself you wouldn't change. That I wasn't enough to make you want to change."

"That implies I was really in need of change. Was I that bad?"

She frowned. "Baby, the big bad wolf could have taken lessons from you."

He winced. "Point taken."

She curled tighter against him. "So I prepared myself for the inevitable and when the first opportunity occurred, I convinced myself it was true and hightailed it west."

He couldn't keep the pain from his voice. It was eight years old, miles wide and unvoiced until this moment. "You didn't even give me a chance to explain."

She sniffed a little, raising her face to the sky so that he could see the tears on her cheeks. "I know. And I'm sorry. That's the biggest regret of my life. That I didn't have the courage or the self-confidence to get in your face and demand an explanation."

If she had, how different might their lives have been? He had no idea, and it was a waste of time thinking about the past, now, when the future stretched out in front of them. At least, he hoped it did.

They fell silent again, just rocking in the moonlight, listening to the bark of the neighbor's dog and the creak of the swing's chain. And then, just when he'd thought she'd say no more, she added, "I'm sorry for doubting you. I know you'd never hurt me."

That was enough for him, the moment he'd been waiting for.

And the moment he knew his future.

CARO WOKE the next morning and slipped from Mick's bed after a night of lovemaking like none she'd ever known. She'd expected frenzy, a hungry grasping of something that was slipping away and might very well be over when she boarded the plane the next day.

But there was none of that. There was long, slow, languorous loving that went on for hours, until she lost sight of who she was and who he was, where her body ended and his began. She moaned and she sighed. She came and she gave. She cried out and she sobbed. And over and over she whispered—if only in her mind—*I love you, Mick.*

When she got out of the shower, she found the bedroom empty. Mick had left her alone, obviously not wanting to watch her pack to leave. "So why didn't you ask me to stay?" she muttered as she returned to her own room to gather the last of her things.

Why hadn't he? How could he make such beautiful, perfect, tender love to her and never once even broach the subject of their future? "Maybe now that the past is reconciled, he doesn't want a future anymore." She stared at her own reflection in the mirror, hating that she'd thought the words, much less said them aloud.

"Caro, you're going to miss your plane," she heard from downstairs.

"Son of a bitch," she muttered, growing angry now, instead of just hurt. She'd poured her heart out. Okay, no, she hadn't poured her heart out. All those "I love you's" had been shouted in her brain, but not even whispered from her lips.

But still, how could he not have heard the silent declarations, when every touch, every move, every kiss and caress repeated them again and again?

"All men are deaf as well as blind," she muttered as she hoisted her shoulder bag over her arm and prepared to go downstairs for her grand exit. That was all she had to carry. Mick had gotten her heavier things earlier, while she'd showered, so there was no more reason to delay.

When she arrived downstairs, he was standing in the foyer, leaning against the banister, a sunny smile on his face.

The fiend.

"You ready?"

"Uh-huh."

"You take anything for the flight?"

"What do you mean?" she asked.

"I mean, I know you hate to fly. Or are you just going to regale us on board with the theme songs from NBC's 'Must See' TV season?"

She gave him a sour look, barely listening, waiting for him to say something—*anything*—to let her know how he felt.

"Here, let me take that," he said, reaching for her carry-on.

Her fingers itched, wanting to smack him for his good mood. Dammit, why did he feel good when her heart was breaking?

But she wouldn't beg. She wouldn't plead.

Nor, she decided, would she leave without admitting, once and for all, how she felt. She wasn't a coward anymore, wasn't willing to walk away with words left unsaid between them, whether they were words he wanted to hear or not.

After she left, maybe he'd think about it, acknowledge that she really did love him. And that maybe he loved her, too. Maybe it would just take some distance for both of them to figure out a way to make this long-distance relationship work.

"Okay, babe, pick up the pace. We got a long way to go."

She dragged herself out the door after him. She barely took note of the beauty of the blue sky, the cold nip in the air that said autumn had arrived in earnest. It was punctuated by the visible puffs of breath she exhaled.

She couldn't concentrate. Not on anything she saw, nor on anything he said, unless it might be prefaced by the words, "Caroline, I love you, don't go."

"Caroline?"

She sucked in a hopeful breath.

"Hope it's a smooth flight."

A particularly savage swearword shot through her brain. "Thanks a lot."

Then she practically stalked to her car, beelining for the driver's side. But the door was locked, and Mick had her keys. "Can you open the door for me?" she asked, walking around to see him unlock the trunk to place her carry-on bag inside.

That was when she noticed something.

The trunk was stuffed. Overflowing. She easily recognized her familiar, tasteful burgundy leather luggage. But there were also a couple of big, tattered, navy blue duffel bags crammed near to exploding.

She looked at the bags. Looked up at Mick. Then back down at the bags. "What is this?"

"What's what?" he asked, slamming the lid shut and giving her a completely innocent look.

She tilted her head, confused, studying his face…and that was when she saw it. That wicked, mischievous, "gotcha" look she'd come to know and love.

"Mick—"

"What's the weather like in California at this time of year, anyway?" he asked, not letting her finish.

"Mick!"

"I mean, I didn't bother with heavy stuff. Until I get my Realtor's license out there I figure I'm going to be a beach bum, anyway. You don't mind marrying a kept man, do you? I promise I'll make it up to you when I can start working out there. Sell a few of those multi-million-dollar mansions to the stars, and we'll be set."

She couldn't help it. She reacted like a total girl. Tears rose to her eyes and she threw her arms around his neck. "Oh, God, Mick!"

He grabbed her around the waist, holding her close, burying his face in her hair. Inhaling her. Adoring her. Telling her without words that he was never letting her go.

"I love you, Caroline."

"I love you, too, you rotten, miserable joker."

He began to laugh. "That's about as romantic a declaration of love as I've ever heard." Then he kissed her forehead, her temple, her eyelids. "And it's the only one I've ever wanted to hear."

She pulled away, staring into his beautiful green eyes that sparked with tenderness and longing, promising the kind of future she'd been dreaming about for eight years.

"I will never let you leave me again." His words were an oath.

"I'll never want to. You're sure you want to come to California?"

He nodded without a second's hesitation. "I do. I really do. It took you coming here, waking me up to the fact that I'd been doing nothing with my life—nothing but existing, killing time—to make me realize I wanted to start *living* it."

She stood up on tiptoe, pressing her lips to his, kissing him with every bit of pent-up love and emotion she'd ever felt for the man. And she began to whisper, "Love you, love you, love you."

He caught her whisper. Whispered it back. Over and over, the two of them were standing there in his driveway, declaring their love for one another.

It was like something out of a TV show.

Finally she pulled away and stuck her index finger in his face. "Why didn't you tell me last night? Why torture me? When did you decide? What about your house? What about your family? What about your business?"

He laughed and grabbed her hand in his, pulling her finger to his mouth for an intimate little nibble.

"I have things worked out with the business. My associates are going to run it until they can earn the capital to buy me out. The house can stay here—"

"For vacations. Holidays."

"Weddings," he added, obviously meaning Sophie's.

"Christenings," she chimed in, already picturing the children they'd have.

He understood her meaning and his eyes grew a shade darker, more intimate, more serious.

"As for why I didn't tell you…I had to be sure. I had to know why you left me. And what would make things different now."

She looked up, not removing her arms from around his neck. Caro understood. Completely. "You needed to know I trusted you."

He nodded.

"I do."

"I know that. And I'll never make you sorry."

She grinned. "I know that, too."

Turning, he put his arm around her waist and led her to the passenger side of the car. He unlocked it, watched her get in, then walked to the driver's side.

Once inside and buckled, he looked at her beside him. "You think I'm gonna like California?"

She nodded. "I think you're gonna love California."

He put the car in gear, reached over and took her hand and looked toward the west.

"Then let's go."

California's most talked about family, the Coltons, is back!

"Just how close to me do you intend to get?"

CLOSE PROXIMITY

by bestselling author

Donna Clayton

When attorney Libby Corbett started receiving death threats, Private Investigator Rafe James whisked her away for round-the-clock protection…and soon realized that the only place she would truly be safe was in his arms.

Coming in August 2004.

"Donna Clayton pens a cozy romance with a lot of humor, heart and passion."
—*Romantic Times*

THE COLTONS
FAMILY. PRIVILEGE. POWER.

Where love comes alive™

From Silhouette Books comes an emotional series
about the quest for family—
and the romance found along the way!

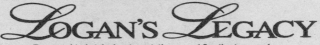

LOGAN'S LEGACY

Because birthright has its privileges and family ties run deep.

Coming in August 2004.

ROYAL AFFAIR

by
USA TODAY
bestselling author

LAURIE PAIGE

One night of impulsive passion changed Ivy Crosby's
life forever when she found herself pregnant—and on
the front pages of the tabloids! Turns out her sexy
stranger was none other than Prince Maxwell von
Husden…who was now proposing marriage!